You Can Have My Back 2

Minami Kotsuna

NewYork

Minami Kotsuna   ILLUSTRATION BY Hitomi Hitoyo

Translation by Aleksandra Jankowska

This book is a work of fiction. Names, characters, places, and incidents are the product of the author's imagination or are used fictitiously. Any resemblance to actual events, locales, or persons, living or dead, is coincidental.

SENAKA WO AZUKERU NIHA Vol.2
©Minami Kotsuna 2021
First published in Japan in 2021 by KADOKAWA CORPORATION, Tokyo.
English translation rights arranged with KADOKAWA CORPORATION, Tokyo, through Tuttle-Mori Agency, Inc., Tokyo.

English translation © 2023 by Yen Press, LLC

Yen On
150 West 30th Street, 19th Floor
New York, NY 10001

Visit us at yenpress.com
facebook.com/yenpress
twitter.com/yenpress
yenpress.tumblr.com
instagram.com/yenpress

First Yen On Edition: November 2023
Edited by Yen On Editorial: Payton Campbell
Designed by Yen Press Design: Andy Swist

Yen On is an imprint of Yen Press, LLC.
The Yen On name and logo are trademarks of Yen Press, LLC.

The publisher is not responsible for websites (or their content) that are not owned by the publisher.

Library of Congress Cataloging-in-Publication Data
Names: Kotsuna, Minami, author. | Jankowska, Aleksandra (Translator), translator.
Title: You can have my back / Minami Kotsuna ; translation by Aleksandra Jankowska.
Other titles: Senaka wo azukeru niha. English
Description: First Yen On edition. | New York, NY : Yen On, 2023-
Identifiers: LCCN 2023004111 | ISBN 9781975363932 (v. 1 ; trade paperback) |
    ISBN 9781975363956 (v. 2 ; trade paperback)
Subjects: CYAC: Fantasy. | Reincarnation—Fiction. | LCGFT: Fantasy fiction. | Light novels.
Classification: LCC PZ7.1.K6828 Yo 2023 | DDC [Fic]—dc33
LC record available at https://lccn.loc.gov/2023004111

ISBNs: 978-1-9753-6395-6 (paperback)
        978-1-9753-6396-3 (ebook)

10 9 8 7 6 5 4 3 2 1

LSC-C

Printed in the United States of America

Contents

Lucas

Ionia's schoolmate and the lieutenant general of the Royal Army. He suspects that Leorino is Ionia's reincarnation.

Josef

Leorino's childhood friend and bodyguard. His androgynous appearance doesn't betray his headstrong personality.

Dirk

Ionia's younger brother. Currently serving as Gravis's adjutant in the Royal Army.

August

Leorino's father. Margrave of Brungwurt. He is concerned about the future of his youngest son.

Ebbo

Ionia's subordinate and the last remaining survivor of the Special Forces. Witnessed Ionia's death.

Hundert

Leorino's attendant. Devoted to his job. Fully supports Leorino

Kyle

The crown prince and Gravis's nephew. He has yet to marry. His personality is rather elusive.

Julian

Eldest son of the Duke of Leben. He falls in love with Leorino at first sight and pursues his hand in marriage.

Theodor

Gravis's valet. As a bloodline purist, he was never fond of Ionia due t his status as a commoner

Ionia
Met Gravis through a strange twist of fate, joined the army, and later died in battle.

Gravis
The king's younger brother and the general of the Royal Army. He has grown bitter since the death of his best friend, Ionia.

Leorino
The fourth son of a margrave. Known for his unmatched beauty, he possesses the memories of the late Ionia.

Character Introductions

You Can Have My Back

The Tea Party

Leorino accompanied his mother and sister-in-law to the estate of the Count of Arhen in the countryside just outside of the royal capital.

The estate was famous for its gardens, located roughly a half-hour ride by carriage from the center of the capital. There, they were to attend a tea party hosted by the countess. They were joined by the maids of his mother and sister, as well as their respective guards, Josef among them.

The countess and all her guests could not contain their excitement at the arrival of the family from Brungwurt, which was the current center of attention in the royal capital. The Countess of Arhen in particular could not hide her elation at the rumored appearance of the fourth son of the Cassieux family, whose beauty had caught even the crown prince's attention during the Vow of Adulthood.

They were led into a drawing room overlooking the count's prized garden, where they were greeted by the count himself. The garden, illuminated by the spring sun, was indeed beautifully landscaped and deserving of its fame.

The Count and Countess of Arhen couldn't wait to countenance Leorino's famed beauty.

Leorino's attire today was simple, consisting of a white shirt with a matching flax-colored jacket and trousers to complement the women's lavish formal daywear. The only ornaments he wore were the silver buttons engraved with the family crest and a small purple iridescent gemstone clip fastened at the base of his throat. However, even in such simple garments, his sophisticated appearance was so striking that he easily stood out among the other guests.

Everyone was gazing at Leorino in rapt attention until Maia cleared her throat and brought them back to their senses, causing them to quickly avert their eyes. The experienced nobles immediately understood the meaning behind Maia's warning.

From that point on, the guests treated them with reasonable indifference, even as the occasional glances continued. Feeling deliberately ignored, Leorino was finally able to relax.

The tea party was to take place in the garden. Several large canopies were pitched under the beaming sunlight, with tables and chairs set up beneath them.

Leorino quickly spotted Josef in the garden. The guards appeared to have all been deployed to different parts of the property.

Leorino's eyes met Josef's.

Instantly feeling reassured, Leorino smiled. Josef smiled back and nodded.

"...Why, Brother, I didn't know you were attending!"

At the sound of Erina's voice, Leorino turned around with a start. There were the smiling faces of Erina's mother, the Duchess of Leben, and Erina's brother, Julian Munster, whom he had grown accustomed to seeing over the past year.

"Erina, Madame, how do you do? And Leorino, what a joy to see you."

"Lord Julian, Duchess of Leben, well met."

Erina must have known her mother would be attending. However, she seemed genuinely surprised by her brother's appearance.

Julian was likely not the sort of man to attend tea parties largely populated by the older generation. Leorino had heard he was sought out at all kinds of social gatherings. Even now, he was attracting the gazes of those around them in a different way from Leorino.

Leorino was blindsided by this reunion with Julian. He couldn't help being self-conscious about what he had said to him when they parted at the soiree. Nevertheless, Julian was behaving like the noblest of noblemen that he was and treated Leorino with courtesy.

After exchanging greetings, the two families were led by the Count of Arhen—who looked nervous surrounded by leading nobles—to a seat with the best view.

Julian and Leorino walked side by side behind the laughing women.

At that moment, Julian quickly brought his lips to Leorino's ear and whispered, "I've missed you."

The whisper felt ticklish, and Leorino couldn't help reacting. Julian offered him a mischievous smile.

"When I heard you were coming, I couldn't contain myself. I simply had to come see you," he whispered in Leorino's ear again.

"Lord Julian, please…"

But Julian chuckled at Leorino's flustered response. "Rest assured, I wouldn't dare do anything that might embarrass you out in the open, Leorino."

Leorino cast his gaze down. He was still unable to give a tactful reply to Julian's suggestive statement. Leorino knew he must do his best, but he looked to Josef as if he could simply swoop in and save Leorino.

When he noticed Leorino's anxious expression, Josef nodded slowly. Leorino didn't know why he had nodded, but he couldn't help being amused by how seriously Josef took his role as Leorino's guard, and Leorino regained his composure.

Leorino looked up at Julian and quietly whispered back to him so that no one around them could hear. "I trust you, Lord Julian. I don't want to cause any trouble for my mother and sister-in-law, so please, *please* don't say anything that might get me in hot water."

He found the courage to say what had been on his mind.

Julian looked at Leorino with narrowed eyes and raised his hands in surrender.

"Well, look at you… I don't see you for a few days, and suddenly you've become something of a provocateur. I give up."

Having offered a successful retort in conversation with another adult, Leorino grew confident.

At the table reserved for the guest of honor, the Duchess of Leben took the reins of the conversation and did not let go, mainly occupying the ladies. The duchess adored Maia and was anxious to please her throughout the conversation. Her cheeks flushed as she spoke.

Julian did not attempt to interact with Leorino, per his request. Despite his nerves, Leorino managed to flawlessly participate in the conversation, nodding along and making small talk whenever it was expected of him.

Having visited each table and greeted each guest, the countess returned with a petite woman.

Erina smiled when she saw her. It appeared that they knew each other.

"How good to see you, Antonia! It's been too long!"

Leorino inclined his head at the sight of the woman. Then, with a start, he remembered. He knew that petite silhouette with reddish-gold hair. It was the same young lady who had stood next to him during the Vow of Adulthood ceremony.

"Lord Julian, Lady Erina, you've met my daughter. Madame Maia, Lord Leorino, may I introduce to you my daughter, Antonia."

The daughter of the Countess of Arhen greeted the guests with a beautifully executed, ladylike curtsy.

"My name is Antonia Klaus. Margravine of Brungwurt, Lord Leorino. It is an honor to meet you."

Leorino returned the greeting with an equally graceful gesture.

When Antonia's eyes met Leorino's, her round cheeks flushed red. "Um, I was standing next to you, Lord Leorino, during the ceremony of the Vow of Adulthood. Although I don't expect you to remember me..."

Leorino smiled. "I remember you. I am sorry that I could not introduce myself properly, as I arrived late. My name is Leorino Cassieux."

"So you did remember me! Oh, I'm so glad."

Leorino's grin made Antonia smile back pleasantly, her cheeks turning even redder.

"Ah, so you've met before. Lady Antonia, please have a seat."

Maia urged her to sit, and Antonia nodded and sat down next to Erina. When her eyes met Erina's, they grinned at each other. Antonia had a small round face that matched her petite frame, a pair of sparkling green eyes, and soft features that gave her a charming appearance.

"So you spoke with my son during the ceremony?"

"N-no, I didn't have the opportunity...but, um, I would never forget Lord Leorino. Everyone in the hall was stunned, uncertain if we were all dreaming. After that, the room was astir with excitement as we wondered if he was really human, made of the same flesh as the rest of us."

Leorino sipped his tea in silence. *What could I possibly be made of if not flesh?*

"…Oh, I apologize."
Antonia had immediately noticed Leorino's irritation.
Leorino replied with a smile that he didn't mind. Erina came to her rescue with a laugh. "Antonia, the same thing happened to us. When we met Leorino for the first time, we all nearly keeled over."
"Oh my. Your family as well?"
"…Sister, please. The Klaus family might take you seriously."
"But she's right, Leorino. We *were* stunned. And Mother was just about ready to faint."
When Julian entered the conversation, Leorino scowled in irritation.

Antonia laughed melodiously. "I can relate. I was so glad that I was called forth before Lord Leorino during the ceremony. If I had been forced to go after him, I might have fallen straight out of my chair when they called my name."
Everyone laughed at Antonia's humorous turn of phrase as she recounted the story.
Leorino was growing quite fond of Antonia.
She was a wonderful young lady, far more open-minded and charming than him. More than anything, Leorino was pleased with how quickly she was able to relax in his presence.

What followed was a pleasant conversation about Antonia's debut in high society and tales of her school days.
"Antonia has such a brilliant mind. She excelled at school, especially in history and mathematics. She was famous throughout our grade."
"Oh, Lady Erina, you flatter me. But it makes me quite self-conscious. It's as if I'm fishing for compliments."
"Oh, but it's true. You were known to argue with the math teacher. One day, the teacher gave her a textbook for the upper grades, telling her to solve the problems inside in hopes of buying themselves some time. But Antonia happily returned a few days later, having solved all the problems, and assaulted them with another barrage of questions. The teacher looked ready to beg the heavens for mercy."

"Lady Erina! They don't need to know that!"

The guests gathered under the canopy adored Erina's anecdote.

When everyone calmed down, the Countess of Arhen said to her daughter, "If you don't mind, Antonia, why don't you show Lord Leorino our rose garden?"

"Mother?"

The Countess of Arhen ignored her daughter's surprise and continued with a smile. "Lord Leorino, we're the only family to grow certain rare species of roses in the royal capital. My daughter will show you around, so why don't you go have a look?"

Leorino glanced at his mother. Seeing her quietly sipping tea with her eyes downcast, he decided this was not an offer he should refuse. Leorino nodded at the countess.

"I'd love to. Lady Antonia, would you show me the way?"

"Of course. Um, Lord Leorino, may I…?"

Leorino held out his hand, and Antonia, her cheeks tinted, timidly took it. The Countess of Arhen seemed pleased by the sight.

As Erina looked on anxiously, Julian smiled gracefully·and offered to accompany them.

"We would love to see the countess's famous rose garden as well. Erina, let us join Lady Antonia."

Antonia led Leorino to the rose garden. A short distance away, the Munster siblings, Erina and Julian, followed, walking arm in arm.

Leorino began in a soft voice in hopes of soothing Antonia's nerves.

"Is the rose garden beyond that hedge?" he asked upon seeing the veritable wall of greenery.

Antonia nodded. "Y-yes. The hedge is double layered. On the other side is the rose garden, and in between there are paths for strolling."

"I see."

Leorino was asking for a reason. He wanted to know how far he would be forced to walk.

Shouldn't be an issue, but it would be polite to let her know.

* * *

"Lady Antonia, due to an accident I suffered six years ago, I cannot walk for long periods of time. I want you to know this, as it may negatively affect our stroll."

"Is that so? I see no issue with your gait right now..."

"Yes, walking itself isn't an issue. My legs only tire from long walks."

Antonia instantly looked apologetic.

"I'm really sorry, my mother's offer was very inconsiderate..."

"No, not at all. It was a lovely thing to suggest. I just wanted to inform you ahead of time that a longer walk may be impossible for me. I'm perfectly fine at the moment, so don't let it bother you," Leorino said with a kind smile, and Antonia seemed relieved.

When they glanced behind them, Erina and Julian waved, smiling. They waved back.

"Then let us go. Show me that fantastic rose garden of which everyone speaks so highly."

"Of course."

They slowly walked down the gently sloping hill. As they approached the hedge, they could no longer see the canopies set up behind them. The air was mild in the endlessly glorious spring sunlight.

Once the rose garden came into view, it became immediately apparent how it had become the pride and joy of the countess.

Roses were planted in a radial pattern, extending from the vine-covered gazebo in the center. Climbing roses of various colors were beginning to bloom on the arches along the path. Many buds were still visible, but some of the seasonal varieties were already in full bloom, threatening to spill over the path.

"It's incredible... I've never seen such a beautiful rose garden."

"Do you mean it? I think my mother would be sincerely pleased to hear you say so."

"Of course. Brungwurt is so far north that only cold-hardy varieties get to bloom at all."

"Oh, I see. Our territory is much farther south, so we see all sorts of other flowers, too."

* * *

From there, they made a slow tour of the rose garden. The circular walkway allowed them to see Julian and Erina following them. Leorino noticed that Antonia had been glancing at the siblings behind them.

"Are you concerned about our pursuers?"

"...Huh?"

Antonia looked up at Leorino with unhidden surprise on her face. She smiled softly and blushed suddenly.

"It's just... It was actually I who asked my mother to give me some time alone with you."

"Is that so? And for what reason?"

"It's, um..." Antonia's face turned bright red as she stuttered. Then, suddenly, she pulled Leorino's arm and urged him toward the gazebo. Leorino had no choice but to go wherever she pulled him.

Her petite body came to a sudden stop in front of the gazebo.

"...Lady Antonia?"

"Yes! I...actually have something I would like to ask you, Lord Leorino..."

"Yes, what is it?"

Antonia fidgeted, rubbing her hands in front of her chest. After a moment's hesitation, she looked up at Leorino with a snap.

"Um... Lord Leorino, are you in a r-relationship with L-Lord Julian?"

"...Excuse me?"

Leorino's jaw dropped at the abrupt question. Antonia's adorable face turned as red as an apple.

"I saw you, at the soiree... I saw Lord Julian walking with you in such an... intimate manner."

"Lady Antonia, I believe that's, um..."

"For a year now, I have heard rumors that Lord Julian had fallen in love with someone. He's very kind to everyone, you see, but...when I saw the look in his eyes as he watched you, I..."

With that, Antonia closed her eyes, wringing her dress as if she was waiting for his verdict.

Why was this near-complete stranger of a woman suddenly asking him about his relationship with Julian?

For the time being, he had to nip the rumor in the bud.

"There is nothing between me and Lord Julian. He is my sister-in-law's brother, nothing more, nothing less."

"Oh, is that so?"

"Yes, that's all there is to it."

As soon as she heard Leorino's answer, Antonia smiled with relief. Leorino knew little of romantic affairs, but that reaction made everything clear.

"You have feelings for Lord Julian, is that the way of it?"

"Ah... Oh, um... No."

"Hm? So you do not have feelings for him?"

"No, I, um... Yes, I love him dearly." Still reeling from Leorino's blunt question, Antonia finally nodded in resignation.

"Are you not going to tell Lord Julian how you feel about him, then?"

"Ugh, Lord Leorino, please. You're too forthright, I hardly know what to say."

"Am I? Well, Lord Julian is a lucky man to be loved by such a wonderful woman as yourself. I hope he realizes it before long."

Antonia sighed. "...Hearing that from an angel, I might just expect a miracle."

At that moment, Leorino had an idea. This might just be a great opportunity to help her.

"Since they're already following us, let us wait for them to catch up. We can switch so that you walk with Julian, and I will escort my sister-in-law. Then you can speak with him until we return to the party."

"Huh...? N-no, I can't... Should we...?"

There was something adorable about a woman in love.

Leorino quickly made up his mind to do whatever he could to support Antonia.

"Let's do it. I hope you will tell Lord Julian how you feel about him."

"Lord Leorino...I appreciate your support...but I cannot do that."

"Hm? Why not?"

"...Lord Leorino, one cannot simply confess their feelings. You must wait until...you get to know each other better."

Leorino reflected on this and agreed. It was one thing to have feelings for someone, but acting upon those feelings was something else entirely.

At that moment, the face of the man who had stolen his lips flashed through Leorino's mind. He felt a sudden pang in his chest.

"I suppose you're right. Then, as you say, you should enjoy a stroll together and get to know each other first."

"...Lord Leorino, you look like an angel, and you really are not of this world, are you?"

"Hm? Do you think so? I was hoping to support you and your feelings for Julian, was that wrong of me?"

"...It wasn't wrong of you... I-I'm glad to hear that. Thank you."

As they waited near the gazebo, Erina and Julian joined them. Acknowledging their arrival, Leorino cracked a smile at the blushing woman by his side.

The tea party ended without issue. Leorino was exhausted from the carriage ride and the stroll through the gardens. Still, he was satisfied with the day's outing. He felt a little more confident now that he had managed to complete a social event without causing a scene.

Seeing him off alongside her parents, Antonia wore a pleased smile on her face. Leorino was happy at the thought that he might just become good friends with her.

Following his mother and sister-in-law, Leorino was about to get into their carriage when he felt a sudden tug at his waist.

When he turned around in surprise, he saw that it was Julian.

"You're coming with me."

"...What?"

Before he could even protest, Julian lifted Leorino by the waist and carried him to his own carriage. Entering after Leorino, Julian pushed him deeper inside.

The carriage doors closed behind Julian.

Instantly, the interior of the carriage turned dark. The afternoon light only reached them through the small windows.

"...Lord Julian?"

Julian knocked on the wall of the carriage. With a loud thump, the carriage sprang into motion.

Leorino sat frozen in shock.

"Finally, we're alone."

"...Lord Julian, why...? Why are you doing this?"

Leorino was frightened. He did not understand why Julian wanted to be alone with him in the first place.

The carriage began to sway at a steady pace.

Leorino shrank back on the edge of his seat, trying to keep as much distance between himself and Julian as possible.

Seeing this, Julian chuckled.

"You may relax. The madame has given me permission to return with you to the capital. Besides, your guard is following us on horseback."

"So we're returning to the capital...?"

He looked at Julian, silently trying to confirm the veracity of his statement with his gaze, when Julian grinned at him.

"Yes. I've been meaning to talk to you."

Julian's tone was perfectly calm. It was hard to believe that he was the same person who had carried Leorino into the carriage against his will.

The royal capital was some half an hour away.

I suppose I don't mind talking for that long...

Leorino had been taken aback, but slowly began letting his guard down. Julian watched him with a somewhat amused look on his face.

"Right, then... I'm ready to hear your excuse."

"Excuse...?"

He wasn't sure what Julian meant. Julian smiled, watching Leorino tilt his head.

"Yes. You tried to play matchmaker with me and Lady Antonia in the rose garden today, didn't you?"

Leorino let out a quiet gasp. He had offered to take over as Erina's escort during their stroll through the rose garden. At that moment, Julian's eyes widened slightly, but Leorino forced a smile and agreed.

What does he mean by "excuse"...?

Julian's tone was as kind as always.

Because of this, Leorino had not noticed the man's silent anger.

"Why did you do that?"

"I was just, um, trying to help..."

"Hmm. Trying to help. Trying to help whom, exactly?"

Help Antonia, of course.

He acted on behalf of Antonia, who looked so lovely with her cheeks stained by her feelings for Julian in the hope that her love would be requited.

He simply figured that giving her some time alone with Julian would make her happy and was therefore a good idea.

"Leorino, look at me."

When he gave no reply, Julian placed his fingers on Leorino's chin and lifted it himself. Leorino had no choice but to lock gazes with this man he was sharing this enclosed space with.

That was when Leorino noticed. Behind his mild expression, Julian's smile didn't reach his eyes. If anything, they hid an irritation that Leorino had never seen before in Julian, who had always been so elegant and kind.

Leorino watched Julian with fear in his eyes.

"Did that...upset you somehow?"

"Not quite. I had no issue keeping her company. She's a sensible young lady. I enjoyed our time together."

Leorino was confused. If his offer had not been the issue, what had?

"Then why do you seem so upset...?"

"Why? You can't tell? Really?"

Leorino shook his head, his chin still in Julian's fingers. If he had enjoyed speaking with Antonia, what could have bothered him so much?

* * *

"I've told you so many times, but it just doesn't seem to stay in your head, does it? …Now, listen. I haven't given up on you yet, remember? I've told you that, haven't I?"

"…O-oh, um, of course."

Leorino shuddered.

He did remember. They were his parting words after he had saved Leorino from his predicament at the soiree. But Leorino's father should have already turned down Julian's proposal.

Although Leorino had hinted it at the soiree, Julian had been cordial today, maintaining an appropriate distance from him the entire time. Leorino had been so reassured by this that he assumed Julian had accepted Leorino as part of his extended family.

"I see you remembered."

"I—I didn't have to remember. I hadn't forgotten. But I thought that you… had come to terms with it by now."

Julian laughed out loud, apparently finding this deeply amusing. "Is that what you thought? What a pity. Is that all my proposal meant to you?"

"No, of course not! But my father told me that he had already turned you down… I assumed that would be the last of it."

"Did you think that just because your father said no, I would simply say 'I see, thank you,' and my love for you would disappear just like that?"

"Well, no, but…"

"Do *you* get to decide how *I* feel?"

Leorino instantly paled as Julian watched him with affection in his eyes even as he verbally drove Leorino into a corner.

"Really, I should pity that young lady. I don't know what she told you, but you must have learned how she felt and innocently suggested that she act on those feelings, didn't you?"

"I…"

"You're the one I long for. Did you give any thought to how she will feel when she learns that she was spurred on by her rival?"

His words came as a shock to Leorino.

Julian was right.

He had simply wanted to support the love of a brave young woman.

But when Antonia learned that Julian still had feelings for Leorino, how much would his prior act hurt her self-esteem?

How...how utterly foolish of me...

Leorino's heart ached with regret, and he clutched at his shirt. Julian was watching him closely.

"You are as innocent as an angel, but unforgivably cruel, too. To think you would not give my love for you the slightest consideration and try to sell me off to someone else. And you have no awareness of it whatsoever."

"I..."

Julian slowly stroked Leorino's trembling chin with his thumb.

"Oh, but you were 'just trying to help.' Ha-ha, best joke I've heard in a while. You're so simple, and *so* insensitive." Julian admonished Leorino's thoughtless behavior matter-of-factly. Still, his tone was calm, and a kind smile graced his lips.

Leorino couldn't bear it any longer and cast his eyes down.

"I'm sorry... Lord Julian, I was foolish... I'm really sorry."

Julian *had* alluded to his feelings earlier that day, but hidden by his decorum, it almost felt like he had been teasing Leorino.

Leorino felt like crying.

He would not have imagined that Julian still held any serious feelings for him.

At that moment, the carriage shook violently.

They appeared to be passing over a rough road that had not seen regular upkeep. He felt the intense shaking particularly hard in his legs and back. Leorino gritted his teeth at the pain of being tossed about in his seat.

"Oh, I felt it on the way there, but this road's quite terrible, isn't it...? Come now."

Noticing the agony Leorino desperately tried to hide, Julian grabbed him by the waist and lifted Leorino up onto his lap sideways.

"Ah..."

"Come now, aren't you more comfortable like this?"

"Lord Julian...!" He immediately pressed his hands against the man's chest and tried to escape. But despite Julian's slender appearance, Leorino could not free himself from the man's arms even as he twisted and turned.

"N-no, it's all right, please let me go!"

"The shaking will hurt your legs. Just sit back and rest. Here, I'll hold you like this."

Julian was right. In the rocking carriage, he felt much better secured in place.

But he didn't want to sit any closer to the man whose marriage proposal he had refused, the man who still had feelings for him.

As Leorino shrunk back in the man's arms, Julian laughed again.

"Are you afraid of me? I would never do anything to you in a carriage, rest assured. We'll be past this road soon, just sit tight for now."

"Still... Lord Julian, I insist. Please let me go."

"No. Learn to accept the kindness of others."

Leorino bit his lip.

He felt sorry for himself for being unable to firmly refuse Julian. He had a feeling that Julian was not going to let him go, no matter how hard he protested.

Just as he had promised, Julian had not done anything inappropriate. He simply held Leorino's body firmly in place.

After a while, Leorino muttered to himself, "...I thought you were upset with me."

"Hmm? Yes, I am upset, of course."

"Then why are you being so kind?"

"Because you're you. How many times must I say it? I'm in love with you. And in any case, this is your punishment. You're quite uncomfortable now, aren't you?"

Leorino frowned in irritation.

No matter how kindly Julian treated him, Leorino could not accept Julian's feelings.

Leorino bowed his head and apologized.

"...Lord Julian. I am truly sorry. I was foolish. I sincerely apologize. I will write a letter of apology to Lady Antonia as well."

"Hmm, a letter? And what are you going to write? You'll say your behavior was inappropriate because the man she's in love with proposed to you? That would be counterproductive. Don't bother."

"...I'm sorry."

Hearing it said so calmly made him more restless than he already was. He didn't know how to apologize to Antonia.

"Oh, you really don't understand the subtleties of the human heart, do you?"

"…I-I'm sorry."

The pain in Leorino's chest caused him to curl in on himself.

They remained silent for a while longer.

"…That reminds me, I heard that you want to become independent. Your brother told me you want to find a job."

Leorino was puzzled by the sudden change of subject.

"Yes. That's why… I'm sorry. I can't marry you, Lord Julian."

Julian smiled at his apologetic refusal.

"I couldn't have known it at the time, but I'm sorry for what I said that day. I admire your determination to be independent. I will support you in your decision."

"Oh… Thank you." Leorino sighed in relief, assuming that Julian had finally given up on marrying him.

"But as it stands, you'll cause heaps of trouble for the people around you."

"…Huh?"

Julian smiled softly. "You may even hurt many people with your innocent insensitivity, just as you did today."

Leorino was flustered. "That's not… That was never my intention…"

"I do wonder. You might even scoff at people's feelings without realizing it. You know…like what you did to me earlier."

Julian's tone was calm, but each word was dripping with venom.

For some reason, Lucas's tormented expression flashed through Leorino's mind.

"So, Leorino," Julian whispered. "Did I hit the nail on the head?"

Leorino turned melancholy, casting his eyes down.

"…I'm sorry."

"Hah. I'm sure you are. But it's not your fault. You're just ignorant of the ways of the world."

"I know I am… But—"

"That's all right. You'll have plenty of chances to learn. Let me show you the outside world."

What does that mean?

"Um, uh, but… You and I, we're not…"

Julian suddenly stroked Leorino's cheek. His touch was perfectly gentle, completely non-threatening.

"Don't worry about the future. And don't concern yourself with how I feel about you right now."

"But, Lord Julian…"

"Hush now. No ifs, ands, or buts. Your mind is still so immature. You need someone to guide you."

"I…"

"You do realize you might end up hurting people again with your thoughtless behavior, like you did today, yes?"

Leorino was oblivious.

Before he knew it, the carriage had left the bad road. Nevertheless, Julian's elegant hand continued to leisurely caress Leorino's slender back.

Leorino remained in his lap, ruminating on his words. Julian watched him with a smile.

"…I hope you'll slowly grow accustomed to me."

"…?"

Leorino hadn't quite caught what Julian said and directed a raised eyebrow at Julian.

"Don't worry about it." The elegant man smiled.

The Winged One

While Leorino and his family were out in the countryside, Sasha, a military doctor from the Royal Army, visited the eldest son Auriano, the current acting head of the Cassieux family, at the Brungwurt residence in the royal capital.

"So His Royal Highness was serious about his offer from the other day..."

Sitting across from Auriano, Sasha nodded as he enjoyed a cup of fine, fragrant tea.

"It was originally my idea. I wanted to support Leorino's independence, and His Excellency agreed to it. So how does the Cassieux family feel?"

"We greatly appreciate the offer...but I doubt the boy can perform work either you or His Highness would find satisfactory, Dr. Sasha."

"That's all right." Sasha shook his head. "We don't want to give him special treatment, but I'll watch him closely and let him start with whatever he can do, so please rest assured. Of course, he won't be a mere decoration; we want him to do real work."

"...Nevertheless, there is also the matter of Leorino's appearance. I hear the Royal Army is a gathering of ruffians, so to speak. No, excuse me...but Leorino is too helpless for a man. It would be like throwing a sheep into a pack of wolves."

Sasha was indignant at the gall required to question the moral character of the Royal Army. "What do you think the Royal Army is? Yes, it may be full of meatheads, but they are not a band of rogues. Besides, in accordance with His Excellency's plan, he would not officially belong to the Royal Army. He would only work in the Palace of Defense."

"Still..."

"The Palace of Defense is composed of civilian officials, is it not? It employs men with the same slender physique as Lord Leorino. You should know women work there as well. Certainly, you'll find few people as extraordinarily beautiful as Lord Leorino...but are you saying these people are constantly being assaulted?"

"No, I certainly didn't say that..."

"I don't think it's a bad idea for Leorino to work at the Palace of Defense. Especially since that's where His Excellency reigns supreme... Or rather, because he is in command, he has more control over the entire hierarchy of the Palace of Defense than the other palaces."

Auriano pursed his lips.

"...Still, Leorino's position would be very weak."

"The general himself has officially invited him to the palace. And he's a son of the Cassieux family, is he not? That's more than enough to make anyone with untoward intentions think twice about troubling him." Sasha laughed loudly, but his smile didn't reach his eyes.

Auriano was distressed.

Although they had not informed Leorino himself, the Cassieux family already had a path in mind for their youngest son to follow, and it was marriage to Julian Munster.

Leorino still thought that August had asked the Duke of Leben to drop the matter entirely, but the two families had merely agreed to put it on hold. August had asked Julian to take things slowly as Leorino's mind matured, and Julian had agreed.

In other words, at this point, the two families had privately established a tentative promise that Julian and Leorino would get married in the future.

These two years were just a grace period for Leorino to establish an emotional bond with Julian. August would marry Leorino off to Julian as long as there were no serious rifts or irreconcilable differences between them.

For Leorino, who genuinely wanted to become independent, his father's secret plot bordered on betrayal. But that was the decision the head of the family had made in order to protect Leorino.

But here comes this offer…

They were told at the outset that this offer was a formal invitation from Gravis Adolphe Fanoren, the general in the Royal Army and a member of the royal family.

When Gravis whispered this to Auriano as he carried Leorino home, he had thought it impossible, but Sasha had finally arrived as the official messenger. And, as it turned out, the general himself had already gone to Brungwurt to speak directly to Auriano's father.

It was the most unusual series of events.

The Cassieux family could not simply refuse an official invitation from a royal. Auriano had to get in touch with the head of the family and confirm his intentions.

Sasha urged the now-silent acting head of the Cassieux family, Auriano, to come to a conclusion.

"Lord Auriano. We're talking about the youngest son of the Cassieux family, yes? Do you really want to risk letting him work anywhere else? With his beauty and his lineage, he would be kidnapped in an instant. That's what you're most worried about, isn't it? I can think of no better place to guarantee his safety than the Palace of Defense."

Auriano considered this.

Regardless of August's thoughts, Auriano personally wanted to abide by Leorino's genuine desire to work.

Leorino would be under the protection of the general, and Sasha would be close by, keeping an eye on him and allowing him to work at his own pace. Moreover, he would be working in the Palace of Defense, arguably the safest place to be.

In terms of a work environment that would ensure Leorino's personal safety, there could certainly be no better conditions.

But Leorino was too earnest for his own good. Auriano could easily imagine him working himself to the bone at his new job.

If that were to happen, he would not be in the right headspace to fall in love with Julian.

Auriano groaned.

He couldn't quite make up his mind. Sasha's eyes lit up as he carefully observed Auriano.

"Judging by that reaction, you never truly intended to let Lord Leorino out into the world in the first place...or am I wrong?"

Auriano's temples twitched.

"...Oh, I see how it is. The engagement with Julian Munster is still on the table, then? In that case, you certainly can't have a boy who will marry into a duke's family working his life away, now can you?"

"It's not official yet. Not to mention...Leorino has no knowledge of it."

Auriano acknowledged Sasha's words as vaguely as possible.

Hearing this, Sasha released a deep sigh.

"...Don't you feel bad for Leorino? He's really trying to find a job, isn't he? He even wanted to go to the employment agency in hopes of finding one."

Auriano bit his lip.

"Leorino is a son of a noble family. If you had told him that both families had agreed to marry him off to Julian Munster, he would have complied. It's a horrible betrayal to make it seem as if the topic has been dropped when you're actively plotting behind his back."

He was right.

Auriano averted his gaze from Sasha.

"...What's wrong? It's not like you. I always thought the Cassieux family cared so much about Lord Leorino."

"...I have nothing to say to you about the decision of the head of the family."

"Well, that's all right, then. I can guess the circumstances that led to the margrave's decision. I can understand the sentiment. But in this case, I will absolutely take Lord Leorino's side."

"Doctor, please! This is our family! Please, let it go!"

Sasha's gaze on Auriano was frightfully cold.

"...Lord Auriano. Do you really think that keeping Lord Leorino from hardship and being so overprotective of him will make him happy? Has he ever asked you or your father to let him live comfortably under the protection of a powerful man?"

"Dr. Sasha, please…"

"I have seen hundreds of deaths on the battlefield. There is precious little we doctors can do to make the difference between life and death. Life and death are God's decisions, a momentary fork in the road… Lord Auriano, you saw him, didn't you? The way he lay there with his shattered body?"

Of course. I still remember it vividly.

That day, Leorino lay on the ground of Zweilink like a doll tossed away by a child who had grown bored of it.

"If His Excellency had not happened to be in Zweilink, and if he had not instantly summoned me to Brungwurt, the boy's life would have certainly ended there. And that was thanks to His Excellency, thanks to me, and thanks to your family! We have all saved his precious life, haven't we?"

"Doctor…"

"It may have been just a series of coincidences that allowed us to save his life…but the damage was so terrible that we were considering amputation. And yet, through Leorino's efforts over the years, he regained his ability to walk, did he not?"

Sasha's eyes burned with anger.

"…That same boy! He told me, 'I want to be able to protect someone, not just be protected,' and he's trying his best to become independent… To become a man worthy of the Cassieux name, just like you!"

Auriano winced.

"His beautiful appearance is the biggest obstacle standing in the way of his independence. Yet still, he refuses to give up. He's desperately trying to find his way in the world!"

"Doctor, please…"

Sasha took a deep breath to quell his own excitement.

"…So, Lord Auriano, we are in the position to support him, and we have the power. We can still keep him from any real danger. He knows it's dangerous out there, but he still wants to leave the nest. Don't you want to let him spread his wings?"

It was finally time for Sasha to state his ultimatum.

"The invitation extended to Leorino Cassieux to work in the Palace of Defense is an *order* of His Excellency the General. I want you to consider the meaning of this and give me an answer within the next few days. Is that clear?"

Auriano could hardly speak. "...Please let me first get in touch with the head of the family. Until then, I will refrain from giving you a formal answer."

"Very well."

"...Dr. Sasha, it is highly unusual for the brother of the king himself to extend a personal invitation to Leorino. I really don't want any strange rumors spreading about my brother."

Without paying any heed to Auriano's desperate rebuttal, Sasha pushed back in a calm voice. "What does it matter? His Excellency will get his way in the end. And he will do everything to protect Leorino, in a way different from yours. I am certain that His Excellency has personally told the margrave the very same thing. Is that not good enough?"

With that, the doctor sipped his tea again, looking very pleased with its flavor.

Auriano sighed as he folded the letter for his father.

What was really happening with his youngest brother?

Ever since his arrival in the royal capital, Leorino had been utterly swept up by the big city. Distinguished men had appeared to intervene in Leorino's life one after another. The peaceful days he'd spent in Brungwurt felt like a dream.

His angelic smile appeared in Auriano's mind.

Will we be able to protect that smile?

Childhood Friends

About half an hour ago, Leorino and his family returned home in two separate carriages, surprising the entire household.

Maia, Erina, and the Duchess of Leben disembarked from the carriage bearing the Brungwurt coat of arms. Next arrived the carriage of the duke, from which Julian Munster emerged, followed by Leorino.

But why did he ride home in a carriage belonging to another family?

When Hundert learned that his master had been alone with Julian during the return trip, he worried that something had happened to Leorino. He quickly inspected his master's body from head to toe and found that his clothes were undisturbed and there was no sign that anything inappropriate might have taken place.

Still, he couldn't fully relax.

There was also the matter of what had happened at the Palace of Defense. Hundert was the only one who knew about the marks a certain someone had left on Leorino's neck.

Leorino had said nothing happened, but Hundert had no doubt that someone had at least attempted to assault him. He only kept it quiet because Leorino didn't want to turn it into a serious ordeal.

At that moment, his eyes met Julian Munster's. Hundert quickly bowed his head. He heard the young nobleman chuckle in amusement. He seemed to have understood the servant's concern.

Leorino was somewhat dazed as he and Julian exchanged parting words. Beaming through the whole encounter, Julian whispered something in Leorino's ear.

Leorino nodded hesitantly.

Returning to his room, Hundert's master sat down on his sofa.

Hundert had heard from Erina that everything had gone well during today's outing. Leorino's beauty had not caused a stir, and he had made friends with a young lady close to his age during the visit.

However, his master seemed far from pleased. If anything, he looked to be in particularly low spirits. It wasn't physical exhaustion—Leorino seemed to be more mentally drained than anything.

Hundert quietly offered him a cup of tea. Leorino thanked him in a soft voice.

In truth, Hundert had been worried about his master ever since he arrived in the royal capital. It was only recently that Leorino, his face flushed with fever, expressed his desire to go out into the world and learn to maneuver it.

Hundert couldn't help worrying about his master's health, wondering if he was straining to keep up with the dramatic change in his environment, having no appropriate outlet for his restlessness.

Leorino looked uneasy, like a child who couldn't find his place in the world.

Hundert bit back the urge to ask him what happened. He had the sense that Leorino would not tell him the truth even if he asked. With this in mind, Hundert decided to ask for the help of a guard who was also a childhood friend of his master.

Back in Brungwurt, Leorino had been mostly confined to the castle since he was a child, even before the accident.

Josef and Leorino may have been childhood friends, but they had not seen each other very often over the past few years. However, since coming to the capital and being placed in each other's care, the two had rekindled their old bond.

Josef was a typical northern man with his blunt attitude, which must have put Leorino at ease. They seemed to share a comfortable relationship.

Having prepared tea for Leorino, Hundert went downstairs. He was lucky to find Josef in the entrance hall.

"Josef! How did Master Leorino wind up traveling alone with Lord Julian? And after I told you to keep an eye on him!"

Josef immediately seemed vexed.

"I know, Mr. Hundert! I didn't want to leave them alone, either, of course!"

"Then why?"

"…It was Madame Maia. She told me not to interfere with their opportunity to speak alone. After that, there was nothing I could do."

"She did…? Fine, what did you see of their carriage?"

Josef shook his head hopelessly.

"Well, I was riding alongside on horseback, but I couldn't see much because of the curtain… Mr. Hundert, I know what you're going to say. I'm upset, too."

Biting his lip, Josef lamented his own helplessness.

"…We're not in Brungwurt anymore. In Brungwurt, I could accompany and protect Leorino wherever he went, but everything is different in the royal capital. I'm a commoner and can only fulfill half of my duties as his guard. At the end of the day, I can't always be by Master Leorino's side."

"Josef…"

"I'm a poor excuse for a guard. I never wanted to be a nobleman, but I hate being so helpless."

Hundert could empathize with Josef's anguish.

The same was true for attendants. Even if they accompanied their master to a soiree, the customs of the nobility dictated that the attendants and guards were not allowed to enter the venue. If anything happened, Leorino would be forced to face it alone.

"Josef, could you go to Master Leorino's room? He seems to be troubled, and…he might talk to you."

"…You don't think that playboy's done something to him?"

"Come now, I told you to watch your language. It doesn't immediately seem like he did anything. Nevertheless…"

Josef nodded fiercely and made to leap up the staircase two steps at a time. "Josef! Wait!"

"I'll find out what happened. Don't worry!"

The old servant grabbed Josef by the sleeve with an agility that belied his age, stopping him in place just in time.

"Hah-hah… Is there nothing in that head of yours? …Now, listen. Don't get so excited, just approach him calmly and join him for tea."

"It'll be fine. I'll take care of it. I'll do it right."

Hundert could only watch with concern as Josef nodded vigorously and left.

"Oh, that's definitely your fault, no doubt about that."

Josef's merciless denunciation threw Leorino into a deep dark hole of self-pity. He hugged the backrest of the sofa and buried his face in it.

"…I know. Lord Julian scolded me, too. I realize I was wrong…"

"Even if you rejected Julian's proposal, it was still horrible of you to try and hook a woman up with a man who's still in love with you."

"…I know."

"And the young lady was happy, wasn't she? You know what happens when you play with a woman's heart."

"…Yes, I know."

The backrest had almost completely swallowed his platinum-blond head by now.

"You have no experience with romance, Lord Leorino. That may be your biggest problem."

"…Yes, I get it, all right?!"

Finally, Leorino fell onto the sofa and hid his head under the backrest.

Leorino couldn't forgive himself for his behavior. He had recognized his mistake and was now overcome with anger, regret, shame, and disappointment in himself.

At the moment, Josef was engaging with Leorino not as a guard serving his master, but as his childhood friend.

He may have been very direct, but it was all part of Josef's plan to get his withdrawn master to spill his guts.

Leorino remained frozen in that position for a while, but finally spoke in a muffled voice: "...Lord Julian told me that I was simple and insensitive."

"...I don't think that's true. You were looking out for your family all through your recovery."

"But he said I was 'unforgivably cruel'..."

"Huh? Is that fancy nobleman such a baby that your words or actions could cut him so deeply? I'd imagine you could have hurt the young lady, but still. As far as the man's concerned, I doubt he's hurt at all."

"...But I still ended up toying with their feelings. That much is true."

Josef got up from his seat and crouched down by Leorino's sofa. He poked him on the head, still completely hidden within the backrest.

"Come, you can show me your face now."

When Leorino said nothing, he added, "I know you're sorry. You know what you need to work on. You've realized your mistake and now you need to move on."

Leorino repositioned his head with a loud rustle to look up at Josef through a small gap in the backrest.

His eyes were glossy with tears.

"What did that ass— No, Mr. Hundert will yell at me again. Lord Julian, what did he say to you? Tell me again, loud and clear."

Leorino's lips trembled.

"That I don't understand the subtleties of the human heart. But he said he would support my independence."

"I see. Maybe he's a better guy than I thought."

"Yes... He is a very kind man. But he scolded me, saying that at this rate I'll keep causing trouble to the people around me, that I would scoff at people's feelings and hurt them unknowingly..."

"I take back what I just said, he's not kind at all... But listen, Lord Leorino, I think he's got it wrong."

"...?"

"Come, no need to hide," he said, and gently pulled Leorino out from the backrest. Josef locked eyes with his master.

* * *

"First of all, I realize that I get myself in a whole lot of trouble all the time, as well."

"…I can't deny that."

"You *could*. Don't be mean. Sure, I know I'm in a very different position from you. I make a lot of mistakes, and I force people to clean up after me more often than not. I'm short-tempered; I reflect on that every day and regret it a lot."

Sitting on the floor, Josef peered up into his master's face.

He firmly caught Leorino's anxious, wavering gaze with his own.

"But you see… You don't hate me, do you, Lord Leorino? You've accepted that I don't have to be perfect to be there for you, haven't you?"

"Josef…"

"You said we should both do our best in the royal capital, remember? Even though we're from completely different backgrounds and positions. Even though I have a filthy mouth, and I'm quick to reach for my sword…I'm aware of that. I have no redeeming qualities besides being your childhood friend and knowing you well…and you thought that was fine, didn't you?"

Leorino nodded. "But you do have redeeming qualities. There are many great things about you."

Josef gently brushed the thin strands of hair stuck to Leorino's temples back over his ear.

"Thank you. That's what I mean, Lord Leorino. Who said you need to be perfect? I mean, you couldn't be perfect even if you wanted to. You're burying your face into the backrest of a sofa while crying your eyes out as we speak."

"Ugh… You're so mean. But it's true."

Josef smiled.

"That's fine, I'm saying this as your childhood friend. But you get it, don't you? Still, I respect you for being such a hard worker and for being able to admit your mistakes. Everyone sees the good in you and is willing to support you, aren't they?"

"Yes…"

"Is being immature a bad thing? Do you think you need to be perfect for the right to be alive?"

Leorino seemed to remember something at that.

"...Father once told me the same thing. That I deserve to be alive even if I'm not perfect."

"If the margrave says so, then it must be true." Josef laughed softly once more.

"...But hurting people is bad."

"That's right. You might mess up at first, but then you can reflect on it, apologize properly, and make sure it doesn't happen again. You can't just give up on yourself the moment you make a mistake and live in fear. We're going to do our best in the royal capital, aren't we? You decided to fight, didn't you?"

Leorino nodded at Josef's blunt but kind words.

"Yes, that's right... I'm going to fight."

"Right? So don't get discouraged if someone criticizes you. Now, what do you want to do about this, Lord Leorino?"

Leorino's eyes had regained their strength.

"I really want to apologize to Antonia for my foolish behavior. But even if I offered her an honest apology, I would only be doing it to satisfy my own ego. It would only hurt her even more...so I'm sorry, but I'll just have to keep the apology to myself this time."

"...Yeah, that makes sense."

"And I'll be really careful not to act so thoughtlessly in the future. I'm afraid that I might hurt someone else, but...I'll do my best."

"There you go. You definitely shouldn't hurt women and children, but... just reflect on your actions and move forward. You're going to be strong, right?"

Josef was slender, but had developed some muscle over the years and now patted Leorino forcefully on his thin shoulder. Leorino groaned in pain, but finally showed a faint smile. Josef saw this and smiled as well.

"Cheer up, Master. I'll work even harder to protect you."

Leorino gave a small nod.

"Thank you, Josef... I said I'd protect my heart myself, but I'm relying on you after all."

"Not because I'm your guard, but because we're childhood friends. Well, with stuff like this...I think that if you get more romantic experience, you'll learn to understand the subtleties of love better. But I don't know... I don't have any experience myself. I could ask my brother."

"Ha-ha, that would be scary in its own way."

They laughed as they reminisced about Brungwurt. Josef's brother Rolf was a famous lover boy back in Brungwurt.

Leorino's heart still ached with regret and shame. Now that he grew aware of his own ignorance, he was even more afraid of his actions unwittingly hurting others.

He remembered Julian telling him he would show Leorino the outside world. Leorino agreed that he might indeed need someone older to objectively guide his behavior in the right direction.

...Maybe I should ask him. Or would that be playing with his feelings? But Lord Julian said he wouldn't mind...

Suddenly, Josef pulled on his arm, making Leorino stand up.

"...Well, first things first, we need to make sure you can keep yourself safe."

Leorino inclined his head.

"What exactly am I supposed to do?"

"Self-defense. We'll start training tomorrow so that, if worse comes to worst, you can at least pack a solid punch."

Sword in Hand

"All right, so...when you're grabbed like this, you lower their elbow...and when your opponent loses their hold, you grab their shoulder with your other hand and send them tumbling in the same motion."

"I understand the principle. May I give it a try??"

Josef looked at his earnest master, nodded, and took a step back. He then quickly closed the distance once more and grabbed Leorino by the front of his shirt.

Leorino applied the technique just as Josef had taught him.

"...Ngh! ...Hah!"

"Whoa!"

Leorino was able to stagger Josef's upper body, even if he couldn't quite throw Josef over his shoulder.

"H-how was that, Josef?"

"You did well. You'd at least surprise them. You managed to throw *me* off-balance!"

"Fantastic! Can I try one more time, please?"

"Sure, now try grabbing me by the shoulder and throwing me."

Just as Josef had declared, he was now trying to teach Leorino some basic self-defense techniques. They had created a space in the living room by pulling chairs and the tea table up against the wall and had been practicing for a little while now.

Incidentally, the move Leorino was learning was a self-defense technique intended to break the enemy's stance and allow him to escape when grabbed by the front of his shirt.

Back when he was Ionia, he had already completed a full range of martial arts training. Thanks to that, Leorino had inherited a vague knowledge of basic techniques.

The problem was Leorino's body.

His body was flexible since he exercised every day to keep his legs in good condition. His limbs had the minimum muscle expected of a young man. Still, his muscles were not strong enough to fight.

Josef was well aware of his master's weakness and hoped he could teach him self-defense techniques that would at least discourage a potential attacker. He wanted Leorino to be able to keep his opponent in check if he was attacked in the dark.

Leorino did not expect himself to become a skillful fighter. Still, he fancied exercising like this for the first time in a long time.

Despite Leorino's heavy breathing and the flush on his milky white cheeks, he seemed to be very much enjoying himself. His violet eyes sparkled with the joy of learning a new skill.

Meanwhile, Hundert stood in the corner of the room, anxiously watching everything play out. He was glad that his master had recovered from his melancholy, but overprotective as he was, he worried that Leorino might get hurt.

"Now, make sure you grab me by the shoulder. And when you have me in your grasp, pull me downward, as if...you're trying to throw me to the ground."

"All right, I feel like I can do it."

"Yeah, that's the spirit. Now show me."

With that, Josef reached for Leorino's chest once more. But when Leorino was about to practice the move and strike the elbow of the arm holding him...

"...What in the world are you two playing at now?"

They both froze in place and turned to the owner of the voice.

"Gauff! Welcome back!"

There stood Gauff, the third son of the Cassieux family, with a look of exasperation on his face.

Even among Leorino's stronger older brothers, Gauff was undoubtedly the strongest, and blessed with an innate talent for martial arts. He was currently serving in the Inner Palace Guard as a member of the Imperial Guard.

Gauff was also Josef's childhood friend.

"What were you two doing?"

Gauff looked around the room, seeing it had been cleared of furniture. Leorino relaxed his stance, greeting Gauff with a smile.

Of his three brothers, Gauff was the one he had always felt most comfortable talking to because of their close age. But Gauff was now on inner palace guard duty and was therefore quite busy, so this was only the third time they had seen each other since Leorino's arrival in the capital.

"Welcome back, Brother. It's good to see you again."

After giving him a light hug, Leorino patted him on his wide shoulder. Gauff seemed pleased to see him as well and hugged his beloved brother tightly.

"I missed you so much. Have you been well? Are you getting used to the royal capital?"

Leorino was immediately reminded of his blunder from the other day but didn't feel the need to bring it up. He smiled sweetly instead. "I recently visited the Count of Arhen's estate. I've become painfully aware of my own ignorance, but I'll do my best to get used to my new life here."

"Sounds great."

His brother stroked Leorino's head in encouragement, his eyes smiling. Gauff had short-cropped dark brown hair and blue-green eyes, much like their father. Leorino suddenly felt a pang of longing for the margrave back in Brungwurt.

"...So can you tell me what you've been up to?"

"Josef was teaching me self-defense."

Gauff glared at Josef, who had been watching their exchange.

"Jo, what are you making Leorino do now?"

"...I'm teaching him some basic self-defense, in case he's ever left alone."

Josef stood there, unflinching under Gauff's gaze, completely unfazed.

"...Right. I don't know what strained logic brought you here, but don't bother. There's no point."

Leorino was indignant at Gauff's words.

"That's so mean! How can you say there's no point? I want to be able to defend myself at least a little."

Gauff scratched his cheek in annoyance and hesitated to respond for a moment.

"What? If you have something to say, then just say it."

"...Ah, Rino, I just think you shouldn't push yourself. You have Josef as your guard now. Let him handle everything."

"...I'm not pushing myself. And I just managed to do it. I want to learn enough to be able to scare an attacker away."

Gauff sighed in exasperation. The next moment, Leorino blinked and his brother's large body suddenly appeared right in front of him. He grabbed Leorino by the front of his shirt.

"...Gau— Wh-wha—?"

"Do what you just did."

Leorino understood his brother's intention. Gauff wanted him to practice the move on him.

Leorino nodded and swung his hand at his brother's elbow joint. As expected, Gauff's upper body shook.

Yes...!

When his upper body folded, Leorino grabbed the clothes around Gauff's shoulder blade. Now he simply had to use inertia to send him tumbling. Gauff was losing his balance. Leorino brought his body close.

"...Yes! ...Ah? Um..."

The next moment, Leorino was being lifted like a piece of luggage onto the shoulders of his muscular brother.

"Huh...?"

"See?"

Leorino had no idea what had just happened.

Josef snapped at Gauff with a fierce expression. "Go easy on him! Obviously he's no match for an actual knight!"

"This is on you, Jo. Self-defense could be dangerous for Leorino. Don't you understand?"

Josef was dumbfounded by the harsh reproach.

"Why? If things go well, it could buy him some time."

"And if things go badly, it would only provoke a potential assailant."

That much was true. Leorino understood what Gauff was saying logically. Emotionally, however, he wanted to try a little harder.

"...Let me try one more time, Gauff."

"Rino?"

After more urging, and with some reluctance, Gauff put Leorino down. Then, after letting his arms hang loose, he nimbly grabbed at Leorino's chest again.

Even with no real strength...I can still make him tumble him to the ground...!

Leorino applied the technique again, but quicker and more carefully than before. He focused, thinking about where to apply his force.

Then, with a beautiful sound, Gauff's huge frame rolled smoothly to the floor.

"You did it!" Josef yelled in delight.

"Hah, hah...! How's that, Gauff? Now take back what you said!"

Gauff was lying on the floor, rubbing the back of his head. Leorino felt guilty for throwing his brother to the ground, but more than that, he was elated that he managed to execute the technique perfectly.

Perhaps there was still hope for his body.

"...And? Rino, where do we go from here?"

"...Where?" Leorino turned his head at his brother's words.

He felt a strange sensation in his leg. When he looked at his feet, he noticed Gauff had suddenly gotten a firm grip on his ankle.

The feeling startled Leorino, and he shuddered.

"Now try to run away."

"...Gauff, please."

Gauff's fingers were not exerting any force, only gently restraining his ankle. If he wanted to shake him off, he probably could.

But if this were to happen in real life...

Gauff watched his pale brother with pity in his eyes.

"...Do you see now?"

There was no way some ruffian would be this kind to him. Leorino's legs—especially his left leg—were not suited for anything more vigorous than walking.

It was just like when he was being restrained by Lucas.

When the lower half of his body was held down, there was nothing Leorino could do to resist, unless he could bring himself to fight back hard enough to risk breaking his own legs.

And in Leorino's case, even one reckless move could spell the end.

Gauff stood up with an exasperated look on his face. He was not injured, and it was clear he had deliberately allowed his brother to execute the technique as intended.

"You said it was self-defense. This kind of self-defense is just a way to buy time to incapacitate the attacker for long enough to escape. That's what you were trying to teach him, wasn't it, Jo?"

His brother was trying to show Leorino the reality of his situation.

"I'll come out and say it. Stalling for time won't do much for you when you can't run away on those legs. That's why you shouldn't provoke your opponent with any strange moves in the first place."

Leorino bit his lip.

"Don't look at me like that. You have to face the truth, Leorino."

Gauff was making valid points.

Gauff looked at Leorino as he hung his head in disappointment, and spoke to Josef. "Jo, you're unmatched with a sword. I doubt anyone in the royal capital could best you... But you see, you're not just protecting yourself anymore. You must get in the habit of thinking about what you can and can't do in the event that the person you're guarding is attacked. That's what it means to be a guard."

As a member of the Imperial Guard, working on inner palace duty and guarding the nobles day in and day out, Gauff's words carried a different sort of weight to them.

Josef winced. "I'm sorry, Lord Leorino..."

Leorino hated every part of this.

Was his body useless after all? Even if he could make a temporary escape with his superficial self-defense skills, he would not be able to run away if he was chased.

What was there to do then?

"I understand... I won't mention self-defense or martial arts again."

Leorino's eyes were filled with fierce conviction.

"But, Josef, in return, I want you to teach me how to use a dagger."

"...Umm, Rino?"

"Lord Leorino?"

"If I can't run away, I might as well learn how to inflict a fatal wound... Yes, that's a better idea."

"What— Rino! Are you out of your mind?"

Leorino shook his head at his shocked brother. "I don't want to always have to be protected. I refuse to be treated like some princess, locked up in a tower my entire life."

"Rino... You don't—"

"Josef will protect me, of course. But Josef won't always be around. I refuse to be completely helpless when push comes to shove."

At that moment, there was a knock at the door. The brothers paused their conversation.

When a servant opened the door, there stood Auriano's personal valet.

"Lord Leorino, Lord Auriano wishes to see you."

"...He does?"

"Yes. He wants you to come with Lord Gauff at once."

Invitation to the Palace of Defense

"...I'm going to work for Dr. Sasha?"

Auriano nodded.

In addition to his eldest brother, his mother Maia, his third eldest brother Gauff, and for some reason Josef were also invited to the study.

"Dr. Sasha has extended you an offer. He has asked if you would like to work at the Palace of Defense as his assistant."

Leorino may have known little of the world, but even he realized that this was a very special offer.

"That was very kind of him...but I don't know anything about medicine."

"Dr. Sasha said that won't be an issue. You're not going to be directly involved in treatment, but a member of the Health Department, mainly doing clerical work."

"B-but..."

Leorino still couldn't believe it.

His eldest brother's expression as he explained the situation seemed to indicate that he himself was bewildered. Auriano's face also revealed some confusion and distress, as if he was hoping that Leorino would turn down the offer.

This was the best offer Leorino could ever hope for. That must have been why his eldest brother was discussing this with him at all.

But...why?

He couldn't get past that question.

He could walk normally, but his legs were not suited for standing and working like a fully able-bodied person. He may have received higher education from his private tutors, but he had never attended school and lacked knowledge that most would consider common sense.

Was there something more to this sudden offer?

Leorino went through all the scenarios he could imagine, but given that he had no power outside of being a son of the Cassieux family, he couldn't see any merit in hiring him.

Or perhaps some secret agreement had been made between the Palace of Defense and Brungwurt?

As part of the arrangement between the royal family and the Cassieux family, the youngest son would fall under the custody of the Palace of Defense... No, why would they do that?

There was a troubled expression on Maia's gorgeous, ageless face.

Gauff had also just learned of this and seemed unconvinced, the furrow in his brow even deeper than their eldest brother's.

"Brother, I'm opposed to this. They can't seriously expect Rino to work in the Palace of Defense."

The eldest brother reassured Gauff after his biting remark. "It would be the safest place for Leorino to work. At the Palace of Defense, Dr. Sasha vowed he will personally supervise Leorino's work while ensuring his safety."

"Even so, Dr. Sasha won't be able to follow him everywhere! What if something happens to Rino in his absence?!"

"Josef will be working with him. We won't make it public that Josef is his guard—he'll be Leorino's colleague. This has been approved by Dr. Sasha."

Standing in the corner, Josef seemed surprised by this. He and Leorino exchanged a look.

"...Brother, such a thing would be practically unprecedented. They would allow Leorino, who has never even attended school, to work at the Palace of Defense and, on top of that, be accompanied by a guard? That's unheard of!"

Gauff was right, and that was also what Leorino wanted to know. It was a very kind offer, but he couldn't understand where it came from.

Auriano sighed at Leorino's inability to hide his inner turmoil.

"...It was Dr. Sasha's idea, but the general himself has said that he will take care of Leorino at the Palace of Defense, and that if Leorino wants to be independent, he wants to support him... I don't know his true intentions behind this."

"The general himself? But why would he possibly...?"

"It appears that he has already spoken with Father. Since His Excellency has gone that far, our family can't exactly turn down the offer."

"...I can't begin to fathom this. What led him to such a decision?"

Vi is calling for me... But why?

Leorino subconsciously brought his fingertips to his lips and pondered the sensation he remembered.

The kiss Gravis had stolen from Leorino in his office. The faint heat, like the touch of a feather tip.

He didn't kiss me because he's interested in me...did he?

Leorino waved away the wishful fantasy. The thought that a mature man like Gravis could have any interest in him was delusional at best. Recalling that conversation, Leorino was suddenly beset with anxiety and sorrow.

Could it be because I have the same violet eyes as Ionia? But...

When Lucas was projecting Ionia onto his eyes, Gravis had told him:

"Look at the boy for who he is. Look at him, at the brilliance of his own life as Leorino Cassieux."

Yes. Gravis was supporting him.

He must have heard from Sasha that Leorino was looking for work and extended a helping hand.

That was the most natural conclusion.

And if that was the case, then it was probably safe to assume that there was nothing suspicious behind this unusual offer and that it was simply a product of Gravis's generosity.

Silently watching the conversation unfold, Maia finally spoke to her youngest son: "Leorino, are you prepared to work in the outside world?"

"Mother... Yes, of course I am. The idea of working at the Palace of Defense simply came as a surprise to me."

"Are you scared?"

Leorino nodded honestly. He may have been surprised, but he was more optimistic than not. However, when it came to actually accepting the offer, he was filled with a different kind of unease.

"No, I'm happy. But I'm not sure how well I'll be able to perform given my legs... I'm worried that I'll cause nothing but trouble for Dr. Sasha after he's been so kind to me."

Maia looked at her troubled youngest son and said, "You don't need to work if it's too much for you, Rino."

"Mother?"

"Your father enjoys living a simple life, so it might be hard to fathom, but we're a wealthy family. You and Gauff will not inherit a title, but you have already inherited a good part of the estate that I brought as a dowry. Even if you never work a day in your life, you will always have food on the table and a place to live."

Leorino reconsidered his family's financial situation.

He had worried that, in comparison to his three older brothers, he could be considered the deadbeat son causing his family significant financial hardship. He was relieved to hear that, although he was still a burden, money would not be an issue.

"If you only want to be independent because you fear financial problems in the future, then you can stop now."

Leorino nodded. He appreciated his mother's words.

But even if he did not need financial independence, he still felt the need to go to work. He needed to work to find out who had been behind the tragedy at Zweilink. In order to learn more about the incident, he desperately needed a place to work and an opportunity to connect with people outside of his family.

In that sense, the Palace of Defense was the perfect place to gather information.

He wanted to accept Sasha's offer after all. He did not know if he would be of any use, but he still wanted to do his best at the job he had been so graciously offered.

Leorino's thoughts were disturbed by Gauff's booming voice.

"Mother! I'm against it!"

"Gauff. This is for Leorino to decide."

Leorino was baffled.

He thought that his third brother had supported his quest to find a job in the royal capital, but he seemed to be opposing it throughout the entire conversation. Was working in the Palace of Defense really so difficult?

But Leorino was shocked to his core by the next words to come out of Gauff's mouth.

"This wasn't part of the agreement! You never told me you were *really* going to put Leorino to work!"

"...Gauff!"

At Auriano's admonishment, Gauff turned to Leorino with a start. He clicked his tongue and looked away.

"...Wh-what do you mean by that?"

But no one offered to clarify.

Gauff refused to meet his eye.

Leorino looked to his eldest brother with pleading eyes.

"...You never intended to let me work? Is that true...?"

"...Leorino."

"You supported me because you thought I wouldn't be able to find work because of my legs anyway? ...Or were you going to oppose me even if I did manage to find a job?"

The family could only offer silence in response.

Leorino struggled to keep his voice from shaking.

"Brother Auriano...was Father thinking the same thing? When Father told me he wanted me to try my best for two years in the royal capital...was that all a lie, too?"

Auriano winced. "Father's support for you is not a lie."

"But he never intended to let me become independent. That's what this is all about, isn't it?"

"Leorino...we're all just worried about you. You remember what happened at the soiree. We worry that you might be kidnapped...that you might be hurt."

Leorino couldn't take it anymore and cast his gaze to the floor. If he hadn't, he would have surely burst into tears. Any mention of the shameful events of that soiree cut him deeply.

"...What, then? Am I to spend the rest of my life cooped up at home?"

"Leorino, listen to me."

"...So, in the end, you just want to marry me off to Lord Julian or any other man who could be my guardian, so that they can protect me and lock me away...? Is that it?"

"...Leorino!"

Leorino shook his head, refusing to listen.

No words could console him right now.

Leorino was painfully aware of his own weakness. But being confronted with that reality over and over again was too painful. The fact that he had believed his family was supporting his desire to become independent only made it worse.

But...this isn't the end. I won't deprecate myself by doing everyone's bidding and staying meekly confined somewhere safe.

He couldn't give up yet. In order to fulfill his purpose in the royal capital, he had to free himself of the suffocating love that kept him caged.

Determination burning in his heart, Leorino raised his face.

"...I will gladly accept Dr. Sasha's offer."

"Don't be stubborn. I'm against it, Leorino."

Leorino shook his head at Gauff's objection.

"Auriano, please tell them that I will humbly accept the offer."

Leorino then looked at every family member present in the room and bowed his head.

"Mother, my dear brothers...thank you so much for watching over me all these years."

"...Rino."

"I realize that I may cause you much concern, but please don't stop me. Allow me to fulfill my original promise with Father and put in two years of honest work. If, by then, I can no longer stand on my own, then I will do as you ask."

With sadness in their eyes, Maia and Leorino's brothers silently watched their youngest, his head still bowed.

Leorino did not change his stance.

Maia's sigh echoed around the room.

"...If you're going to accept the offer, then be sure to display the spirit of the Cassieux family and work hard, Leorino."

"Mother?!" Gauff yelled.

Leorino raised his head and looked at his mother.

She beckoned him to come closer and squeezed his hands. Seeing her up close, Leorino saw the wrinkles in the corners of his mother's eyes. Her hands were fair and thin, just like his own, but Leorino was struck by how much larger his hands were than hers.

"We were too overprotective of you... You've gotten so big and you're well on your path to adulthood...and yet we wanted you to remain our sweet little angel forever. That was so selfish of us."

"Mother. I'm sorry for worrying you."

Maia nodded and told him in a firm voice.

"Do your best. Show us that you can do it."

"Mother..."

Maia gently pulled him closer and pressed their foreheads together.

"If you ever get the chance, you should ask your father what he thinks. You have the right to walk your own path in life, but you also have obligations. As a member of the Cassieux family, you are obligated to adhere to the decisions made by the head of the family."

"…Of course."

"You are a member of the Cassieux family. Like your brothers, you've inherited the royal bloodline of Brungwurt. You also have the blood of the Fanoren royal family flowing through your veins. One day you may have to make a difficult choice. When you do, remember of your duty."

"…Yes, Mother. I understand."

Leorino turned to Josef, who had been watching them in silence, and asked, "Josef, will you come to the Palace of Defense with me?"

Josef nodded dutifully.

"I would follow you anywhere, Master Leorino."

At his reassuring words, Leorino smiled like a flower blooming after a long winter.

The Palace of Defense

"Useless trash!"

Leorino bit his lip at the malicious whisper tossed his way by the passing men. He kept facing forward; he did not look back.

"What was that, you bastards?! What did you just say?!"

Walking next to Leorino, Josef turned around and yelled at them instead. The young men were fellow desk workers in the Health Department. They were running away.

"Josef, let's go."

Josef was still angry, but he heaved a sigh when Leorino placed a hand on his arm.

They were headed for the archives at the far end of the Palace of Defense. It was somewhat of a detour, but they always chose to walk the less populated corridors.

After a while, Leorino looked up at Josef and murmured, "...If you get angry at every little thing they say, you'll never see the end of it. They call me useless because that's what I am."

Josef's beautiful face twisted in anger. "They're just jealous of you."

"I know, but you can't blame them. I'm exempt from doing chores. Dr. Sasha *is* giving me special treatment, that much is true."

Leorino hung his head. Josef clenched his teeth at his master's crestfallen appearance.

* * *

Out of consideration for Leorino's condition, Sasha gave him a job that would keep him from attracting undue attention.

"You're in a different position from them, Lord Leorino."

"Josef, that's where you're wrong. As employees in the Palace of Defense, our relative social standing is of no import... In any case, I can only keep working as hard as I can. I hope they will understand that in time."

"Lord Leorino..."

"Don't worry. I'm not going to give up, no matter what they may say," Leorino said, and smiled. His face appeared thinner than it had been.

Having worked at the Palace of Defense for a month now, Leorino was suffering daily.

"Mr. Kaunzel, it's me, Leorino."

The Palace of Defense's archives smelled of dust and old paper.

Despite the large window facing the courtyard, the room was somewhat dim due to the many bookcases filled edge to edge with documents.

Important classified documents were kept in a locked vault deep within the archives. The documents and records stored in the front of the archives were accessible to everyone who worked at the Palace of Defense.

Leorino and Josef acknowledged the man they had become familiar with over the past month who sat at the large desk by the window. Dust glistened in the light surrounding the man.

The man they called Kaunzel seemed to be intently reading some document. When he looked up at the sound of his name, he finally noticed their presence.

"Good afternoon, Mr. Kaunzel."

"Leorino, Josef, good to see you. Are you doing more research today?"

"Yes, sir. Today, I would like to look into the records of the dispatch of medical units and supplies from the Health Department to the mountains. I would like to ask for permission to see the documents from the Zwelf invasion eighteen years ago, and from the large-scale subjugation five years ago, respectively."

"Of course." Kaunzel nodded with a kind look on his face. Leorino relaxed his tense body and smiled slightly.

*　*　*

It had been a month since he began working in the Palace of Defense. Leorino was under constant stress, feeling like his every move was under close surveillance. To him, Kaunzel was a valuable presence who offered him no special treatment while maintaining a reasonable distance.

Worn down by walking on eggshells every day, going to the library was the only chance Leorino got to heal. Both him and Josef had grown fond of Kaunzel's gentle disposition.

"Would you like to look in the vault in the back?"

Kaunzel raised his large frame from the chair and touched the bunch of keys at his waist with an audible jangle.

When the generous man stood, he was about two heads taller than Leorino. But the left sleeve of his military uniform was missing the vital part that should have been there.

Kaunzel had originally been a soldier in the mountain troops. But having been wounded in the war eighteen years ago, he lost an arm, retired from the front lines, and had been placed in charge of the archives at the Palace of Defense ever since. Sasha, however, insisted that he was still strong enough to take down active members of the army with one arm alone.

Kaunzel had become a sort of watchdog of the archive, protecting the greatest secrets of the Palace of Defense.

This was the second time that Leorino and Josef had been allowed to enter the vault.

It was darker and cooler than the main room of the archives, given its lack of windows, and smelled of old paper. Inside, it was separated by several layers of gates. Multiple keys were required to reach the deepest part.

The documents that Leorino wanted to see were of relatively low secrecy.

"Documents from twenty years ago should be around here, so the stuff from the war eighteen years ago should start here. The documents from five years ago should be in this area. There's quite a lot, but let's take them back to the archives first, shall we?"

"Yes, thank you so much, Mr. Kaunzel."

But Leorino decided to make an additional request.

"Mr. Kaunzel, if possible, I would like to see the detailed procurement of weapons and foodstuffs for the same period, along with a record of each unit's activities."

"Huh. That's quite the research project. What does this have to do with the Health Department?"

"Is that a no?" Leorino tilted his head.

"What do you want to look into?"

"I, um… I'd like to investigate the damage to the units and how it relates to their preparedness for battle."

Kaunzel looked at Leorino with naked curiosity. The young man had worked in the palace for only a month, but was already offering an interesting perspective.

Sasha had told Kaunzel that Leorino had never gone to school, and that due to his incredibly sheltered upbringing, he understood precious little of the real world.

When they finally met, the young man was indeed a beautiful, otherworldly being who could be easily mistaken for an angel, just like he had been told. Even Kaunzel, who was confident in his inability to be surprised by hardly anything anymore, was moved beyond words when he witnessed Leorino's beauty for the first time.

However, as he gained more opportunities to talk with Leorino over the past month, he observed him beyond the thin veneer of his appearance and realized he was a very thoughtful young man. He may have been unworldly, aloof, and far too earnest, but he wasn't a fool, either.

Still, he possessed an interesting point of view. Kaunzel cocked his head, wondering how he had arrived at the idea.

"Did Dr. Sasha tell you to do that?"

"No, Dr. Sasha said that the management of the on-site procurement of personnel and supplies of the Health Department had been careless and asked me to organize it. The latter part of the request is…a pet project of mine…"

Leorino's tone gradually wilted as he grew self-conscious. Kaunzel offered him a reassuring smile.

"Do you *really* want to look into it?"

"Yes, sir. I understand if that won't be possible, but…I thought that if we could find a way to improve lateral cooperation, we might be able to minimize the damage on the front lines... Is that presumptuous for someone of my status?"

Kaunzel shook his head. To the former frontline soldier, Leorino's enthusiasm toward research was more than welcome.

The issue was that the documents Leorino wanted to see were under the jurisdiction of General Staff, and working within the Health Department, Leorino would need additional permission to view them.

"Those are highly classified, so you will need permission from the General Staff. Can it wait a little?"

Leorino's face immediately brightened at that. His smile was so beautiful that Kaunzel felt he could look at it forever. Leorino's honest display of emotion was adorable.

Kaunzel scratched his head bashfully.

"I'm weak to that angelic smile of yours. I can't promise they'll give you permission, but I know some people in General Staff. I'll see what I can do."

"Thank you, Mr. Kaunzel!"

Kaunzel looked at Leorino warmly, as if he were his own grandchild.

"Some documents can't leave the archives, but some can be taken out within the Palace of Defense. Would you like to take them with you now?"

"Yes, please. I'll work on them in a vacant room in the Health Department."

"Oh, in that case... I suppose you won't be able to carry all that on your own. Let me put them in a box for you. You can send someone to pick it up later."

Leorino's expression turned somber.

"...Um, if you don't mind that it takes a while, Josef and I will manage on our own."

"Lord Leorino, I don't mind making a few round trips."

Their exchange made Kaunzel realize something. Leorino was still alone in the Palace of Defense.

He was always smiling in the archives, but his face seemed even thinner than when they had first met. He must have lost weight due to the stress of his work.

Kaunzel had heard from Sasha about the difficult situation Leorino was in.

* * *

As the Cassieux family had feared, Leorino's presence was more conspicuous in the outside world than they had expected. Because of his extraordinary beauty and otherworldly aura, he stood out like a sore thumb in the Palace of Defense.

The backlash had come from the younger generation.

To them, Leorino's presence was, metaphorically speaking, like that of a royal princess. They could gaze at him from afar just fine. In fact, as far as gazing was considered, there was nothing more suitable for admiration than his radiance.

However, Leorino had entered the Palace of Defense as their colleague. Even in the Health Department, working for the Royal Army was not easy. For commoners and the young men and women of the lower nobility, it was a coveted profession that they had worked hard to acquire.

They were jealous of Leorino, wondering why he was given special treatment. And when they saw Leorino in person, they feared they might fall for his all-encompassing beauty.

As a result of these mixed feelings, Leorino ended up completely isolated from his colleagues.

"I was hoping it would go better than this," Sasha had lamented. Kaunzel was also well aware of the situation, but like Sasha, he watched on in silence.

What Leorino needed now was not sympathy nor words of comfort. It was support for his eagerness to fulfill the mission he had been given.

Kaunzel offered whatever help he could.

"You can work here as long as you want. You're free to use that corner."

Leorino smiled brightly. "Thank you so much! Then, um… I'll work here starting tomorrow, if you don't mind."

He bowed his head. His swaying platinum hair shimmered in the light streaming in through the window.

"But you'll have to wait for the weapon procurement logs and field records until you get permission from the General Staff."

"Yes, sir. Thank you!"

Kaunzel was struck by Leorino's commitment and enthusiastic nod, filling Kaunzel with the immense desire to support him.

After the meeting, as the top brass stood from their seats, Stefan Stolf, the head of General Staff, approached Sasha, the head of the Health Department.

"By the by, the fourth son of the Cassieux family who joined at your behest, Dr. Sasha, is quite the interesting fellow."

Sasha inclined his head. "Lord Leorino? Why, he must have done something very special to capture *your* attention."

"Well, there's his beauty, of course. At first, I thought it was entirely a token invitation, but he seems to be doing some interesting research of his own, so he's caught my eye as of late."

"Oh, yes, about that! Thank you for allowing him access to your documents. He certainly brings an interesting perspective to the table."

Besides Sasha and Stolf, Gravis, Dirk, and Lucas remained in the room. Lucas winced slightly at the mention of Leorino's name.

"So what's Leorino working on?"

Sasha answered Dirk's question. "Right now, I'm having him organize the system managing the deployment of medical units and supplies."

"Huh. Very impressive. But that's a difficult job to begin with...and he's only been here for a month. I know he's clever, but can he really handle that?"

"I think he can. Dirk, you really think Leorino is just an ignorant little princeling, don't you?"

"Well, am I wrong?"

The most gifted doctor in the kingdom grinned at Dirk's skepticism.

"Dirk, you really take him for a fool. He may not have gone to school, but he *is* from Brungwurt, which means...he's as educated as any graduate—if not more so. He's, for lack of a better word, perfectly useful."

"Wow! Good for him. But even so, I doubt he understands the ins and outs of the Royal Army just yet. You made him tackle a real challenge as his first assignment."

Sasha inclined his head at that.

"See, that's the strange thing. I don't know what they were teaching him, but he already has a better grasp of the army than the recruits who joined earlier this year."

"What do you mean?"

"Hmm. He's not used to working, but he doesn't seem to have any questions or confusion regarding the organization of the army or how it works."

Gravis stopped gathering his belongings and listened to the doctor.

"I don't know where he got his knowledge from, but he quickly found his way with actual work. I was surprised, too. Though he still sticks out like a sore thumb."

"We spoke briefly once, and he was rather knowledgeable. I wonder if he was always enamored by the Royal Army."

Dirk also cocked his head.

"The fact that the Health Department's management methods are sloppy is obvious to anyone who sees them. But, you know, when I asked him to organize the documents, he read them carefully. 'Why is there no uniform way to manage personnel and supplies?' he asked me, very politely."

The paperwork-hating doctor scratched his head in defeat.

Stolf widened his eyes at Sasha's words.

"My. Quite incredible of him to offer such a perspective after only a month in the palace... Hey, Bergund. He might be even better than you were when you first joined."

Stolf was Dirk's former superior from his days in General Staff. Dirk forced a smile at the teasing of a man who knew him well when he was younger, but nodded in agreement.

"When I first joined, I was struggling just to learn the organizational structure. He might actually be something special."

That seemed to capture Stolf's interest.

"When I heard about his request, I was skeptical, but...I might actually want him in the General Staff."

"Master Stolf! Absolutely not. I wouldn't even dare joke about sharing Lord Leorino with you. He is not strong enough to endure the hard work of the General Staff. I've actually been worried about him, because he's lost a lot of weight due to his new lifestyle."

* * *

Gravis, who had been quietly listening to his subordinates, spoke up for the first time.

"Is he in good health?"

"Yes, he's fine. He must have lost his appetite due to the hardships he's been facing."

"Hardships? Caused by what exactly?"

"Oh, there Your Excellency goes, being overprotective again. Well, I saw it coming from a mile away, but he stands out from his peers more than I'd expected."

Everyone remaining in the room fell silent. Thinking of the person in question, the reason became obvious.

"Well, to put it bluntly, it's his relationship with his colleagues. There's no open conflict, but they certainly don't get along. Rather, they ignore his existence."

"Why does the Health Department allow this to go on?!" Lucas demanded.

But Sasha shook his head. "If we intervene at this point, it will only make things worse. If Leorino is to live in the outside world, he will have to overcome such obstacles eventually."

The Chief of Staff groaned. "Hmm... Indeed, with his good looks and upbringing, it would be difficult for him to fit in with others."

"Yes, but he hasn't lost heart yet. Josef told me as much. He is trying his best to find a place for himself. I just want to believe in his efforts a little longer."

"What about the Cassieuxs? Have they said anything?" Gravis asked Sasha.

"No. He's Brungwurt's prized jewel, after all. They've been a little on edge, but...he's been diligently coming to work every day."

"Huh, he's got more backbone than I expected. I assumed him to be soft based on his appearance, but he's no fool... Forgive me, but honestly, I didn't think he could be of any real use, but alas."

Sasha agreed with Stolf's words.

"Oh, I've always believed in Leorino's grit. I, too, was surprised about his work ethic. I had planned to start him off with simple clerical work, but he suddenly pointed out the most sloppy management problems in the Health Department. His work is slow but thorough."

Stolf chuckled.

"And that's when he decided to look into the deployment of troops to the Baedeker Mountains and Zweilink eighteen years ago? How very diligent."

It was Gravis who found fault with the Chief of Staff's casual remark.

"...Stolf, what's this about? What did Leorino say to you?"

"Sir. He has submitted an interesting request through Kaunzel, the archivist. He asked for access to classified documents relating to the deployment of the mountain troops in the war with Zwelf eighteen years ago."

Gravis's gaze grew slightly more intense.

"...Do you know why Leorino was interested in the deployment of the mountain troops?"

"In the process of sorting out the management issues of the medical units, he figured that if we strengthened the horizontal cooperation between the Health Department and the General Staff, we could reduce the damage received."

Dirk was surprised to hear his former superior's words.

"Wait a minute. Bright as Leorino may be, this is not the kind of idea that a layman who has only worked in the palace for a month would come up with."

The former superior and subordinate from the General Staff looked at each other and groaned.

"That's the point. That's why I was interested in him. Is that the result of Brungwurt's education? But no, Kaunzel had said it, too; his perspective is not that of a rookie. At this rate, he's going to find inadequacies in General Staff, too."

"So what's your response?" Gravis asked Stolf again.

"Sir. The records of the deployment eighteen years ago, although classified, contain no information we have any reason to hide. The General Staff has given him permission to view them."

Gravis pondered this for a while.

He then beckoned to his second-in-command. "Dirk."

Dirk quickly complied and approached Gravis. He brought his ear to the general's mouth. Dirk widened his eyes at the whispered instructions.

"Y-yes, that should be fine...?"

Gravis nodded toward his second-in-command. Then he looked around at the remaining officials.

"Keep me informed on the progress of his research."

Lucas had followed Gravis, saying he wanted to talk. Gravis dismissed Dirk, leaving him alone with Lucas.

"You want to talk about Leorino?"

Lucas's face stiffened. His amber eyes had a terrible, threatening glint to them.

"I would like to ask once again why Your Highness invited Leorino Cassieux to the Palace of Defense."

"What do you intend to do with that information?"

"...If this is somehow related to Ionia, I have a right to know."

Gravis sighed.

"My inviting Leorino to the Palace of Defense has nothing to do with Ionia."

"But Your Highness also found what you just heard strange, didn't you?"

"It could be a coincidence."

"A coincidence? If he is not the reincarnation of Ionia, why would a child who has just reached adulthood and has never been exposed to the outside world be interested in a military expedition from eighteen years ago?! Is that not enough 'coincidence' for you?!"

Gravis did not change his expression even as Lucas stifled his anger.

Lucas was indignant.

"Your Highness...you said it yourself the other day. You told me that you hold the same feelings as I...but I don't believe you. Only I am still haunted by his death."

Starry-sky eyes caught Lucas's gaze.

"I'm not like you...! Your feelings for Ionia are different from mine."

In spite of Lucas's pained scream, Gravis's expression remained unchanged.

"...If that boy had some connection to Ionia, what would you do?"

Lucas clenched his teeth at Gravis's question.

Gravis's starry-sky eyes watched him intently.

* * *

"...If he's the reincarnation of Ionia, I can't give up on him."

"Then what if he has nothing to do with Ionia...? What if he *is* just Leorino Cassieux?"

Lucas was perplexed by the question. He consulted the feelings stirring inside him.

"What if he's just Leorino Cassieux...?"

"Yes."

Lucas said nothing.

Leorino was unbelievably beautiful, of course.

But that was not the reason Lucas was drawn to him.

Lucas desired one thing and one thing alone: the presence of that red-haired young man.

"...I suppose that's your answer, then?"

Gravis seemed slightly irritated at Lucas's inability to reply.

"If you do not care for Leorino himself, whether he's Ionia reincarnated or not, he will never be yours."

"Why not?! ...If he really were *him*, I have the right to him!"

"Right? You have no right to anyone."

"And you do?!"

Gravis shook his head.

"Of course I don't. He's his own person."

"Then..."

"But he will be mine in time."

"...!"

Lucas looked at Gravis in disbelief. The man wore a faint smile.

Gravis's tone was as dispassionate as ever, but Lucas couldn't help noticing that his eyes were glowing gold.

"You heard me."

"Your Excellency... But the boy..." Lucas swallowed, trying to argue. "But if he really is the reincarnation of Ionia..."

This time, Gravis actually laughed.

"That would change nothing for me. Frankly, I'd prefer if he weren't—saves me the trouble of fighting with you. I want *Leorino*."

"...Then, if I were to fall in love with Leorino himself, what would you do?"

"Now, that's a different story... Who knows."

Lucas clenched his teeth. He felt like the man's calm intimidation would have overwhelmed him if he hadn't.

"I thought you invited him to the Palace of Defense to help him become independent..."

"I can do several things at the same time. He will work within my reach. I have the power to do that."

Gravis smiled in a way that Lucas had never seen before, a smile that seemed almost tender.

"...What's with that face? Were you actually doubting me? I told you...I'm just like you."

"Your Highness..."

"Lucas. You're very special to me. I would even consider you my closest friend."

The intensity of Gravis's gaze made Lucas shiver.

"If you desire Leorino himself, fine, we'll see who he chooses. But if all you want is whatever traces remain of Ionia, don't even think of touching him."

Lucas had no answer.

"If you use Leorino as a substitute for Ionia, then..."

His starry-sky eyes flashed gold.

"...I'm afraid that's where you and I will part ways."

Malice

"Leorino. We will finally speak today."

"We will not."

"Leorino!" His third eldest brother, Gauff, banged on the table. The attendant serving them jolted upright from the shock. Leorino looked at his brother in exasperation.

"Brother, where are your manners? I wish you wouldn't frighten the attendants."

"To hell with manners! ...You're going to listen to me."

"I already know what you're going to say, and I'm fine! Leave me alone, please."

"You are far from fine! Just be honest. You've lost so much weight... You're clearly having a hard time working at the Palace of Defense."

"There's nothing wrong with my weight."

"Like hell there isn't! You're withering away in front of our eyes!"

Leorino finished his after-dinner tea and hastily stood from his seat. Gauff's voice echoed after him.

"Leorino! Wait! I'll tell Father!"

Leorino finally stomped his foot. "You...! Fine, tell him! Now, if you'll excuse me!"

"Leorino!"

After the departure of his mother, eldest brother, and sister-in-law, the Brungwurt residence was growing more vicious by the day. It was no wonder—ever since Leorino had started working in the Palace of Defense, this exchange had been repeated day and night between the three older brothers and the youngest child of the family. This argument had gone on for almost two months now.

Spending time at home slowly became agonizing to Leorino. His older brothers continued to be overprotective and over-involved in his life. In particular, Gauff, the brother closest to him in age, still hadn't accepted Leorino's new occupation.

He knew that his older brothers' meddling was a product of love. He didn't want to dismiss them, but the truth was that he felt increasingly irritated by their behavior.

I appreciate them, but...I'd prefer if they could just silently watch over me right about now...

Leorino met up with Josef, his guard, in the entrance hall.

"Good morning, Josef. Looking forward to another day of working with you."

"Good morning, Lord Leorino."

When Leorino smiled at him, Josef smiled back. Josef, with his sword strapped to his slim, lean body, was very good-looking.

"I've thought this for a while, but you're really attractive, Josef."

"Huh? Where did that come from? I don't know what you want, but you won't get it with flattery."

"It's not flattery."

Leorino had meant it. Josef looked very good in the uniform of the Royal Army. The ascetic navy blue military uniform only served to highlight his slender yet toned physique. Combined with his feminine features and threatening expression, he looked rather impressive.

Josef may have been a young man with a rather puzzling personality, but with a sword in hand, he was a nearly peerless prodigy back in Brungwurt.

Leorino looked down at himself, wishing he looked as strong as Josef.

There's so much empty space around my belt... I'm too weak.

As Leorino rushed to fasten his belt, Hundert, who was about to see them off, gently stopped him.

"You mustn't show how thin your hips have become."

"Hm? But it looks bad. If I don't wear it properly, people will take issue with my appearance."

"No, it looks just fine on you, my lord."

"Mr. Hundert is right. You just need to put on some weight. Let's go, Lord Leorino."

Leorino wasn't satisfied with that answer, but he got into the carriage as instructed.

Feeling like riding up to the Palace of Defense in their carriage would have been inappropriate, they had gotten into a daily routine of getting off at the front gates of the royal palace and walking to the Palace of Defense from there.

But it was true—ever since Leorino had begun working at the Palace of Defense, he had become visibly thinner.

At first, he lacked the stamina necessary for the daily outings to which he was not accustomed, especially considering the fact he had to work all week without any time to rest. Ever since the incident six years ago, he had often been bedridden, and his fragile body was starting to give out. His legs in particular felt completely numb by the end of the day. He only managed to get by thanks to Hundert massaging life back into them regularly.

Sasha had exempted him from standing work that all newcomers were required to do in the Health Department from the very beginning. That alone had reduced his physical burden considerably. Leorino realized that getting exempted from physical labor meant he was receiving very special treatment. He also knew that his coworkers felt slighted because of this.

He couldn't help noticing the sort of clear hostility they displayed, whether he liked it or not.

His colleagues had at first distanced themselves from Leorino, but recently stopped trying to hide their hostility.

Although they never dared to touch him, they hid things from him on a daily basis and refused to relay messages to and from him. They also often verbally abused him in passing.

Recalling the face of one of the young men who had set his eyes on him, Leorino felt melancholic this morning.

* * *

"Are you thinking about that blond guy again?"

Sitting across from him, Josef sensed Leorino's anguish.

"That blond... Wait, how did you know?"

"I just do. Your face is all doom and gloom, you know. I know you're depressed to think you'll see him at today's debriefing, aren't you?"

He made an attempt at comfort by adding, "Don't worry about him."

"No, I don't give a damn! I'm over it, but I really wish he would stop hiding my messages. It interferes with my job. That's just unacceptable, isn't it?"

"If he were capable of listening to reason, he wouldn't have harassed you in the first place. He simply hates you because he's jealous. Don't you understand?"

Leorino nodded.

"I understand. It's because I'm a special case and Dr. Sasha gives me preferential treatment."

"It's not just that. Everyone in the Health Department must have fawned over that handsome face of his. But now that someone as beautiful as you has arrived, he's envious of the attention you're getting as well."

"And now everyone is fawning over me instead of him? Where in the Palace of Defense is that supposed to be happening? No, I've certainly experienced no fawning so far. If anything, I'm being treated rather coldly, don't you think?"

"What, you think they'd *openly* fawn over you? No one would dare. They could never be so chummy with you. I would actually respect them if they approached you so nonchalantly."

"...Josef? That's not what we were talking about."

"I know, that's different. But don't you get it?"

Leorino was at a loss. He knew that he wasn't very perceptive or tactful, but he really didn't understand what his guard was implying.

"Well, worrying about them won't change anything anyway, Lord Leorino."

"Yes, I'll just keep my head down in the archives today so as not to provoke them."

Josef nodded.

For the past twenty days or so, Kaunzel had graciously allowed them to work in a corner of the archives. With Sasha's permission, the two of them had been spending most of their time there recently.

After seeing their carriage off at the gates of the royal palace, Leorino hid his face deep within his hood on his way to the Palace of Defense. It was a conspicuous thing to do, but it was much safer than leaving his face uncovered. Although Leorino found it beyond frustrating that Josef could show his face off without fear.

"But I must say, I was so surprised when Mr. Dirk came to help us."

"Oh... Him. I don't like him."

"Why not? He's a lovely person." Leorino inclined his head at Josef's scowl, recalling his time with Dirk with a smile.

It was the day before yesterday when Gravis's second-in-command showed up in the archives.

"My former superior from the General Staff told me about you, so I'm here to help."

Dirk appeared before Leorino and Josef with a mischievous smile on his calm face.

He had indeed mentioned that back when he was a student, he had studied the war with Zwelf of eighteen years prior, and that it was because of this that he had joined the General Staff. Leorino was delighted that Dirk had offered to help.

At the same time, he felt a little guilty.

Leorino had not told anyone the real reason why he wanted to look into the mountain troops' deployment and the records of their activities from eighteen years ago.

Of course, now that he had access to the documents, he would use them to examine ways of closer coordination among the units once he organized the management methods of the Health Department.

But his real aim was to investigate the past of Edgar Yorke, who was deployed and integrated into the Special Forces at the same time as Ionia. The Marquis of Lagarea had reported to Leorino's father, August, that he had been unable to trace any of Yorke's movements in the capital. However, the marquis could no longer be trusted.

Leorino wanted to personally search for information that would lead to a clue as to who Yorke was connected to, however slim the possibility might be. He did not expect to come across potential clues so soon after arriving at the Palace of Defense, but he had to make the most of this opportunity.

I must make sure Dirk doesn't suspect anything...

Leorino had to focus. Around Dirk, he struggled to keep himself from asking all sorts of questions and wanting to bond with him.

"But we're making steady progress, aren't we? You should be able to report to Dr. Sasha soon, right?"

"Yes. I think we have enough for our first report. As for actual work, there are many things I just don't understand, so I'm hoping to have it ironed out by the concerned parties to finally end up with something practical. From here it's more of a collaborative effort with the people in the field."

"I really admire how you're so reserved and kind, but you're still working your ass off in the Palace of Defense, Lord Leorino."

Leorino laughed awkwardly. "Ah-ha-ha, Josef, language! I think you're just biased."

The only reason he had such a good understanding of the Royal Army and was able to immerse himself in the administrative work was thanks to Ionia's memories. He was lucky that even eighteen years later, the basic institutions of the Royal Army had not changed much.

He figured he had an unfair advantage. Still, he would never tell Josef about his past life as Ionia.

He already had a good idea of the new plan for the management of personnel and supplies of the medical units.

In border areas far from the capital, such as the mountainous region and Zweilink, transporting personnel and supplies from the capital took too much time and was too wasteful, so several intermediate bases had been set up. This research was conducted to correct the uneven management of communication between these bases and the Palace of Defense.

* * *

Leorino had memories of life in the mountain troops. Ionia had hated it, especially in winter when the mountains were covered with snow.

The mountainous area in the northwestern part of the country was particularly difficult to operate in and prone to causing injury. There were several bases in the towns leading up to the mountains, and Leorino intended to discuss their best usage.

The supplies stockpiled at the bases should be distributed on a gradient according to the number of troops deployed. In addition, there was a regular communication network between the bases set up by the General Staff, but the Health Department had not been able to take advantage of it.

Up until now, the Health Department had only managed the coordination between the royal capital and each base. If the Health Department could optimally distribute supplies and personnel between bases by utilizing the General Staff's regular communication network, it would be able to streamline their function at the front lines.

A combination of such small improvements would at least slightly reduce the sacrifices on the front lines. Leorino knew this from Ionia's memories. He had lost many men, colleagues, and superiors alike in the snowy mountains and at Zweilink.

He wanted to estimate the effects of this improvement based on actual combat records to provide a basis for proposing his plan.

A proposal from a low-ranking officer with no previous accomplishments like Leorino would otherwise never be given a second thought. If he showed them actual numbers, they were more likely to listen to him. That's how organizations worked, after all.

It was also the price he had to pay for access to records that would allow him to follow Edgar Yorke's movements.

Leorino and Josef headed to their usual small room in a section of the Health Department.

They brought the documents Leorino compiled every day back from the archives and stored them in this locked room before leaving. But the moment they unlocked the door and entered that very room, Leorino and Josef's faces turned grim.

"…What is this…?" Josef growled.

The shelves in the room had been ravaged, even though they were certain they had locked the door before returning home the previous day.

Documents were scattered all over the floor. Someone had broken in and ransacked the room. They were clearly being harassed.

Leorino rushed to the locked shelves. There he found the research materials he had been compiling. Relieved, he flipped through them just to be sure. That was when he realized a part was missing.

He knew who could have done it.

"Lord Leorino…do you think it was them?"

Leorino bit his lip. He wouldn't have cared if it had been a personal attack. He'd endure that if he had to.

"…But this is unacceptable."

A fierce anger brewed in Leorino's eyes.

As soon as Leorino and Josef entered the main office of the Health Department, all eyes were on them.

Normally, Leorino kept his head down, avoiding eye contact as much as possible, but today, he fearlessly lifted his chin as he scoured the room with his gaze. Boldly displaying his beauty, Leorino's presence was overwhelming. A silence fell over the office.

But a few men sitting in the center of the room stood out immediately.

As soon as Leorino and Josef had entered, they'd smiled wickedly. Looking at Leorino, they kept whispering something to each other and snickering. Their laughter echoed strangely through the silent office.

"So it *was* him…"

In the center of the group of men was the blond with short-cropped hair that Josef had mentioned earlier—Balto Entner. He was of relatively short stature for a man in the Palace of Defense, with blond hair, blue eyes, and an overall beautiful appearance. He was the second son of a viscount, one year older than Leorino. For some reason, he had made Leorino his archnemesis ever since he arrived at the palace.

Following Leorino and Josef's gazes, the people in the office looked to

Entner and his cronies. They sneered, seemingly unperturbed by the attention of the entire office.

You're basically admitting you did it...

Leorino was appalled, realizing the man had no intention of hiding what he did. He may have wanted to harass Leorino no matter the cost, but vandalizing a room in the Palace of Defense was a much greater issue. He could even be punished for it.

Did they not think about the consequences of what they had done out of their petty hatred for Leorino?

Leorino heaved a small sigh. Standing beside him, he met Josef's gaze. Josef looked back at him calmly, but his lips were quirked in a faint smile.

"...Josef, you seem calm."

"No, I'm just thinking about how I'm going to beat the living crap out of him... What a fool."

Leorino agreed with that last part.

"For the sake of our peace, let's keep beating the crap out of people a last resort. I'll try speaking with them first."

Josef nodded.

"It's your maiden battle, Lord Leorino. I'll be watching over you."

Leorino chuckled at that.

Then he headed straight for Entner and his lackeys.

The remaining people in the office watched the scene play out in silence. Entner and his cronies had been smirking at first, but hid their fiendish smiles and showed alarm at the sight of Leorino coming straight at them.

"I need to talk to you, Mr. Entner. May I have a moment of your time?"

"...What's that? I don't have anything to say to you."

Entner turned away childishly.

...What???

* * *

Leorino was baffled. In no world was this attitude appropriate for a military man to express toward his colleague. Combined with Ionia's memories, Leorino had never seen a more childish person in the Royal Army. Or was it that those who did desk work were never exposed to the taking of lives, and thus did not feel the need to abide by basic rules?

Leorino was stunned, unable to understand the thought process of people like Entner, but for the time being, they would get nowhere without talking. Besides, Leorino had his own reasons for wanting to keep things quiet and resolve the issue without causing a fuss.

He wanted to talk somewhere out of sight, so he decided to employ a threat or two.

"If you don't mind me saying what you did, we can speak right here, right now."

"Hah...?! How rude of you! What are you claiming that I did?"

Leorino kept his expression fixed.

"Very well, let's speak here... Here, where *everyone* can hear us. That's fine by me."

Entner shot Leorino a deadly glare, then gruffly got up from his seat.

"Fine, let's go...!"

He patted the shoulders of his cronies around him, and the men who had been watching their exchange with somewhat guilty expressions stood up as well.

Leorino nodded, turned on his heel, and left the room with Entner and his men.

They stopped at the landing of an empty staircase.

"Fine, we're here, now what do you want?"

Leorino turned around. The men were momentarily lost for words as his beauty took their breath away. Noticing the dazed look on his companions' faces, Entner elbowed them with a scowl, immediately turning them self-conscious.

I don't know how to talk to them... I'll be polite, I just need to get them to return my documents.

* * *

Leorino exhaled quietly. He was not equipped with the ability to judge people's feelings and get what he wanted from them.

In the end, he decided to get straight to the point.

"Mr. Entner, do you have any idea where my research materials are?"

"Hah...? Is that what this is about?"

"The room where I kept my materials was ransacked, and some of them went missing. Do you have any idea what happened to them?"

"Hah! So you're calling me a thief. I will not take such slander, not even from the son of the Margrave of Brungwurt!"

"My family has nothing to do with this. If my status gave me any power in the Palace of Defense, we would have already dealt with you differently."

The men behind Entner seemed alarmed by Leorino's words, but it was Entner who finally let his anger off its leash.

"You truly believe your pedigree grants you no privileges here?! You can clearly walk normally, and yet you are exempted from physical labor because of your legs. And you *dare* act like you don't get preferential treatment?! Or did you use that pretty face of yours to cozy up to Dr. Sasha?"

Leorino focused on speaking matter-of-factly.

"It is true that I'm exempt from certain duties, I won't deny that. However...I would ask you to retract what you said about Dr. Sasha. He doesn't deserve such slander."

But the next moment, he put some strength into the corners of his eyes and glared at Entner and his cronies.

"...But that has nothing to do with my current issue. I would like the documents you stole from my room back. They're part of an important research project."

"Hah! Your incoherent scribbles? Important research? How far up your own ass can you be?!"

And there it was.

"Spoken like someone who has actually seen said 'scribbles,' Mr. Entner." Entner bit his lip, seemingly realizing his mistake.

"Please return my documents. If you give them back now, I'll forget this ever happened."

"...I told you, I don't know anything!"

Leorino sighed deeply. The conversation was not progressing toward a peaceful resolution.

"...Mr. Entner, do you understand what you have done?"

"I didn't do it!"

"...If you want to bully me out of the Palace of Defense, fine. You can hate me all you want."

Leorino caught Entner's gaze with his violet eyes.

Entner was overwhelmed by his silent gaze, and for the first time, he seemed to falter.

"You may have been trying to damage my reputation. But no matter what work is done at the Palace of Defense, neither the process nor the results are the property of the individual in charge. It all belongs to the Palace of Defense."

Entner said nothing.

"You don't know the details of my work, do you? Perhaps they are just scribbles. My research may not be useful after all. But what you stole is not mine. It belongs to the Palace of Defense."

"...! Like I said...this is a false accusation!"

"Please. Please just give me back my documents."

Leorino bowed his head.

The men's eyes widened at the sight of this nobleman of a status so incomprehensibly higher than theirs bowing to them.

"If you insist you don't know where they are, that's fine. I just... I hope to see the materials in question back in that room by the end of the day. That's all."

Josef, who had been watching silently until then, stepped up next to Leorino, still bowing his head.

"You heard him. If Lord Leorino reports to your superiors that his room was ransacked and the documents stolen, it would become a major incident concerning the entire Palace of Defense.

"...You wouldn't—!"

"I mean, it would be a report from a powerful nobleman's privileged son. You can feign ignorance all you want, but there's only so much you can hide. Besides, a theft in the Palace of Defense would tarnish the reputation of the Royal Army—do you really think they would let you get away with that?"

Entner and his men shuddered. They finally realized that what they had done was more than just a prank, but a malicious breach of the law.

"What now...?" Entner's cronies began to waver.

Will they just give them back now...? I'm not so sure. That's all I really want.

Listening to Josef's words, Leorino raised his head. His eyes met Entner's, whose face twisted in humiliation.

"...Why do you get all the easy work and preferential treatment? ...You might just be 'special,' but I loathe spoiled brats like you!"

Was that how he truly felt?

Leorino clenched his teeth.

He knew they harassed him because they hated him, but it still hurt to hear it said to his face.

"I understand that my presence may be discouraging. If Dr. Sasha decides that I'm no longer needed here...I'll abide by his word."

"You better...! And I'm not the only one, everyone agrees with me! We don't want a rich boy like you barging into our world!"

Leorino calmly lowered his eyes.

That was when Josef patted him on the back.

"Lord Leorino, don't listen to them."

Leorino looked at Josef with gratitude.

Josef had sworn to fight with him. He was Leorino's dear childhood friend, and now he was also his guard.

Yes, if I reach out, I will find someone who will stand by my side...just like Ionia did.

Ionia had also had a family who loved him, and a best friend who supported him. Having something so precious within reach was more than enough. This thought brought him comfort and strengthened Leorino's heart.

He met Entner's hateful gaze without fear.

* * *

"What are you boys doing here?"

A voice suddenly echoed from upstairs, causing everyone on the landing to shudder.

When they looked up, they saw Sasha, the head of the Health Department. Omar, his adjutant, stood behind him.

"I went to the office just now, and everyone was chirping about how you two had left together. That's quite the unusual rendezvous, isn't it?"

"Dr. Sasha…"

Sasha's voice was calm, but his smile did not reach his eyes.

"So what were you discussing here? Something you can't talk about in the office?"

"H-hey… Entner, what now?"

But Entner gave no reply.

It was Entner and his cronies who were beginning to break out in a cold sweat, but Leorino wasn't happy with this situation, either. He had wanted to settle the matter as amicably as possible.

What would happen if his family found out his colleagues were bullying him? His overprotective family would surely stop him from working at the Palace of Defense—Leorino wanted to avoid that at all costs.

"I'm sorry, Dr. Sasha. I just…wanted to discuss something with Entner about my research."

"…Oh, is that so? And that's something you can't discuss in the office?"

Sasha and Leorino watched each other silently. The usually mild-mannered Sasha's blank expression filled him with fear.

While Leorino struggled to find a way out of the situation, a relaxed voice that didn't fit the tense atmosphere addressed him from downstairs.

"Oh? Lord Leorino? What are you doing here? Weren't we supposed to meet in the archives soon?"

It was Dirk, looking up at the landing with a quizzical look on his face. Leorino panicked, realizing that it was indeed almost time for their meeting in the archives.

"Oh, Dr. Sasha, you're here, too. Is the Health Department gathering here now?"

"I-I'm sorry, Mr. Dirk… Um, I'll be right there."

But Sasha, looking down at him from the stairs, addressed him again.

"I'm not finished talking with you yet, Lord Leorino."

"Dr. Sasha…"

His gaze darting between the top and bottom of the stairs, Leorino racked his brain for a way to amend this situation.

In Leorino's stead, Entner answered in a low voice from behind him. While Leorino was still reeling, Entner had regained his mask of composure, as if he hadn't just been fuming with rage.

"As Lord Leorino said, we were just talking."

"…Hmm, I see. Would you say that's an accurate description, Lord Leorino?"

"Y-yes." Leorino could only nod.

"Well, we have some work to attend to, so we'll take our leave now," Entner said, getting ready to walk away with his cronies. "Let's go!"

Twisting his body, Leorino suddenly grabbed Entner's arm as he walked past him.

"Um… Please do the thing we discussed!"

"…Ugh! Fine! Let go!" Entner shook him off as hard as he could.

"…Ah."

Leorino's body lurched backward.

Oh no…!

He quickly reached out for something to grab onto. But his hand found no purchase.

He could see the shock on Entner's face.

"Lord Leorino!"

"Leorino!"

Josef's scream echoed through the staircase. In the distance, he could also hear Sasha and Dirk's cries.

The next moment, he felt something solid and warm wrap itself around him.

Falling through the air, Josef still holding him in his arms, Leorino's body bounced with the impact as they slammed into the floor below.

Crime and Punishment

Suddenly, he was conscious again.

"Don't move his head... Dirk, can you lift Leorino? ...Gently now, keep them both as still as possible."

"Yes, sir."

Someone had picked him up.

"...Ugh."

"Lord Leorino, you're awake. Thank god. Can you speak? Are you in pain?"

The voice belonged to Dirk.

Immediately, Dirk laid him on the floor once more and stepped away.

Leorino felt a flurry of movement around him, his head spinning, likely due to the impact of the fall.

"Dirk, keep talking to Josef. Is he waking up?"

"No, sir."

"I see... Entner, boys! Bring the stretcher!"

He heard a rush of footsteps running down the hall.

What are they talking about? Who...?

"I'll examine Lord Leorino first. Lord Leorino, ah, you're awake. Good, can you answer me?" It was Sasha's voice now. "You fell down the stairs. Do you remember...? I'm going to touch you now."

...I fell down the stairs... Right, I lost my balance...and Josef...

His whole body was numb from the impact. As Dr. Sasha examined him, Leorino's mind gradually began to clear. He desperately tried to get his eyes to focus.

"…Doctor…I'm sorry."

"It's all right. Does your head hurt? Can you feel your legs? Are you in pain?"

He was terribly dizzy, but his head didn't hurt.

Next, Leorino turned his attention to the lower half of his body and moved his toes.

"…I'm okay. I'm sorry."

"Thank god. I don't want an apology right now, so hush. We'll discuss this later. I need to look at other parts of your body now."

Sasha swiftly checked Leorino's entire body.

Leorino shuddered when he felt Sasha touch his left wrist. The sharp pain fully brought him back to his senses.

Right…Josef saved me…!

"Doctor…"

"Oh, you sprained your wrist. But it's not broken. You're lucky—it's all thanks to Josef."

"Doctor…how's Josef…?"

"…You mustn't move yet. Lord Leorino, I'm going to examine Josef. I'll have to leave you. Omar, hold Leorino so he doesn't hurt himself any further."

Sasha left Leorino in the hands of his adjutant and moved to Josef.

Leorino struggled in Omar's grasp and managed to turn his body sideways. He saw Josef lying there, unconscious.

Dirk knelt next to Josef with a concerned expression on his face. He had taken off his jacket and placed it under Josef's head.

"Josef…! Josef…!"

Leorino frantically called his guard's name.

Dirk heard his hoarse voice and turned to Leorino with pained eyes.

* * *

With another rush of footsteps, Entner and his men returned with a stretcher.

For a moment, Leorino's eyes met Entner's, but Entner quickly averted his gaze. Leorino could only watch, still unable to move his body.

Lying there, his face pale, Josef looked so frail. Leorino couldn't stop shaking. He was only lightly injured thanks to Josef's quick wits and his wrapping himself around Leorino to save him from the impact.

"Dirk, can you lift Josef carefully? Yes, like that, thank you. Now gently place him on the stretcher... There."

"I'll carry him. Hey, you there. Help me."

Dirk pointed to a well-built man, one of Entner's cronies. The man, flustered, followed Dirk's order and took one side of the stretcher.

"Omar, will you be able to carry Lord Leorino?"

Sasha's second-in-command gently picked him up. No matter how desperately Leorino reached for him, the stretcher carrying Josef grew more and more distant.

"Josef... Josef..."

"Lord Cassieux, calm down, you must rest."

After another intense bout of dizziness, Leorino lost consciousness once more.

When he awoke, Leorino found himself in an unfamiliar room. He could see an unadorned wood plank ceiling above him.

"...Are you awake?"

Accompanied by the deep, smooth voice was a large hand placed on his forehead. The slightly cool fingers gently stroked his bangs.

I've felt these fingers before. I'm not afraid of their touch. These fingers are...

"...Your Excellency."

Gravis was sitting by his bedside. When he caught Leorino's gaze, the man nodded slowly.

Why was Gravis here? And where was "here" anyway? There were so many things Leorino wanted to know, but when he managed to squeeze his voice out of his parched throat, he asked about the most important thing.

"...Sir, my guard... Josef, is he—?"

"He's fine. Sasha came to report that he had just woken up. He hit his head, but it's nothing serious."

He was so relieved that he nearly fainted again, but the feel of the palm on his forehead gently held Leorino's consciousness in place.

"...Thank you."

Having expressed his gratitude, Leorino stared into space for some time. All the while, Gravis continued to stroke his head slowly, not saying a word.

Gradually, his feelings took shape.

"I'm sorry for the trouble I've caused you. Your Excellency, how did you—?"

"Dirk reported to me. I was chilled to my core when I heard you fell down the stairs. I'm glad you weren't seriously hurt, but I see you injured your wrist."

Gravis grasped Leorino by his left elbow and gently lifted his hand. Leorino's wrist was wrapped in a thick bandage.

It didn't exactly hurt, but he could feel a pulsating heat throb within.

"Sasha and Dirk told me what happened. You were discussing something on the landing with those boys from the Health Department. Do you have anything to report?"

Leorino immediately denied it.

"Nothing, sir... We were discussing...work, you see..."

"Sasha's second-in-command told us that the room where you kept your research materials had been ransacked."

"...No, that's—"

"I'm going to ask you once more. Is there anything you want to tell me?"

Leorino shook his head again.

He was no longer sure why he was being so stubborn, but he didn't want people to think he was the kind of man who would so easily tell on a colleague to his superiors.

"...I see. Then I'll judge based on what I know and punish him myself. That won't be a problem, will it, Sasha?"

Gravis called Sasha's name. Leorino searched the room and saw Sasha standing behind Gravis, hidden in the shadow of his large body.

Leorino rushed to sit up, only for Gravis to push him back onto the bed.

Feeling guilty for everything that happened, Leorino frantically apologized to Sasha.

"Doctor…I'm…really sorry for all the trouble I've caused you. And thank you so much for helping Josef."

Sasha smiled, looking a little tired.

"As you may have heard from His Excellency, Josef is going to be fine. He's stronger than he looks. He fell on his back while protecting you with his body, but he didn't break or sprain anything."

Leorino was relieved to hear his trusted doctor's words.

"I see… Thank god."

"He did hit his head hard; I admit I was worried about that. He just regained consciousness. He's communicating without issue and showing no concerning symptoms, so I don't think there's anything to worry about, but things can worsen quite suddenly when you've been hit on the head, you see… We'll keep him in our custody for tonight and see how he feels."

"Thank you. Um… Will Josef feel better soon…?"

Sasha nodded emphatically.

"Yes. The fall took a toll on his body, and he's got a big bump on the back of his head, so he'll be in pain for a little while. Well, we'll watch him for a few days, and if he shows no further symptoms, he'll be fine. Which is a relief… He fell from quite a height with a person in his arms. He could have been seriously injured."

Leorino was so full of regret, he couldn't bring himself to look up. He felt sorry for himself, wondering why he always had to cause so much trouble for others.

"It was all my fault. I forgot about my legs and moved without thinking… I can't even begin to apologize."

"Rino…"

"Doctor. I do not have the right to remain in the Health Department after all the trouble I've caused. Would you allow me to keep working here?"

The answer to Leorino's desperate plea came not from Sasha, but from Gravis.

"You won't be the one leaving the Palace of Defense."

"...Sir?"

"The man who injured you, Entner, was it? He and his cronies will have to go."

"...What do you mean?"

The fingers caressing Leorino's forehead trailed down his cheek. Leorino shivered at the touch and questioned Sasha behind Gravis with his gaze. Sasha wore a sour expression.

"I'm going to dismiss Entner and his cronies. Sasha will suffer a pay cut, too."

Leorino was so shocked by Gravis's statement that he sat up.

"Wh-why, sir...?!"

"I invited you here, and whatever the reason may have been, you were injured. That's absolutely unacceptable."

Leorino suddenly grabbed Gravis's fingers.

"Wait...! Your Excellency, please wait...!"

That was preposterous.

It was true that Entner had stolen Leorino's documents, but even so, Leorino had lost his balance and fallen down the stairs, injuring himself all on his own. He never expected them to be punished for that.

Leorino couldn't believe what Gravis was saying, and tried desperately to argue his case.

"Sir, dismissing them...?! And punishing Dr. Sasha, too...?! It was my own carelessness that caused me to fall down the stairs! They are not to blame!"

Leorino looked at Sasha.

"Please say something, Dr. Sasha...! You saw what happened... I just made a misstep and lost my balance!"

But Sasha shook his head.

"Lord Leorino, His Excellency already knows the details. He also knows that your room was ransacked by Entner and his cronies."

"But still... It was my own fault I fell down the stairs. Dr. Sasha had nothing to do with it."

"I knew they were harassing you, but ignored the situation and didn't intervene. As a result, you and Josef fell down the stairs. We're lucky that you weren't seriously injured, but it is true that I was negligent in my supervision."

Leorino felt like crying. He had caused this horrible situation.

"No, sir! I was the one who called them there. And then I fell... I should have reported it to Dr. Sasha instead. And yet..."

Gravis wrapped his large palm around Leorino's imploring hand.

"Leorino, this is also your punishment."

"...My punishment? B-but..."

"You must learn that as a result of your actions, others may be punished instead of you."

"I..."

Leorino was shocked.

"My inviting you here means just that much... Don't underestimate your own value, Leorino."

Hearing Gravis's words, he couldn't stop shaking.

"But... But, sir...! Please. This isn't nearly serious enough to dismiss them over it!"

Gravis gently lifted Leorino's bandaged hand once more and closed his fingers around it.

Gravis's starry-sky eyes blinked coldly, numbing Leorino's nerves with fear.

"Are you going to question my decision?"

"...! N-no, sir. But..."

...But it doesn't mean I'm the only one who should get preferential treatment...!

So he desperately pleaded with him.

"If you're going to dismiss Mr. Entner and the others, please punish me, too! Please dismiss me as well!"

Gravis smiled slightly at Leorino's frantic protest. He then calmly asked Sasha, "Sasha, a penny for your thoughts?"

"...Sir, I knew of the harassment, and I only stood back and watched. I am responsible for everything. They are promising young people with much potential. I will keep a close eye on them from now on, so I would like to beg your forgiveness this time."

"I see. I will consider it."

His words exhausted what little strength Leorino had left.

Although Gravis had not made any promises, Sasha might have just made room for consideration regarding the treatment of Entner and his men.

"But, Leorino, your punishment will be different."

Gravis slowly lifted Leorino's body.

His arms were gentle, but with his body grating at the smallest movement, Leorino involuntarily moaned in pain.

"Your Excellency...! The impact of the fall has affected Lord Leorino as well. You must be careful...!"

Looking back at Sasha, Gravis smiled.

"Believe it or not, I *am*. You'll have to live with the pain of the bruises for now."

"...Yes, sir."

"Your guard will stay here tonight so that we may monitor his condition."

Leorino was already surprised at being picked up so suddenly, but this feeling turned to dismay when he learned that he would be leaving Josef.

"I'll stay with Josef... Please, let me stay here with him tonight."

"Absolutely not. It is almost evening. The security here is too weak for you to stay."

It must have been early in the morning when he spoke with Entner and his cronies. Leorino turned to the window, but the curtains were drawn, so he couldn't tell the time by the color of the sky.

Gravis peered into his face.

"Or would you rather I take you home?"

Leorino didn't want to go home.

He felt he wouldn't be able to convincingly explain to his family why his wrist was injured and why Josef would not be coming with him.

In any case, he wanted to stay with Josef—being told not to worry did not change that.

"I will not go home today. I will keep my head down in his hospital room...
so please let me stay here."

Leorino desperately tried to persuade Gravis, but he replied only with "I
see," and not a word more.

With Leorino's body wrapped in a white fabric, Gravis held him tightly
once again.

"Sasha, I'm taking him with me."

"...He has just fallen down a flight of stairs. Please keep an eye on him."

"Please, who have you taken me for?"

Unable to keep up with the conversation between the two men, Leorino
questioned them with an anxious look in his eyes. Gravis seemed smitten
at that.

"You can relax. Sasha is going to take care of your guard. If he says Josef
will be fine, then it must be true."

"...Yes, sir. But I would still like to stay with him... Please."

The grip of the strong arms holding him up with no effort at all tightened
around Leorino for the briefest moment. He instinctively shuddered.

"No. You're coming with me."

The blanket enveloping Leorino's body fluttered.

Leaving a white mirage, the two disappeared from the hospital room, dis-
solving into thin air.

Leorino felt like his organs were being squeezed, and the next instant, still in
Gravis's embrace, he noticed they had appeared in a room of a luxurious
mansion.

He looked around the room anxiously.

The room, composed of midnight blue accented with teal and gold, had a
high ceiling like the royal palace. The pillars and ceiling were intricately decorated, making it clear it was no ordinary mansion. The furniture in the room
was all large, stately, and imposing.

Leorino could see the sky through the ceiling-high windows. Seeing the
light fade on the horizon, he realized Gravis was right—it was already evening.

Where are we...?

"This is my palace."

"Huh…?"

So this was one of the detached palaces of the royal family. It was no wonder, then, that it was so grand and opulent. But Leorino still didn't know why he had been brought to the palace of the king's brother.

With Leorino wrapped in a blanket in his arms, Gravis stepped toward the bed centered against the wall in the back of the room.

"Sir…?"

He held Leorino in one arm and pulled the top cover down with the other. Dexterously peeling the fabric off Leorino and tossing it to the floor, Gravis laid his slender body on the bed.

"Stay here and rest."

Gravis brought the covers over Leorino and pulled them up to his neck. He then sat down by his bedside.

"I can't let you sleep in the Palace of Defense with no guards around."

"Josef is there."

Gravis chuckled.

"Don't be silly. What good will an unconscious guard do you?"

Leorino did not offer a reply.

"This place is far more secure. I must return to the palace to take care of some business, but until I come back, you should get some sleep here. Can you do that?"

Leorino was so confused, he couldn't think straight.

"Leorino. Answer me."

"Yes, sir…"

"Good boy." With a casual stroke across Leorino's forehead, just the same as he had done in the hospital room, Gravis stood up.

"Theodor."

"Yes, my lord?"

Leorino startled when he noticed the man standing by the door. He had no idea when he had entered the room. The room was so large that Leorino could not see the man's face from where he lay.

But his name and voice sounded familiar.

Of course, Leorino remembered. He was Gravis's valet. He hailed from the family of the Count Moreau.

...So he's still Vi's valet, then?

He remembered that Ionia had been shunned by Theodor for being a commoner. As Gravis's valet, he must have found it scandalous that a commoner could feel so comfortable next to royalty.

"I will let Leorino rest here for a while. Bring him a medicinal infusion."

"Yes, sir. But may I ask who this gentleman is?"

"Right, I suppose you've never met before. This is Leorino Cassieux, the fourth son of Brungwurt. He has been in my care at the Palace of Defense since last month."

"...I see. He is one of the sons of the Cassieux family?"

"Yes. I'm certain you'll be seeing him again in the near future. When he wakes up, make sure he eats something. Oh, and his hand is injured. Tell the doctor to prepare a new compress for him."

"I shall, my lord."

The Cassieux family was of higher status, but as the son of a count and valet to the king's brother, Theodor held a higher official position than Leorino.

Leorino rushed to sit up and greet Theodor, but Gravis's arm blocked his way and he was pressed onto the bed once more. It may not have been very polite, but Leorino at least managed to greet him laying down.

He wondered if Theodor had heard him. The servant quietly left the room without another word.

Seeing Leorino's apparent confusion, Gravis offered a small smile.

"Don't worry about it. You must rest first. Can you do that?"

"...B-but—"

"I'll check on your guard again on my way home."

"Thank you, sir...but why am I in Your Excellency's palace?" Leorino was finally able to ask what he had been wanting to know since they arrived.

"I told you. I can't leave you unprotected in the Palace of Defense, and you said you don't wish to go home, either. My only remaining option was to bring you here."

"I would have been happy to stay with Josef in the palace."

"And I told you I can't allow you to do that. Don't make me repeat myself. What do you expect of me, Leorino? You'd have me assign a whole squad just to keep you safe?"

Leorino gasped at the rebuke. He hadn't even considered that extra personnel would be forced to protect him.

"You haven't thought that far ahead, have you?"

"I'm sorry…"

"Besides, I haven't even had a chance to punish you for this mess yet. Or have you forgotten about that already?"

Leorino's lips quivered slightly, as if he wanted to say something, but couldn't. The corners of Gravis's mouth turned up slightly at the sight.

Leorino tried to sit up, but was once more pressed into the sheets by Gravis.

"I told you to rest. Why do you keep trying to get up? How many times will you make me say it?"

"A man about to receive punishment should not be allowed to rest so comfortably in Your Highness's palace."

"It's fine. You're staying. I brought you to my palace because it suits me."

"…B-but, sir—"

"…If I threaten you any further, you'll be too anxious to rest. We'll discuss punishment when I return."

Gravis stroked Leorino's forehead once more and brought his face closer.

Leorino's violet eyes, wide with fright, and Gravis's starry-sky eyes watched each other at this breathtaking distance.

"You are a precious treasure entrusted to me by Brungwurt, and you were hurt in the Palace of Defense. That's an issue I cannot overlook."

"Please, it's not nearly that serious… It was my own carelessness that caused my injury!"

"That was just the end result. The issue is that someone caused you to find yourself in that position. Do you understand?"

He did not.

Leorino was too baffled to form a coherent thought.

* * *

"Another reason is my wrath. I want to keep you in my sight until my anger subsides."

"Sir...?"

"You don't need to understand. I'm just being selfish."

Leorino could only nod.

"I'll inform your family that I'll be looking after you for the time being. You'll stay here until your guard recovers."

"...Huh?"

"You can commute to the Palace of Defense from here."

Leorino could hardly believe his ears. "Th-that would be unacceptable."

"Unacceptable? To whom?" Gravis cocked his head.

To whom? ...To whom indeed...

Leorino argued, half stunned. "...I—I don't believe my father would allow me to stay in your palace."

"The Cassieuxs' opinion matters not. I have given my permission. Who else's permission do you need?"

"But isn't this, well..."

Once again, a large palm was placed on his forehead. Gravis smoothed back Leorino's bangs, only to ruffle them again.

"Isn't this what?"

Leorino suddenly felt like crying. He had no idea how to respond.

Finally, Gravis chuckled.

"Are you saying it's inappropriate? You're not even allowed to spend a night away from home? You're an adult now, you know."

"That's true, but..."

"I know you're sheltered. You've never really spent time away from your family, have you?"

Blood rushed to Leorino's face. He felt embarrassed to be teased about his age.

"...It's true, I've never stayed with anyone other than my family. But what I'm trying to say is..."

"Yes, I know. I didn't mean to call you a child, rather the opposite. I think you've finally realized how people see you."

In other words, he was trying to say that someone as beautiful as Leorino staying the night with him could be misunderstood in a certain way.

"…I want to be a little more trustworthy; more manly."

"Regardless of what anyone might think of you, in the future I don't think you'll ever spend a night anywhere without someone protecting you."

Leorino bit his lip. It hurt to be reminded of his own helplessness like this.

At that moment, Gravis whispered to him in a voice so low that it nearly melted into thin air. "Do you wish to carry a Power in your hands once more…?"

Leorino's violet eyes blinked.

"…What did you…?"

Their gazes met again.

Gravis said it was nothing and raised the corners of his mouth slightly.

"…I'm not happy with this. Perhaps I'm too helpless to be called manly, but—"

"I admire your spirit, but it's also true that most young ladies are more adept at worldly affairs than you."

"Yes, well…"

"Are you afraid to be here?"

Leorino couldn't escape Gravis's gaze.

"I'm asking you if you're afraid to be near me."

Leorino shook his head like it was the most natural thing in the world.

This stirring in his chest was not fear. It was something far sweeter, far more ghastly than fear itself. Gravis's beautiful face so close to his, the warmth of his body, all of it made Leorino's heart throb.

For some reason, Leorino wanted to escape Gravis's gaze. He wanted to hide. But Leorino couldn't move a finger, held in place by the man's eyes.

Leorino was confused by his own overwhelming emotions, wondering if this was really how women felt. He knew that he had feelings for Gravis. Was that the reason for this stirring in his chest? Or was it just his feminine disposition?

But even if he remained silent, he could not escape the sharp gaze of the man before him.

In the end, he could only offer an honest answer.

"…I am not afraid of you, sir."

Gravis nodded at Leorino's quiet reply.

"If you're not afraid, then you should be able to stay here just fine."

"Is it really all right for me to be here?"

"Why wouldn't it be? Just keep getting used to me like this… Ah, here comes your medicine."

Leorino was startled again. Theodor, holding a cup of what appeared to be a medicinal infusion, was standing behind Gravis before Leorino knew it. He couldn't sense Theodor's presence at all.

Finally seeing Theodor up close, his face had certainly aged, but his slender, solemn appearance remained unchanged.

"Sir…aside from my wrist injury, I'm fine. I don't even have a fever."

"Your condition might not be as serious as your guard's, but you fell down a flight of stairs. You should drink it to be safe."

That didn't leave him much of a choice.

He sat up, supported by Gravis's arm. Theodor handed Gravis the medicine and immediately left the room. Urged by the man, Leorino drank the bitter infusion and lay down on the bed once more.

As he watched Gravis stand, Leorino asked about the issue remaining on his mind. "Sir, and my punishment…?"

"We'll worry about that when I return. Get some rest until then. Can you do that for me?"

With that, Gravis vanished.

Left alone in the unfamiliar room, Leorino let his mind wander.

How in the world had he ended up in Gravis's palace? He was told that he couldn't be left alone in the Palace of Defense, but the entire royal palace was heavily guarded at all times. He and Josef would simply stay cooped up in a hospital room.

He couldn't imagine he would face any danger serious enough to concern

Gravis, but the thought that Gravis would be at fault for increasing security for Leorino's sake made him consider that perhaps he had been naive.

The fact that a member of the Cassieux family had been invited by the general himself to work in the Palace of Defense may have been a much bigger deal than Leorino had imagined.

He lay down as he was told and explored the room with his gaze.

The bedroom alone was about four times the size of Leorino's room. Rough measurements aside, it was huge.

A starry night sky had been painted on the tall bed canopy and the even taller ceiling. The design had likely been inspired by Gravis's eyes.

As he lay there looking at it, the midnight blue wallpaper and curtains made him feel as if he was outside under the veil of night.

Slowly, his body grew heavier.

The medicine must have contained a sedative. Leorino was intimately familiar with the sensation forcibly pulling him to sleep.

A faint scent of a winter forest hung in the room.

Vi's scent...

Leorino's consciousness began to fade in earnest.

He really wanted to see Josef. Being told that he was fine was not enough; he wanted to see Josef himself and make sure he was all right.

I shouldn't be here.

Leorino wanted to see his cherished guard who had protected him and return to his regular life as soon as possible.

"Josef, I'm sorry... I'm so sorry... I can't wait to see you again..."

With that, the wave of sleep finally pulled him under.

Lips Wet with Sin

Feeling fingers stroking his forehead, Leorino awoke with a start.

Slowly opening his eyelids, he saw Gravis sitting by his bedside.

The man had removed the jacket of his uniform, and now remained in a loose white shirt and black trousers.

A large shadow blocked the candlelight.

Leorino's golden eyelashes quivered like butterfly wings as his violet eyes looked up at the man.

"...Welcome home."

Gravis raised an eyebrow at that. Leorino hadn't realized he had unconsciously greeted the man as he would a family member.

"It seems you had a nice nap, but you haven't even eaten. How do you feel? Any pain?"

Leorino's mind was foggy from sleep, but he felt around his body. He felt somewhat sluggish, but except for his wrist, nothing hurt too badly.

"...I'm fine. Thank you."

"It's gotten late, but I'll have Theodor prepare you something to eat."

Leorino shook his head.

He hadn't eaten lunch, but he didn't feel particularly hungry. He had no appetite and figured he wouldn't eat even if they gave him food.

He felt himself grow more awake.

"I'd rather you tell me my punishment already."

"Well, you certainly waste no time."

* * *

Leorino sat up. He was about to get off the bed when Gravis stopped him, but Leorino refused.

"I will get up. Let me speak with you properly."

"...Very well."

Gravis nodded and lifted Leorino by the underside of his knees.

"Sir...?! I can walk by myself!"

"You're going to walk with no shoes on?"

His words forced the breath out of Leorino's lungs.

Come to think of it, he was barefoot. Of course he was. He had been sleeping.

Gravis finally set Leorino down on a settee in his parlor. Gravis sat in the chair across from him.

Gravis had a muscular physique that most men would look up to. Despite this, there was nothing brutish about him, his refined movements so captivating that one could suspect he owed this special trait to his noble lineage in some way.

Leorino remembered his manners and straightened his back.

He braced himself to accept his punishment, wanting to remain unshaken no matter what he was told.

Gravis's eyes no longer contained the affectionate gaze he had shown Leorino, instantly turning cool and distant instead.

"Very well, you can make your case first."

He had no choice but to confess. Sasha had said it, too. Gravis already knew everything.

"...I didn't want to exacerbate an issue caused by the friction between myself and Mr. Entner. That's why I tried to resolve it through a private conversation."

"Why?"

Leorino just barely managed to keep himself from casting his eyes down from the sheer intensity of the man.

"...I didn't want Dr. Sasha or my family to know that I was being harassed by my colleagues. If it became a whole ordeal and my family learned of it, they would surely object to my working at the Palace of Defense."

"And what happened as a result?"

"…My guard Josef was injured. I myself was injured as well. It became an even greater issue that I could no longer conceal. All because of my short-sighted decisions."

"…Then what do you think you should have done instead?"

Leorino audibly gritted his teeth. He was already aware that he had made all the wrong choices.

He should have reported it to Sasha when he discovered his room had been ransacked. He criticized Entner and his cronies for breaking the rules but tried to deal with them personally when he should have addressed the issue according to established regulations.

Josef had said it, too. Even if it was just mischief on their part, ransacking a room in the Palace of Defense and going as far as stealing documents was a malicious act that undermined the authority of the Royal Army. In other words, it was a blemish on Gravis's authority.

"…I should not have attempted to tackle it on my own. I should have instead reported the room being ransacked to my superior, Dr. Sasha. I apologize."

Leorino bowed deeply.

"Correct. Whatever the circumstances, you tried to cover up a theft in the Palace of Defense for your own petty reasons. That's a clear violation of the rules… What else?"

"What else…?"

Gravis calmly repeated himself.

"What else do you think you've done?"

Leorino thought hard. But no amount of thinking helped him arrive at an answer.

"…I don't know, sir."

"You're not even aware of it? I suppose you wouldn't be. If you were, you wouldn't have made such a simple mistake in the first place."

"I apologize, sir…"

"You disputed my punishment of Entner and his cronies. Don't you remember?"

"I..."

"You dismissed your superior's decision."

Leorino's face instantly paled.

"Do you have to say anything for yourself?"

"...No, sir."

Gravis's overly soft, calm voice stung Leorino like a needle.

Of course. In truth, the difference in status between Gravis and him was like heaven and earth. An unranked secretary trying to overrule a general's decision was a serious crime.

Why had he forgotten his place so badly that he thought he could make such demands of the man? Were Ionia's memories to blame? Had he unwittingly reverted to what they had back then?

No, that's not it... It was my fault. I just forgot myself...

"Please dismiss me as well," my ass.

"What's more, you unconsciously placed your worth on the line and used it as a bargaining chip against me. I almost laughed out loud at that adorable attempt." Gravis chuckled. "But it was a good attempt nonetheless. In a sense, it wasn't the wrong strategy, either."

Leorino felt himself cringe at his own foolishness.

"...I'm sorry... Sir— Ah!"

Gravis had stood up gracefully, scooped up Leorino's body, and placed him in his lap.

"I told you to know your own worth. So I can't exactly blame you for using yourself as a bargaining chip against me."

"I did that...?"

"You didn't even notice?"

Leorino couldn't help thinking about how close Gravis's masculine beauty was to him now, when the man smiled wickedly.

"You're worth just that much to me. I think you've subconsciously accepted that."

And here he had thought Gravis was accusing him of narcissism.

Leorino turned pale and hung his head.

"I'm not complaining. It's an improvement."

Each gentle word tightened around Leorino's heart like a thorny vine.

"Leorino, look at me."

Gravis lifted Leorino's chin gently but resolutely. Leorino was forced to show the man his remorseful, shame-stained expression.

"So my punishment is...?"

"The dismissal of Entner and his cronies. Sasha will also be held accountable, of course."

"But that's..."

Leorino was stunned by this revelation when the man had earlier said that he would take his opinion into consideration.

"You put yourself in danger by failing to do the right thing in your initial response. As a result of your foolish actions, you have cost Entner and his men their future in the Palace of Defense. That's it."

"Your Excellency...I will leave the Palace of Defense. So please..." Leorino strained his voice.

"Absolutely not. I invited you to the Palace of Defense, and I will be the one to decide whether or not you leave. Your resignation will never again be a bargaining chip, Leorino."

"No... Please. That's not..."

He hadn't meant it that way. He didn't think that his own position would be worth anything, much less a bargaining chip against Gravis.

"Now everyone will know what happens to people who trifle with you. They will treat you differently. You'll have to live with that and continue to work as hard as ever at the Palace of Defense."

"...Please, punish me."

"That *is* your punishment. It's not easy getting special treatment, is it?"

Tears silently spilled from Leorino's eyes.

"Listen. You don't want to rely on the kindness of others, you want to be independent—fine. But you need to stop making bad decisions based on such foolish thoughts... And no more secrets."

Gravis lifted Leorino's sprained hand and removed his bandages. The wrist beneath had lost its original delicate shape and was horribly swollen. Gravis's cold lips touched the injury.

It didn't hurt. But the cool sensation on his hot skin made Leorino shudder.

Gravis said that Leorino was valuable to him.

But what was this "worth" he spoke of? What had he meant by that? If their relationship were merely that of a general and a secretary at the bottom of the food chain, they would not be as close as they were now.

Whenever Gravis drew the line in the sand, he got so close to crossing it himself that Leorino had no idea what to think.

That was what made it so confusing. That was why he kept misjudging the appropriate distance between them.

Leorino did not possess the skills to remedy this confusion. He gasped in breathless agony.

"...I won't allow anyone to hurt you ever again, not even you yourself."

With the very lips that condemned Leorino, Gravis gently wiped the tears that trickled down his fair cheeks.

I want to blame this man for everything.

Gravis's lips, wet with tears of contrition, closed around Leorino's own trembling lips.

Tears of Sweetness and Salt

Leorino gasped at the intense sensation. Gravis's thick tongue slipped in through the gap between his lips.

"...!"

A lewd sound escaped his lips when their tongues met. Leorino's slender body bucked at the feeling of someone exploring his mouth for the first time in his life.

Leorino was confused.

He shook his head, trying to free his lips.

But with his face turned up, Gravis discovered every last source of pleasure inside his mouth. Leorino's small tongue shrunk away but was captured by Gravis's, gently licking and nipping at its underside.

How...? Why?

Gravis's skillful tongue relentlessly poured poisonous pleasure into Leorino's body. The sensation was so sweet and obscene at the same time that it made Leorino's head swim as he struggled to take it all in.

He didn't know how to catch his breath. Slowly, he felt his vision grow dark. Leorino dug his slender fingers into Gravis's muscular shoulders, frantically trying to convey his distress.

Noticing Leorino's anguish, Gravis parted his lips just slightly to offer him some reprieve. Leorino greedily gulped down the air he so desperately needed.

But his gasping lips were again mercilessly captured by Gravis's.

"Nn...hnn... W-wait..."

"...You're fine, breathe through your nose."

"I—I can't..."

Leorino cried, his nose stuffed.

Gravis looked at him with unhidden affection. Smiling, he gave Leorino the occasional reprieve and encouraged him to breathe. He could take in air through his nostrils, but the man's lips would not release his.

Leorino was overwhelmed by the immense pleasure flowing into his body through his mouth.

I'm scared... This feels too good... Vi... I'm afraid.

It threatened to expose some*thing* that lived inside of him, something he didn't truly know himself. He didn't want any more stimulation.

Leorino frantically patted Gravis on the shoulder, silently pleading for him to let go. He couldn't help groaning at the pain from his sprained hand.

Gravis's long arm snaked around his back, grabbed his elbow, and fixed it in place. With that, he could no longer move his arm.

Even sitting in his lap, Leorino's head only reached the tip of Gravis's nose. That was the extent of the size difference between him and Gravis.

"Why... Why, this...?"

Demand as he may between breaths, his helpless resistance meant nothing. Gravis's unyielding but sweet assault on Leorino's senses continued.

Gravis's fingers slowly traced up his spine as if counting every vertebra beneath, before they gently grasped the back of his head. Leorino's face was turned upward, and once again, the man's lips were on his, further deepening the kiss.

Leorino's small mouth was filled to the brim with the man's tongue.

"Come... Open your mouth..."

"I...can't... Hng..."

Whose was the sweet liquid filling his mouth? Leorino felt like he was drowning.

He was panting, not knowing what to do with the fluid in his mouth, until it finally spilled out from the edge of his lips.

Leorino's throat twitched in embarrassment and tears spilled down his cheeks. Gravis smiled, wiping Leorino's face with his fingers.

"You taste so sweet."

Leorino cast his eyes down, unable to look directly at Gravis's tongue as it licked Leorino's saliva off his fingers.

"Ha... Don't choke now."

"...Kh... Nn..."

"Here, swallow."

He stroked his throat with his thumb.

In tears, Leorino swallowed as instructed.

Gravis raised the corners of his lips in satisfaction and immediately covered Leorino's lips with his own once more.

Wh-why? ...I did as you asked...!

"...Please... Nkh..."

"...Let me have some of yours, too."

Feeling Gravis's hands around his body, Leorino found himself straddling him. Supporting the backs of his thighs, the man pressed Leorino's thin body tightly against his muscular torso.

"Kh... I—"

Leorino looked down at Gravis for the first time in his life. Even now, Ionia's memories stormed his mind. Leorino had no control over it.

Ah, it's Vi...

He could still see the boy with the starry-sky eyes in the man's face. Those gleaming starry-sky eyes remained unchanged despite Gravis's advancing age. Memories of the first time he saw those eyes came flooding back. His chest suddenly felt tight.

"Leorino…"

He couldn't resist the gentle but bold arms pulling the back of his head. Gravis's skillful tongue scooped up his, softly biting and sucking on it.

Leorino could feel the saliva filling his mouth.

The thought of having Gravis swallow his saliva was unbearably embarrassing, but Leorino had no way to resist.

Gravis drank the liquid pouring out of Leorino. He chuckled, practically showing off.

"You really are sweet."

"Ah… Pl-please… Wait…"

Leorino placed his hands on Gravis's muscular shoulders, struggling to support his faltering body.

The kissing continued in a manner so vigorous—far too intense for his first time. The sensual exchange was so lewd that Leorino finally began to grow dazed.

Tears spilled from his violet eyes and fell onto Gravis's cheeks.

"You're getting a little heated down here."

For a moment, Leorino didn't understand what Gravis was saying.

It was only when Gravis's strong arms pulled Leorino's hips against his chest that Leorino noticed his own arousal.

"Ah… W-wait!"

"I suppose you're a man after all. You must have really enjoyed that kiss."

Before he knew it, heat had pooled in his abdomen.

Having his hips rocked against the man's body, directly delivering him intense stimulation, made Leorino arch his back.

"Ugh… This is so—"

"What's wrong? Are you afraid?"

"Y-yes… I'm scared… No more…"

He was frightened by the sex act he had suddenly found himself in the middle of. Leorino was so innocent, he was afraid of Gravis's strength, of his own reaction, of everything happening to him.

In the face of the rawness of the exchange, Ionia's memories were of no use at all. At the end of the day, their experiences were entirely their own.

* * *

"Please… Let go of me… I'm scared." Leorino answered honestly.

He could not allow himself to expose his raw desires to Gravis.

He didn't know what would happen to him if he did. That was the most frightening and embarrassing thing. The more he imagined what would await him if he laid his desires bare, the more it scared him.

Leorino's consternation had reached its peak.

Why is he doing this to me…? This is almost like…

Gravis lifted Leorino's chin and peered into his tearful eyes. Beyond Leorino's fear hid something carnal. Something sensual was budding beyond the shame and confusion of the inexperienced young man. Gravis enjoyed this sight.

Leorino, however, instead of indulging in the feeling, felt terribly frightened and continued to cry, his throat twitching.

Perhaps taking pity on Leorino as he sobbed in the daze of the new experience, Gravis released him from his arms and sat him down in his lap once more. He wiped Leorino's tearstained cheeks.

Leorino's chaotic emotions gradually subsided as he regained his composure. After a little while, when his sobbing waned, Leorino looked down and mumbled, "…You do this to me and then act surprised when I forget myself around you… I fear I'm presuming on your kindness far more than is appropriate."

"As you should."

Leorino felt incredibly indignant at these words.

Had Gravis not *just* reprimanded him for forgetting his place?

If Gravis truly cared about him, he would have listened to Leorino's wishes and resolved the situation with Sasha, Entner, and Entner's cronies amicably. Gravis even told Leorino to live with the special treatment he would receive in the royal palace. He said that would be Leorino's punishment.

Perhaps Leorino would be lonelier than ever. But if he was willing to accept special treatment, Gravis should do whatever Leorino wanted in return.

Leorino told the man off in his mind.

"You say that, and yet...you're not making my life any easier at all."

"And here I thought I was spoiling you rotten."

Leorino bit his lip.

No... If I stay here any longer, I'm going to say things I must not say...

He writhed in the man's arms. Gravis let go of him.

Leorino wobbled to his feet.

"Where are you going?"

Leorino felt the cool carpet under his bare toes.

"I can no longer stay with you, sir... I'm clearly too foolish to maintain the appropriate distance from you."

"No."

Leorino quickly shook off the hand that grabbed him. He immediately regretted it, but he couldn't control himself. Under any other circumstances, such behavior toward a superior would have been unthinkable, but he no longer cared. It was Gravis who had overstepped in the first place.

He couldn't stay there a second longer.

Leorino's inexperienced heart had been driven to the very edge.

"And where do you plan to go, barefoot and without a coat?"

"Anywhere. I can walk barefoot just fine."

Leorino staggered through the large room and struggled with the door. It was heavy. He had never opened a door by himself in his life. He was keenly aware of this fact.

The wide hallway was silent. Several large doors lined the dim, candlelit corridor. Leorino walked forward, guided only by his impulses.

He walked as fast as he could.

Behind him, the sound of leisurely footsteps followed.

"It will take you at least an hour to walk from here to the Palace of Defense."

Leorino shook his head, still facing forward.

"...I'll crawl back if I have to."

"And what if you're assaulted by some ruffians like you were at the soiree the other night?"

They walked down the long corridor and reached the stairs.

Leorino's legs made him unable to run down them. Still, he descended as quickly as he could, and in his rush, he tripped over his own feet.

Without missing a beat, a strong arm reached out from behind to catch him.

"Slow down. You'll fall down the stairs."

"…Let go of me!"

Leorino was crying. He felt pathetic. He was upset beyond belief.

Halfway down the stairs, several guards appeared without a sound to block his path.

Leorino glared at the armed men, tears streaming down his face.

"…Please, let me pass."

"We cannot, sir." One of the men answered on behalf of the others.

Leorino finally screamed. It was the first scream of his life. "Let me through! I'm leaving!"

He tried to force his way through the crowd of men.

The Imperial guards were dismayed. They were not certain if they were allowed to touch the beautiful weeping guest directly. The soldiers extended their arms, doing everything not to injure the thin body impulsively coming at them.

"Don't touch him."

At that moment, Gravis reached forward and scooped up Leorino's slender body in his arms.

"That's enough, Leorino."

"…No! I'm going back to Josef… Let go of me! I'm leaving!"

"You're not going anywhere."

Leorino frantically struggled to escape the man's arms, but it was for naught. In an instant, he was taken back up the hallway he had spent so much time walking down.

Leorino could not stop crying.

When they returned to Gravis's quarters, Leorino was carried straight to Gravis's bedroom and somewhat roughly lowered onto his bed.

"Ow…!"

A moan spilled from Leorino's mouth. He had felt the fall in his injured arm.

"You think *that* hurts? No brute would ever be this gentle with you."

Frustration welled in the pit of Leorino's stomach at the sound of the cold voice mocking him.

Gravis placed his hands on both sides of Leorino's head and leaned in. Leorino placed a hand on his chest.

"You will not refuse my hand," said Gravis.

"No… Please! Not now! Don't come any closer! Don't touch me!"

Leorino sensed a silent anger in the man above him. Frightened, he resisted desperately.

"…Let go of me!"

"No."

"Gh…! No! Why…?!"

He tried to push back, but Gravis easily caught his arms.

"D-don't touch me… Please, don't do this to me anymore."

"You don't like me touching you?"

Gravis wouldn't budge. The only resistance Leorino could muster now was covering his eyes.

"…It's not that, I just… Not now, please."

Gravis took Leorino's arm and pulled it away from his face. His tear-stained face now exposed, he could only glare at Gravis and cry.

"If so, why do you push me away? Are you angry with me for bringing you back here?"

"…I don't want you to use your power to set me free, sir. When I am with you, I can't do anything. It hurts to be reminded of my powerlessness every time I'm around you."

Leorino heard a small sigh fall from Gravis's lips. Leorino's heart ached as if it were going to burst.

"…I don't know what you expect of me," Leorino complained in a feeble voice.

"I've told you time and time again, haven't I?"

"But you've explained nothing. I don't want this anymore… I don't want you to confuse me any further... If that's how it's going to be, I don't care anymore!"

Gravis grabbed Leorino's chin and forced Leorino to look at him.

"Because you don't seem to care about your own safety."

"I'm doing all I can!"

"Accept your own weakness already, Leorino!"

Leorino instinctively shrank in on himself. It was the first time Gravis had yelled at him.

"What's wrong with being weak? Why do you turn away from who you are like that?"

"I..."

Leorino's violet eyes wavered. Gravis did not allow him to look away. He glared at him, silently ordering Leorino to look at him.

"What is this 'power' you're obsessed with?!"

"The power I'm..."

"Is being physically weak something to be ashamed of? Is physical weakness a sin? You're so beautiful, what could you possibly complain about? Why are you ashamed of yourself? Why are you so stubbornly trying to be strong?!"

"No! I just, I want to be..."

The two men glared at each other from so close that their faces appeared blurred.

"Why do you care so much about being physically strong or having a manly physique? Why do you feel the need to be traditionally strong like me or Lucas?"

"I just...! I don't want to be weak!"

"But you are! So what, does that mean you don't deserve to be alive?"

"Your Excellency wouldn't understand!" Leorino shouted.

Gravis looked down at the panting young man, his brow furrowed.

"You wouldn't understand..."

This was the first time Leorino had ever thrown such a tantrum.

He knew it was childish and stupid. He was beyond himself with worry that Gravis would finally grow disillusioned with him.

But he couldn't hold back the rage that surged in his heart.

"I've *tried* to come to terms with it! I tried to accept that I was born this way, that I was injured, but...to hell with this body!"

Gravis sat up.

The pressure on Leorino disappeared, and he felt relieved and lonely at the same time. He hated himself for having such unmanly feelings at all.

Leorino rejected the hand Gravis offered him, twisted around, and threw himself onto the bed.

"Leorino...accept reality."

Leorino shook his head, pounding the bed with his fist.

"No! I'm an adult and I'm not even allowed to leave the house alone. To hell with this body! ...To think I'd spend the rest of my life being protected... when all I really wanted was..."

I wanted to be strong enough to protect you.

"I may be weak and I may be helpless, but I don't want to live in a world where someone is always protecting me..."

Gravis patiently watched as the young man released all his fury.

From what Sasha had told him, Leorino was supposed to be calm, gentle, and quiet. He had endured the pain of his injuries, never complained about his exercises, and patiently persevered through it all.

When Gravis met him in person, that impression remained unchanged. Leorino was a delicate, fragile thing who would be snatched and hurt by some brute the moment Gravis took his eyes off him.

However, the Leorino lying in front of him now was struggling against the fate imposed on him, wishing with all his might to overcome it.

His tearful face resembled that of a child throwing a tantrum. His hair was disheveled, his face flushed, his eyelids swollen. His cheeks were covered with visible stains from all the tears he'd spilled.

But even in such a state, Leorino was beautiful.

"Leorino..."

"No... Don't!"

Gravis opened his fist and laid his palm on top of his. Leorino struggled desperately to free his interlocked fingers. His resistance was so faint that it resembled that of a small bird.

His thin limbs were so helpless, Gravis caught him in an instant without much effort on his part.

"Whatever you're doing...please stop."

Compared to the intensity of Leorino's feelings, the overwhelming fragility of his body filled the man with pity.

"Leorino..."

Gravis wanted him to spread his wings freely. And just as much, he wanted to wrap Leorino in his arms and protect him from the faintest wind.

Gravis bit back the emotion that threatened to spill from deep within his chest.

"...Please, stop resisting and accept my protection."

Leorino's thin throat trembled.

He was surprised. Gravis was pleading with him.

"I want to respect your desire for independence. That's why I invited you to the Palace of Defense."

Leorino could only listen as Gravis continued.

"But I can't compromise any further. It may be cruel to you, but I cannot give you any more freedom in the Palace of Defense unless you agree to stay under my protection."

Another wave of tears welled in Leorino's eyes.

His quivering lips were heartbreaking. But Gravis did not mince words.

"You don't yet know the true dangers of life or the horror of having your freedom taken away. But...even if you want to face those dangers yourself, I won't allow it."

"Why? Why do you care so much for me...?"

"Can't you tell?" Gravis whispered, watching him intently. "Because I've decided that, this time, I'm going to protect you with my own hands to the very end."

"This time...?"

"I once made a mistake that I can never undo. I will not make the same mistake again."

Gravis's eyes were dark.

In his mind, Leorino asked Gravis if it was Ionia who he had failed to protect. Behind the man's beautiful eyes, he felt he could see a glimpse of a deep wound.

Leorino's heart ached more than he could say.

Vi... Vi...

Gravis gently held his thin body as he began to hiccup.

"I know better than anyone the frustration of having to be protected by the very person you want to protect."

Leorino shut his eyes tightly.

"I...I was once protected by someone I deeply cared about, but I couldn't save them. I have gnashed my teeth and despaired at my helplessness more times than I can count."

"Sir... I...I just—"

"So I'll never be able to turn a blind eye to your getting hurt... Even if you don't want my protection."

Gravis tenderly looked down at Leorino's tearstained face and gently brushed his fingers through his damp bangs.

"Leorino, listen to me. You have value, no matter what. Stop deprecating yourself and accept yourself for who you are."

The weight of his words overwhelmed Leorino.

"...I just wanted to be strong."

"I know. I know that feeling all too well."

Even in this life, he couldn't escape his destiny.

He fell in love all over again with the man to whom he had once sworn his blood and loyalty.

All he wanted was to have the right to stand next to Gravis as himself, as Leorino. It may have been a hopeless wish, but he thought that if he made progress, little by little, he might be of use to him someday.

I wanted you to entrust your back to me again...

But perhaps it was time to give up.

"You're defenseless and you don't take care of yourself. That frightens me more than anything."

"S-sir..."

"Leorino, accept my power. Don't push me away. I don't want to force you into anything."

Once more, Gravis embraced him tightly.

"Please, let me protect you this time."

Gravis lowered his cool lips to Leorino's tearstained face. His lips tickled Leorino's clumped lashes and trailed down his wet cheeks, wiping away the tears.

"You're so brave and beautiful—stop rejecting it. Your heart is beyond strong enough as it is. Don't you agree? And you're surprisingly stubborn, too."

With that, Gravis pressed his forehead to Leorino's with a little too much force.

The sweet pain shattered Leorino's heart into a million pieces.

"...Then please, don't do this to me anymore. I still don't know what I should do."

Gravis said nothing.

Why do you touch me like this...?

"Wh-what exactly am I to you, sir...?"

"Do you need me to spell it out? Once I say it, there'll be no going back."

With that, he brushed his lips against Leorino's. Just as quickly, his heat pulled away.

I want to know. But I'm afraid to learn the truth.

Leorino's heart finally burst, and all his reason left with it. Overwhelmed by an intense dizzy spell, Leorino finally whined in earnest.

"No. No more... I'm sc-scared..."

"I understand. I scared you. I won't do anything else. I promise."

But his consideration changed very little now.

Leorino's emotional faucet was completely broken.

Gravis could tell by the way he sobbed like a child that Leorino had truly reached his limit.

"I've gone too far... Do you want to take your medicine again?"

Unable to speak, Leorino only shook his head.

Gravis stroked his head for a while longer, hoping to calm him down, and slowly, Leorino's eyes turned vacant.

With Gravis watching, his eyelashes slowly closed, like a butterfly resting its wings.

"...Leorino?"

The poor little bird in his arms fled into sleep so quickly, it was as if he had fainted. Gravis released his body as gently as he could so as not to wake him with his movement.

Gravis went to get the compress and bandages that had been left on the desk. He still had to change Leorino's dressing.

He sat down on the edge of the bed and lifted Leorino's slender wrist. Then, with a careful hand, he began to apply the treatment.

Leorino's small face stained with tears. His sniffles. His still-quivering lips.

Gravis felt sympathy for him, worrying he had pushed him too hard.

Leorino was so inexperienced that Gravis's actions had overwhelmed him. The sight of the state Gravis had single-handedly driven Leorino into made Gravis feel sorry for him.

Leorino had feelings for him.

This was evident in the sweetness of his lips, and in his trembling the first time Gravis touched his skin.

Leorino's heart was too inexperienced to respond to Gravis's games, but his receptive body was another matter entirely. His mind was still frightened of receiving pleasure from Gravis, but his body had already accepted him. He wasn't even aware of it, and even if he had been, he did not possess the skill to hide it.

This cluelessness was pitiful and precious all the same.

* * *

It would have been easy for Gravis to capture Leorino's young mind and body with his mature wiles before Leorino even knew it was happening. Gravis could simply wrap him in silks and protect him while acting like the gentle guardian.

But he didn't want that.

Leorino had been protected from the world for most of his life, until now. He was tucked away in the depths of the family castle like a precious jewel.

However, a young man who had just left that padded cage and attempted to become independent couldn't be placed in another cage without his consent. It was important for Leorino to *choose* to enter Gravis's arms on his own.

After all, Leorino would not have any physical freedom going forward, either. It was absolutely impossible for Leorino to live as a normal boy. He would have to realize this sooner or later.

Leorino was completely unaware of the weight of the Brungwurt blood. The same was true of his own worth.

That gem of a human being would need absolute protection for the rest of his life, whether he wanted it or not.

No matter how hard Leorino tried to flap his wings, he would only be allowed to fly freely within the safe confines established by Gravis.

Gravis had thoroughly taught Leorino this lesson with this incident.

Leorino had tearfully asked what he meant to Gravis. Gravis already knew his answer.

But before that...there is a mystery to be solved.

As long as the secret Leorino was hiding lay between them, neither Leorino nor Gravis could move forward.

The key to the mystery lay in a certain red-haired young man.

Gravis gently stroked Leorino's platinum hair.

"...Show me the secret inside you soon, won't you?"

When he awoke, Leorino was lying in bed alone. A ray of the morning sun was bleeding through the heavy velvet drapery.

Right… Last night, I dozed off right then and there…?

He couldn't remember falling asleep. He blinked several times as he lay there, trying to expel the drowsiness that had settled in the back of his eyeballs.

He must have cried far too much last night. He had just woken up, but there was a throbbing deep in his temples. His eyelids also felt heavy.

But despite his physical condition being far from good, his mind was strangely calm. The fury he had felt the previous night felt almost like a dream now. Enjoying the warmth of the bed, Leorino ruminated on the night's events.

Gravis had told him to accept his power; that unless he agreed to live under Gravis's protection, he would not be given any more freedom. With these words, Leorino finally learned the conditions for continuing his work at the Palace of Defense.

The Gravis Adolphe Fanoren from Ionia's memories was nowhere to be found. In his place was a perfectly mature man who dominated Leorino with his overwhelming power and arrogance.

What little Leorino had left of his fighting spirit was crushed in Gravis's grip. The lingering memory of the humiliation and arousal that Leorino had been subjected to was still smoldering deep inside his body.

The morning sun shining through the gap in the curtains slowly grew brighter. He lifted one arm to shield his eyes.

He wanted to enjoy the warmth of the bed a little longer.

Vi…

No matter how tightly Leorino closed his eyes, the image of Gravis burned into his eyelids would not disappear. The memory of Gravis's flawless beauty appeared ever more vivid.

Leorino hated how pathetic he felt.

He had been so indignant at Gravis's overbearing, self-righteous behavior. He had rejected Gravis's touch, not wanting to rouse his oversensitive heart.

And yet, when he woke up after fainting from his immense daze, all that remained in his empty chest was a maddening, bittersweet joy.

No matter how much his heart resisted, Leorino could not refuse the touch of Gravis's hand. Leorino was frightened and delighted all the same by the pleasure Gravis had forcefully poured into him.

He had felt it in his dreams many times, but they were only dreams at the end of the day. Experiencing it in real life was far too overwhelming.

Leorino had been so innocent that a larger man leaning on him was instinctively frightening, positive or negative feelings aside. But Gravis had also drowned Leorino in his sweetness and drank his in turn without mercy.

It was the first time in Leorino's life that parts of his body reacted involuntarily.

What would have happened if he had not asked him to stop?

But I can't push him away. I love that man… I'm in love with him.

The light shining through the gap in the drapes changed angles and finally fell on Leorino's cheeks.

He had to get up.

No matter how much he didn't want to deal with reality, the sun would rise and shine down on the earth, and soon the world would be covered by a starry night, and then morning would come again.

That was how it always went.

In Ionia's life and in Leorino's, no matter how difficult life got, the morning would always come.

That's how he had made it this far, one day at a time.

That's all I can do. I can only keep going.

Leorino slowly sat up, looking out for his injured hand.

He felt around his body, checking its condition. He had made it a habit since his injury. He was relieved to find that he was able to move without issue, even if he felt a slight ache in his limbs here and there.

Thanks to Josef, his wrist had been his only injury.

*　*　*

"Right…Josef…!"

Leorino reached for the curtain.

As if someone had been waiting for the right moment, the curtain was pulled away from the outside.

"Ah…"

The bright light assaulting his senses made him close his eyes.

"You're awake."

Leorino's body shuddered at the sound of the deep, smooth voice.

"How do you feel? Any pain?"

But Leorino did not respond.

Self-conscious of what had happened the night before, he couldn't bring himself to speak.

"Leorino."

When Gravis called his name, he felt compelled to reply. But more than anything, he felt awkward.

Leorino reluctantly reminded himself that it was expected of nobility to behave with respect to one's status and decorum, even if it was toward the person who had been so mean to him last night.

"Good morning. I'm all right."

His voice was hoarse and trembling. It betrayed his conflicting feelings about Gravis.

"Look at me."

Leorino silently refused. He knew such behavior toward royalty was unacceptable, but he didn't want Gravis to see his face when he had just woken up, especially when it was swollen from all his crying. Not to mention he hadn't even bathed last night.

On the floor was a pair of small indoor shoes.

He glanced at them, and Gravis urged him to put them on.

Last night, in his agitation, Leorino had stomped barefoot down the hallway. In retrospect, he couldn't believe his own outburst, wondering how he could have done such a thing.

He gratefully placed his feet in the shoes he had been given. As he tried to stand, Gravis supported him by the elbow. Instantly, he felt a twinge of rebellion, but in the end, Leorino accepted his hand.

In the absence of his attendant at his side, he was genuinely grateful for the support of Gravis's hand. Leorino's left leg would go numb without notice, and when he woke, his posture was unsteady, and he would stagger.

Despite the excessive care he was receiving from Gravis—a royal, no less—Leorino refused to look up.

He wouldn't dare put it into words, but he wanted Gravis to know he wasn't pleased with him. Leorino was completely unaware that this thought itself was already a sign he had accepted the man.

On the other hand, Gravis was laughing inwardly at his spoiled stubbornness. He found Leorino's unwitting acceptance of him endlessly amusing.

After everything Gravis had told him yesterday, Leorino was still unconsciously trusting and relying on Gravis's affection. He thought he was rebelling of his own volition, but in reality he was presuming on Gravis's kindness, knowing instinctively that no matter how he behaved toward Gravis, Leorino would never be told off for it.

Though Leorino was angry at his own disability and frightened by him, Gravis couldn't help but love the little bird that had begun to stretch his tiny wings in his arms.

"Heh... You must be embarrassed after crying in front of me."

"...I—I am not!"

When Leorino looked up to glare at him reproachfully, Gravis smiled, looking very proud of himself indeed.

When their eyes met, Leorino winced, realizing he had already failed.

"Your eyes are swollen. Did I scare you last night?"

"...I'm fine. Yesterday, I..."

"You can spend the day at the Palace of Defense next to your guard. It will depend on his condition, but in any case, you'll be going home today."

"...Yes, sir."

Gravis's fingers grasped Leorino's chin, and he caught his gaze. Leorino was puzzled, but didn't look away and met Gravis's eyes.

"...Have you calmed down yet? Are you still afraid of me? I didn't think you'd cry in fear like that. I shouldn't have yelled; I must have really scared you."

Gravis was so gentle now, as if the events of last night had never happened.

Leorino nodded, accepting the man's apology.

He was calm now and felt more embarrassed than anything.

In truth, he still felt a little like running away. Last night, he had been pushed to his mental limits. But when he considered his own feelings, he found that he didn't really want to escape Gravis's grasp.

Leorino had been scared, but he didn't want to leave Gravis. It was a twisted feeling he found himself unable to control.

So he decided to be honest.

"I'm not afraid of you, sir...but you bring nothing but chaos to my heart. That's what scares me."

Leorino met Gravis's gaze as he gave his levelheaded answer, and Gravis's eyes seemed to smile. He must have been concerned about Leorino's feelings in his own way.

"You seem better than I expected. I worried you'd be too scared of me to leave the bed. For someone who appears so delicate, you're surprisingly bold."

"...Like I just said, I am not afraid of you, sir."

Leorino looked around the large room.

Gravis's bedroom appeared the same as the previous night. It was decorated in solid midnight blues, teals, and golds, but with no extravagant ornamentation. Everything seemed simple and sturdy, but certainly of the highest quality.

That was when Leorino noticed something. He had been sleeping in the master bedroom. Leorino suddenly felt sorry for having driven the royal master of the palace out of his own bedroom.

Leorino gingerly looked up at Gravis, who did not appear to be particularly upset about this.

The entire palace with its dozens of rooms belonged to Gravis. Leorino dismissed his previous train of thought. He didn't want to say something silly and get teased again.

Leaving the bedroom, he found himself in an even larger parlor.

"...Um, may I use your washroom?"

He remembered his physiological needs, but most of all, he couldn't bear the thought that he hadn't bathed since yesterday. He wanted to refresh himself at least a little.

Gravis nodded and pointed to the door on the opposite wall. Leorino thanked him and hurried to the washroom.

The moment he entered, Leorino gasped in awe.

It left him with no doubts that he was in a royal palace. The washroom alone also served as a dressing room and was large enough to easily fit Leorino's room within its perimeter. It was incredibly spacious.

A door at the back led to a bathhouse fitted with natural stone from floor to ceiling.

The stone walls of the bathhouse glistened in the bright sun streaming in through the skylight. The large circular bathtub was filled to the brim with hot water despite the early hour, dense steam rising from its surface.

Leorino wanted to take a bath, but the bathhouse belonged to a royal, after all. For the time being, he settled for washing his face.

He washed his face with the water in the wash basin and groomed himself as best as he could. That alone made him feel considerably refreshed.

A small knock sounded on the door, and Theodor, Gravis's valet, entered the room.

I see Theodor still looks as stern as ever.

"I have prepared a change of clothes for you, Lord Leorino. Please wear this today."

The servant offered him a tightly folded military uniform and a brand-new shirt. He had also brought a pair of shoes. But how had he managed to get Leorino's exact measurements when he had only arrived last night?

Pondering this, Leorino politely thanked Theodor as he promptly laid out Leorino's clothes.

"Is there anything else I can do for you?" asked Theodor.

"...Um, could I possibly use the bathhouse? I would like to take a bath," Leorino asked, intimidated by the polite man. He wanted to get himself clean. He was also very curious about that huge bathhouse.

"Of course."

"Thank you… And, um, could you please send someone to help me? My, um…my hand is injured…"

Under normal circumstances, Hundert, his full-time attendant, would help him bathe. Now that he had injured his left wrist, he needed all the more assistance.

He knew that it was a tall ask, but Theodor nodded and quickly disappeared.

Leorino breathed a sigh of relief.

In any case, he wanted his bath as quickly as possible. Hoping he could at least take off his shirt on his own, he eagerly made an attempt on the buttons.

That was when he heard the door to the bathroom open once more.

Theodor must have immediately sent a servant to assist him. Struggling with the buttons, Leorino addressed the servant.

"…I'm having some difficulty undressing. Could you help me?"

"I could."

A deep smooth voice echoed in the washroom. Taken aback, Leorino instantly turned to face him.

A man dressed in a simple shirt and black trousers stood in the entrance to the washroom with his arms crossed.

"…? …S-sir, why—?"

Gravis approached him with large strides. Panicking, Leorino took a step back.

"You asked Theodor to find someone to help you bathe, didn't you?"

"Yes. But… But—"

Gravis's long arms reached for him, his hands finding their way to the buttons of Leorino's shirt.

"W-wait, wait, please…!"

Leorino rushed to restrain his hand, but Gravis made quick work of the front of his shirt.

His fair skin lay exposed under the morning sun.

Leorino was dizzy with confusion and shame all at once.

How, why…?

* * *

Leorino looked up at Gravis in disbelief.

But the owner of the manly beauty far above his head still refused to let Leorino read his expression.

"I asked Theodor to send…a *servant* to attend to me! Wh-why would Your Excellency choose to do something like this…?"

Gravis cocked his head.

"Are you suggesting that I can't do it? I usually bathe alone; I'm used to it by now."

"Th-that's not what I meant… You mustn't. How could I ever allow Your Excellency to serve me…?!"

He felt dizzy.

Would Gravis, the country's royalty and highest-ranking man in the army, seriously assist him in bathing?

Leorino frantically pulled the edges of his open shirt together. But as he held it down with his uninjured hand, the man undid the hook in the front of his trousers.

"Wha— Ah!"

Leorino immediately grabbed his large hand, but Gravis gently shook him off.

"Don't use your injured hand."

"But—"

"I don't know what you're expecting, but I won't do anything."

"I wasn't…I wasn't *expecting* anything!"

He realized he was being teased, but couldn't help reacting. While his face was turning red with frustration, Gravis turned him around and stripped him of his trousers and underwear at the same time.

In no time at all, Leorino stood in front of Gravis in his birthday suit.

No! This is so…unbelievably embarrassing!

He didn't mind if servants saw him naked.

But he couldn't bear the thought of exposing his feeble nude body to the man he loved. If that wasn't bad enough, the perfect body of this particular man was the envy of all.

"No! I-I'm embarrassed… I don't want you to see my pathetic body…!"

Leorino desperately pushed Gravis away, his heart burning with shame.

"You have nothing to be ashamed of. Size aside, my body and yours are the same."

That was a technicality.

Leorino frantically tried to cover himself up, but his resistance was in vain, and before he knew it, he was being led into the bathhouse. Gravis asked Leorino to sit on a step at the edge of the bathtub, and suddenly poured hot water over his head.

"Pfft…"

Leorino brushed away the hair sticking to his face and looked up at Gravis, who only mercilessly poured more hot water over him. His large hand brushed back Leorino's wet platinum hair.

The rising steam turned Gravis's hair and clothes damp before Leorino's eyes. Combing back his dripping wet hair, Gravis revealed his prominent forehead.

The gold in Gravis's eyes was shimmering. Leorino's heart skipped a beat at the beauty of his eyes reflecting the morning sun.

"Sir…"

The still-glowing ember in Leorino's abdomen was slowly beginning to smolder inside him.

Leorino was trying his hardest to shrink away from Gravis's gaze.

"I wasn't planning on playing your attendant, but then again, I would never allow a servant meeting you for the first time to touch your naked body. This is my palace, after all."

Having said that, Gravis seemed very pleased as he watched Leorino's fair, snow-white skin slowly flush pink before him.

"…Were you planning to expose your beautiful body to a man other than me in such a vulnerable state?"

Tears began welling in Leorino's large eyes.

"Come, I thought you were feeling better, no need to cry. You're all right, relax."

Inspecting Leorino's naked body, Gravis bit back his disappointment.

...Of course, it's not there.

Gravis ran his fingers along Leorino's slender midsection. Leorino shivered. The fair, china-like skin glistened as the hot water slid off it, but the mark Gravis was searching for was nowhere to be found.

He recalled the night of the graduation ceremony, the one and only night when he and Ionia had made love.

Ionia had been pursuing his own pleasure in Gravis's embrace. On that moving body of his, a scar stretched from his stomach to his back, a mark from when he had been pierced by a sword.

The scar was proof he had protected Gravis.

They had placed their hands on the scar and rocked their hips for so long that they could both feel the other's pleasure.

Gravis's fingers could still remember the bumpy texture of that scar.

If there had been even the slightest trace of that mark on Leorino's fair skin, how much clearer could the path to the truth have been. Gravis had never truly given up hope.

Life can never be that easy, can it?

"Sir...?"

Leorino was puzzled by Gravis's behavior.

Leorino would surely feel humiliated if he learned of the man's true purpose. Not even Gravis could muster enough gross disregard for Leorino's dignity to forcefully strip him naked and then act disappointed when he couldn't find anything that looked like Ionia's mark on his body.

"...Sir, I'm embarrassed to be seen by you like this. I don't want you to see my...my infirm body."

Leorino's desperate attempts to hide his slender body inspired feelings of guilt and pity in Gravis.

"Why not? Your body is gorgeous. You have nothing to be ashamed of."

He meant every word. Leorino's body was beautiful.

"But it's…it's not the body of a warrior."

"Perhaps not, but the same could be said about many men. Why do you always seem so concerned about that?"

"I understand that…but…"

Gravis could not comprehend why Leorino was ashamed of his body.

He may have been small, especially in comparison to Gravis who was larger than most men, but his height was average at worst. He may have lacked breadth, but his shoulders were well defined, and his limbs were particularly slender and gracefully long.

He also had muscles, however faint, where they should be, likely a product of his exercises. His waist was so thin that Gravis felt he could fit it in one hand, but he was not nearly as unsightly as he seemed to believe he was.

Perhaps he wasn't masculine, that much was true.

"Have you ever grown a beard?"

"…A beard…?"

Leorino contemplated Gravis's question.

Gravis chuckled, realizing how foolish of a question it was.

He lifted Leorino's arm and peered into the young man's armpit. That area was as regrettably smooth as his chin.

It must have been simply his natural disposition. He certainly possessed the features of a man, but he could hardly be described as manly.

Not only was what little body hair he had a bright platinum color, almost the entirety of it was vellus hair. His pubic hair was so modest that one could easily see the skin beneath.

Leorino himself may not have been happy about it, but his entire body was fair and smooth, like a porcelain doll.

…No, he's no doll.

His nipples were small and pale, in clear proof that no one had ever touched them. Beneath the clump of soft hair, his genitals rested innocently.

Every part of Leorino's body was smooth and fit comfortably in Gravis's hands. It was perfectly pure, and yet exuded a hint of eroticism that roused Gravis's carnal desires.

It was a living, breathing, sinful body.

When Gravis slowly lifted Leorino's left leg, Leorino's body stiffened.

Extending from his small knee down his fair shin ran a straight line of scars and marks left by stitches that reached all the way down to his ankle.

It was the scar he had received six years ago.

Back when he was treating Leorino, Sasha had said the bones in the left leg were broken below the knee, and the tendons had been damaged. The scar was irregular, likely because the broken bones had pierced his skin.

"...This is from the wound from that day?"

"Yes."

Gravis gently traced the scar with his fingers. The thin skin was bumpy in places and indented in others, lacking smoothness.

It looked very similar to the scar on Ionia's belly.

Gravis stroked the scar once more.

"...If only I had been able to reach you in time, you wouldn't have had to suffer such a horrible injury."

"Please... If you hadn't immediately brought me to Brungwurt, I would not be here now, sir. That's what my father and Sasha always told me."

Gravis smiled at Leorino's gratitude.

It was the only flaw in his perfectly beautiful body. And yet there was nothing ugly about it at all.

If things hadn't gone as well as they had, the leg might have been amputated. Now it was strong enough to walk. It wasn't as sturdy as his right leg, but it had regained its muscle. What more was there to ask for?

But more than anything, Leorino must have invested a lot of blood, sweat, and tears to have been able to make such an incredible recovery.

"The scars may be ugly, but..."

"How could they ever be ugly? I'm impressed you can walk after such a serious injury. You've worked very hard."

There was nothing sexual about Gravis's fingers as he traced the scars. Leorino had relaxed and allowed the man access to his leg.

"...Thank you. Dr. Sasha and my family also helped me a lot. Thanks to them, I am now able to walk... I'm really grateful. Although I...I can't run anymore."

"Who says you need to run? Walking is more than enough. I can't remember the last time I ran myself."

Leorino smiled faintly at the man's words.

"That's because of your Power, sir... You have even less need for running than me."

"My Power grows stronger with age. I can travel all across the country without breaking a sweat... Come to think of it, I don't ride my horse much, either."

"I envy you. I would love to be able to go anywhere without depending on anyone."

Gravis smiled.

"You envy my power, hm...? No one's ever told me that so forthrightly."

"Really? I think everyone envies you."

"You don't have to envy me. You can go anywhere you please as well, even if you have to walk slower than most people, on your own two feet."

"Yes, sir..."

"You should be proud of what you've accomplished."

Gravis's expression didn't change, but there was a soft glow deep in his eyes as he gazed at Leorino.

This meant the world to Leorino.

"So stop deprecating yourself by comparing the fragility of your body to others. You are beautiful. So is the scar on your leg, and so is every other part of you. Be confident."

"Yes, sir..."

"When I said I didn't want anyone else to see you like this, I meant it. Don't expose your beautiful body to anyone."

"...Yes, sir. But I think at least my full-time attendant will still have to see me," Leorino retorted quietly.

Gravis nodded with a small smile, saying he could accept that.

Gravis plunged a wooden bucket into the tub, scooping up the hot water with a loud splash.

"Come, I'll wash your hair. Now put your head down and close your eyes."

"...To think Your Excellency would go out of your way to help me like this... You will surely get in trouble."

"Get in trouble with whom? I want to take care of you, what's the issue? Just sit there and humor me."

Gravis generously poured warm water over Leorino's now-lowered head. Unlike Leorino's attendant, Gravis's hands were a little rough, but free of any sexual intent, allowing Leorino to relax and comply.

Spilling shampoo on his palm, Gravis rubbed it into the soft platinum-colored locks until it formed a fluffy lather. The platinum hair seemed to disappear into the white foam, and soon the foam itself seemed to glow.

He scrubbed Leorino's head with his large hands. As he put some strength into it, as if he were washing his own head, he heard a moan. He saw Leorino's small head visibly swaying.

Gravis immediately eased the pressure in his fingertips.

He poured hot water over Leorino's head several times to swiftly remove the foam, revealing the contours of his shapely scalp.

Leorino's forehead was streaked with shiny, wet hair. Gravis ran his fingers through it. When he brushed Leorino's bangs back to clear his vision, Leorino's eyes lit up with gratitude as he smiled.

Gravis's heart was instantly filled to the brim with love for the young man behaving as obediently as a baby bird.

"...You're truly..."

"Sir...?"

"No, it's nothing."

Gravis combed his long fingers through Leorino's wet bangs once more. He also stroked Leorino's smooth forehead with his thumb. Leorino's face, which had already been tinged pink, turned a bright red.

"Time to wash the rest of you."

He urged Leorino to turn around. His fair back was exposed before Gravis's eyes.

The contours of his spine extending from his slender neck. His symmetrical shoulder blades. The fair, smooth skin stretching from the narrow waist to his soft buttocks. He looked so delicate and beautiful that Gravis hesitated to touch him.

And still, the mark was nowhere to be found.

Gravis swiftly washed Leorino's body. Feeling Gravis nearly reach his genitals, Leorino refused his hand, his face red, insisting that he could manage alone.

He began to scrub his body with one hand, though he wasn't very good at it.

When Leorino was fully covered in bubbles, Gravis ordered him to get into the bathtub.

Leorino eagerly submerged his body in the tub and let the bubbles dissolve. The remaining bubbles floating on the surface drifted away with the overflowing water. Finally, he could catch his breath.

"Don't put your left wrist in the water. It'll hurt if exposed to heat."

Gravis's shirt was soaking wet.

"You're soaked, sir... I'm sorry."

Leorino apologized, but Gravis did not seem to be bothered as he left the bathhouse.

Leorino breathed a sigh of relief and relaxed in the bathtub. With his entire body concealed in the hot water, he was finally able to unwind completely.

That was so...so nerve-racking...!

He would have never imagined that a royal like Gravis would help him bathe, let alone wash his entire body; perish the thought.

Unlike Leorino's servants, Gravis's hands were rough, but he didn't sense any sexual intent in Gravis's touch.

If anyone found out that he had Gravis wash his body, Leorino would be in major trouble. But Gravis had ordered him not to show his body even to his servants. With one of his hands incapacitated, he had no choice but to rely on Gravis.

Leorino dunked his face in the hot water and ruminated on what he had just experienced. His heart had been in a state of constant turmoil since the previous day. Just when he thought everything had finally calmed down, he found himself in this impossible situation.

As his thumping heartbeat gradually slowed, Leorino realized that he was disappointed.

Despite his fear, somewhere deep inside, he had been hoping that those long, graceful fingers would perhaps dare to do unspeakable things to him.

"I'm so self-conscious, it's embarrassing…"

He had been afraid of what happened last night, but in the end, he had taken pleasure in it.

That made him feel pathetic.

He just barely managed to keep the heat from building in his abdomen with each touch of Gravis's fingers. It was no wonder, as he wasn't used to physical contact.

Leorino was a man, too, and had all the desires expected of one.

He had been horrified at the thought that his body might react to Gravis's touch.

At the same time, he was genuinely relieved to see the faint excitement in Gravis's gaze. If he had looked at Leorino's feeble body with pity, he would have only hated himself even more than he already did.

He looked to his scars. The pink mark on his fair leg looked even more grotesque in the hot water.

He remembered the feeling of Gravis's fingers gently stroking the ugly scars.

"…He told me I worked very hard."

He felt like those words alone made it all worth it.

It was the same last night.

He had never been able to share his frustration with anyone.

Gravis accepted Leorino's anguish, which he had never even told his family about.

"You must accept your own weakness," Gravis had said. Leorino was scared to believe him and accept his words, but there was hope there, too.

…If I told him I was Ionia reincarnated…would he believe me? Would he be disappointed?

Leorino grew ever more hopeful that Gravis might be willing to accept him as he is.

The door to the bathhouse opened and Gravis called: "Leorino, your wrist will hurt. Come out already."

"Y-yes, sir...!"

Some time must have passed as he was lost in thought.

Leorino quickly looked up. Gravis watched him with some exasperation as he blew bubbles in the water. Perhaps Gravis thought he was childish. Leorino's flushed face turned even redder.

The next instant, Leorino's eyes widened.

A large cloth was spread out in Gravis's hands.

He couldn't possibly allow Gravis to play the role of his attendant any longer. But what else was there to do?

"Come, we don't have all day."

"Y-yes, sir..."

He couldn't exactly just stand there naked forever.

In the end, Gravis wrapped him in the piece of fabric he had been holding.

"...Choosing to walk right into my embrace? That's a good sign."

"...Sir?"

Leorino tilted his head and Gravis laughed quietly, saying it was nothing.

Gravis's somewhat rough hands wiped the water droplets off Leorino's skin. When he was mostly dry, Gravis picked him up, the fabric still around him.

Returning to the washroom, Gravis brought him to the large settee where he sat Leorino down.

"Wait here. I'll go wash myself now."

"Oh?"

Gravis swiftly removed his wet clothes, unabashedly revealing his robust muscles, and disappeared into the bathhouse.

Leorino was left alone on the settee, dumbfounded. He was overwhelmed by the sight of Gravis's nude body in all its splendor.

He seems so much bigger than I remember. His arms and legs are so thick, so sumptuous...

Gravis had trained his body to perfection, as evidenced by his rippling muscles, making him the epitome of the word *handsome*. He was breathtakingly beautiful.

"Hah..."

Leorino glanced down at his own body before he could help it. Although Gravis called him beautiful, he was depressingly skinny and helpless in comparison.

Leorino patiently waited on the settee. How long would he have to stay naked? Given the warm season, he wasn't exactly cold, but there was no sign of an attendant coming to help him get dressed.

At that moment, Leorino had an epiphany.

"...N-no, he wouldn't."

He worried that Gravis was planning to help him get dressed, too.

He decided he would do his best to dress himself on his own, and searched for the clothes that had been laid out for him. Even with an injured wrist, he could still move his fingers.

Leorino stood up, the fabric still wrapped around his naked body, and headed for the clothes.

"...Huh?"

The set of clothes he had received was missing any undergarments.

Leorino was at a loss.

That was when he noticed a lovely scent rising from the fabric covering his body. Leorino sniffed it.

"This smell..."

The scent was like the bark of a tree towering over frozen earth, an exciting fragrance tinged with something animalistic on a slightly damp winter's night.

It was a noble, enigmatic, complex scent—a scent he had come to know and love before he could help it.

It's Vi's scent... But why?

* * *

It was then that he realized something with a start. Leorino sniffed at his arms.

The smell was coming from his own body. Of course. It must have been the scent of Gravis's bespoke soap.

"I...I smell the same as Vi now...!"

Leorino's entire body flushed with unspeakable embarrassment. He couldn't help the silly thought that it was almost like being embraced by Gravis. And with such unseemly thoughts, Leorino's body became even hotter.

"...Huh?"

Leorino noticed something had changed about his body.

"Wait, wait. No, not now, don't be stupid...!"

His skin was growing hot under the fabric. As he began sweating, the scent grew ever stronger. The desire he had managed to stifle during his bath slowly made itself known under the influence of Gravis's scent. Leorino was beginning to panic.

"No, stop... Idiot! Stop reacting!"

He pressed down on his stiffening flesh from on top of the fabric in admonishment, but his inexperienced body reacted to that stimulus and asserted itself even further.

He rushed back to the settee and cowered on it.

Leorino wanted to cry.

His young body grew hotter at the slightest movement, at the same time intensifying the scent that got him so excited in the first place.

As he sat there, Leorino's arousal had grown to the point of no return.

What now...? What do I do...?

That was when Gravis returned from the bathhouse, with a "Sorry to have kept you waiting."

Leorino's gaze turned dark with despair.

Gravis swiftly wiped his wet body and wrapped the fabric around his waist. Leaving his muscular torso carelessly exposed, he quickly began to dress himself.

Leorino watched him in a daze.

But why was Leorino still naked when he had left the bath before Gravis?

"Come, Leorino. I'll dress you."

Gravis finally turned to him. His pronounced muscles were peeking through the gap in his unbuttoned shirt. Leorino could clearly see everything, from his toned abdominal muscles to the hair on his lower abdomen, only partially hidden by his undergarments.

Gravis's immense sex appeal made Leorino incredibly dizzy.

"What's wrong? Come," beckoned Gravis, but there were circumstances that prevented Leorino from moving from the settee.

"I... Um..."

His body had calmed down a little, but he was still in no condition to walk. Leorino did not possess the skill to quell or hide his arousal.

Leorino cast his eyes down, trying to distract himself from the man.

Right, Josef is waiting for me...!

"What are you doing?"

"Hyah!" Leorino jumped with an embarrassing scream when Gravis suddenly appeared beside him.

"What's wrong? You're acting strange. Was the bath too hot for you?"

"I... Um..."

Gravis knelt in front of the settee and combed his hand through Leorino's damp hair. Gravis's fingers grazing his skin only excited him further. Leorino trembled violently at his touch.

The man's body was so close to Leorino now, and his sweet, tormenting scent was thick on him. Feeling his body temperature rise, Leorino shrank away.

Unlike Gravis, Leorino was still completely naked, wrapped only in the thin fabric.

Leorino's body ached. He felt beyond miserable. The morning sun shone down on him through the washroom window.

* * *

In broad daylight of all times! I'm such a deviant...!

Gravis's bare chest tempted him with its enticing smell.

Following the strange urge, Leorino reached for Gravis's chest. Feeling the need to hide the source of what was driving him crazy, Leorino brought his fingers to the edges of Gravis's shirt and suddenly began to button it.

"...What exactly are you doing?"

Gravis cocked his head at Leorino's strange behavior.

"Y-your shirt is undone, sir... I wanted to help."

But Leorino's fingers were not used to helping people, even when his wrist wasn't injured, and already struggled with the first button.

Gravis sighed.

"You don't have to do it."

Leorino's fingers were scrambling but not producing any results, when Gravis finally held them, putting his attempts to a stop.

"That's Theodor's job. My valet seems to have his own special way of styling my clothes."

"I—I see... Then I had better let Mr. Theodor handle that."

"More importantly, you're still naked. We should get you dressed already. Don't use your injured hand. Come now, stand up."

At the sight of the hand gently urging him to get up, Leorino finally resigned himself to his fate. Without lifting his gaze, he managed to address his current predicament.

"...I'm very sorry. I can't get up right now."

"What's wrong? Are you in pain?"

"No... I'm, uh... I—"

Gravis frowned. "I told you not to stutter."

Tears finally began to well in Leorino's eyes at the rebuke.

"Leorino."

But Leorino said nothing.

"...What's wrong?"

Gravis finally noticed that something was different about Leorino.

At closer inspection, Gravis noticed that his entire body was fidgeting in agony. His face, neck, and shoulders peeking out of the fabric were also flushed.

Leorino's eyes were tearful and his breathing shallow. There was also his gaze, looking up at Gravis in a somewhat pleading manner. Something sensual was hidden within.

That was when Gravis realized the predicament Leorino was in.

"You're aroused, aren't you?"

He didn't mean to tease him, but Leorino's face turned red at his words, and he hung his head, looking as if he was about to burst into tears.

"I-I'm sorry..."

He wilted in embarrassment. He looked pitiful and precious all the same.

"Ah... Sir!"

Gravis sat himself down next to Leorino and lifted his body onto his lap. He held Leorino from behind so as not to embarrass him, but Leorino still shrank away, unhappy even with that position.

"What happened? Was my washing you *that* exciting?"

"N-no, sir..."

"You must be quite pent up. Well, you *are* eighteen. At that age, anything vaguely shaped like a human body will get you all hot and bothered."

"Pent...? No, sir...! I was just sitting here, and I realized I smell like you... It just happened."

"Smell?"

Leorino nodded timidly.

"...I was missing some clothes, so I had to wait here like this...and then..."

"Hmm. Then what?"

"I was still naked, and I got the impression my body smelled the same as Your Excellency, so I sniffed it and...I was right, so my body began feeling hot and then...and then I ended up like this."

Gravis looked up to the heavens in disbelief. Quickly, he covered his mouth to conceal his expression.

The young man had just shyly admitted that he lusted after Gravis's scent.

"I'm sorry... There must be something wrong with me."

With no concern for Gravis's growing possessiveness, Leorino complained about his predicament, his voice ridden with guilt. Such nonsense.

* * *

Gravis brought his nose to the soft skin of Leorino's neck and inhaled. Leorino's thin body trembled at the man's warmth.

Leorino did indeed smell like the soap Gravis always used. It was blended with his own unique fragrance.

"...You're right, you smell just like me. It's a nice scent when mixed with your own."

"Yes, well..."

Leorino was covered in his scent now. This fact brought Gravis immense satisfaction. The familiar scent mixed with Leorino's own lush flowery fragrance smelled divine.

The smell was so delicious that Gravis pressed his lips to Leorino's beautifully long neck before he could think better of it.

"Ah..."

His freshly washed skin was sweeter than Gravis had imagined. Not to mention unbelievably soft.

Could such skin really belong to a man?

As Gravis tasted Leorino's pale skin with his lips with no hint of hesitation, Leorino began to panic.

"Your Excellency! Sir! Please...!"

"...What's wrong?"

"Sir, if you could just give me a moment, I would like to, um...d-deal with *this*."

Is he begging me to let him jerk off here?

Do I even need to say it... He's unbelievable.

Gravis couldn't take it any longer and nuzzled his face against Leorino's thin shoulder to stifle a laugh. How pure, how naive could he be?

"Oh, I can't keep up with you, can I?"

"I'm so... Sir, I'm...I'm sorry."

Gravis's strained laugh dismayed Leorino.

"Leorino, I may be quite a bit older than you, but I'm not *that* old."

"Y-yes... Uh? Old, sir...?"

"Did you think that if you asked me to let you 'deal with it' with that pretty mouth of yours, I would just sit back and let you relieve yourself alone?"

"Huh? ...S-sir...? Wai—"

The next moment, Gravis lightly covered Leorino's lips with his own.

"...?"

He twisted around and laid Leorino down on the settee. His nearly dry platinum hair fanned out across the seat.

Leorino's eyes—a mixture of lust, confusion, and fear—looked up at Gravis in a silent question.

"Open your legs."

"Ah... Wh—"

Gravis spread Leorino's knees and settled himself between them.

"Wh-why...?"

Gravis was very careful not to put any weight on Leorino's weak legs. Although, even aside from his disability, it would be easy for a man as large as Gravis to crush Leorino's slender body if he leaned on him without thought.

"This position is so embarrassing!"

Leorino suddenly began to resist. He really had been raised to be docile.

Now that they were this close, Gravis could feel it touching his abdomen. Indeed, Leorino had gotten quite firm under the fabric. Leorino was unconsciously rocking his hips against Gravis even as he struggled to escape.

"Ah, I can feel how hard you are. Hah, must be nice to be so young."

"Ahh... Wait."

When Gravis ground his hips against Leorino, his violet eyes clearly moistened with lust.

"Sir...I can manage on my own...!"

"You really think I'd leave you alone in this state?"

Leorino shook his head from side to side in fear.

He attempted escape, but of course, Gravis had no intention of letting him go.

Gravis pulled down the fabric covering Leorino's chest to reveal the fair skin beneath.

"...Wh-what are you doing?"

His nipples were tucked away in the pale areola above his slightly tensed pectoral muscles. They were so small that Gravis couldn't even hold them between his fingers, their color even lighter than Leorino's lips.

Gravis rubbed them with the pads of his thumbs, hoping to rouse them to a more accessible size.

"Wait... Ah!"

Gravis licked his neck, at the same time gently stimulating both areolas, causing Leorino's small head to shake. But, paying him no mind, Gravis toyed with them a little harder, and soon the small, soft buds began to stiffen and make their presence known.

Pulling away from Leorino's body and gazing down at his chest, Gravis saw that the areolas had swollen and his small nipples were eagerly standing at attention. Gravis couldn't help noticing how sensitive Leorino's body was and figured it would certainly be worth exploring.

"They're small, but still nice and receptive."

As Gravis rubbed Leorino's nipples in a circular motion, Leorino gasped quietly and arched his back.

"Ahh, wh-why...? Why there?"

"Touching you here should make you feel good down there, too. Just enjoy it."

"Sir, that area is, um, not really relevant right now... What I'm struggling with is, as you may have noticed, a little lower. You know, my... Mmph."

Leorino looked like he was about to cry when he very nearly said something scandalous.

"...That's quite enough."

"Nn! ...Hng..."

Gravis descended upon Leorino's lips.

He wasted no time, using his tongue mercilessly, licking and lapping at the places he had learned Leorino enjoyed last night, flooding them with pleasure.

After a few moments of Gravis's elaborate tongue work, Leorino's body completely relaxed. His arousal pressing into Gravis's abdomen was so hard now that they couldn't turn back if they tried. The way he unconsciously rubbed himself against the fabric in hopes of obtaining any stimulation was adorably lewd.

Gravis had intended only to offhandedly give him some pleasure to offer him release, but Leorino's innocent submissiveness stirred something inside him and made Gravis want to touch him in earnest.

Gravis whispered in his deep voice.

"Look, you don't need to say anything."

"Sir…"

"Just enjoy yourself and it'll be over in no time. You've got nothing to be afraid of."

Having been ravaged by Gravis so thoroughly, Leorino's lips struggled to form any coherent words. His thoughts also seemed to dissolve in a blur of pleasure, and Leorino looked at the man absentmindedly with dazed eyes. The sight filled Gravis's heart with love.

His own body was beginning to share Leorino's arousal, but Gravis clenched his teeth and held himself back.

It had been eighteen years since he had felt this affectionate lust for anyone.

Am I betraying Ionia?

Gravis thought what he had felt for Ionia was a once-in-a-lifetime love.

He had thought that his fixation on Ionia, too maddening to truly call love, had died on that day eighteen years ago, tearing out the only tender parts of his heart.

But hopelessly yearning for Leorino in his arms, he couldn't lie to his heart.

I love him. I love him more than I can say.

This feeling was so clear now that Gravis felt foolish for continuing to search for traces of Ionia in Leorino.

Gravis scoffed at himself. Perhaps this affection was a pardon for the crimes his heart had subconsciously prepared for him.

But that's fine. I want to make this soft, sweet young man mine already.

Should I take him here and now?

But just as he thought that, Leorino's unblemished abdomen caught his eye.

"Hah…"

The image of the red-haired young man bleeding profusely from his stomach flashed across Gravis's mind.

Leorino ferociously fueled his love and possessive nature. At the same time, Gravis still held onto his unfulfilled desire to find out the truth.

His lust was ready to run out of control, but his rationality held him back just in time.

"Not yet, Leorino. I won't steal you away just yet."

"Nn… Ah."

But what would Gravis do when he arrived at the truth? Would it change anything when his heart pined for Leorino so much?

Leorino… When I'm finally able to say that I love you for who you are with complete certainty, that's when…

That's when he would beg for Leorino's love with all the words he could find. He would never again be at the mercy of fate. He was different now.

He made his own fate now.

He would not make the same mistakes he had made in the past.

"…I haven't told you anything. So I will not steal you away yet."

"…Sir?"

"Do keep your pretty mouth shut—don't make me lose my head any further."

Tears spilling from his eyes, Leorino nodded and placed his fist in front of his mouth.

The gesture nearly burned away Gravis's reason all over again.

This time, he brought his fingers directly to Leorino's arousal, waiting for release under the fabric.

Leorino arched his back, accepting the pleasure he was being given. His turgid member spilled drop after clear drop, desperately longing for the moment of release brought about by Gravis's fingers.

Before long, Leorino's small fist was not enough to contain the sweet moans escaping his mouth.

The Meaning of the Word "Shield"

In terms of time, it may have been just a few moments. But for Leorino, it was like being tossed about by a storm.

For the first time in his life, Leorino learned the sensation of being driven to climax by a hand other than his own.

A large hand gripped around him gently urged him to spill his seed. All the while, Gravis kissed him on his panting lips, his trembling shoulders, and his swollen nipples. He felt like he was going to melt from the waist down.

Leorino's ragged breathing slowly returned to normal. Gravis's fingers had been stroking his cheek, but finally pulled away.

In a daze, Leorino followed the man's back with his gaze.

Gravis returned with a hand towel. Leorino lifted his leaden arms to stop Gravis's hand from reaching out to clean his body. The realization of his own foolishness returned to Leorino along with his reason, coming to haunt him with regret.

"...I can do it myself. I apologize for the inconvenience."

"All right."

Leorino slowly sat up. He endured the shame as he silently wiped the wet area with the towel he received.

His whole body was still filled with a sweet numbness. The sensation of being touched in a sexual manner by the hands of another *in real life* was incredibly intense.

Leorino hid his nudity, wrapping the fabric around his body. He was grateful that Gravis left him alone, only watching him without saying a word.

"Leorino, I arranged a change of clothes for you. Can you dress yourself alone? Oh...but before that."

Gravis approached Leorino with his graceful, weightless gait once more. In his hand he held a compress and a bandage.

"Let's get you patched up. Here, give me your hand."

"Of course... Thank you."

Leorino offered Gravis his hand. After covering the injured area with a medicine-infused compress, Gravis deftly wrapped it with the bandage.

Leorino thought Gravis used to be more royal, somehow.

He wondered absentmindedly what had changed Gravis, why he was so eager to take care of him.

As Gravis wrapped the bandage neatly around his wrist, Leorino's mind had calmed.

No matter how many years had passed, Gravis's flawless beauty had not waned with age at all. If anything, he had only matured, his masculine beauty veritably radiant. But Leorino already knew that when Gravis smiled, small wrinkles appeared in the corners of his eyes.

Leorino and Ionia were not the same person.

Leorino felt that they were two separate people living very different lives, even if they were connected through memories played back in his dreams.

But his soul could be doomed to remain forever trapped because of the man before him.

I love him. He's special. He always will be...

Gravis was royalty. He was also the symbol of Fanoren's power.

Leorino was born a nobleman. He was fortunate enough to meet Gravis again, and happened to be able to stay in his vicinity. That was all there was to it. Leorino had no special powers and could not fight in the royal army.

If he were to fall in love with Gravis, those feelings would never amount to anything.

But even so…if Gravis has even the slightest fondness for me…

I want to be there for him. I have only one wish: Let me be by your side until my dying breath. This desire welled in Leorino's heart.

It didn't matter if the feeling wasn't mutual. He only wanted a pretext to stay by Gravis's side forever.

…If I told him I have Ionia's memories, would he let me stay by his side like he did back then?

With equal parts hope and worry in his eyes, Leorino peered at the man imploringly. Sensing Leorino's gaze, Gravis looked up.

Their eyes met.

Leorino's hidden desire turned into a storm inside him, demanding release. He couldn't contain his feelings.

"Sir…"

Leorino finally opened his throat, nearly gasping for breath.

"I have something to tell you."

"Yes?"

"You may think I'm crazy. But the truth is, I…"

Gravis's eyes glowed gold as he silently waited for Leorino to finish.

…Please accept it. Please believe me.

Leorino desperately tried to squeeze out the words, his throat tight with nerves.

"Sir, I—I have…"

A sharp knock sounded in the parlor. The tension that had been building between them immediately snapped. Leorino was brought back to reality all at once, as if doused with cold water.

"Your Highness, it is nearly time." Theodor stood in the doorway. "Lord

Leorino, we must get you dressed as well. His Highness is very busy and has very little time."

"...Y-yes, of course. I apologize."

When Leorino pulled back in a panic, at that moment, Gravis tightly squeezed his fingers.

"...?"

"Theodor, leave."

Gravis watched Leorino with horribly serious eyes. Leorino's heart was pounding.

"Out, now!"

At Gravis's command, the door closed instantly.

Once more, they were alone. Leorino's heart thumped away in his chest.

"What were you going to say?"

Gravis squeezed his hand tightly. He wasn't holding back his strength now.

"...Ow."

"Leorino, tell me. What were you going to say?"

But Leorino only silently shook his head.

The courage that had been swelling in his chest was instantly popped by the needle known as reality.

Gravis urged him to continue with a stern expression.

"Leorino, say it."

"It's nothing. We should be leaving, it seems... I apologize for wasting your time."

With that, Leorino kept his eyes firmly on the floor and did not look up.

Gravis finally gave in.

He heaved one heavy sigh, trying to hold back his raging emotions.

"...You're right. We're out of time."

Gravis stood up.

Leorino quietly bit his lip as the man's warmth pulled away from him.

"Do you need help getting dressed?"

"...Thank you. I'll be all right. I might only need a servant to help me with the buttons." Leorino answered in a firm voice, his eyes still downcast.

He couldn't embarrass himself any further. After the intense confusion and pleasure Gravis had brought him, it was time to return to reality.

His life as Leorino would continue. As a son of the Cassieux family, he couldn't escape the yoke of his duty.

"Leorino, let's speak more some other time. I'll see you soon."

With that, Gravis turned on his heel.

Nodding at his back, Leorino regained hope.

One day, he might have the opportunity to confess his secret.

When that day came, he would have the courage to reveal that he possessed Ionia Bergund's memories.

Then he would plead with Gravis to let him stay by his side, insisting that he would make himself useful to the best of his ability.

Leorino set his sights on his goal.

Gravis stifled his irritation and headed for the valet waiting for him in his bedroom.

Leorino had wanted to say something.

He was dying to know what it was, but Theodor must have already refrained from interrupting them for as long as it was feasible. It was true, Gravis had no time to spare.

Theodor had prepared everything and waited in silence. Gravis approached, nodded, and the man promptly began preparing his master for the day ahead.

Under normal circumstances, it had been the job of the fitter to dress Gravis for the day. But ever since an assassin had disguised himself as a fitter when Gravis was still a young boy, Theodor had taken on the responsibility.

The valet deftly inserted Gravis's shirt into his trousers and buttoned it up so that the contours of his perfect muscular body would show.

"What do you intend to do with him, Your Highness?"

He looked down at the valet, who was roughly a head shorter than him.

"Theodor, what is the purpose of this question?"

Gravis locked gazes with the light blue-eyed valet.

"He is a son of the Cassieux family. If you intend to make him the target of your next conquest, I would suggest you reconsider."

"You dare question what I do?"

Gravis warned that he was overstepping in a low voice.

Theodor worked calmly, paying Gravis no mind. The valet knew his master's boundaries better than anyone, now moving his hand to the ornament at the base of Gravis's sleeve.

"Even I can recognize those eyes... You sensed *him*, did you not?"

"Theodor."

Theodor stopped his hands and apologized.

"Forgive me. But I do feel the need to know exactly what Your Highness intends."

Theodor was the only attendant who had accompanied Gravis since he was little and had remained by his side until now. If the man who had sworn his absolute loyalty to him was going to be this insistent, Gravis decided it was only right to address Theodor's concerns seriously.

"What do you want to know? We don't have much time."

"Yes, sir. I'll just ask while I get you ready, if you don't mind."

Gravis nodded his head in approval.

"Do you intend to keep Lord Leorino by your side from now on? Just as you did with Ionia Bergund in the past?"

But Gravis remained silent.

"Judging by his appearance, Lord Leorino is so fragile that he could never wield a sword. Apart from his beautiful appearance, I highly doubt he possesses the necessary skill to serve at Your Highness's side."

Frowning at his comment, Gravis replied in a low voice, biting back his irritation. "You're right. The boy can't fight. I wouldn't entrust him with my back in *that* sense, either."

Theodor reached for the other sleeve and fastened the decorative cufflinks.

"Do you intend to keep him by your side regardless?"

Theodor examined his master's body once more, making sure Gravis was fully presentable, as was his job as his valet.

Gravis was silent for a moment longer, before finally slowly nodding to Theodor.

"Hmm... I suppose I will."

"May I ask why?"

Gravis turned his head, pondering this.

"Theodor, I no longer need a shield nor a bodyguard. I am far stronger than I was back then, am I not?"

"Yes, sir. Right now, Your Highness is the strongest man in the land."

"That I am. That's why I don't expect him to play Ionia's part. If anything, I want the opposite."

"Which is?"

Gravis smiled softly.

"Like I said, the opposite. I want to become *his* shield. I want him to entrust his back to me. That's what I intend to achieve."

Theodor was shocked. In all his long years of service, the valet had never seen his master speak about someone with such a gentle expression on his face.

"Your Highness..."

"You mentioned his physical weakness. You're not wrong, but his body is the only weak thing about Leorino."

"Is that so? Somehow, I doubt it."

"He may remain physically weak, but his heart is strong. He is persevering and hardworking. He's also stubborn in some ways. If he can see his own value, he will surely grow stronger in the years to come."

Theodor said nothing to that.

"I will be his shield. I will protect him. Fighting is just about all I can do... but I do have the power to protect him."

Theodor remained silent and finally attached the cloak to Gravis's shoulders.

"...I had assumed you longed for those violet eyes of his."

"...I see. You saw it, too, then."

Theodor nodded.

"I was quite shocked. Seeing those eyes, I was ready to believe *he* had been reborn."

"I can't deny that I'm looking for a trace of him in that boy. But that's always been the curse hanging over Lucas and me."

Gravis finally took the sword and belt Theodor handed him and slung it around his own waist. This was the only task the man always performed himself.

"But...I suppose it's true. Truly, that boy is nothing like Ionia." .

Theodor blinked silently.

"I want to let him spread his wings freely. And, just as much, I don't want to let him out of my arms for a single moment if I can help it—that's what he means to me."

Theodor's eyes widened for a moment, but his serious expression quickly returned. Gravis chuckled at the way Theodor maintained his reputation as Gravis's valet.

"It's fine, you can laugh. Tell me I'm not acting my age. I myself am surprised at how much I've changed."

"It's not that, sir. There's just something touching about the thought that Your Highness has once again found someone you can feel so strongly about."

"What do you mean?"

"Back when Ionia Bergund was around, I...I believe I failed to fully grasp the extent of your feelings, sir."

Gravis remembered Theodor when they were younger, back when Theodor held nothing but contempt for Ionia.

"I see," was all Gravis said before he turned to head for the washroom to reunite with Leorino.

"Theodor...I want you to be as mindful of him as you are of me. Can I ask that of you?"

Theodor responded to this command with a deep bow.

Watching as Gravis left to the parlor, Leorino had stood up as well. He began to prepare himself, struggling with his aching left hand. He wasn't very good with his hands, but somehow he managed to dress himself all alone.

"...Yes! I don't look sloppy, do I? ...No, I think I did well. If it's not presentable enough, I'll ask for help."

Leorino opened the door to the parlor to ask the attendant to put the finishing touches on his outfit.

Through a small gap in the door, he caught a glimpse of Gravis and Theodor. Leorino was about to open the door further and join them when he stiffened at the contents of their conversation.

"Apart from his beautiful appearance, I highly doubt he possesses the necessary skill to serve at Your Highness's side."

Leorino was the topic of conversation.

His temples began to pulse with dread.

Then Gravis answered his valet, "You're right. The boy can't fight."

Leorino's vision went dark.

Gravis continued in a cool voice.

"I wouldn't entrust him with my back in *that* sense, either."

At that moment, the resolve and hope Leorino had just rekindled in his heart were snuffed out.

He quietly closed the door. He couldn't bring himself to continue listening to their conversation any longer.

Gravis's words echoed in his head.

He assumed that, even if he had been reborn as Leorino, if he did something of merit, Gravis would eventually recognize him for who he was... He hoped that he would once more be able to offer Gravis his blood and loyalty, just like Ionia had.

Regretting his own foolishness, Leorino resented the man who had given him such vain hopes.

At the same time, he was heartbroken.

So when you said there's nothing wrong with being weak, I suppose you never really meant it...

Despite the warm spring sunshine, his heart grew cold. And deeper inside him, somewhere beyond the rhythmic heartbeat, all warmth was replaced with melancholy.

Leorino stared blankly at his hands; his soft hands that had never been used to fight.

Eventually, the door opened and Gravis reappeared, now in his military uniform. He looked at Leorino and smiled.

The affection in his eyes must have been an illusion created by Leorino's greed.

He had been longing for something he could never have.

From now on, he would know his place.

Leorino hid the pain in his chest and burned Gravis's expression into his mind.

Like Ships in the Night

Josef had fallen down the stairs while protecting Leorino, but was now able to stand up on his own. In fact, he was already fully dressed in the uniform of the Royal Army.

"Josef... Thank god...!"

"Lord Leorino? What's all this?!"

As soon as they reunited in the hospital room, the guard was shocked to see Leorino rush at him in a way usually unthinkable for a noble.

"You got hurt because I was careless... I'm really sorry."

"No, I'm glad I was able to protect you, Lord Leorino."

"Are you feeling all right?"

Josef laughed uneasily as his master ran his eyes over Josef's entire body.

"I got a bit of a bump on my head, but I wasn't bleeding. Dr. Sasha said I should be fine. My body... Well, I hurt all over...but I can move no problem, so I'm all right."

Josef tried to flex his muscles to reassure him, but his face twisted in pain. Leorino's large eyes immediately welled with tears. Josef was at a complete loss.

"L-Lord Leorino, I really am all right."

"You must have been in a lot of pain. If only I had been able to hold my ground back then... I'm so sorry for being such a sorry excuse for a master."

"...Lord Leorino?"

* * *

Something was wrong with his master. Leorino seemed somehow worn out, as if he had been the one protecting Josef as he fell down the stairs.

There was a bandage around his left wrist, but other than that, his master appeared to be uninjured. But Leorino's usually perfectly shaped eyes were swollen and red, as if he had spent the night crying. Upon closer inspection, they were lined with faint dark circles.

Josef wondered if he had been crying the entire time since the incident.

"You seem…more exhausted than me, Lord Leorino."

Josef turned to Sasha and Dirk, who stood behind him. The men also seemed to notice that something was wrong with Leorino.

Josef placed his hand on Leorino's shoulder, hoping it might cheer him up.

"What's wrong, Lord Leorino?"

"Josef… Josef…"

Then, perhaps subconsciously, Leorino seemed to wither on the spot as he made himself small and crawled into the arms of his guard.

"Are you in pain?"

"I'm not…"

Shaking his head, Leorino hugged Josef even closer. Leorino was a modest man, but right now he was not at all shy about asking for comfort in the presence of others.

Sensing something strange about his behavior, Josef glared like a lioness protecting her cub at the man behind him, who must have been the cause.

Behind Leorino stood the general, his arms crossed on his chest.

Seeing the general up close for the first time, the man had an air of supremacy about him that proved he was no ordinary man. Josef felt sweat run down his back. Even the most fearless of men couldn't keep their knees from trembling in Gravis's presence.

Then again, Josef's middle name was "reckless." He glared at the general, pulling Leorino closer protectively.

Josef was convinced that something had happened between them.

Sasha had told him that while he was resting in the Palace of Defense, Leorino had not returned home, instead staying at the general's palace.

"...General, what did you do to Lord Leorino?"

Leorino jerked upright in Josef's arms.

"...Josef! You can't speak like that to the general!" Dirk admonished, but Josef only clicked his tongue. He narrowed his cat-like eyes harder, glaring up at the man standing behind Leorino.

Gravis, on the other hand, only frowned down at Josef with cold, inscrutable eyes.

As soon as he saw Josef, Leorino was unable to contain himself. He clung to his guard in full view of others.

Leorino realized that Josef was desperately putting up a brave front against Gravis. He rushed to pull away, feeling bad for Josef, but Josef only kept his arms wrapped tightly around his master's back.

"Just look at him... What have you done?"

Gravis was the most powerful man in the country, second only to the king. His influence was hardly limited to the Kingdom of Fanoren. His name was known all throughout the continent. Few could confront him and keep their composure.

But Josef was always ready to go on the offensive for the sake of his cherished master.

Josef tensed his core. With his gaze, he silently questioned the man wearing an air of supremacy that intimidated everyone around him. He had to know what this man had done to Leorino.

Gravis quirked an eyebrow at that. It appeared he had taken an interest in Josef.

"You're very bold, I'll give you that. What's your name?"

"...Josef Lev of Brungwurt, sir."

"Lev... There was a man of that name in the Brungwurt Autonomous Army. You're his son?"

"Yes."

"Your quick wit in protecting Leorino during his fall is commendable. Well done."

Josef had been glaring at the general with a belligerent look on his face, but the sudden compliment completely threw him off.

"Th-thank...you?"

"But if Leorino attempts something reckless, it is also your responsibility to admonish him. Keep that in mind and keep up the good work."

"...Yes, sir. But I would still like to ask you a question, general. What did you do to Lord Leorino?"

Dirk was quick to chide him.

"Josef! How dare you speak like that to His Excellency?!"

"Has the man left his manners in Brungwurt?" Gravis asked his second-in-command.

"Hah... I can see how you'd come to that conclusion, sir, but Josef has always been like this."

Gravis and his adjutant both looked at Josef. Josef stirred, feeling ill at ease under the men's scrutiny.

"What can I say—if you have the mettle and the skill to protect Leorino, I couldn't care less about your manners."

"Josef is technically not a member of the Royal Army, after all. We're both commoners, so I'll give him some guidance, but I don't doubt his commitment to protecting Leorino."

Leorino quickly pulled away from Josef and bowed to Gravis.

"...I apologize for my guard. Please forgive his insolence."

Leorino was pale. Considering that he was already fragile, his crestfallen look worried everyone in the room, including Gravis.

"What's wrong, Leorino?"

"...Nothing, sir. I just wanted to apologize for the behavior of my servant."

Leorino could tell his overly formal answer had upset Gravis. Sasha and Dirk stiffened.

"Your Excellency...Lord Leorino seems to be tired as well. May I send him home with Josef for the day?"

Gravis nodded.

"Of course. But first, I need to talk to you. Leorino, come."

Leorino hesitated for a moment, but finally obeyed the order. Gravis grabbed him by his healthy arm and pulled him closer. It wasn't a violent motion, but Leorino was thrown off-balance by the force of the movement.

"Hey!" Josef yelled in protest, but Dirk immediately intervened. He felt nothing good could come from provoking Gravis any further.

"Leave us alone for a moment."

Gravis's irritation was palpable.

When Josef tried to raise his voice in protest once more, Dirk silenced him by covering his mouth.

Sasha furrowed his brow deeper than usual.

"Your Excellency. Please be careful with him, Leorino is—"

"I know. I just want to talk."

Gravis coldly repelled the doctor's reproachful gaze, signaling that he had no interest in discussing the matter any further.

Leorino looked somewhat at a loss, and Sasha wondered if he should leave the room. However, a closer look into the eyes of the man looking down at Leorino revealed a gleam that was at once more rational and concerned than Sasha had expected.

"Your Excellency, please keep your upcoming meeting in mind... Dr. Sasha, Josef, let's go." With that, Dirk left the room with the doctor and Josef, holding Josef's arms behind his back even as he struggled to break free.

Gravis and Leorino were left alone in the now silent hospital room.

When he felt the slightest hint of fear from Leorino, Gravis lowered his eyes, perching on the bed so as not to frighten him. Sitting down, it was easier to make eye contact with Leorino, whose head only reached up to Gravis's shoulders.

"...What's wrong?"

When Gravis gently shook the arm still in his grasp, Leorino finally met his gaze.

Leorino's violet eyes had been lit up like jewels just a few moments ago, but now turned melancholy, his heart completely closed off to Gravis.

"...It's nothing. I am truly sorry for the trouble I have caused Your Excellency."

"That's not what I wanted to hear… What's the matter? Why are you so dispirited?"

Just a few moments ago, Leorino's slender body was shivering in Gravis's arms, wet with tears of pleasure the likes of which he had never tasted before.

When Gravis stroked Leorino's cheek as he watched Leorino slowly descend from the heights of bliss, perhaps unconsciously, Leorino narrowed his eyes like a kitten, his long eyelashes quivering.

He had laid bare both his body and his heart to Gravis.

Gravis had taken his eyes off Leorino for just a moment, and in that time, Leorino had put up a wall around his heart and shut himself away behind it.

Something had caused Leorino to close himself off to him. But Gravis couldn't figure out what. He hated not knowing.

There were faint dark circles around Leorino's eyes, making it clear how tired he was.

Gravis's heart ached at the sight of him. Gravis spoke slowly, trying to sound as gentle as possible.

"You were trying to tell me something this morning. Is that the reason?"

"…No, sir. It's really nothing. I just think I've presumed on your kindness far more than is appropriate."

Gravis frowned. "And I told you I'm fine with that."

Leorino shook his head. "I've come to realize that's not good enough."

Gravis said nothing to that.

"You're right, sir. I have unwittingly…allowed myself to get too comfortable in your presence. I seem to have completely forgotten my place as a servant of the Palace of Defense, as your subject. I have finally come to that realization, and I am sorry."

Gravis heaved a small sigh. Leorino's shuddered, as if frightened by it.

Gravis gently hugged Leorino's thin body to reassure him.

"…What's wrong? Leorino, why are you so distant? What happened?"

Leorino twisted uncomfortably, trying to escape from the man's arms.

"Leorino."

"Please don't concern yourself with me anymore. Please don't treat me like this anymore. I—I can't... I don't..."

Gravis scowled. Leorino took one deep, desperate breath and clenched his fists to hold something back, trying to regain his composure.

Leorino's heart was inexperienced and delicate, only now learning about the outside world for the first time. Gravis realized he had been manhandling that tender heart far too much since last night.

Seeing Leorino's reaction, Gravis slowly loosened his arm so as not to further upset the young man.

His intuition told him that he shouldn't push Leorino any further.

Leorino and his guard returned home early.

Leorino's heart ached at the sight of his anxious servants and the worry he had caused the entire household.

He apologized especially to Hundert, who must have spent the entire night worrying about him. Hundert took care of him more diligently than usual, examining every inch of his body.

Hundert noticed Leorino's injured wrist, and his face twisted in pain. After managing to calm Hundert's fussing about calling the doctor, Leorino was finally left alone in his room.

Leorino sat in an armchair, ruminating over the events of the morning.

While Gravis and Josef had been staring each other down, Leorino was so busy suppressing his own chaotic emotions that he could not afford to focus on his surroundings.

Leorino found himself deeply attracted to Gravis.

Whenever he was near Gravis, he was all Leorino could think of.

No matter how much chaos Gravis introduced to his heart, Leorino struggled to distance himself from Gravis. He couldn't help but be drawn to him; to his overwhelming, one-of-a-kind presence.

But Leorino's heart was inexperienced and incredibly fragile.

His defensive instincts subconsciously made him want to keep his distance from Gravis. He dreamed of escaping back to the safety of Brungwurt, where no one could hurt him.

And yet, without Gravis's arms around him, he felt despair.

"Vi..."

Leorino couldn't stand it anymore and buried his face in his hands.

A knock sounded on his door.

"Leorino, I need to talk to you. Could I have a moment?"

It was his second oldest brother, Johan.

Johan's blue-green eyes were so dark that they appeared pitch-black. Leorino had never seen his second brother, the gentlest of them, so angry in his life.

Leorino felt desolate as he faced his brother, wondering how Johan, who had always been so kind to him, had come to wear this sort of expression.

"I heard that you stayed at the general's palace last night. I was shocked when a messenger arrived from His Excellency's residence."

Leorino tried to keep his expression firm.

"...Yes. He very kindly invited me to spend the night."

"Right. But the messenger told us that Josef was injured and placed in Dr. Sasha's care, and that the general would take custody of you for your own safety. We received no further details."

"I see. Then the messenger told you the truth."

Leorino had no intention of telling his brother what had happened. Right now, he was filled with frustration at his own stupidity and naïveté, and a heavy feeling he would not be able to explain even if he tried.

Little by little, the secrets between Leorino and his family grew.

As he watched his brother in silence, Johan sighed. Faint dark circles lined his eyes, and he looked exhausted.

Seeing Johan like this, Leorino again felt guilty for causing his family undue stress.

"...I'm sorry for worrying you."

"Oh, we were worried all right. We wondered if something had happened to our angel. Especially Hundert, he almost collapsed from anxiety. Am I right?"

Johan turned to the attendant. Leorino apologized to his brother and his attendant once more.

"So are you not going to report that injury?"

"...It's nothing serious. I received treatment at the palace, and the swelling is improving."

"And how did you get hurt?"

Leorino thought of the most innocuous answer.

"I lost my footing and nearly fell down the stairs, but Josef saved me. It was thanks to him that I only sprained my wrist."

He wasn't lying. Johan frowned.

"I'm glad he was there... And you didn't hurt anything apart from your wrist?"

Seeing his youngest brother nod, the furrow in Johan's brow finally disappeared. Leorino also relaxed at that.

"God... Consider yourself lucky that Auriano and Gauff aren't here, Leorino."

"You're right. Unlike you, they worry over every little thing. Gauff sprains himself all the time."

Johan forced a smile.

"That's true. But if they found out that you were harmed by your colleagues in the palace, they would have told Father and had you sent back to Brungwurt immediately."

Leorino gasped at that.

As he stared at his second brother in astonishment, Johan laughed.

"How did I know? You're curious, aren't you?"

Leorino didn't reply.

"An old poacher makes the best keeper, Leorino. If you think I'm just some provincial nobleman with no connections in the capital, you're wrong."

The most gentle and mild-mannered of his three brothers suddenly appeared incredibly fearsome.

"Johan..."

"You are our treasure, our beloved family. This time, His Excellency is going to exact a punishment, otherwise we would not have kept quiet about the matter." Johan inclined his head. "Entner, was it?"

* * *

Leorino clenched his fists.

If he already knew everything, there was no point in hiding it.

"...Johan. Yes, we've had a few arguments, but it was not his fault that I fell down the stairs. It was because of my poor balance."

"Oh, I'm aware of that, too. If he had intentionally pushed you, even I would have had to reconsider some things, my soft spot for you and all."

Leorino bit his lip.

"...Will you tell Father about what happened?"

"If this reckless behavior of yours continues, I might. I have agreed on that point with His Excellency."

"...What do you mean?"

"I have just received a messenger from His Excellency the general, and he sends his apologies. He said that it was a private apology and that he would not make it public, but that he would be more attentive to your affairs in the future."

At his brother's words, Leorino's whole body felt heavy as if it had been packed with sand.

Gravis must have known that the Cassieux family was already aware of the situation. Beyond that, he must have anticipated that Leorino would not be able to conceal it and delivered his apology ahead of time.

Whatever was happening, it all went over his head.

Everyone is trying to lock me in a cage, as if I'm some weakling.

Feeling his self-loathing swell within him, Leorino was despondent.

"...Yes, I've already promised His Excellency that I'll be careful and stay out of trouble."

Johan nodded and stood up.

"Then I'll keep this matter to myself. Think you'll manage to have some dinner?"

Leorino shook his head and turned to watch his second brother leave the room.

"...Oh yes, Hundert. Please hand that to Leorino." Johan said, and Hundert, who had been waiting by the wall, presented an envelope to Leorino.

He could recognize the family crest in the wax seal.

"A letter to me from the Munster family...?"

"Yes, it's an invitation to a soiree hosted by the Duke of Leben. Be sure to send a reply. Oh, I also heard you have plans to go out with Julian. When I saw him the other day, he said he would come by to invite you soon."

"Of course..."

After his brother left the room, Leorino sat down in his chair again, staring thoughtfully at the letter in his hand.

When he opened the invitation, he found, as Johan had said, a typically phrased letter inviting him to the soiree, written in a flowing, ornate script. The soiree would be held at the duke's residence in a month's time, and it would likely be a very large and lavish affair.

The invitation itself did nothing to improve his mood.

Below the standard text, an extra line had been added in a distinctly masculine hand: *I will come around to invite you within the next few days. I look forward to seeing you again.* Alongside was Julian's signature.

Right... Lord Julian had said it, too. I must learn about the outside world.

Leorino hesitated.

He had refused Julian's marriage proposal, but Julian told him not to worry about it. Leorino wondered if he should take Julian at his word, but it would also be in his best interest to spend time with Julian, who was technically his relative now, since his family wouldn't try to stop him.

Besides, if he could get in and out of the Duke of Leben's house, he might be able to obtain some information about their close relative, the Marquis of Lagarea.

Such were Leorino's private hopes.

...I must focus on what I can do for now.

Leorino made the decision to accept Julian's invitation. If he sent a reply, Julian would surely visit him soon.

"Hundert. Please send word that I will accept Lord Julian's invitation."

Beside Solitude

Balto Entner and two of his colleagues in the Health Department had been officially discharged from the Royal Army for violating military regulations.

Although the specific nature of the infraction was never made public, everyone in the know understood that it had been targeted harassment toward Leorino Cassieux.

Leorino again apologized to his superior, Sasha, and asked to be punished himself. Sasha offered Leorino a three-day suspension on the grounds that his involvement in the incident was failure to report the offense.

Leorino felt humbled, suspecting his true intention was to give his guard, Josef, a chance to recover.

Ever since the incident, Leorino had become a pariah in the Palace of Defense even more than he was previously. Due to his extraordinary beauty and pedigree, a wall had always existed between him and his colleagues since he first stepped foot in the palace.

But solitude was not a punishment for Leorino.

It must have been unimaginable to his colleagues who had attended school in the royal capital, but Leorino had had few opportunities to interact with people of his own age in his life.

And while he might not have been aware of it, Ionia's memories had a profound effect on his social skills. Having the Power to destroy a human body in an instant, and having actually used it, Ionia had avoided physically harming anyone by building walls of his own.

Leorino was also terrified of ruining someone's life with his actions.

He immersed himself in the research project he had been given and spent most of his days in the archives.

Despite these circumstances, Leorino experienced a slight change in his relationships.

Dirk began to visit the archives on a regular basis. This was a great joy for Leorino.

Dirk visited him in the archives to check on the progress of his research and gave him sound advice every time. His advice was based on the entirety of his knowledge from his time in the General Staff and his position as the general's second-in-command, which gave him a good view of general military strategy. He was particularly generous when sharing his vast knowledge of the cooperation between the General Staff and the Health Department.

Leorino had a fondness for Dirk, but Dirk seemed to take a liking to Leorino and Josef himself. Perhaps due to his close proximity to Gravis's perfect beauty, Dirk recently stopped taking notice of Leorino's appearance, naturally treating him like a younger colleague.

Perhaps because Ionia's memories of Dirk ended when he was still a boy, Leorino grew attached to him as if Dirk were an older relative.

The task Sasha had given him was slowly taking shape.

Ignorant as he was, Leorino was aware of the implications of his research.

He was secretly afraid that his research was too specialized for a newcomer like himself, but somehow no one ever brought this up.

Dirk also assured Leorino that if his research was put into practice, it would greatly increase the efficiency of the provision of medical units and supplies. He even speculated that collaborating with the General Staff could increase the survival rate of soldiers.

Leorino felt there could be no better reward than his research being of use to someone.

At the same time, Leorino continued to search through the records of Edgar Yorke and his movements in secret without arousing suspicion.

Tracing the records of a lowly soldier in the mountain troops was quite the challenge. Much to Leorino's dismay, he had learned very little.

Edgar Yorke had been severely injured at Zweilink and had taken a long time to heal. Leorino had no doubt the injury in question had been the effect of Ionia's Power applied to Yorke's stomach just before his death.

In the end, everything linked back to the fact that Ionia had been unable to kill Edgar at that moment.

If he had not survived, the possibility of finding the mastermind behind the Zweilink invasion would have remained forever buried in darkness.

On the other hand, because Edgar survived, he jumped off the wall of the outer fortress with Leorino in tow six years ago, making him unable to ever run again.

He had found the address of Edgar's brother and his wife, his only known family. However, the couple appeared to have died several years prior.

Like Ionia, Edgar possessed a special ability.

There must have been someone who had taken notice of it and made contact with him.

Leorino vowed to look into Edgar Yorke's brother and sister-in-law in the near future, hoping it would serve as a clue.

The issue was finding a way to do just that.

Thanks to his overprotective family, Leorino was under near-constant surveillance. Every day he traveled to and from the royal palace by carriage, and within the palace he was always accompanied by his guard.

When he returned home, he was under the watchful eye of his family and their servants. He had no way to secure any free time for himself without anyone noticing, and frankly, he didn't know how to go out into the city all alone, either.

* * *

In an effort to gain some experience functioning in the outside world, Leorino decided to accept Julian's invitation.

As soon as he sent a reply to the soiree invitation, Julian invited him to a rendezvous. His next day off would mark his first outing with Julian.

He had not met with Gravis since that day.

Leorino glimpsed him from afar several times. There had been a handful of times when he thought their gazes had met. But the distance between them never grew any closer.

Unaware of Gravis's growing irritation, Leorino was focused on getting by in his day-to-day life.

The Horse Auction

Julian had brought Leorino to a horse auction on the outskirts of the royal capital.

It was the first time he had seen Julian since the tea party. Seeing him behave like that gentle, kind, perfect gentleman he had always been, Leorino slowly relaxed in his presence.

"Lord Julian, will this be all right?"

"Oh, it should be fine. It hides your face well, so make sure it stays that way."

"Of course."

Julian gently patted his head from over the cloak.

Leorino's spirits slowly lifted. Sitting across from him, Julian smiled and watched as Leorino's cheeks flushed as Julian grinned.

Just as he had written in the invitation to the soiree, Julian invited Leorino out shortly after receiving his reply.

He was a little apprehensive when he learned Julian wanted to take him out for some "adult entertainment," and he certainly hadn't expected it to be a horse auction. From what he had heard, Julian had suggested several locations to Johan.

In the end, Johan had given his permission to bring Leorino to this auction.

When Leorino was told about this, he couldn't help clutching his head in his hands at how overprotective his brother was. Leorino's cheeks flushed with embarrassment as he asked if this had taken Julian aback.

"No, I'm just glad he agreed. This auction is held only twice a year. I wasn't sure what I would do if Lord Johan had rejected this idea as well."

"I'm sorry about him…"

"Ha-ha, trust me, I hardly mind. I got to bring you here in the end. We're sure to see some fine stallions at the auction, so look forward to that."

"I will." Leorino smiled.

Before his legs were injured, he was taught the basics of horse riding. He was elated at the thought he would soon be able to see horses up close once more.

He would never be able to ride through the fields by himself again, but if there was even a sliver of possibility, he wished he could once more become one with the horse's throbbing muscles and relish the wind on his skin.

After leaving the city walls surrounding the royal capital and riding the carriage for half an hour or so to the countryside, they arrived at the auction. They could already hear the spirited noises from their carriage. Leorino could not contain his excitement.

"Lord Julian, may we go now?"

"Ha-ha, you're just raring to go, aren't you?"

"Yes! I have never been somewhere so bustling with life."

Julian chuckled at the sound of Leorino's excited voice.

"Everyone is desperate to get their hands on a good horse, after all."

"I see. Will you also be looking for a new horse today, Lord Julian?"

"Who knows? Perhaps, if they present some outstanding colt. My family owns some fantastic horses as it is. Most of them are back in our territory, but we have brought some of them to our residence in the capital. You're more than welcome to come and see them sometime."

"I'd love to. They must be wonderful horses—they belong to the Duke of Leben for a reason."

Julian placed his hand on the door and turned to face Leorino.

"It won't be just nobles here. Commoners will be attending as well, so don't let your guard down. There's a security system in place throughout the venue, so it's safer than not, but you never know what might happen. Do not leave my side under any circumstance. Is that clear?"

"Of course."

* * *

Josef did not accompany them on this outing. The Duke of Leben had offered to provide a full escort, so there would be no need for his services. The Cassieuxs were far from pleased, but in the end, Leorino had boarded the duke's carriage alone.

Having been informed just before the outing, Josef was upset, but Leorino thought leaving the house without him would be good practice for the future.

"I don't mean to scare you, and you can rest assured that my family's guards will be there to protect you."

Leorino nodded. He would do everything Julian asked, he just wanted to go out into the auction already. Julian smiled at him as if he could hear his thoughts.

"All right, then, shall we?"

Outside of the military, Leorino had never seen so many horses in one place before. It was also the first time he had ever stepped foot in such a noisy place filled with so many people.

Careful not to let his hood slip down, he couldn't help glancing around restlessly.

"Come now, relax. I don't want you getting lost."

Julian pressed his hand into Leorino's back.

The auction was bustling with visitors, from aristocrats to merchants. Young horses over a year old were sourced from the southern plains—a region famous for their fine horses—most of them bred for riding.

"Look... Can you see the horses in that enclosure? Careful now, don't get swept up by the crowd."

There were a number of horse enclosures placed around the venue. A large tent was set up in the center, and it was there that the auction took place.

Julian skillfully wove his way through the crowd, bringing them close to the fence.

Leorino was told that the Duke of Leben's guards were securing the perimeter, but the crowd was so large that he couldn't spot them.

There were some ten horses beyond the fence. The enclosure was large enough for the horses to walk about it freely. Many visitors stood in a circle around the fence, chatting excitedly and keenly watching the horses that were about to be auctioned off.

A chestnut mare was grazing calmly. A black colt was shaking his head. Some of the horses appeared rather agitated, stomping their hooves. Several caretakers in the enclosure were observing the horses and calming the nervous ones.

All the young horses were so beautiful and full of life. Their glossy coats glistened in the sunlight. They could surely run as fast as the wind, and Leorino found them absolutely breathtaking.

Leorino was so engrossed in the sight of the horses that his hood began to slip off, but Julian noticed and immediately fixed it for him. Leorino turned to Julian and offered him a bright smile from under his hood.

"Lord Julian, look at them! They're all so beautiful!"

Julian laughed at Leorino's inability to conceal his excitement.

"Each enclosure has its own price range for horses. I suspect these horses are for the merchants and the lower nobility. The prices are pretty standard for the horses they have on offer this time around."

"Really? But they're so beautiful."

"The further we go, the more expensive and pedigreed the horses will be... Come, have a look for yourself. See how there are fewer horses there? Those are more valuable."

Leorino looked in the direction he was pointing, and sure enough, there were fewer horses in one enclosure. He couldn't see them clearly yet, but there were four horses beyond the fence farthest from them.

"So those horses at the far end are the most expensive?"

"Yes, the horses in that enclosure are the main attraction of the auction. They must be the offspring of some of the most renowned horses in the country. Would you like to go and see them?"

Leorino nodded.

The horses inside the fence were all strong and full of life. To Leorino, they all looked inexpressibly beautiful.

But when they finally reached the far end of the venue after wading through the crowd, the four horses were so striking that even Leorino, who knew little of horses, could tell they were special.

They were perfect steeds, gorgeous and powerful.

Leorino was so moved that the sight rendered him speechless for a moment.

"How do you like them? Aren't you glad we came?"

"Yes… The horses are all so fine, but I can tell these are very special."

"Which one is your favorite?"

Leorino tilted his head at the question.

All the horses were so wonderful that he struggled to choose, but Leorino's eyes were naturally drawn to the dapple gray horse in the back. It was a graceful mare with a silvery coat. Her body was relatively large and toned, making her appear very imposing.

She was calm in a way that belied her age as she smoothly raised her head. She flicked her shiny tail there and back good-naturedly.

"I think the dapple gray mare is simply stunning."

"Yes, I thought you'd choose her. She is a delightful girl indeed. Would you like to see her up close?"

"Can we do that?"

When Leorino looked up at him in surprise, Julian smiled wryly.

"Who do you think the owners would most like to present their horses to?"

At this remark, Leorino remembered that Julian was the heir to the Duke of Leben, the richest man in Fanoren.

Indeed, with the Duke of Leben's wealth, he could buy up all the horses at the auction and it would hardly make a dent in his coffers. That must have been the reason Leorino had felt eyes on Julian from all around them. But it appeared that few people could approach Julian directly, given his status.

"Shall we have a closer look? Assuming you're not afraid of them, of course."

"I'd love to. But would that be all right? Wouldn't we be inconveniencing them?"

Julian laughed.

"Aren't you just adorable. It's a standard request for anyone who wants to bid on a horse, so it's not like they're going out of their way for us."

"But I don't have any money of my own, so I won't be able to participate in the auction myself."

"That's all right. I'll be with you. And we came out here for you to enjoy yourself, after all. Now wait just a minute."

Leorino had never done any shopping and didn't even know if he had any money he could use for his own purposes. Nor was he accustomed to exercising his noble privileges in public.

But the temptation to get a closer look at his favorite horse was too great for him to resist, and he decided to take Julian up on his kind offer.

When Julian raised his hand, a caretaker inside the fence approached him. When Julian whispered something to the man, he nodded and immediately signaled to a stable hand near the gray horse. The stable hand then took her reins and began walking toward them.

"Whoa... Whoa...!"

Leorino gasped in admiration at the beautiful horse approaching them with her graceful gait. The majestic steps of the dapple gray mare had the air of a queen who made humans drop to their knees before her.

The mare stopped so close that Leorino would be able to touch her if he extended his hand just a little.

"Ah, she's even more beautiful up close. Where was she born?"

The stable hand replied to Julian's question with unhidden pride. "Yes, sir. She's from the lands of Hexter. Isn't she a real beauty?"

"Yes, she's quite the head-turner. And it's no wonder. Speaking of Hexter, is she from the line of the famous Eloquente?"

"Yes, sir. Her father is Eloquente and her mother is Gâre."

"Oh, so Gâre is the mother? Now I see, her coat is just like her mother's."

"She certainly got her large body from Eloquente. She has fantastic legs, as all of Gâre's offspring do. Without a doubt, she's a head above all the foals born last year."

The conversation between Julian and the stable hand went right over Leorino's head. Leorino only watched the dapple gray horse intently, completely entranced.

Then, suddenly, Leorino seemed to catch the horse's attention, and she closed the distance between them with a shake of her head.

Leorino slowly placed his palm on the fence so as not to scare her. The horse brought her nose close to the fence and loudly sniffed at him. Her warm, wet breath tickled his skin.

Leorino giggled in excitement.

"I see you two beauties have already taken to each other."

Leorino looked up at Julian and smiled.

"She's very gentle. May I ask her name?"

Leorino turned to the stable hand, who politely answered the young man's question, even as Leorino's face remained obscured from view.

"My good sir, she has no official name yet. Her new owner will be the one to name her."

"But that's... It's a shame to think she's never heard anyone call her name yet."

At the sound of Leorino's disappointed voice, the stable hand hurried to explain. "Oh, no, sir, they all have names, they are simply temporary."

"Oh, I see. Then what was she called until now?"

"Amancera, sir. She was born at daybreak, so she was named after the light of dawn."

"...Amancera. What a lovely name." Leorino murmured, calling her name and holding out his hand once more.

Amancera responded to Leorino's call by shaking her head and pressing her nose firmly against his palm. Despite her regal appearance, she was a very friendly horse.

Leorino laughed sweetly.

"She seems pleased to hear her name."

"Ha-ha, I'm very happy to meet Amancera as well. Thank you for showing me such a wonderful horse."

Leorino thanked the stable hand and the man bowed deeply. He then returned Amancera to a spot where she could be seen by the gentlemen surrounding the fence.

Leorino sighed with satisfaction as he admired the horse's grace from every angle.

"Did you enjoy that?"

"Yes, very much! Thank you so much for bringing me here today, Lord Julian."

Then, suddenly, Julian asked something he couldn't have expected.

"Do you want her?"

"Huh? No. She's a lovely horse, but I don't have any money of my own, so I can't take part in the auction."

Leorino inclined his head, and Julian smiled.

"Heh... I've only ever had partners who tried to take advantage of my status and wealth, so your unselfishness is precious to me."

"What do you mean?"

"I mean that I would bid on that horse for you."

Leorino was shocked.

"Absolutely not! You mustn't!"

"Why not? I have my own money, and plenty of it. I could buy her and give her to you as a present. Money is of no issue."

"Yes, I'm aware. But even I know that horses are very expensive. I wouldn't dare accept such an expensive gift from you, Lord Julian."

"Oh, please. Are you saying you can't accept my kindness?"

Leorino was at a loss. Julian's eyes seemed to be smiling, but he appeared to be somewhat upset.

But a horse was certainly too expensive. If Julian was this insistent, he would surely pay any price for Amancera, no matter how high. However, if Leorino received such an extravagant gift, the Cassieux family would struggle to return it.

Leorino shifted his cloak a little, enough for the people around him to see his face, and peered up at Julian's face, roughly half a head above his own.

"Bringing me here was already more than kind enough of you, Lord Julian."

"My god. Not a hint of greed in you, is there?"

"No, hardly. I'm just pragmatic."

"What do you mean?"

"The stable hand said it himself. Amancera's legs are fantastic...

Therefore, she should belong to someone who can ride her at full speed. She would be wasted on a cripple like me."

Julian's irritation disappeared from behind his eyes, and his face turned serious.

"I'm sorry. I hadn't considered that."

Leorino shook his head.

"No, I'm very grateful for your offer, but it wouldn't be right of me to own that horse. She deserves a better master. I hope to see Amancera running like the wind one day, but I won't ask for anything more than that."

"I see. If that's what you insist."

Leorino was relieved that Julian seemed to accept his reasoning. He was glad that he was able to refuse him without hurting his ego.

"Right, then, are you tired? They have some stalls here. Would you like to take a peek?"

"Stalls? So they sell more than horses here?"

"Oh, right, I suppose you've never been to a stall. They sell small things, refreshments among them. Well, let's have a look. If you get tired, there is a rest area as well. You want to see the auction itself, don't you?"

Leorino did feel a little tired. He nodded at Julian.

At that moment, a man approached them from behind. "Lord Julian."

Leorino shivered at the sound of that voice. The strong, husky voice made his heart clench. Leorino didn't need to turn around and look at the man's face to know who he was.

"Oh... If it isn't Lieutenant General Brandt. Well met."

The man Julian had just exchanged pleasantries with was Lucas Brandt, the lieutenant general of the Royal Army.

...Right! They said Amancera was from Hexter lands, so this must mean...

He recalled the conversation between the stable hand and Julian.

Lucas was the second son of the count of Hexter. Lucas's older brother must have already succeeded the countship by now.

* * *

This was the first time Leorino was meeting Lucas in person since the day he dragged Leorino into his room. He had seen him from afar in the Palace of Defense. But, perhaps because Lucas had been avoiding Leorino, they never ended up running into each other.

That day, Leorino's heart was violently shaken when he was forced to witness Lucas's overwhelming love for Ionia still smoldering inside him.

That day, Leorino was at his mercy, unable to mount any resistance against the much larger man.

Lucas had a maniacal obsession with Ionia. What Leorino glimpsed was the product of the eighteen-year-long agony of a man who still anguished over a love that was suddenly cut short.

Leorino was racked with guilt toward Lucas after the incident. It was the guilt of concealing his true identity from Lucas, and the woe of being unable to reciprocate his feelings.

Whenever he thought of Lucas, he felt a piercing pain in his chest. He felt it now, too.

But he couldn't hide forever. Leorino looked for an opportunity to greet him.

Lucas and Julian begin to talk amicably. Perhaps because of the hood over his head, Lucas hadn't noticed Leorino.

"I apologize, I must have surprised you. I heard from the caretaker that you were interested in a horse of ours, Lord Julian."

"Oh, so that's what I owe this conversation to. Did you also come here to look for a steed, Lieutenant General?"

"No, I'm here on behalf of my brother who remains in our territory. He asked me to watch over the bidding for Amancera."

"Ah, that does explain it."

Leorino gradually grew puzzled by Julian's uninterrupted conversation.

Leorino worked at the Palace of Defense. Lucas was his superior. Julian must have known this, but for some reason he would not let Leorino greet the man.

Lord Julian... Why?

* * *

Unable to interrupt and greet him, Leorino had no choice but to listen to their conversation in silence.

"Horse husbandry has been a favorite pastime of my brother's—he's a bit of a horse fanatic, you see, and he's mastered it over the years. This year's horses are particularly fine, don't you think?"

"Of course. The one we saw just now was simply perfect. She inherited the best features of both her parents. I can't wait to see who will bid on her."

Lucas raised his eyebrows in surprise.

"I assumed you had taken an interest in her."

"Yes, I have considered it."

"Does that mean you won't be bidding on her? Oh, though I don't mean to pry. My brother told me that if no good buyer appears, I should bid for Amancera myself."

"Oh my. Ha-ha, Count Hexter is quite the devil of a man, isn't he? In that case, why put her up for auction at all?"

"I suppose that's the complex mind of a horse fanatic who has tried his hand at breeding. He wants to know the price she could fetch at the auction, but I suppose he's very selective about who should actually get to own her... I'm certain my brother would be relieved to know she ended up in a stable of the Duke of Leben."

Julian shrugged.

"Unfortunately, my companion told me they were happy simply to behold the horse. We're only planning to observe today."

Prompted by these words, Lucas cast a glance at the young man standing next to Julian.

"By the way, who has joined you today, Lord Julian?"

Leorino thought this was his moment. He tried to pull down his hood to greet him, but Julian pulled him by the shoulder, making him unable to raise his arms.

"Yes, he's my sweetheart."

"Oh..."

Julian's sudden statement startled Leorino.

He looked up at Julian before he could help it, but the next moment, Julian grasped his shoulder tighter. The pain made Leorino swallow his protest.

Why? Why would Lord Julian lie like that?!

"…I thought you were courting Leorino Cassieux."
"Ha-ha, so you've heard that rumor as well, Lieutenant General?"
Julian responded with a dry laugh, but did not deny the rumor itself. Lucas frowned.

Leorino completely missed his opportunity to deny Julian's statement.
He had lost all courage to pull down his hood and greet Lucas at this point. Now he found himself shrinking back, trying to keep Lucas from seeing his face.

"…You mean the rumors were just that, rumors?"
Lucas's voice was low and tinged with irritation for some reason.
"I'm simply enjoying myself today. I would appreciate your understanding in this matter."
This only seemed to anger Lucas further. Sensitive to his anger, Leorino drew his head back.

But there was a reason for Lucas's irritation.
Julian did not deny his courting of Leorino, but on the other hand, he said that his current companion was here so that he could "enjoy himself." In other words, he implied that the man he brought with him today was simply his partner in a casual affair.
Leorino, sheltered and ignorant as he was, could not have guessed what Julian had meant by this. But Lucas understood everything.

Lucas was disgusted at Julian's comments, so disrespectful of Leorino's situation. But Lucas wasn't in the position to denounce Julian.
Lucas felt a stirring in his chest, but only nodded silently to Julian.

"Well, I believe it's time for us to take our leave."
"…Right. My apologies."
"No, Amancera is a lovely horse. I pray she finds a good buyer."
Lucas nodded in agreement.

"Thank you. Though it's a shame the next heir to the Duke of Leben won't be bidding on her."

Julian nodded and replied in a remorseful tone.

"Oh, I fully agree. But I have no doubt that the horse will fetch an excellent price."

"The bidding will begin shortly. Farewell, Lord Julian...and your companion, of course. Enjoy your time here."

Lucas left without ever noticing Leorino.

The distinguished presence of the lieutenant general renowned for his valor was quite conspicuous even in the middle of the crowded marketplace. As Lucas walked, the crowd naturally parted before him. It was truly a sight to behold.

Once the man's back was out of view, Leorino could finally relax. His knees nearly buckled beneath him.

"Ha-ha, it appears that the lieutenant general didn't recognize you."

Leorino twisted out of Julian's grasp. He bit his lip to calm his stirring thoughts.

Leorino glared at Julian from inside his hood with protest in his gaze.

"...Why would you lie like that to the lieutenant general?"

"Did I offend you?"

"No... That's not the issue. If anyone finds out about it, we may never recover."

Julian inclined his head.

"Like it or not, you stand out far too much. If you show your face at the wrong moment, the auction will devolve into chaos. That could be incredibly dangerous, especially considering the crowds. Or were you hoping that showing off your face will grant you some much needed attention?"

Having this explained to him so calmly made Leorino think that perhaps he was being unreasonable.

"I *don't* want that, actually... In any case, I'm not pleased about lying to the lieutenant general."

"It saddens me to think that you so hate the notion that people might think we're together."

"I—I don't *hate* it, I just..."

As Leorino bit his lip in frustration at his inability to express what he meant, Julian cracked a smile.

"If you don't hate it, why the long face? Just be glad it didn't turn into a whole ordeal."

"Lord Julian…"

Julian was dodging his concerns on purpose.

Leorino was frustrated, but figured it would be unbecoming to continue arguing out in the open like this and held himself back.

"Come, people are starting to gather now. Shall we go watch the auction? Or would you like to get something warm to drink at a stall?"

Leorino was torn. The stressful situation had tired him out, not to mention that some negative feelings toward Julian still lingered inside him. He was in no mood to go around the venue and enjoy himself.

"Leorino?"

"I'm sorry, Lord Julian. Could I rest in the carriage, please?"

Julian furrowed his beautiful eyebrows.

"Did what I said upset you?"

It did, but there was more to it than that.

"No, I'm just a little tired. And look at these crowds… I don't think it's safe for me to… Ah!"

Someone had bumped into him.

The visitors were beginning to move toward the tent in the center where the auction was to take place. Some were rushing to the tent to get a good spot, to see the horses from as close as possible.

Leorino was pushed by the crowd and stumbled forward. People bumped into him from left and right and he found himself unable to maintain his position. No one paid any mind to Leorino, his presence obscured by his cloak.

Leorino wasn't strong enough to hold his ground and was in danger of falling over.

"…You're right, it's not safe. Let's get out of here."

"Yes, let's… Ah!"

Just a few steps away from Julian, Leorino's slender body was tossed about by the crowd. Julian reached for him with a stern look on his face.

"Leorino! Stay with me! It's dangerous, come here."

"R-right."

Leorino nodded and was about to approach Julian when a loud trumpet echoed through the venue.

"The auction is about to begin!"

Excited voices rose from all around them, and the visitors began to move toward the tent all at once.

Leorino couldn't hold his ground.

No...!

"Leorino! Give me your hand, quickly!"

"Lord Julian...!"

Leorino desperately reached for him. But Julian's hand was just out of reach, and he found himself swept backward. The sound of Julian calling his name was drowned out by the noise of the men surrounding them.

Before he knew it, Leorino had been swept up by the crowd.

He was separated from Julian, but that was still far better than falling over and getting trampled. Leorino moved his legs frantically, following the ebb and flow of the crowd.

After being tossed about for a while longer, Leorino found himself flung out of the crowd.

A straw-filled cart was stopped nearby. He moved, propped himself up on it, and let out the breath he had been holding.

"Hah... Hah... That was insane... I'm so glad I didn't fall over."

He crouched down weakly where he stood. The first crowd he had ever experienced had been horrifying.

Desperately trying to calm his pounding heart, Leorino took one deep breath after another.

* * *

I need to find Lord Julian...

The visitors were still moving. It would be easier for Julian to find him if he stayed in one spot, Leorino thought as he crouched.

Julian and his guards must have already been looking for him. The people in the venue were relatively wealthy merchants and nobles. He should be safe for the time being.

"Hey, kid... What's wrong? Are you all right?"

A man had approached him from behind.

"Oh... Yes. I'm fine."

Leorino was caught off guard and looked up at the man defenselessly. When the man who appeared to be a merchant bent over to check on him, their eyes met.

"Whoa... Look at you...!" The man exclaimed in admiration, seeing Leorino's beauty up close.

Leorino hid his face in a panic, but it was too late.

"Wait, let me see that pretty face of yours again."

Leorino rushed to leave, but the man stopped him.

Leorino was caught between the cart and the man, unable to move.

"Hey, I won't hurt you. Just show me your face."

The man sounded excited as he bent down to try to peek under Leorino's hood.

"Ah...!"

Leorino frantically turned his face away, but he had no way to avoid the man peering into his face.

Gazing intently at Leorino's beauty, the man again gasped in wonder.

"Wow, just wow! ...Are you a man? You *are* a man, aren't you? I've never seen anyone as beautiful as you in my life. I can't believe this... It's like I'm seeing a faerie or an angel."

The man's eyes were spellbound and filled with heat.

He began to undress Leorino with his eyes and appraise his entire body. Leorino recognized that gaze.

The men who surrounded him during the soiree all looked at him the same way. They were the eyes of a hunter evaluating him like a piece of meat with no regard for his personhood, a predator who would put his mitts on Leorino if he so desired.

Leorino braced himself.

He couldn't afford to show any sign of fear. Judging from the way he spoke, the man must have been a merchant. In that case, Leorino decided to remain undaunted in hopes of reminding the man of his status and his place in relation to it.

Leorino pushed away the hand the man had placed on his hood.

"I don't recall giving you permission to touch me. Keep your hands to yourself."

The man's eyes widened in surprise. Leorino's tone of voice must have made his status clear, but that only prompted the man to make his approach more flirtatious.

"Huh, so you're a princeling then? Not only are you beautiful, you've got the pride to go with it."

"…I appreciate your checking on me. But I'm here with someone, so you'll have to excuse me."

"Oh, come now, what's the rush? Tell me, what does the little prince like to be called?"

As he was about to slip past the man, he placed his hand on Leorino's shoulder. His touch was so startling that Leorino found himself frozen in place. The man saw this and instantly grinned.

"I'll stay with you until your friend finds you."

"No, thank you. He should be here any minute now."

"Ah… God, you're *such* a looker. You're as bright as a star… Come on, can't I stay? Are you also taking part in the auction, little prince?"

The man refused to shut up, and when he finally closed the distance between them, Leorino was finally left without recourse.

Leorino wanted more than anything not to be touched and frantically did all he could to avoid the man's tenacious hands, but the man was persistent. Slowly, the man moved closer and closer, so close that Leorino could feel the man's breath on his skin.

"Stop right there."

Leorino glared at him. The man's cheeks flushed, and he backed away slightly in embarrassment.

Leorino put his hand on the dagger he carried on his chest.

Josef had been teaching him how to use it since the day he decided he wanted to be able to defend himself. Ever since he had learned to handle it well enough not to injure himself, he always carried the dagger on him when leaving the house.

He had never hurt anyone physically yet, but he had memorized where all the human vitals lay.

If he produced the blade, it would cause a commotion, but it might be easier for Julian and the guards to find Leorino if he made a bit of a scene.

With that in mind, Leorino reached into the pocket under his cloak and wrapped his fingers around the dagger.

But just as Leorino was about to draw the blade, the man was flung backward by a thick, strong arm that suddenly appeared between them.

The lush smell of grassy fields in the sun filled his nostrils.

"What is this?"

Luca...?

Leorino looked up and saw a wide, broad back. Lucas had walked away from him just a few minutes earlier, but now made himself a wall between Leorino and the man.

"This man is with the next Duke of Leben. He has no reason to give a puny merchant like you the time of day."

Lucas leaned in close to the man with a cold, stark look on his face. Intimidated by his menacing appearance, the man stepped back, making some excuse or other.

"N-no, the young prince didn't seem to be feeling well, so I simply approached him out of the kindness of my heart..."

"Well, young man, would you say that's an accurate assessment of the situation?"

Lucas turned around, asking about the man's excuse. When he finally saw him, Lucas's eyes widened in surprise.

"...Leorino... Why?"

"...Lieutenant General."

They watched each other for a longer moment before Lucas quietly clicked his tongue, took one look at the merchant, and in a low voice commanded: "...I'll forget this ever happened. Now go."

"Y-yes, sir...!"

Leorino watched in blank amazement as the man ran off into the crowd. All the while, Lucas's gaze never left Leorino.

The hardened hands of the warrior lifted Leorino's hand with a careful touch, as if he were handling something fragile.

The firmness and warmth of the swordsman's fingertips made Leorino tremble slightly.

He remembered this warmth. Etched into the memories he inherited from Ionia, he knew how kind and compassionate Lucas was, how his hands had gently comforted his aching body.

"...Come. I want to talk."

If he had wanted to escape, he could have.

But Leorino could not bring himself to shake off Lucas's hand.

They had moved out of the bright sunlight into a spot in the shade of a tent.

The neighing of the young horses had been so close to them just a few moments ago, but was now far away. They could hear the hustle and bustle of the men waiting for the auction to begin coming from the huge tent.

Leorino pulled down his hood to reveal his face to Lucas. Lucas gazed at his exposed beauty with a somewhat bitter expression on his face.

"...I wanted to save you because I'd assumed you were Julian's companion, but I never expected it could be you."

"I apologize."

Leorino bowed deeply.

But the words he expected to follow the apology never materialized. Lucas had brought Leorino under the shade of the tent, but now seemed to be at a loss for where to begin.

"...Why didn't you reveal yourself earlier?"

"Back there, I...I thought I missed my moment to greet you. I am truly sorry."

"Are you in love with Julian? Are you already engaged?"

When Leorino lifted his head in shock at those questions, he saw that Lucas was looking at him with a complex array of feelings in his gaze. Leorino shook his head frantically. This was the one misunderstanding he felt the need to address immediately.

"We are not engaged. I'm not in a relationship with Lord Julian, either. He just wanted to give you that impression..."

"He did? Why did he feel the need to hide your presence from me? Why would Lord Julian lie to me?"

Lucas no longer hid his anger. Leorino shook his head frantically.

"...I don't know what Lord Julian intended, either. He just didn't want me to draw attention to myself in public."

"Is that why you hid your face?"

Lucas took that as an excuse and scoffed at him in a low voice.

"...That, or you didn't want to see me."

Leorino's eyes widened.

"No! No, of course not! Lieutenant General, why would I avoid you like that?"

"Because I did something that would make it natural for you to feel that way. And you... Look."

"I..."

When Lucas suddenly reached his hand toward him, Leorino reflexively shrank away from it. Seeing his reaction, Lucas's face twisted, and he let his arm hang loosely by his side. Leorino's heart ached.

"I realize I did something that would make you fear me... Words can't convey how much I regret hurting you that day... Though that's nothing but an excuse now."

There were so many things Leorino wanted to say swirling in his chest, but he felt he couldn't properly articulate any of them.

Luca... I'm not afraid of you.

Leorino couldn't bring himself to hate the man who was still madly in love with Ionia, even eighteen years after his death.

The man who had been Ionia's best friend, his accomplice whom he liked to call his significant other. The very same man who had known for whom Ionia's feelings were reserved, and who gave him his enduring love until the day he died nonetheless.

The man who had also been physically closer to Ionia than anyone else.

So, even for Leorino, he was a special man whose presence was deeply rooted in the soft parts of the memories he shared with Ionia.

Just when Ionia had realized he loved Lucas in a way different from how he loved Gravis, they had been separated forever. His feelings for Lucas had burned that day at Zweilink alongside his body.

The vestiges of the feelings Ionia was never able to convey still clung to the memories tormenting Leorino.

Lucas was like the sun, generous and openhearted. That man was now hanging his head remorsefully.

Leorino felt like crying, knowing he had made Lucas like this.

Leorino had noticed. What Lucas was looking for in him was whatever remained of Ionia.

His perception distorted by his mad love, Lucas saw Ionia in Leorino.

But Leorino was not the redheaded warrior whom Lucas loved with all his heart and soul. He may have inherited Ionia's soul and his memories, but he was just a helpless weakling now, living his life as Leorino Cassieux.

"Lord Lucas..."

Leorino looked up at Lucas with anguish. The top of his head only reached the tip of Lucas's shoulders.

Back then, they could have smiled at each other with just a slight lift of the chin. They could have reached out and brought their arms around each other.

But now, no matter how hard Leorino looked up at Lucas, their eyes would never be at the same level unless he bent down.

Lucas did not love Leorino Cassieux. That was why Leorino could not respond to his feelings. He didn't have the right to.

They were in different positions and at very different ages. They could never return to being best friends or romantic partners. To have to face Lucas like this despite everything was heartrending.

Please notice, Luca. I am not the man you loved. I am worthless to you. Please stop looking so hurt. Please, just…give up on me already.

Leorino finally opened his mouth.

"Allow me to restate: There is absolutely no way that I could ever dislike you, Lieutenant General."

He wanted the man filled with self-reproach to at least know that much. Leorino focused his feelings into his gaze as he looked into Lucas's amber eyes.

"Leorino…"

"I already received your apology that day. I accepted it. I have put that all behind me now. I've just felt empty and guilty ever since…and that's why I couldn't bring myself to see you."

"…What do you mean?"

"This entire time, I have felt guilty because I could never be the person you wanted me to be."

Saying this, Leorino gripped his chest. That was where he kept his hidden dagger.

Leorino held out his palms in front of Lucas.

"Please, look at my hands."

Lucas watched his fair, slender hands intently.

"My hands…can't do very much, can they?"

"…Leorino."

"My hands are not as strong as the one you seek, sir. I can only wield a dagger at best."

"…How do you know that Ionia was strong?"

Leorino hesitated a little.

"His Excellency the general told me."

"…Right. His Highness Prince Gravis… He told you about him."

After watching silently as Lucas laughed at himself, Leorino spoke once more.

"…And the way you handled me at the time was very…intense. I simply put two and two together."

Lucas had nothing to say to that.

"If you could have considered the size difference between you and me, I'm certain you wouldn't have treated me like that."

Lucas gasped at his words.

"…I—"

"I think that at that time, you saw in me some remnant of Ionia. I'm certain he was much, much larger and stronger than me… I assume you must have thought I could take some rough handling."

Leorino looked a little sad.

"…I wanted you to notice, Lieutenant General, that I am not Ionia…

"You may find this pathetic, but I am certain that I would be frightened by anyone reaching toward me."

"…Leorino."

"Just now, I was very afraid of what that merchant might do to me. I was also somewhat prepared for what might happen if he resorted to force. Of course, I was planning to resist as much as I could."

When Leorino confessed what he was thinking while the man drew near him, Lucas furrowed his thick eyebrows.

"So the reason I reacted to your hand earlier had nothing to do with you. Any strong man puts me on guard."

The fear of being made to submit to a man by force had already taken root in Leorino.

"…But my behavior that day is part of the reason, is it not?"

"Perhaps it is. I *was* scared at the time. I was powerless, fully at your mercy… All I could do was cry. As a man, I felt pathetic and humiliated."

"…I'm sorry."

"No, it's just…"

Leorino's voice was sweet and husky.

"I'm just that weak."

He tossed the words between them, and Lucas picked them up silently and reflected on them deep inside him.

"Lord Lucas... Could you look at me once more, please?"

Despite his insistence that he be addressed by name, the moment Leorino called him "Lord Lucas," he became extremely flustered.

Their gazes met.

"Leorino..."

"Who do you see before you?"

The violet eyes looking up at Lucas were tinged with the color of sorrow.

"Is it me you see?"

"Leorino... You..."

The image of the young man gradually began to take shape in Lucas's mind.

"You are..."

Except for his violet eyes, the slender young man standing before him bore no resemblance to Ionia.

Leorino was only tall enough to reach Lucas's shoulder, and he couldn't have weighed more than half Lucas's body weight. Leorino could hardly be compared to Ionia's strong, muscular physique. He was a frail, fragile young man who would surely break if not handled with care.

"I'm sorry... I'm not Ionia."

Back in his office, Leorino had apologized through tears.

Lucas had felt it from the moment he met him: Ionia had returned. There was no mistaking those unique violet eyes. Even now, Lucas couldn't ignore his intuition.

But, in reality, the person standing before him was not Ionia. He could look at him over and over again, and he would never be Ionia.

At that moment, Lucas finally became aware of how much the eighteen long years of deep-rooted delusion had warped his fixation.

I have continuously invalidated this young man in my fruitless search for Ionia... What a fool I've been...

Lucas had projected his significant other with the body of a warrior onto such a frail young man and handled him as roughly as his heart desired. He had completely shut the fact he was Leorino out of his mind.

"Look at the boy for who he is."

Gravis's words from that day made Lucas's chest tighten all these weeks later.

All Lucas had wanted was for *Ionia* to return to his hands. He had, frankly, never considered Leorino's thoughts and feelings on the matter.

Gravis had been right.

Even if Leorino was in some way connected to Ionia, he had no right to touch this young man without his consent.

He had involved this young man in his eighteen-year-long pursuit of his lost love.

"You are Leorino, aren't you?"

Leorino nodded with a puzzled expression on his face.

Lucas's heart ached at the sight of Leorino's thin, weak neck.

As if to convince himself of Leorino's existence, Lucas gently scooped up his outstretched hands once more. Leorino did not shake him off.

His hands were like porcelain.

Compared to Lucas's hands, large even for a man of his size, Leorino's were so small and slender that he could easily crush them.

Leorino's hands gently squeezed Lucas's hands back. The faint heat of his skin filled Lucas with guilt that made him want to clutch at his chest.

"I wanted to be strong."

"...Leorino."

"My body is a lost cause, but at least I have my mind. But...I will have to live with the body I have... Please understand that."

Eyes of the same color. The same conflicting emotions.

But what Lucas saw before him now was a young man struggling to live a strong life with a body so frail that it looked as if a stronger gust of wind could break him.

It was the moment Lucas first faced Leorino head-on.

At that moment, the sound of several footsteps approached.

Lucas pulled Leorino to him. Sheltering him in his arms, he glared in the direction of the footsteps. It was Julian.

"Leorino! There you are!"

Leorino's slender body shuddered in Lucas's arms.

Julian dashed toward Leorino with a terribly worried expression on his face. Behind Julian, men dressed like merchants followed. It was clear from the way they carried themselves and the threatening look in their eyes that they were not merchants. They must have been the guards arranged by the Duke of Leben. They have been looking for Leorino with Julian.

"Lord Julian, I'm sorry."

Slipping out of Lucas's arms, Leorino saw Julian run up to him and wrap him in an embrace.

"...Lord Julian."

"Didn't I tell you to stay with me? I was so worried about you."

"I'm sorry. I couldn't hold my ground and got swept away by the crowd."

"Were you all right? Are you hurt?"

"I'm all right. The lieutenant general saved me."

Leorino looked up at Lucas with gratitude in his gaze. At the sight of Lucas, Julian frowned slightly, disturbing his usual graceful beauty. He thanked Lucas in a stiff voice.

"Your Excellency. Thank you for saving Leorino."

"...It was nothing."

"And I apologize for trying to hide him from you earlier. I hope you can understand."

Lucas's expression stiffened.

His expression equally firm, Julian hugged Leorino to his chest once more and pulled Leorino's hood back over his head.

"Lord Julian?"

"Leorino, go back to the carriage. We should head home for the day. I'll be right there."

"But…"

"I'm your guardian today. Come, my guards will escort you back to the carriage."

Julian handed Leorino over to the men behind him.

"Oh, um, I want to say good-bye to the lieutenant general."

Surrounded by the guards, Leorino looked up at Lucas with concern.

"Lord Lucas, thank you for saving me."

Lucas raised one hand in response.

"Leorino."

"Y-yes, sir?"

The corners of Lucas's eyes wrinkled as he smiled softly.

"I can show you our military training next time, if you'd like. It should be quite the spectacle."

Leorino's eyes widened in surprise.

Then, as soon as he understood the meaning behind Lucas's words, he grinned.

"Yes! By all means, I'd love to witness it myself."

"That and…I'll make sure you'll get to see Amancera again."

"Yes, by all means. I would love that."

Leorino didn't understand what Lucas meant by the comment about Amancera, but he could tell that Lucas was trying to meet him halfway.

The clumsy way in which Lucas showed him his kindness made Leorino's heart flutter in his chest.

He didn't know what kind of relationship he would come to have with Lucas in the future. He was a superior officer of a much higher rank than Leorino. Their relationship could remain limited to their positions in the military.

But that was fine, too.

As long as he could reconnect with the man from the soft part of his memories, now as Leorino in a new type of relationship, he would be happy.

"Thank you, Lord Lucas."

A smile bloomed on Leorino's lips.

Leorino did not notice the bitter expression on Julian's face as he listened to their exchange.

Leorino left with a charming smile and returned to the carriage, surrounded by guards.

With that, Lucas and Julian were left alone.

"Right, then." Julian turned back to Lucas. Behind his smile, Julian's eyes were awfully sober. They glared at each other silently for a while longer. Finally, Julian pursed his lips.

"You seem to have something to tell me, Lieutenant General Brandt."

"…Not exactly. Leorino told me about your intention behind keeping me from him. And that he is not engaged to you."

"Yes, Leorino is allowed to believe that."

Lucas frowned at his words.

"What do you mean?"

"Exactly what you think I mean. Allow me to make it clear that Leorino will be mine sooner or later. The rumors are true."

"Leorino denied it."

The handsome young man donned a wry smile.

"I mean that a path has already been paved between my family and the Cassieuxs."

"…Does this arrangement consider Leorino's wishes at all?"

"That's not for me to say." Julian shrugged, and Lucas watched him with disgust.

"Your Excellency saw him yourself. I'm certain you can understand. He can't be left alone for even a moment considering his beauty and his infirmity. He aspires to independence, but in reality he is, for all intents and purposes, an innocent, naive little princess."

Lucas was angry now.

But he could not deny Julian's words. It was true that Leorino attracted unwanted attention the moment one took his eyes off him. The young man was too beautiful to be left alone.

"I do pity him, but with such a beautiful appearance, he can hardly expect anyone to treat him like a normal boy. That's why it is necessary for those around him to make certain arrangements for him in advance."

"...And that's what his marriage to you will be?"

He could understand where Julian was coming from, but he could never accept treating Leorino like a fool who couldn't even decide his own future.

Leorino had opened his heart with sincerity. Although he had only recently outgrown his boyhood, he did his best to empathize with Lucas's pain.

This allowed Lucas to keep himself from falling into the depths of his twisted obsession.

"Your claim is an insult to Leorino. He's doing his best at the Palace of Defense. You should believe in him and let him have his freedom."

Julian quirked an eyebrow.

"Leorino is a child of the Cassieux family. I don't think you understand what the Cassieux family means to this country, Lieutenant General Brandt— though I suppose that's all I can expect from the second son to a count."

Lucas clenched his fists to contain his anger.

"I suppose what matters most to you, Lieutenant General, is that Brungwurt is a key military point for our country..."

Julian's eyes flashed.

"...but that's not the case for us. For those of us who value bloodlines, the Cassieux family line is incredibly precious."

"What does that have to do with anything?"

"Oh, it has everything to do with it. The Cassieuxs, as you know, are the former royal family of Brungwurt. For two hundred years, they have been in close blood relations with the Fanoren royal family, which makes them the second royal family of this country, so to speak. The royal blood runs so pure in them, they cannot begin to be compared to dukes or other noble families."

Lucas forced himself to listen in silence.

"Even among them, Leorino is special. His appearance makes it clear he's of the lineage of his grandmother, Princess Eleonora. Leorino's exceptional beauty is even keener than Madame Maia's and veritably unparalleled on the continent. He is the very symbol of the fusion of two royal bloodlines... If he had been a girl, how priceless he would have been."

"...You deny that Leorino is a boy at all?"

Julian chuckled lightly.

"No, of course not. If anything, his being a boy is a godsend. If he had been born a girl, he would certainly have been summoned to become the queen consort of the crown prince Kyle. A royal princess would have been married off to a foreign country, but his bloodline will never leave Fanoren."

Lucas felt something cold in Julian's smile.

"There are no princesses among the children of the current head of the family. That means their blood will never leave the Cassieux family. But Leorino is the way he is. Despite being a boy, he needs a spouse who can be his protector, which is why this opportunity for me to get my hands on him has arisen at all."

Lucas gritted his teeth. It sounded as if Julian desired and respected Leorino's lineage, but not *him* as a person.

"Do you love Leorino at all?"

"Love...?"

Julian inclined his head in thought and considered this for a moment. Lucas held back his irritation, waiting for Julian's answer.

"Now, how should I put this... Hmm. Let me be honest. I have never desired anything so strongly in my life. Mostly because I have always gotten what I wanted."

"...I'm sure you have."

Julian smiled dryly at Lucas's bitter sarcasm.

"I know it's an arrogant thing to say, but it's the truth. I've always received all I wanted; things, people, anything."

Lucas had nothing to say to that.

"But after getting everything I wanted, my life has become incredibly dull—no object, no person can excite me anymore."

Julian looked into the distance, in the direction of the carriage where Leorino was waiting.

"But when I took one look at Leorino... When I beheld his pure, unadulterated beauty, I was so moved that I felt like my world had been thrown off its axis. I couldn't believe he was flesh and blood."

Julian's cheeks flushed slightly.

"From the moment I saw him, I knew I simply needed him. So I impulsively proposed to my father that I wanted to marry Leorino. I knew that I could no longer hope to inherit the dukedom, but I still wanted Leorino with all my heart...and for the first time in my life, my father told me that there was a chance that I might not be able to have him."

Lucas listened as Julian went on.

"I am not referring to the obligation to create an heir. The Cassieux family has enough authority to reject the duke's offer. If anything, it would be much easier to marry a royal princess. That's just how precious that bloodline is... and that is why I so desperately want to own it."

"You want to *own* it...?"

Lucas felt as if Julian had just described his own feelings toward Leorino.

They ignored Leorino's personhood, only valuing his existence as a projection of their own desires.

"As things stand, there is a good chance Lord August will let me have his hand in marriage. I plan to take great advantage of this situation. I will not let anyone stand in my way."

"And what of Leorino's feelings?"

"...I do want to be considerate of them, of course, but I can worry about that after he's mine. Once I have that precious gem, I will cherish it for the rest of my life, never letting anything touch him. Is that not love, Lieutenant General?"

Julian's question was almost innocent.

Lucas did not understand.

Lucas had devoted his heart and soul to a commoner, and could not comprehend Julian's deep-rooted fixation on bloodlines.

Lucas had met Ionia when he was twelve years old.

Ionia had just turned half-fledged, silently trying to fulfill his role with a firm determination in his eyes. Lucas was attracted to his courageous, earnest way of life.

His status was of no matter to Lucas.

Ionia was a commoner and a man, and Lucas could not stop loving him regardless.

Lucas knew that he would never be able to have Ionia for himself. Lucas wished he could at least own Ionia's body, but always regretted the forceful way in which he had claimed him…and though he knew Ionia would never feel the same way about him, he loved Ionia more than life itself.

For Lucas, love was a selfless offering. He knew that love came in all shapes and sizes, and it wasn't his place to compare them, but Lucas would never believe that Julian's feelings for Leorino were true love.

"…Whatever it is you feel, it can't be called love."

"Oh, is that so? If this obsession is not love…perhaps I don't know what love is after all. But I hardly care either way—all I want is that boy. And so…" Julian glared at Lucas with cold eyes. "Lieutenant General. I want you to stay out of my way. I wouldn't want to turn you into my enemy."

"I respect Leorino's wishes. That is all."

The two men glared at each other coldly once more.

"I shall take my leave, then. Thank you for protecting that boy… You have my gratitude. Now if you'll excuse me."

With that, Julian gracefully turned on his heel.

Footsteps of Fate

"Huh, so that's what it's all about after all... Though I'd already noticed that Lord Julian is obsessed with Leorino myself. Besides, that engagement is still on the table, isn't it? I really do feel sorry for Leorino; he's working so hard to be independent."

In the general's office, Gravis's second-in-command, Lucas, and Sasha the military doctor, were all present.

Looking beyond chagrined, Sasha sank down onto the sofa uncouthly. Contrary to his usual cheer, Dirk now furrowed his brow as he listened.

"The bloodline of the Cassieux family... That world is beyond comprehension for a commoner like me."

"You and me both, Dirk. I'm a lowly nobleman at best, so I have no connection to that world... Honestly, this is why I can't stand these bloodline supremacists."

"Your Excellency. I hate to ask, but is the Cassieux family really worth that much? They're not even a dukedom."

Gravis nodded at the adjutant's question.

"What Julian Munster said is true. For Fanoren, the most important noble family always was and still is the family of the Margrave of Brungwurt."

Dirk was shocked. At the same time, he cocked his head.

"But the margrave is not particularly involved in central politics, is he?"

"That's because for generations the heads of the family have been calculatingly keeping to themselves in that region. The bloodline that had ruled the former kingdom of Brungwurt has been given autonomy over the vast frontier and was allowed to have its own army. Strictly speaking, they are the only noblemen in Fanoren who own land outside of the royal family."

"Hmm? Meaning?"

"Every nobleman's domain is granted to him by the crown. You could say it's a loan that comes with the title. When the title is taken away, the land also reverts to the crown."

"Huh…"

"But Brungwurt is different. Their lands rightfully belong to the Cassieux family. They possess the exceptional right to autonomy. Conceptually, our relationship is closer to an alliance. That's the state of Brungwurt…and of the current Cassieux family."

Dirk sighed.

"I didn't realize they were so special…although they certainly don't act all high and mighty like you might expect."

"The honest and unpretentious nature of the family is likely a result of its geographical location. The land is one of the most geographically complex areas on the continent. Hardly anyone but them could rule that region while maintaining the balance of power with the rest of the world. You love your history; you should know this."

"Yes, sir… Well, to be fair—"

"If Brungwurt were allowed to become independent, or if some other country were to take that land, the situation surrounding Fanoren would change dramatically. It's a pivotal point that could easily tip the balance of power."

"Which is why…the royal family regularly sends their hostages there."

Gravis nodded at Sasha's sarcastic remark with a wry smile.

"It's true. About once every three generations or so, the royal family engages in intermarriage to add variety to its blood. They always choose a good bloodline to keep its blood as pure as possible. Hence, the Cassieux family, despite the status of the margrave, in actuality possesses more royal blood than any of the dukes. In other words, royal blood is the price for the family's loyalty to our kingdom—a tribute."

Dirk had known this, but it hardly made sense to a commoner like him.

"Let me put it simply. The grandmothers of the queen dowager and Margrave August were half sisters. That makes them second cousins. At the same time, they are also second cousins to Madame Maia. Madame Maia is a cousin of my father's, which makes the Cassieux brothers and I second cousins. The brothers are directly of Fanoren royal blood on both their father's and mother's sides, and are quasi royalty themselves, so to speak."

Dirk sighed. Absolutely no part of that explanation was simple. But it did clarify that they were close blood relatives to the Fanoren royal family. Having learned the details for the first time, Dirk was speechless at the quality of the Cassieux family's bloodline.

Realizing once more how noble the blood of the brave and gentle Leorino was considered in this country, he paled.

If we allow such a precious young man to get injured while he's in our care, I can definitely see how it would ruin His Excellency's reputation. Scary stuff...

As far as the series of incidents in which Leorino and Josef were injured were concerned, Dirk privately thought that the dismissal of Entner and his cronies was too severe a punishment.

But considering what he had just learned, it made perfect sense now. The punishment was also a political consideration for the Cassieux family.

"After two hundred years of intermarriage, the royal blood flowing through the brothers' veins is far purer than that of the current royal family. After all, Madame Maia is also of royal blood through direct lineage especially on the side of her father, the Duke of Wiesen. The only princess of a royal bloodline purer than hers is her mother, Princess Eleonora. So for the bloodline purists, the Cassieux family is the next most precious bloodline they cling to after the royal family."

Lucas and Sasha listened to Gravis's story with mixed feelings.

The current king, born of a concubine from a lower noble family, and Gravis, born of the queen consort from the Francoure royal family, who also inherited the Fanoren royal bloodline herself. Gravis and his brother were both aware of the succession issue between them that had been sparked by the bloodline purist nobles.

"It is no coincidence that their daughters marry into the royal family. If Leorino had been born a girl, he would certainly have been summoned to become Kyle's queen."

"Wouldn't their blood be *too* closely related?"

"No. Unlike me, Kyle's grandmother was Lady Brigitte, a concubine from a lower noble house, and his mother is Lady Emilia of Francoure—his blood would be of no consequence. The same cannot be said for me. My mother is also a direct descendant of the Fanoren royal family. Direct bloodlines should mix only once in several generations, so if Leorino had been a girl, it may have been impossible for us to marry."

"I see," was all the men could reply.

"But for some unknown reason, it's rare for girls to be born in that family. They have had no daughters for the past few generations."

"Now that you mention it, the only women in the Cassieux family were princesses who had married into it."

Dirk cocked his head at that. Gravis nodded.

"That must have been what Munster meant. The blood of the Cassieux family has never been released into the world outside of the royal family. Neither have the boys lost the name of Cassieux. To him, boy or not, Leorino is like a jewel that has been put on the market for the first time—he's worth his weight in gold."

Gravis's voice was calm, but the irritation in his eyes was clear.

Lucas raised his voice, biting back his anger.

"In any case, I…I cannot accept what Julian Munster said."

Gravis raised an eyebrow.

"Lucas?"

"Lord August must be out of his mind. He must have been deceived by Julian's sweet talk!"

Observing Lucas's indignation, Gravis noticed something.

Lucas's obsession with Leorino had completely disappeared. It was as if his curse had been lifted, and he was genuinely livid at Leorino's treatment. Gravis felt he could glimpse the true depth of Lucas's emotion.

"No, the margrave must already know. What he is most concerned about is the next war. He had Leorino evacuated to the capital in advance, just in case. The engagement between Julian and Leorino was also arranged with Leorino's affairs in mind."

"Did Your Highness know of everything?"

Gravis nodded. Seeing this, Lucas twisted his lips and spat, "My point is, I hate to see Leorino be deceived by Julian Munster."

But Sasha shook his head at his statement.

"If he chooses Julian, we're in no position to disagree, Lieutenant General. It's true that Lord Julian is very kind to Lord Leorino, is it not? Just because he made his ulterior motive clear to us, it does not necessarily mean that he will make Lord Leorino unhappy. If anything, he would likely do just as he said and cherish him like a precious jewel."

"But isn't that just like a collector buying a horse for a high price?!"

Sasha's face twisted at the terrible analogy.

"Lieutenant General, we have no right to involve ourselves in Leorino's private life... Am I wrong, Your Excellency?"

Sasha turned to Gravis with an implicating look. The veteran doctor had already noticed the general's obsession with Leorino from the occasional glimpse he managed to catch.

And the way Leorino had Gravis on his mind more often than not.

Sasha observed with his doctor's eye to see if he could read any fluctuations of emotion from the man before him, but Gravis certainly didn't make it easy for him.

"Dr. Sasha."

"Yes, Lieutenant General?"

"I'm going to send some of my men to guard Leorino."

Sasha and Dirk both inclined their heads at Lucas's sudden declaration.

"He's new to the army and a nobleman at that. I'll have them protect Leorino at soirees and other occasions where that cocky commoner guard of his can't accompany him. How does that sound, Dr. Sasha?"

"Lieutenant General...as I have just said, you are inserting yourself far too much into Leorino's private life. In the Palace of Defense, Leorino hasn't even been assigned a rank; he is nothing but a secretary. Under what pretense would you assign Lord Leorino an escort from the Combat Division?"

"I'll let Schultz think of an appropriate excuse. So how about it?"

"Excuse me?"

Aware that Dirk had been glancing at him for his reaction, Gravis listened to their exchange with his arms crossed on his chest.

When Gravis returned to his palace late at night, sensing his master's presence with his usual sensitivity, the valet immediately greeted him.

"Welcome back, my lord."

Theodor helped Gravis change into something more comfortable for his time in the private residence. Feeling the cold ire of his master, Theodor kept his hands moving without missing a beat. That was when Gravis muttered in a low voice, "...Theodor, get *them* moving."

The servant's fingers froze.

"Which country will you be sending them to this time?"

"No, that's not what I meant."

"...What are your new orders?"

"Is anyone who can mind speak available?"

The servant already understood what his master intended by that point.

"I will send him to Your Excellency as soon as he's ready... And this person will be assigned to that gentleman, is that correct?"

Gravis nodded.

"If anything comes up, he is to send me a mind-message. And Leorino must not find out."

Theodor bowed his head in acknowledgement.

He silently moved his hands once more, in his mind picking out the best man for the job from the shadows serving the royal family.

After spending the day off with Julian, a new recruit of his age was dispatched to Leorino from a unit under the direct control of Lieutenant General Lucas Brandt.

When Sasha informed him of this beforehand, Leorino racked his brain trying to deduce Lucas's intention behind this. He couldn't comprehend why Lucas would send someone from the Combat Division to serve him.

It was Lucas's adjutant, Schultz, who brought the newcomer to him that day.

This was the first time Leorino had faced Schultz since he first came to the Palace of Defense. Standing before Leorino, Schultz appeared somewhat ill at ease.

Dirk, his fellow adjutant, watched the situation unfold with his arms crossed on his chest and a grin on his face.

When Schultz introduced the man to Leorino, Leorino couldn't help the gasp of surprise that escaped his lips. It was Kelios Keller, son of the Viscount of Hafeltz, who had arrived just barely in time to sit next to him at the coming-of-age ceremony.

Kelios was about half a head taller than Leorino, with dark brown hair and eyes. The young man had a somewhat restless air about him. He stood there with a smile on his face.

"I'm Kelios Keller. I've been assigned to you for the time being by order of the lieutenant general. Thanks for having me. Feel free to use me however you like."

Wanting to understand what Lucas had been thinking, Leorino asked Schultz. "I don't mean to be presumptuous and pry into the wishes of the lieutenant general, but may I ask...why? My research doesn't exactly require the support of the Combat Division..."

Leorino's question was valid. Anyone would agree. Dirk and Schultz exchanged glances before they could help it.

The sense of urgency Lucas had felt was related to Leorino's private life, and explaining that to his face was erring on impossible.

Looking as if the entire ordeal caused him physical pain, Schultz gave him the sanitized version of the facts. "...The point is, the lieutenant general thinks it necessary to provide you with another guard. Keller here may be new, but he is skilled enough with the sword to gain Lord Brandt's approval."

Leorino felt he understood less with every word.

Leorino had spent most of his time in the archives since the incident. Unless he had some errand to run, he only showed up at the Health Department when he arrived for work and left for the day. Since he submitted regular reports, Sasha had nothing to complain about, either.

Even after starting work at the Palace of Defense, Leorino's world hadn't expanded by much.

Where in such a peaceful life could be the danger that Lucas was so concerned about? As Leorino pondered this, Kelios extended his hand to him.

Kelios's eyes seemed to light up as he waited to shake hands with Leorino. His expression did not attempt to conceal his interest in Leorino.

"We sat next to each other at the coming-of-age ceremony! Nice to meet you. I'm Kelios Keller."

"N-nice to meet you. I'm Leorino Cassieux."

Leorino reflexively took the proffered hand and shook it. That was when Kelios began waving their joint hands around excitedly. Caught off guard, Leorino was swung around with the man's full force.

"Whoa! Look at the destructive force of that kid!"

"H-hey! Keller! Let go of him! And shut your mouth!"

Leorino's mouth dropped open at Kelios's strange behavior. Schultz and Josef reached out from the side and forcefully pulled Kelios's hand away from Leorino's. Leorino finally came to his senses.

"Holy crap! I actually got to touch him!"

Kelios was clutching at his chest, holding up his right hand—the same hand Leorino had just shaken.

Searching for help, Leorino looked to Josef and Dirk in turn…and finally turned to Schultz. He inclined his head slightly, asking what he should do.

"I'm sorry…"

Schultz looked tired as he bowed to Leorino. He still understood nothing, but he couldn't stand to see Schultz wear himself out any further.

"Oh, um, it's all right… I have yet to fully grasp what the lieutenant general was hoping to achieve, but please tell him I appreciate his consideration."

"…Thank you. I assure you, Keller is worthy of your trust, despite his, ahem, character flaws."

Dirk was well aware of how this situation came about and was left to sympathize with Schultz as his fellow adjutant. But he had to confirm something, just to be absolutely sure. Dirk had to follow orders from his own superior, too.

"To think he'd assign him such a rookie, of all people."

"…I'm sorry. He's the best swordsman among the new recruits. Once he settles in, he'll be a real asset…or so I hope."

"Huh. If you ask me, that inspires anything but confidence."

Schultz was at the end of his wits.

"Lieutenant Colonel Bergund... I've heard that you come here regularly to help Leorino with his research. I would appreciate it if you could keep an eye on Keller. I'm sure you're busy as it is, but you see..."

"No, I don't mind. Though I can't stay here all day, either. If he behaves like that whenever he's around Lord Leorino, what's even the point of having him as a guard?"

Dirk's words aggravated Josef.

"If he does anything to Master Leorino, I'll kill him in a heartbeat."

"Okay, Josef, deep breaths. I believe I told you already, but it's forbidden to draw your sword in the Palace of Defense except in case of emergency. If you lose control and do something silly, your master will be the one getting in trouble, so be a good boy."

In the end, it was Kelios himself who dispelled all their concerns. He made his case with a sharp look on his face.

"No need to worry, Lieutenant Colonel Bergund. I have no unsavory intentions toward Lord Cassieux, and of course I would never do anything to him."

"You were *just* losing your mind over shaking his hand. Let's just say your self-assessment isn't entirely reliable."

"That's just fanboying, sir."

"...Huh? Kelios, pray tell, what does that mean?"

Dirk blinked.

"Well, just imagine. If you always admired something beautiful from afar, and you finally got to see it up close, anyone would get excited, don't you think?"

Everyone except Kelios considered this for a moment.

"Huh? I guess. Hmm? Unless?"

"That's just it, Lieutenant Colonel. My earlier reaction went more or less like: *I got to see Lord Cassieux, this incredibly beautiful person up close and personal! And I touched him! Whoa!* which took the form you saw. Nothing more, nothing less, so please rest assured."

They were all speechless.

* * *

Schultz no longer hid his embarrassment, openly pinching the bridge of his nose.

Dirk pointed at Kelios and glared at Schultz suspiciously.

"Mr. Schultz...are you *absolutely* sure you didn't grab the wrong person on your way out of the Combat Division?"

"I wish I could say I did...but I did confirm with His Excellency Brandt that Keller is up to the task."

"Yes, well, I'm sure our good general would be *furious* if he found out," Dirk grumbled. Josef also glared at Kelios with disgust.

"What the hell was that huge lieutenant general thinking, sending us such a weirdo?"

"Oh, come now, Josef. Watch your language. And you're the last person who should be calling others 'weirdos.'"

Leorino had hardly anything to say himself.

He also wished he knew why he always ended up with the most idiosyncratic guards around.

Kelios straightened his back.

"I may be young, but you should know I already have a beloved fiancée, so please rest assured."

"Huh? At your age? Really?"

"Yes. And even if I were to lose myself to Lord Cassieux's beauty, I would be too afraid of the consequences to actually do anything. I'll keep certain things to my fantasies."

Dirk quirked an eyebrow.

It was a rather peculiar turn of phrase, but the newcomer seemed to understand exactly where Leorino stood and who stood behind him. His intuition seemed good enough, and Dirk adjusted his perception of Kelios slightly.

Sensing he had dispelled Dirk's distrust, Kelios suddenly smiled daringly.

I see. There must be more to this young man than it seems.

"I don't know what you're working on, Lord Cassieux, but I should be of use as a guard to you. Maybe even more so than that foul-mouthed fellow over there."

The young man's jab enraged Josef once more.

"…What was that? You bastard with your stupid face… You think you're stronger than me?"

"Whoa, whoa! Settle down now!"

"Josef! Calm down!"

Dirk and Leorino tried to pacify Josef as he grabbed at Kelios.

"I'm here to perform my duty, so I'll be with you for the foreseeable future. Looking forward to it, Lord Cassieux!"

Slightly taken aback by Kelios's unflinching smirk and his strong personality, Leorino finally said yes.

In the end, he remained uncertain about Lucas's intentions behind dispatching Kelios.

With the exception of combat training, Kelios had spent most of his time with Leorino, Josef, and Dirk ever since.

His suspicious behavior aside, Kelios was really good at growing on people. And as far as organizing documents was concerned, he was far more helpful than Josef.

Incidentally, Josef—who had given up on helping Leorino with paperwork from the very beginning—was mostly killing time doing nothing in particular, occasionally joining the conversation.

At first, Leorino had a hard time getting used to Kelios's presence. It was the first time he had been so intimately involved with a colleague his own age and the first time he was interacting with someone so easily excitable.

Above all, Kelios was simply bizarre. He was peculiar in ways that Josef was not. Every time he saw Leorino, he squealed things like "His eyelashes are so long!" or "His hair is so shiny!" and clutched at his chest, driving Leorino up the wall.

Leorino was simply baffled by Kelios's behavior; it was Josef who yelled things like "That's enough!" at him, followed by Dirk's chuckle and some calming phrase such as "I completely and utterly get it, but no screaming, please."

Their corner of the archives became very noisy all at once when Kelios joined them. Sometimes, when things got too loud, the guardian of the archives would appear and mercilessly drop his fist on Kelios's head to silence him.

It took five days or so for Leorino to finally grow accustomed to having Kelios around.

One day, Kelios came to him bearing news.

"Lord Leorino, the day after tomorrow, the Combat Division will be holding some training exercises. The lieutenant general has asked me to invite you and Josef to come along to observe."

Leorino's face lit up when he heard this. Lucas had remembered the promise they had made at the auction.

Witnessing Leorino's bright smile at such close proximity, Kelios gasped at how blinding it was, shielding his eyes. But Leorino had already mastered the art of ignoring Kelios's eccentricities, so it hardly upset him at all. Or rather, he chose to disregard his behavior on purpose.

"Oh, I'd love to! Josef, you'll go with me, won't you?"

"Master Leorino, I'll go wherever you go."

"Kelios, you'll be participating in the training, yes?"

"That I will. So I'm sorry, but I won't be there to guard you that day. Oh, and—" Kelios smiled goadingly at Josef for some reason. "His Excellency, the lieutenant general, asked if you would like to participate in the training yourself, Mr. Josef."

"Huh? Josef?"

It was a completely unexpected offer. Josef seemed stunned, too.

Leorino tilted his head and looked at Josef as if to ask, "What are you going to do?" Josef looked back at his master and angled his head in the very same way.

Dirk and Kelios found the sight incredibly heartwarming. Leorino, with his delicate, pure beauty, and Josef, with his feminine features that looked so gentle when he was silent, both tilting their heads at each other was adorable; a true feast for the eyes.

"I'm allowed to take part in the Royal Army's training, when I haven't officially joined the army?"

Josef seemed interested in the offer.

He had actually worried that his current training regimen was insufficient compared to the one he had in Brungwurt, and that his body would get rusty if this continued. He also wanted to see what the soldiers of the Royal Army were capable of.

"Do you think I could take part?"

"Of course, they invited you. I'll keep to myself and stay out of trouble." Leorino smiled and agreed. He could see that his guard was unusually excited.

Leorino was filled with gratitude to Lucas for giving them this opportunity.

"Lord Kelios, do you know if the lieutenant general will participate in the training that day?"

"His Excellency? He will be overseeing the event, so of course he will be there, but I don't think he will participate in the training himself."

"Then I'll stay close to the lieutenant general. That way you won't have to worry, right, Josef?"

"All right. But if anything happens, you're my first priority, Lord Leorino." Josef nodded. That settled it.

Leorino was looking forward to the day after tomorrow even more now that two people he knew, Josef and Kelios, were both going to participate in the training.

"But what is the purpose of this training? Are you just exercising?"

Dirk answered Leorino's question.

"The army is in the process of reorganizing its units. We are training to test the skills of the combat units in light of that."

"Reorganizing?"

"Yes. Under the direction of the general, we are verifying the reorganization and redeployment of the combat units. The mountain troops normally deployed in the Baedeker Mountains are also subject to this. Since they can't leave the region all at once, they will return to the royal capital in shifts, platoon by platoon. Several units of theirs will be taking part in this training as well."

Leorino blinked restlessly.

"The mountain troops will be...in the royal capital."

"Yes. They're our elite forces, after all. I'm certain the training will be a sight to behold."

The mountain troops were the most elite troops in the army and were deployed from the Baedeker Mountains in the northwestern part of Fanoren all the way to the southern border, standing at the forefront of the Combat Division. They hardly ever returned to the royal capital.

The platoons of the mountain troops were numbered from one to one hundred, with the lowest numbers being the most elite, operating in the harshest areas. They were the strongest soldiers that any young man in the Combat Division could aspire to be a part of.

It was also the unit to which Ionia had once belonged. The Special Forces, of which Ionia was the commander, were officially part of the mountain troops.

With Ionia at its helm, the Special Forces gathered commoners who possessed special abilities.

Tobias Bosse, who could discern the quietest sounds from large distances; Xavier Erdland, who could restrain the movements of his opponents without touching them. Ebbo Steiger with superhuman strength. And Edgar Yorke, a wind manipulator who had stoked the flames around Zweilink, setting the fortress ablaze.

Leorino placed his hand on his chest. Something stirred within.

Was his heart pounding in anticipation or apprehension?

Leorino subconsciously sensed the footsteps of fate approaching from the border.

At the Training Grounds

The Royal Army's training grounds were located on the outskirts of the capital.

Josef and Kelios left the royal capital early in the morning to prepare for the training. The issue of Leorino's safety during the trip was resolved by having Dirk accompany him in a carriage as his escort.

Dirk was easy to get on with, but he held a considerable position in the royal army as adjutant to the general. Leorino felt undeserving of such company, but he could not refuse Dirk when he said it had been the general's order.

In the end, he and Dirk traveled to the training grounds together.

From a distance, the training grounds looked like a stone castle.

Colossal. That was the only word to describe it.

Beyond the gate was a vast space, dust rising from within. It was not a castle, but a gallery built around the empty central space.

As soon as Leorino and Dirk arrived, Schultz was waiting for them near the gate and led them to the upper gallery. The gallery surrounding the training grounds on all sides was so long that it was impossible to see the end of it. A series of arched windows overlooked the courtyard, but they didn't have the time to gaze through them. They were forced to walk for so long that Leorino began worrying about the condition of his legs. After turning the corner twice, they finally reached the far end of the building.

* * *

They arrived at a large balcony-like space that opened out onto the courtyard.

Under the brilliant early summer sun, Leorino spotted Lucas.

His muscular frame was wrapped in silvery armor instead of his usual military uniform. His presence overwhelmed everyone around him as always. His golden hair shimmered in the sunlight like a mane.

Leorino looked upon him with fondness. The sight reminded him of Lucas in his youth, still etched in his memory.

Today, Leorino wore a hood to keep a low profile. He made to lower his hood, but Dirk stopped him.

"If you show your face where everyone can see you, Lord Leorino, it'll cause a scene. Perhaps you should keep your hood on until the lieutenant general gives you permission to take it off."

"But…isn't that inappropriate for a greeting?"

"Not at all. Don't worry, the lieutenant general will know it's you."

Dirk was right.

Lucas looked at the slender silhouette and immediately recognized Leorino. Small wrinkles appeared in the corners of his eyes. His smile helped Leorino relax a little.

"Leorino, you're here."

Leorino bowed.

"Yes, sir. I'm very glad for this opportunity to see your work."

"No need to be so formal. Come join me already."

Lucas beckoned for Leorino.

Behind Lucas stood a row of high-ranking, muscular men who clearly belonged to the Combat Division. All of them looked imposing as they watched the young man in the cloak—Leorino—with interest.

Under such circumstances, he could not summon the courage to stand next to Lucas.

As Leorino hesitated, a hand gently pressed into his back. When he looked up, Dirk was looking down at him with a mischievous smile.

"His Excellency invited you here. You should make the most of it and get the view from the front row."

"...But everyone here is so distinguished, it wouldn't be right for me to put myself on the same level..."

Dirk knew that the top brass had been notified of Leorino's visit in advance. He also knew that they had been instructed beforehand not to bother Leorino with their curiosity.

"It's all right. There's nothing rude about it."

"Are you certain?"

Leorino was still hesitant, but Dirk nodded reassuringly. With his encouragement, Leorino walked up to Lucas resolutely.

With everyone armed for training, Leorino's outfit, completely covered by his cloak, appeared quite out of place. But the top brass knew it was Leorino. No one challenged him for walking up to Lucas.

Leorino bowed deeply before Lucas.

"Your Excellency, thank you for inviting us today."

"Yes, I'm glad you came. I can't offer you much time today, but I hope you have a good look around. You've never seen so many armed soldiers wielding swords at once before, have you?"

Leorino smiled noncommittally.

"I'm certain you'll discover a lot just by watching. Now come, look down. It's already started."

Leorino nodded at Lucas's words and approached the edge of the balcony.

"Dirk, I see you've done well on your guard duty."

Dirk smiled and bowed at Lucas's praise.

The men began talking in low voices, but by then Leorino was already transfixed by the scene below.

"Do you enjoy seeing our soldiers train? Aren't they incredible?"

"Yes, sir...they are! I can feel the heat from here."

Leorino nodded deeply at Lucas's words. His voice was hoarse with excitement.

The training grounds did not appear in Ionia's memories. Ionia had been immediately sent to the front lines and never got the chance to train here. Leorino observed the venue with great interest, every part feeling so new to him.

The large training area was divided into sixteen sections, each populated with several dozen soldiers.

There was a space in the middle of each section where several pairs of one-on-one mock battles were held. Cheers, jeers, and ear-splitting sword fights could be heard from all over the place.

Leorino was overwhelmed by the excitement and enthusiasm of the soldiers. He felt the battles from his memories coming back to him. Slowly, he could feel the blood rushing through his veins.

Oh, wow... I wish I could fight, too!

Leorino's violet eyes gleamed feverishly, and his golden lashes twitched restlessly. His cheeks were rosy, conveying the degree of his excitement.

Lucas watched him with a smile.

Leorino looked up at Lucas with a grin. His violet eyes were nearly bright enough to blind.

"I didn't realize the training grounds were so large!"

"Yes, the facility can accommodate up to five hundred people training at the same time. If we count all the people who could be contained in this building as well, it could fit a thousand people at once."

They were currently standing on the observation platform where royalty and other dignitaries could follow the training, and where they had the best view of the courtyard. The stone galleries were also used for various purposes in different places.

Lucas carefully explained the structure of the buildings in the training grounds, pointing to each of them as he did.

"Wow... Wow...! I'm quite overwhelmed by the grandeur of this place, sir."

"I can see. You're a boy after all, huh? Ha-ha, it's exciting, isn't it? You're all red."

In a teasing voice, Lucas poked at Leorino's flushed cheeks with his finger. The next moment, the rest of his face also turned red.

"I apologize for...being so childish."

"What? I've grown used to this sight, but it's great seeing you enjoy yourself so much, ha-ha. Clearly, inviting you was the right choice."

Leorino looked up at Lucas with gratitude in his eyes. Lucas's amber eyes met his gaze and looked back at Leorino with a sort of tenderness.

"...Aren't you glad you started working at the Palace of Defense?"

Leorino nodded deeply.

"Yes, right now, I'm very glad. I'm dazzled by everything I see."

"That's great."

Lucas patted Leorino on the head over his hood. Despite his fierce appearance, the look in his eyes allowed Leorino to glimpse Lucas's compassionate nature, filling Leorino's heart with something warm and melancholy.

Lucas had gazed at Ionia in the very same way when they had last embraced in their quarters at the Palace of Defense. The way he looked at Ionia was so boundlessly cherishing, so unconditionally affirming of his existence, that it suddenly brought Leorino to the verge of tears.

"Is there anything you want to ask about?"

Lucas's question brought Leorino back to his senses.

Lucas's presence, the smell of dust, the sharp sound of clashing swords, and the voices of the men excited to fight seemed to pull Leorino back into the memories of his past life.

"Well, I...I was wondering if there is any significance to the way the training grounds have been divided."

Lucas nodded and pointed to a small entrance on the opposite side of the venue.

The gate he pointed to was the size of his thumb. It had been huge when they passed through it.

Leorino was once more in awe of the sheer size of the training grounds.

"The training area is divided by experience and skill, from the entrance you came through all the way to here. Normally, the area near the gate is for new recruits. The closer you get to the observation platform, the more elite the soldiers."

"...Does that mean that Kelios and Josef are in the section at the far end?"

Leorino strained his eyes, but the people by the entrance looked like ants. He could not see Josef and Kelios at all from this distance. Leorino felt a little disappointed, wishing he had been able to observe them in training.

* * *

They had walked a considerable distance from the entrance to the observation platform. For Leorino's legs, it was a distance too great to consider treading it back and forth.

Perhaps sensing Leorino's disappointment that he might not be able to see the two men fight, Lucas tapped him on the shoulder.

"I figured it wouldn't be very interesting if we didn't get to see Keller and your guard training, so I made an exception and put them in a veteran's group in the front, far right. Look...they're right there. Can you see them?"

Leorino leaned over the parapet and looked to the aforementioned section.

"Y-yes... Ah! There they are. They're both there!"

Leorino's eyes lit up. Just as Lucas had said, he spotted two familiar figures among the strong soldiers who had been clearly hand-picked for the occasion.

Leorino was delighted to see that both of his guards were close by. But despite being much closer than he expected, their section was still unfortunately far from where Leorino stood on the observation platform. He would hardly be able to appreciate their swordsmanship as closely as he'd hoped.

I wish I could get a closer look.

As Leorino happily leaned forward and watched, Lucas suddenly brought up a difficult topic. "Has Keller been bothering you?"

Leorino turned around with an expression that made it clear Lucas had just rained on his parade. His angelic beauty instantly took on a human quality.

"Bothering, no, not at all... I just think he's a very—how should I put this—interesting person."

The hesitant expression on Leorino's face finally made Lucas laugh out loud at his diplomatic answer.

Leorino rushed to change the subject.

"But...the section closest to us is filled with powerful warriors, isn't it? I wonder if Josef and Kelios will be all right going up against them."

"Oh, changing the subject, I see? They'll be just fine. Keller is a strange young man, but he's so far above his peers with the sword that we've been hearing about him since before he even graduated. And from the looks of it, your guard should have no issues, either. If anything, he seems to be causing quite the stir already."

"That's great! I'm relieved to hear that Josef doesn't seem to be causing any trouble!"

Lucas nodded in satisfaction.

"No, I honestly underestimated him. His physique is rather unassuming, but…his speed and accuracy with the sword is extraordinary. And it appears he's just getting warmed up. I'm impressed."

Dirk had been listening to their conversation from the sidelines and now hummed in surprise.

"If the lieutenant general is singing such high praises, I would love to see Josef's skill in action."

"Of course. You said his name is Josef Lev? He brought the tip of his sword to the neck of one of our elite soldiers in the time it takes to count the fingers of one hand, and he did it with time to spare."

Seeing Dirk's impressed reaction in his periphery, Leorino intently watched the section where the two men were fighting.

That was when he noticed that the armor of the majority of the soldiers gathered there seemed awfully familiar to him. He felt his heart skip a beat.

"…Are Lord Kelios and Josef sharing their section with soldiers from the mountain troops?"

"Yes, they should be. That's the third platoon over there. Your guards must be very skilled if they can hold their own against the third platoon."

Lucas crossed his arms and smiled at Leorino.

"That guard is more than qualified to keep you safe, isn't he?"

"Yes, sir. I trust him."

"I wanted to see your guard's skill for myself. This was the perfect opportunity. Brungwurt has trained him well."

Leorino was filled with pride and joy at Lucas's words of praise.

"Oh, absolutely! Appearances aside, Josef is incredibly skilled! I am very glad to see you could recognize it, Lord Lucas."

"Lord Leorino, please."

"Yes, Mr. Dirk?"

When Leorino looked up at Dirk, Dirk forced a smile and furrowed his brow pointedly.

"I know you're excited, but you're in the presence of the lieutenant general."

Dirk gently reminded him to correct his tone, and Leorino realized his blunder. The top brass were also glancing at him by now.

Leorino rushed to apologize.

"I'm so sorry!"

Leorino was so caught up in the moment that he had begun speaking to him in a way that was far from appropriate. He had also called him by his first name in public instead of the usual "Your Excellency."

Ignoring his mistake, Lucas placed his hand on Leorino's head once more.

"...Sir?"

"Your hood is sliding off. Be careful. You shouldn't expose your face to these ruffians."

"Oh, thank you, sir."

Leorino nodded and pulled the hood low over his eyes again. Lucas nodded in approval.

At that moment, Schultz, his second-in-command, approached Lucas from behind.

"Your Excellency, I hate to interrupt, but it's nearly time."

"Hm? Oh, time really flies, doesn't it?"

It appeared that Lucas had somewhere to be. Leorino had held up the busy lieutenant general for long enough.

"I apologize for taking up your time."

"Not at all. I must head off for now, but you can stay here and have a good look around. I'll speak with you later."

"Yes, sir. Thank you for this opportunity."

Lucas was about to turn on his heel, when Leorino exclaimed, "Oh, right! Um... Lieutenant General?"

"Yes?"

"I would like to watch Josef and Lord Kelios from a little closer, if at all possible. May I?"

* * *

Lucas considered this. He wanted to fulfill Leorino's wish, but he also didn't want him to move from this safe place, where only his trusted top brass resided.

Many of the soldiers in the Combat Division were deployed to the front lines and did not know the people working at the Palace of Defense. Even within the military, they were known for their uncouth temperaments. Many of them were commoners who knew nothing of nobility and were now worked up from the training. It was far from a safe environment.

Seeing his adjutant growing impatient behind Lucas's back as he lost himself in thought, Dirk offered a helping hand.

"Your Excellency, I'll go with Lord Leorino."

"Hm, you will? I'm not certain you'll be able to handle it alone."

Dirk smiled wryly at these words.

Dirk possessed quite an impressively toned body himself. He still kept up with his basic training. However, from the perspective of the man who stood at the helm of the Combat Division and boasted military prowess and physical strength, it made sense that he would appear somewhat insufficient.

Leorino quietly waited for permission, his large eyes filled with anticipation. Lucas was overcome by the expectant look in Leorino's eyes and settled for a compromise.

"I won't allow you to go down to the ground floor. But you can go to the gallery above that area—right there. You should have a good view from there."

He pointed to the right end of the gallery overlooking Josef and Kelios's section.

The second floor of the gallery where Leorino and Dirk stood was very quiet, with few soldiers passing by despite the bustle in the courtyard.

With his hands on the railing, Leorino continued to watch the training in rapt attention. It must have been at least half an hour by now. Leorino and Dirk had arrived late so as not to disturb them, so the training was already coming to an end.

"You must be tired, being on your feet all day."

"...Sorry?"

Even as Dirk spoke to him, Leorino kept his eyes on the ground. He was fixated.

"Lord Leorino?"

"Yes...? No? ...I'm sorry. I got carried away, I wasn't listening."

Leorino's mind seemed to be somewhere else entirely. He did react, but Dirk's question seemed to have gone in one ear and out the other.

"Hm, Lord Leorino, you're really enjoying this, aren't you?"

"Sorry? ...Just now! Lord Kelios has shown the extent of his skill again! Did you catch it?"

Leorino was entirely consumed by the training. Dirk couldn't help but chuckle at that.

He really is just a boy. He's loving this.

"Wow...! I knew Josef was amazing, but Lord Kelios is very strong as well. They're absolutely incredible! Just look at them. Look, look, look, Dirk! Oh, how I wish I could burn this sight into my mind."

Leorino was talking to himself, his eyes bright, clearly thrilled to be there.

Dirk didn't hold it against Leorino, even as his polite tone vanished into thin air.

The ignorant young man, who had lived his entire life under the over-protective eye of his family, was truly savoring his first combat training. Forgetting his manners here and there was no big deal.

Dirk himself often spoke more casually than others, and his language wasn't nearly bad enough to deserve reprimanding.

He's keeping himself together far better than when I first met him. It's been a while since I've seen him so relaxed.

Leorino must have been truly relishing this. He was leaning out the window and earnestly watching the training. There was something comforting about how he stood on his tiptoes.

"I'm so glad Lord Lucas invited us here! I've never been to the training grounds before."

The smile peeking out from his hood was so bright that it seemed to be emitting its own light.

I suddenly understand what Kelios meant.

A young man, so beautiful that it made one wonder if he could truly be just another human, stood so close, a smile blooming on his lips. Dirk figured he should be used to it by now, but still, no matter how many times he saw him, Leorino was still beautiful enough to take his breath away.

Below them, Josef was beginning yet another duel. He unleashed his sword on his opponents with the same skill every time. He was so fast they couldn't follow the tip of his blade. Despite his slender physique, he seemed to have endless stamina.

Josef's brawny opponent was at the mercy of his deft sword, which soon found its way to his throat.

Dirk groaned at the sight.

"Oof! Josef is genuinely brilliant."

"He is, isn't he? Josef is incredible."

"His speed and poise are just as good as they were at the beginning of the training session. If it were me, I would definitely lose."

Leorino nodded repeatedly with a wide grin on his face. Seeing that his hood was beginning to slide off, Dirk rushed to pull it back on. Just to be safe, Dirk also looked around to make sure no one could have spotted Leorino.

"I've never seen such quick swordplay. If that's the standard of the Brungwurt Autonomous Army, that's very impressive."

"Josef was the strongest back in Brungwurt. But I believe the soldiers of the Autonomous Army are just as skilled as those of the Royal Army."

Leorino looked somewhat proud as he said this.

"I could see that." Dirk nodded in agreement.

They were the same fearless fighters who had been defending that key border point since the days of the former kingdom.

"So they're that good, huh? Now you've piqued my interest in the Brungwurt Autonomous Army."

"Well, I've only seen them in training myself."

"That reminds me, what did Josef do before he became your guard? Was he in the army?"

"Oh? No, I...I don't really know. I think he wasn't doing much of anything."

"Much of anything..."

Leorino nodded as if he wasn't all there.

One has his head in the clouds and the other used to be a freeloader... Match made in heaven.

"Josef is the son of the commander of the Autonomous Army, but he never officially joined it."

"I see. Oh, but with all the skill he's shown, the mountain troops will be tripping over themselves to recruit him into their ranks."

Leorino shook his head.

"With Josef's personality, I don't think he'll ever be able to join the Royal Army."

Dirk couldn't help but nod at the confidence of that statement.

Leorino turned back to the training grounds.

"Ah, this time it's Lord Kelios! But his opponent looks so big and strong—"

"Oh, you're right. That's an older soldier. I can't tell his rank from here, but... Lord Leorino?"

The moment Leorino saw Kelios's opponent, he forgot how to breathe.

That's...!

The sight of the mature soldier confronting Kelios instantly brought back memories of grief and pain. He felt as if his blood was flowing backward. Leorino was pulled back into the memory of the fire at Zweilink.

"Close the gates!"

Ionia's voice echoed through the battlefield. A wounded man from his unit turned to him with a look of despair on his face.

"I can't... I won't leave you!"

*   *   *

Tears of grief streamed down the man's blood- and soot-stained cheeks. They both knew that if they were separated there, they would never see each other again. They realized their lives were doomed.

Oh my god, you're alive…!

"Just go! Use your Power and close the gates!"

Ebbo…!

No matter how many years may have passed or how much his appearance had changed, there was no mistaking him.

The man who had closed the gates that day, following Ionia's orders while spilling tears of grief. The man who was likely the final survivor of Ionia's Special Forces.

Ebbo Steiger, the man with superhuman strength, stood there, covered in claw marks etched into his flesh by the ruthless flames.

The Dice Are Cast

The elation that had filled Leorino suddenly vanished.

Below him stood a man who had once belonged to Ionia's unit. He was now the only man in the world who could share with Leorino what had happened at Zweilink that day.

Leorino closely observed Kelios's opponent. He had been older than Ionia at the time, so he must have been in his forties by now.

Ebbo was fighting with a sword, likely suppressing his Power. Leorino remembered that, back then, Ebbo had chosen to use his fists over a sword more often than not. But even with his advancing age, the sword he drew from his powerful, hulking frame was still heavy, and Kelios seemed to be struggling with its weight.

He could not let this opportunity pass him by.

Ebbo belonged to the mountain troops, and Leorino lived in the royal capital, surrounded by walls upon walls. If they parted ways here, they would likely never see each other again.

...What do I do? How can I get downstairs without Dirk following me?

Leorino discreetly glanced at Dirk. He was watching Kelios fight with interest, his arms crossed.

Next, he ventured a look at the corridor behind him.

Leorino and Dirk stood at the far right end of the gallery, where the observation platform jutted out. A little further ahead, there was a staircase in the corner. The spot where they stood was empty and quiet compared to the bustle and heat below.

Clenching his fists, Leorino frantically considered his options.

Even if he went downstairs without permission, he could never outrun Dirk.

Perhaps he could just say he wanted to go say hello to Josef and Kelios?

No, that wouldn't qualify as a valid reason.

Dirk was a bighearted, kind man, but mere good-naturedness would have been far from enough to make him Gravis's second-in-command. He must have been appropriately strict in following orders from his superiors.

Even if Leorino politely requested it, Dirk would likely never allow him to go down to the ground floor teeming with soldiers from the Combat Division.

Think... Think!

If he could, he would yell Ebbo's name. "Come here," he would say, "I must speak with you immediately." But he couldn't. Leorino and Ebbo Steiger had never even met before.

Still, he couldn't afford to miss this opportunity.

In the training area below, the mock duel continued. The old warrior swung his sword down weightily. Kelios bent down and placed his hand on the back of his sword to catch the blow. Their strikes sliced through the air and echoed in the second-floor gallery.

Leorino leaned out the window without much thought. That was when he felt something hard between the stone wall and his chest. Leorino's breath caught in his throat. *This is it*, he thought.

He would have one shot, and he had no choice but to take it.

"Kelios! Hang in there!"

Leorino placed his hand on the railing and suddenly leaned forward with all his might. The arched window opened wide to the outside. Leorino's upper body lurched forward so far he thought he might fall.

"Watch out! Leorino! Don't lean forward so hard!"

Startled by Leorino's movement, Dirk rushed to grab Leorino by the waist. Leorino's upper half hung in the air.

"...! Leorino! What—?!"

But as Dirk tried to pull him back inside, Leorino let out a small shriek and twisted in his arms, trying to reach for the ground.

"Ah, my dagger!"

"...Stop! You'll fall!"

Dirk recognized what had fallen from Leorino's chest as it glinted in the sunlight. But he had greater concerns at the moment.

Dirk forcefully lifted his slender waist. Leorino's hood slid down in the process, revealing his platinum hair. Dirk pulled him away from the ledge and pushed Leorino's body against the wall. Leorino's breath caught in his throat at the violent motion.

Dirk was as tall and strong as Ionia used to be, though still smaller than Gravis. Leorino was instinctively frightened by the strength of the large, angry man.

Finally, Dirk exhaled roughly in relief.

"How harebrained can you be?! I know you're excited, but you must be more careful!"

Dirk scolded Leorino more harshly than ever before. But despite his strict tone, his eyes were filled with worry and relief.

Leorino's chest ached with guilt, but his act was far from over.

"I'm sorry. Lord Kelios was about to lose, so I just..."

Dirk sighed once more and relaxed his hands pressing Leorino into the wall. He then scratched his head.

"I never thought you'd do something so foolish. Did you consider what might happen if you fell from this height?"

"...I'm really sorry. I won't do it again, Mr. Dirk."

Dirk heaved another deep sigh. He must have thought Leorino had forgotten himself in his excitement.

This endeavor was forsaking all of Dirk's trust in an instant. After all was said and done, Dirk would never trust Leorino again. That sad truth was hard to swallow. He wanted to put an end to his silly performance already.

* * *

But Leorino gritted his teeth. This was the moment of truth.

"Mr. Dirk...I dropped my dagger."

"Yes, I saw. That's what you get."

Dirk looked out the window with a grim look on his face, still holding Leorino's arms. He seemed to have spotted the dagger immediately.

"...Did anyone get hurt?"

"No, it's fine. Is that dagger important to you?"

Leorino nodded, dispirited.

"My father gave it to me when I left for the royal capital. It was the dagger he used in his youth. He told me to take good care of it."

It was not.

He had chosen that dagger at random from among the ones Josef had prepared for him with his grip in mind.

"I'm scared to think what my father might say when he learns I lost it..."

Leorino hung his head with a deflated look on his face. In truth, he felt like throwing up from the guilt of lying to Dirk.

Playing the part of a lifetime, Leorino desperately fought the urge to confess.

Please, believe me, Dirk...

Dirk took three deep breaths and grumbled, "We wouldn't want that." He leaned out the window to check for the dagger.

"...Dammit. Someone picked it up. Hey! Bring it back!"

Leorino couldn't see it, but after it had fallen into the courtyard, someone must have found it.

"...Damn, they can't hear me."

Dirk clicked his tongue in irritation.

Please... Please... Dirk, please, please leave me alone for just a moment.

Dirk pulled the hood over Leorino's head and crouched down to look him in the eye.

"...Do you *really* need that dagger back?"

Leorino nodded with a heartbroken expression.

"Right. What if I… Fine, perhaps I'm the wrong person. What if the general were to give you a new one?"

"I'm sorry, Mr. Dirk…but I can't lose that dagger."

Dirk glanced around and clicked his tongue once more.

"Just when I've got no one to leave you with, huh."

"I'm really sorry. Please, let me go fetch it."

"I can't. You're not allowed to go downstairs."

Dirk hesitated for a moment, groaned, and closed his hands around Leorino's shoulders a little tighter.

"…Fine. I'll go get it for you. I'll be right back, and while I'm gone, can you promise me you'll stay here?"

"…Yes, I promise."

"Do not go *anywhere*, all right? That's an order from your superior officer. I'm trying to keep you safe. Do you understand?"

Leorino nodded, doing his best to ignore the pounding in his chest. He prayed that his face did not show any signs of guilt.

"All right. I'll be right back. And you stay right where you are!"

With that, Dirk turned on his heel and ran down the stairs at the corner of the gallery.

Leorino was left alone.

His chest felt like it was about to burst, and he held it with trembling hands, exhaling the breath he had been holding.

It worked… I'm sorry, Dirk.

The dagger fell directly below them. Dirk would be back soon.
Leorino had no time to waste.

I must go… I must see Ebbo…!

Leorino immediately took off.

For a moment, he thought about going down the stairs right away, but Dirk would find him before he got anywhere.

He nestled close to the wall of the corridor.

He brought his ear to one of the doors lining the corridor. He couldn't hear anything or sense anyone inside. Leorino guessed the room must not have been currently in use, given the overwhelming absence of people in the area.

He placed his hand on the door just around the corner.

Quietly, slowly, he turned the handle. The door was unlocked.

He opened the door. The room was empty, save for the high shelves stacked with supplies.

Leorino slid into the room and hid behind a shelf next to the entrance.

Dirk ran down the stairs, biting back his annoyance.

He quickly spotted the soldier who picked up the dagger. When he tapped him on the shoulder, the soldier turned and frowned at Dirk's unarmed appearance, but when he saw his rank insignia, he straightened his back and saluted.

"Lieutenant Colonel, sir!"

"At ease. I apologize for interrupting your training. My name is Dirk Bergund."

The soldier seemed to recognize him as the general's second-in-command.

"What can I do for you, sir?"

"You can start by returning me that dagger... Yes, that one. My companion dropped it from the gallery above. Thank you for picking it up."

"No, I'm glad I could be of service."

The soldier handed him the dagger. Dirk felt something was wrong the moment he received it.

It seemed to be sharp, but it was a simple, unadorned dagger, for something that was supposed to belong to the margrave. Dirk doubted that a family as major as his would use such a blade. But remembering Brungwurt's unaffected and sincere nature, he figured such a thing could indeed be possible.

At that moment, Kelios and Josef noticed Dirk and came running.

"Mr. Dirk! Did you watch our duels?"

"That I did. I'd love to talk more, but I must go. I'll see you later."

Dirk's expression was firm as he said this.

Kelios and Josef frowned at Dirk's strange behavior, given how amicable he usually was.

The man turning on his heel in a rush had a dagger in his hand, a dagger Josef knew well.

"Isn't that Master Leorino's dagger?"

"Oh, Lord Leorino got so excited that he dropped it from the gallery above. We've been watching you from up there until now... I'll see you later." Dirk said over his shoulder and turned on his heel once more.

Kelios stood there speechless, but Josef quickly followed after Dirk.

Chasing after Dirk, as he leaped up the staircase two steps at a time, he asked:

"You said Master Leorino dropped it?"

"Yes. He got a little distracted watching you two duel. He lamented dropping the precious dagger Lord August had given him."

Josef frowned. He had picked out that dagger at a craftsman's shop in the royal capital himself.

Master Leorino lied to Dirk... But why would he do that?

But Josef had no time to ask questions. They had already arrived at the second floor.

"...God dammit!"

Leorino should have been patiently waiting for him there, but he was nowhere to be found. Dirk's face twisted as he swore profusely, when Josef asked:

"Hey... Where's Master Leorino?"

Dirk met Josef's glare with empty eyes.

"...Your master was here until a few minutes ago, and now he's gone. He either left on his own, or he was kidnapped."

"Wh-what the hell...? Are you serious?"

"Yes, and it's my fault."

Dirk looked down at Josef with a strange intensity. He clearly wasn't joking. Josef understood that Leorino was truly gone.

"Damn you...! Seriously?! Why did you leave Master Leorino alone?!"

"...Lord Leorino promised me he would stay put."

Dirk's anguished reply made Josef turn pale. He imagined the worst.

"...Master Leorino always does as he's told. He knows his place. He wouldn't just run off on his own."

Dirk nodded in agreement.

"...In that case, there's a good chance he's been kidnapped."

Dirk and Josef looked at each other with grave expressions.

Dirk said in a low voice, "I'll leave all my apologies for later. Right now, we must ensure Lord Leorino's safety. Josef...please help me find him."

"...Of course, he's my first priority."

"It's only been a few minutes. Lord Leorino would surely resist a kidnapper. And I was on the ground floor. No one came down the stairs."

"That means that either Master Leorino went down the corridor himself or was taken by someone."

At that moment, a figure approached from the direction of the central observation platform. Dirk immediately checked the rank on his chest. The man outranked Dirk.

"Excuse me! Did you happen to pass someone walking with a young man in a cloak? He's about this tall, his cloak is gray. His hair is platinum blond."

The man seemed surprised by the sudden question, but finally shook his head.

"No, I haven't crossed paths with anyone like that."

Dirk scrutinized him. He had no reason to believe the man was lying.

"...Then he must have gone the other way. All right, let's focus on this side—Josef, start with these rooms. I'll go on ahead."

"All right." Josef nodded.

Dirk ran to the other side of the corridor and began to search, opening the door closest to him. Josef turned to opening the doors one by one and checking inside.

He did not care who might be in the rooms.

The rooms in the area were used to store weapons and equipment. They smelled of iron and dust and were dimly lit.

"Master Leorino! Are you there?"

Every room he checked was empty.

Josef's uneasiness grew. He frantically searched for his master.

"Master Leorino!"

It was when he opened the third door. For a moment, he thought he could smell Leorino.

But the room was silent, and Josef's call received no answer. Was he so desperate to find Leorino that he'd imagined his scent? Josef shook his head in dismay.

"Dammit... Where are you?!"

Josef stifled the urge to start screaming and slammed the door to continue his search elsewhere.

Leorino picked up their faint voices and was heartbroken to have betrayed them.

I'm so sorry... Dirk, Josef... I'm sorry.

"Master Leorino!"

The door to the room where Leorino was hiding was flung open with a bang. Leorino nearly jumped at the noise and desperately covered his mouth to kill any sign of his presence. His heart was pounding in his ears.

"Dammit... Where are you?!"

Josef's quiet cry made Leorino painfully aware of the worry and distress he was causing him.

Josef... I'm sorry.

Soon, the sound of a door slamming shut followed. The light from the outside disappeared and the room turned dark once more.

At that moment, a bell rang, signaling the end of the combat training. The heavy sound traveled through the stone walls and shook Leorino to his core as he sat with his back pressed against the stone.

The sound of the bell was fate's way of telling Leorino that this was his only chance. If he squandered it, he would likely never see Ebbo again.

The sound of the bell steeled his resolve.

The die had already been cast. There was no turning back. No matter how grave his betrayal, nor the pain he was putting his friends through, he had to follow through on his convictions now.

"I must do this. It's now or never."

This was the reason he had been born with Ionia's memories. Finding Ebbo here must have meant *something*.

When the sound of Josef's footsteps faded away, he slowly opened the door. Glancing left and right, he saw no one. Leorino quietly descended the stairs, making his footfalls as light as possible.

The ground floor corridor was so busy that the silence of the second floor felt almost unreal. The passage quickly filled with soldiers returning from the training grounds. Praying that no one would see him, Leorino kept to the stone walls and pressed on.

Perhaps Leorino's prayers had been answered, or perhaps he was simply fortunate that the corridor was so crowded, but he managed to blend in despite the suspicious hood pulled over his eyes.

No one spotted Leorino as he continued to search for the man.

Ebbo's appearance was burned into his memory. The back of the man he had last seen through flames and smoke. The fact that he had just seen him in person made it all the more vivid.

The armor of the men that day was dark with blood, soot, and mud. Now, even after all that training, Ebbo's armor still maintained its dull white shine.

There he is...! It's Ebbo...!

He quickly spotted the back of the man he was looking for. He was lucky the training area was just a few steps away from the staircase. Leorino breathed a sigh of relief and slowly closed the distance between them.

Ebbo was walking at a leisurely pace down the corridor, conversing with several men. He gave off a sense of post-training fatigue.

Leorino frantically weaved his way through the crowd. Finally, he caught up with Ebbo.

The man's back was huge up close.

He was at least as tall as Lucas, perhaps even larger. He towered over Leorino now in a way he never had in his memories. Leorino felt overwhelmed by his grandeur.

But of course he would be different now. Ionia would have been able to make eye contact with him without much difficulty, but for Leorino, Gravis and most of the other men in the army were so large that he had to crane his neck just to look at them.

Approaching that large back, Leorino hesitated.

What should I say to him...? How will I explain myself?

He had recklessly concocted this twisted scheme just to see Ebbo, but hadn't had the mind to think of what he should tell him once he actually found him.

Racking his mind on what to do, the distance between the two of them grew again, and Leorino began to panic.

Dirk and Josef were looking for him. He had no time to hesitate.

Throwing all caution to the wind, he quietly approached him from behind. "Um, Mr. Steiger..."

But his voice must have been too quiet for the man to hear him. Leorino again raised his voice a little.

"Mr. Steiger."

Finally, Ebbo turned around. Leorino's heart skipped a beat.

At the sound of his name, Ebbo turned around. Far below his line of sight, he spotted a slender figure hidden in a hooded cloak. Judging from his attire, he was a man.

Ebbo frowned, wondering if it was this hooded man who had called his name. His voice—unfamiliar, gentle, and sweet—was hoarse with nerves. Just going by his voice, he must have been quite young.

The man called Ebbo's name again, trembling ever so slightly.

"Who the hell are you?"

"Oh… Um, I'm sorry to bother you out of the blue. I have come to speak with you."

The way he spoke revealed that this young man hiding his face was an aristocrat. The slender body the cloak couldn't fully conceal made it clear he wasn't a soldier participating in the combat training. If he were, he would not have hidden his face in a cloak in the first place. But a mere civilian couldn't just waltz into the training grounds, either.

Unable to arrive at any conclusive answer, Ebbo was puzzled by the young man's mysterious offer. His colleagues had also stopped and looked at the cloaked young man with interest.

"What do you want with Ebbo?"

"Hey, Ebbo, you know this strange kid?"

The man who had described the young man as strange tried to peer into his face under the hood. The young man, however, did not appreciate this, hiding his face by gripping the edge of his hood.

"Ebbo, a buddy of yours?"

"…No, I don't think so."

The young man's shoulders shuddered at Ebbo's response.

"I'm really sorry to bother you, but I was wondering if we could speak privately?"

Ebbo raised an eyebrow at the young man's demand.

"…I promise, I'll explain everything later. But please, not here."

The young man's desperate request got the men excited, perhaps thinking that he had some illicit relationship with Ebbo.

They knew that Ebbo's appearance—especially his face with its severe burn scars—had kept him away from love.

"Well, damn, Ebbo. I guess you get around after all, huh?"

"You've been in Baedeker the entire time, so when did you get yourself such a youthful beau in the royal capital, hmm?"

"You carrying a torch for Ebbo, kid? Well, come here, show off that pretty face."

The young man shrunk away at the men's teasing. Surrounded by strong men, he seemed to be at a loss for what to do with himself.

* * *

At that moment, the young man mumbled something to Ebbo. But his voice was drowned out by the teasing of the ruffians, and Ebbo couldn't catch his words.

"What's wrong? What do you want to tell me?"

Ebbo felt sorry for him and bent down a little to get a closer look. The young man reached out a slender hand from inside his cloak and touched the back of Ebbo's hand, whispering something again to him as he brought his face closer.

Ebbo's colleagues gasped at the sight of his hand. Unlike the coarse hands of the soldiers they were accustomed to seeing, his hands were fair and dainty.

But Ebbo didn't have the presence of mind to look at them. The moment he heard the young man's whisper, a shock shot through his entire body.

"What...?"

He had not misheard. The stranger had truly said, "I want to talk to you about that night at Zweilink...and what happened that day before you closed the gates."

"...How would you even...?"

His eyes met the bright eyes concealed by the darkness of the hood. At that moment, Ebbo felt himself go numb.

His head went blank, and soon his vision turned red, colored by a phantom flame.

The plains of Zweilink, ablaze. The night when many soldiers were felled and engulfed in flames. The smell of blood and soot that blocked out all else. His friends, disappearing one by one. And finally, the violet eyes of the man who sent Ebbo out through the gates.

Ebbo was bewildered.

The memories of eighteen years ago came back to him so vividly. At the same time, questions swirled in his mind.

Why had this young man suddenly brought up the events at Zweilink? How could someone so young know that it was Ebbo who had closed the gates of Zweilink back then?

The Dice Are Cast

This fact had never been put to paper. There were very few who could have known of it.

"E-Ebbo... Please, I don't have much time."

The young man leaned in close and pleaded desperately in a quiet voice, "I know this is sudden and I know you find me suspicious, but please, let me speak with you. *We* don't have much time."

Ebbo grabbed the young man by the shoulders and asked in a trembling voice: "...Where should we go?"

The young man's slender shoulders shook.

"...Anywhere. As long as we can speak alone."

The voice that answered him was quivering, too.

Ebbo nodded.

Leaving his startled colleagues where they stood, Ebbo walked down the corridor, holding the shoulder of the young man who had suddenly brought him back to the events of eighteen years prior.

The room Ebbo took him to was similar in construction to the one on the second floor. It was almost directly below the room he had just hidden in. It was dark and dusty, with the only lighting being the sunlight filtering in through the small window.

"...Show me your face."

Leorino hesitated for a moment, but finally removed his hood. Steeling his resolve, he raised his chin.

Ebbo was dumbfounded.

He had never seen such a beautiful human being before. Ebbo couldn't believe he was made of the same flesh and blood as himself. His beauty was a thing of legend.

But more than his physical beauty, it was his eyes that truly astonished Ebbo. Extraordinary violet eyes, like a ray of dawn across an indigo sky. Ebbo could never forget those eyes.

A chill ran down Ebbo's spine. It was a feeling akin to fear, as if he were facing something that couldn't, *shouldn't*, be real.

"...Who are you?"

"Ebbo..."

"Your eyes, but how...?!"

"Ebbo, I'm...I'm..."

The Special Forces had been decimated.

The only other survivor besides Ebbo was Edgar Yorke, who had been found on the verge of death from ruptured internal organs.

So there was no way such a young man could have known what had happened on that tragic night. How could he?

"How do you know my name...? How do you know that I closed the gates?"

"Please, just give me a moment. I'll explain everything... I'm, well... You may not believe me."

The young man's lips quivered. It was painful to watch him swallow his words over and over. But Ebbo, impatient and frustrated by his indecision, twisted his face in annoyance.

"You brought up something that no one is supposed to know... Who the hell are you?!"

The burn scars on Ebbo's face were terribly taut. Seeing this, the young man's face turned somber, and he clutched at his chest as if trying to hold something back.

"The scars are...so much."

"...What about my scars? What do my scars have to do with you?! What could you possibly...?!"

Ebbo was flustered. The young man had been watching Ebbo, and before he knew it, his cheeks were wet.

"You were injured so badly... Your burns are from that night, aren't they?"

Tears filled his violet eyes and slowly rolled down his fair cheeks.

"That must have been so horrible..."

Ebbo's memories came flooding back.

The captain ordered the gates to be closed.

Closing the gates until reinforcements arrived: That was Ebbo's final mission. The order of his superior, telling him to go through with it even if it meant forsaking the lives of his comrades, was absolute.

That was why Ebbo used his superhuman strength to close the gates even if his Power took what little remained of his life; even as burning pillars fell on his head; even as the chains of the iron gate, heated by the flames, burned and melted the skin and flesh of his hands.

And it was as *he* had said. The gates kept the enemy at bay until reinforcements arrived, and Fanoren won the battle.

The burns on Ebbo's body would serve as evidence of this as long as he lived.

Although his appearance had been damaged, he was still able to fight. His scars did not diminish the man's pride. The burn scars were proof that the Special Forces brought victory to Fanoren in return for the lives of the captain and his men in the battle eighteen years ago.

Rumor had it that Edgar Yorke had also passed away several years ago. Now Ebbo was the only living witness to what had happened at Zweilink that day.

Ebbo watched the violet eyes that kept shedding tears in blank amazement. And when the young man's fair hand reached for him, he accepted it without a thought.

His slender fingers gently traced the scar on Ebbo's temple, as if handling something fragile. From his left temple to his ear. The shaking fingertips ran over every inch of the burn scar that stretched to his neck.

His small hand gently lifted Ebbo's large hand. He softly stroked the burn scars on both the back and the palm of his hand.

"...You must have been in so much pain. And yet you continued to defend the gates... You obeyed orders to the very end."

Ebbo couldn't believe it could be true.
"You can't be..."
Violet eyes shattered Ebbo's feelings.
"Am I dreaming...?"

He, with his red hair and eyes a unique hue of violet, appeared in Ebbo's mind.

He was still a young man. But his captain's age had never concerned Ebbo. Only those with special abilities could understand the loneliness they felt.

The unit *he* had led was the only place where Ebbo could find solace.

The ghastly back of the young man who continued to slaughter his enemies while his entire body was covered in blood and viscera. Ebbo loved and respected the fighting spirit of the young captain of his unit. Ebbo and the other members believed in him and followed him wherever he went.

The young man weeping before Ebbo now appeared to be the polar opposite of *him*. He looked powerless and fragile, a being of pure white who had never been forced to bathe in blood.

But...his eyes were just like *his*. They were exactly the same as the eyes of the man who gave Ebbo his final orders, filled with grief and trust.

The next moment, the young man leaped into Ebbo's chest.

"Ebbo...!"

Gasping in surprise, Ebbo caught his body. The young man clung to Ebbo's chest with all his might, as if in prayer.

"Ebbo... Oh, Ebbo...! I'm so glad you're alive...!"

He was so slender that Ebbo worried he might break him without ever using his Power.

"...Are you a ghost coming back to haunt me from the past?"

The young man shook his head at Ebbo's feeble question.

"I'm not a ghost. Look, I'm warm, aren't I...? I'm a living, breathing person."

With that, he hugged Ebbo tightly once more, and finally let go of his body.

"I am *not* Ionia."

The older man's body shuddered. Then violet eyes lit with the rays of dawn caught Ebbo's gaze.

"...But I was born with Ionia's memories. So, in a sense, *he* lives on inside me."

Ebbo's eyes widened.

"My name is Leorino Cassieux. I am the son of August Cassieux of Brungwurt. I have memories of my previous life, of...Ionia Bergund, who had the same special Powers as you, who fought by your side, and who died at Zweilink. I keep them here."

Saying this, Leorino pressed his hand to his chest.

"That's why I have come to see you. Ebbo, I have come to tell you of Ionia's final wish."

It couldn't have been true.

"...But how, how could that be?" Ebbo groaned.

Leorino watched as Ebbo held his head in his hands in anguish and confusion, and apologized.

"I'm sorry for confusing you. But it's true, Ebbo... I have inherited Ionia's memories. That's why I came to see you. I really needed to speak with you."

"If you had the captain's memories, why did you come to see me *now*?"

"Ebbo..."

Ebbo's scream was agonizing. It was the cry of a man left behind, a man who did not get to die alongside his friends.

"You can't rewind time! ...Nothing can be done anymore! So why would you drag that up after all this time...?!"

"Ebbo, I'm sorry... I'm sorry, but you have to listen to me!"

"...Please, leave it be. You and all our friends are dead. They're all gone, and they've left me behind. It's all over now...Captain."

Leorino looked at Ebbo with tearful but determined eyes.

"It's not over yet, Ebbo."

"...What do you mean?"

"It's not over yet. I know who betrayed us that night and brought enemies into Zweilink."

Leorino nodded at Ebbo's shocked expression.

"The traitor is the only other survivor of that night...Edgar Yorke. I came to you to learn the truth about that traitor."

The Price of Fate

Ebbo listened in shock to Leorino's unfathomable confession.

"Edgar... He would never! How could someone so timid betray us?"

"But he did. After you ran beyond the gates, Ionia...*I* was prepared to die as I watched the gates close, never to return to the inner fortress again. But...*I* was still standing. *I* was perfectly conscious. It was Edgar who thrust his sword into *me*, ending my life with one blow."

The man's face, taut with scars, twisted in pain. Leorino knew he was forcing him back into those dreadful memories.

Ebbo... Ebbo, I'm sorry... I'm so sorry.

Leorino, too, felt an intense pressure as Ionia's memories filled his mind.

Never before had a memory come back to him so vividly, as if in a waking dream. It was as if he were no longer himself, as if he were being commanded by fate itself.

The boundary between past and present gradually blurred in Leorino's mind.

"When Edgar stabbed *me*, he also said...'This will be the end of you, too... They won't know what I've done.'"

"He said...what?"

"*I* was so desperate to mow down our enemies that I let him go. But I had already noticed by then. I had seen him use his Power to fan the flames set by the enemy and burn the plains of Zweilink to the ground."

Ebbo was astonished. He could hardly believe his ears.

"It may have been Zwelf soldiers who had started the fire, but it was Edgar who set fire to our men."

Many soldiers had died in those flames. The smell of burning human flesh. Blood and soot.

I'm not Ionia... I'm certain I'm not... So why does it hurt so much...?

Leorino groaned in pain.

"His sword, it went right through here..."

"Captain Ionia..."

"He laughed, you know. He looked me in the eye and laughed at me, at the wound that would surely kill me."

His mind filled with the color of blood.

The feeling of the sword piercing his solar plexus—a pain Leorino had never truly felt before—assaulted his senses. He bit his lip and endured the phantom pain.

Pale and holding his stomach, Leorino reached for Ebbo before he could think better of it. Cold sweat formed on his fair forehead.

"Are you all right...Captain?"

Leorino groaned and smiled. The word Ebbo used was familiar and comfortable. It might have been unintentional, but he was so happy to hear Ebbo call him, small and insignificant as he was now, "Captain."

"...I am no longer your captain."

Ebbo gasped at these words. Leorino extended his hand to Ebbo.

"...Look, Ebbo. My hands have no Power. How do they compare to your captain? Could I replace Ionia?"

But Ebbo did not offer an answer.

"Of course not. I was always ashamed of that. In fact, I still am. Not to mention..." Leorino looked at his legs. "I can't even run anymore. Did you know that Edgar Yorke died in a fall six years ago at Zweilink? I was there; he tried to take me down with him as he jumped off the outer wall."

Ebbo must have known of Edgar's death. He nodded, before the full weight of Leorino's words finally hit him.

"...He...he did *what*?"

"The fall shattered my leg. The doctors told me it was a miracle that I didn't have to have it amputated and that I can walk at all now."

Tears welled in Ebbo's eyes.

"...That's horrifying."

"It was my own fault. When I met Edgar, the memory of his betrayal suddenly came back to me. I was too young at the time to understand the significance of the memory or the danger of revealing it to Edgar, the culprit. Because of that, I foolishly pushed him into a corner...and Edgar went mad at the revelation of his crime."

"Did he kill himself?"

Leorino shook his head.

"I don't know anymore. Was it a suicide, or did he just fall in his delirium...? I lost most of my memories of the events before and after the fall. Even now, I can hardly remember anything that happened just before the incident. All I know is that along with my healthy legs, I lost my path to the culprit and the mastermind behind him."

A single tear rolled down Ebbo's scarred cheek.

It was heartrending to see him like that. He hadn't intended to make himself look like the tragic hero. His former subordinate had already suffered enough—he didn't want to torment him further.

"It was only about a year ago that I remembered everything again...and I've wanted to get to the bottom of his betrayal ever since. That's why I came from Brungwurt to the royal capital. But I've been so coddled the entire time that I haven't made much progress yet..."

Leorino was absolutely exhausted.

Confessing to Ebbo may have unshackled his mind.

Leorino had continued to hide the fact that he possessed Ionia's memories for so long. He was so tired of lying; he only wanted to finally free himself of this burden.

"...I have not given up yet. Reckless as it was, I decided to uncover the truth about the betrayal that day on Ionia's behalf."

But this was not a burden.

It was fate. It was Leorino's destiny, one he could never escape.

"Ebbo... Ebbo Steiger."

"Captain..."

Leorino clung to the man's hand and pleaded:

"...I can't let it go on. Ionia's memories keep me shackled to the past. I must expose the mastermind behind the traitor who sold out our kingdom to the enemy... *He*, Ionia, will haunt my dreams until I do."

Leorino's desperation shook Ebbo to his core. Forgetting his strength, he squeezed Leorino's slender shoulders tightly.

The pain that felt as if the bones in his shoulder were about to shatter was the price Leorino had to pay for the cruel fate Ionia had inflicted on Ebbo. Shedding tears, Leorino accepted the intense pain.

"Captain... Captain!"

"...Ebbo, please. I need you to help me. I know it may be painful to recall that day, but you are the only one who knows about Edgar Yorke now... So please, I beg of you."

That was when he heard the sound of multiple footsteps thundering down the corridor. Leorino came to his senses with a start.

Right! Dirk and Josef... They're still looking for me!

Leorino quickly pulled himself away from Ebbo.

"Ebbo... I'm out of time. There are people looking for me. If they find me here with you, they will misunderstand what happened and punish you."

Apart from the phantom pain in his stomach, his shoulder throbbed in Ebbo's unrelenting grip.

"I cannot reveal the truth about my memories to anyone else at the moment...especially not to my enemies. I absolutely cannot let the mastermind find out that I have Ionia's memories, and that *my own* memories have *returned*."

"...Captain. What should I do?"

Leorino frantically considered his options.

"How long will you be in the royal capital, Ebbo?"

"About a month. We are in the process of reorganizing the troops, and I don't know where I will be ordered to go when I receive my next assignment."

"Where are you staying until then?"

"I'm here at the training grounds more often than not, but I sleep in a temporary lodging in the royal capital."

"The temporary quarters in the Palace of Defense?"

Leorino assumed it must have been where Ionia stayed when he returned to the royal capital from the mountains, but Ebbo shook his head.

"Those are the officers' quarters. Regular soldiers like me stay in the commoner district."

Leorino nodded.

"I see. I promise...I will go see you. So wait for me. We'll continue this conversation later, I promise."

But Ebbo's face crumpled.

"Captain...I don't think I'll be of much help. Edgar was my only surviving companion... Until now, my last companion. And I...I still have a hard time believing your words. That period eighteen years ago is mostly a blur to me now. I don't know if I can be of any use."

Leorino's face twisted in pain as he heard Ebbo's anguished groan.

"That's all right. Please, Ebbo. We need to meet again and talk. The key is the mastermind behind Edgar, and that mastermind may still be at the center of our country's politics."

Ebbo raised his head with a start. Leorino nodded.

"Just...try to remember as much as you can about how Edgar was behaving up to that day. I'm so sorry for all the pain I've caused you, but I need just one more thing. Please. Please help me. Please, Ebbo...!"

Leorino watched Ebbo with desperation as he hesitated.

"...I understand, Captain. If you were to be reborn and appear before me again...I would always follow your orders once more."

"Ebbo...!"

Leorino's body relaxed as relief washed over him.

"Thank you... You should go now. Don't tell anyone that you saw me here. I'll sneak out and be sure to get back to you."

Ebbo hesitated.

He watched Leorino with a concerned expression.

"Is it safe to leave you here alone?"

The young man before Ebbo was clearly a nobleman who had nothing to do with combat. He looked pale, as if he was about to collapse.

But Leorino offered him a small smile and nodded.

"I'll be fine... Please, you must go!"

When Leorino confirmed that Ebbo had disappeared down the corridor, he slumped down to the floor where he stood.

He had to return to the gallery. He had to apologize to Dirk and Josef, who were still frantically looking for him.

But that didn't matter much when his body, exhausted by the stress and overexertion, refused to move.

He wondered if he should lie, pondering potential good excuses. If they learned Leorino had chosen to do something so reckless on his own, he would surely be punished by Gravis. He would likely not even be allowed to leave his own house anymore.

It would be difficult to contact Ebbo as it was, and he did not want to become any more of a caged bird, surrounded by walls upon walls.

But he didn't want to think about anything anymore.

He didn't want to lie anymore. He didn't want to deceive the people he cared about.

On the other hand, he had to keep his secret carefully concealed. At all costs, he had to avoid the Marquis of Lagarea's ability to erase all his memories.

Leorino realized he had been irresponsible. He knew he had caused trouble for many people. But he had made progress, incremental as it was. Leorino wanted to think that he had done what he had to do.

And yet, for some reason, Leorino was assaulted by regret and anguish.

He was too preoccupied with his own worthless pride to tell Gravis and Lucas the truth. He knew how foolish it was.

Even at a time like this, the only thing that appeared in his mind was Gravis's face.

I'm sure Ebbo will help me...so I'm certain I did all I could today.

Leorino was determined to see this through for the sake of this kingdom that Gravis was protecting.

He was. So why was he so miserable when he had finally made some progress?

He felt sorry for his own weakness and couldn't stop crying.

"Ugh... *Hic...* Vi... Vi."

Leorino buried his face in his knees and continued to shed big fat tears.

Leorino was crouched down on the floor with no energy to move when the door suddenly opened.

Leorino lifted his tearstained face, thinking that he had finally been found, only to widen his eyes in horror the next moment.

"...Whoa, fellas, you gotta see this!"

A vulgar whistle echoed through the room. It was the soldiers who had been walking with Ebbo earlier who now invaded the room.

"...And here we thought it was unfair for Ebbo to be having a good time all by himself, and we decided to mess with him...but look at that."

"And Ebbo's not even here."

The men barged in one by one, and the small, dusty room was filled with the smell of the men's savage sweat.

"...I knew it from the moment I saw those dainty, snow-white hands. And look, I was right. He's unbelievably beautiful."

The small room was tightly packed with the large men.

Leorino's thin body began to tremble. The men looked down at him in amusement, enjoying the sight.

"Aww, don't be scared... No need to cry, sweetie."

"Hey...pretty thing. We'll be nicer to you than that ugly man with the burns."

Blocked by the large soldiers, the light coming through the door did not reach Leorino. If anything, even darker shadows surrounded him now.

Leorino could not move.

And the last man to enter closed the door behind him.

The Shadow's Secret Orders

When Dirk and Josef reconvened, they were panting, their shoulders heaving.

They were confident in their stamina reserves, but the training grounds were simply too large. Running up and down the long corridors, they were both drenched in sweat. And despite their best efforts, Leorino had yet to be found.

"He's not on the second floor."

"Clearly... We've scoured the entire floor. We've sealed all three gates, but no one has left through them in the last half hour. These training grounds are the only thing for miles; it's all plains beyond these walls. As soon as they leave, we will know."

Unlike Josef, Dirk had the authority and the mind to take all the measures he could while searching.

Privately grateful, Josef bit his thumbnail anxiously.

"Assuming he hasn't gone downstairs, what are the chances he's on the third floor?"

Josef's shoulders slumped.

"...It's my fault for taking my eyes off him. I'm really sorry." Dirk bowed in apology.

He was fully prepared for Josef to cuss him out, but what reached his ears was only his dejected voice.

* * *

"Yeah, you're right. This is all because you took your eyes off him...but maybe you're not the only person to blame."

Josef was still thinking about the fact that Leorino had lied to Dirk about the dagger.

Leorino's personality made it unlikely for him to disobey. Josef was also searching for him so desperately because he genuinely believed he could have been kidnapped.

At the same time, he suspected that Leorino had chosen to vanish.

The only issue was that he didn't know why.

"...Have you told the lieutenant general yet?"

Dirk nodded at Josef's question.

"Yes, I just asked Schultz to inform the lieutenant general. He should get the message shortly."

"Once the lieutenant general finds out...the search for Master Leorino will become a huge ordeal."

"What else can we do? This place is far too large for us to search alone. Some things should be reported immediately. If anything, the later he learns of it, the angrier the lieutenant general will be."

It was then.

The air rippled, and the space next to the two men warped. Josef stumbled backward from the immense pressure, but Dirk was already familiar with the sensation.

"No..."

Tearing the fabric of space in two, a tall man appeared.

His dark cloak fluttered in the silent corridor. Josef felt as if his vision had been instantly shrouded by the veil of night.

"Your Excellency...?!"

Dirk bowed as respectfully as he could at the sudden appearance of the general. Watching Dirk and Josef, the man's eyes were endlessly dark and cold.

"Leorino is downstairs."

Dirk and Josef were startled by the man's words.

"H-how do you know where he is?"

But Gravis did not grace Dirk's question with an answer. Without addressing the two men, he silently turned on his heel and headed for the stairs.

The two men rushed after the general.

Why had Gravis suddenly leaped from the royal capital at this very moment? How did he know Leorino's whereabouts?

Cold sweat trickled down their spines at the unfathomable man.

But Dirk and Josef couldn't possibly have known.

They couldn't have known there was a shadow operating under Gravis's secret orders, watching over Leorino from the darkness, nor that the shadow had secretly followed Leorino as he descended the stairs and disappeared into a room with one of the soldiers. Nor could they know that the shadow had a voice that could directly convey what he saw and heard to Gravis.

And to Gravis, physical distance made no difference.

"Make haste. Leorino is with soldiers from the mountain troops."

Leorino frantically gathered his strength and glared at the approaching men. He felt around his chest under his cloak, but couldn't feel the hard object that was usually there.

He bit his lip with a start. He had deliberately dropped his dagger to meet with Ebbo.

The men who had been assigned to the very front of the venue were powerful warriors. The dagger would likely have made little difference for Leorino, but he was significantly worse off being empty-handed.

Feeling a chill run down his spine, Leorino glared at the man closest to him. If he showed any more signs of weakness or fright, that would only excite the men further.

"…Do not come any closer."

At these words, the smirking men stopped. Leorino focused his strength in his core to keep his voice from shaking.

"I'm…an old acquaintance of Ebbo's. If Ebbo learns of this, he won't let you get away with it."

"Oh, is that so? Weren't you crying just now?"

"Ebbo will be back soon."

Leorino said the first thing that came to mind.

Quite some time must have passed already. He wanted to stall for as long as he could, hoping that Dirk and Josef would find him soon.

"You know as well as I do... You know the Power Ebbo possesses."

The men stiffened.

Thank god. They knew about Ebbo's ability.

"If he wielded his superhuman strength in earnest, you'd quickly regret your choices... Not to mention the lieutenant general is also present at this training session. If anything happens to me, he *will* punish you."

The man closest to him clicked his tongue.

"You've got more nerve than I thought."

Unimpressed by Leorino's threats, the man quickly closed the distance between them and peered into Leorino's face.

Leorino held his breath.

Frightened as he was, Leorino kept himself from turning away. He could not show his weakness before the men at all costs.

"I guess you're really no stranger to Ebbo if you know about his Power."

The man suddenly reached for Leorino's chest.

Unable to take it any longer, Leorino shuddered.

The man's fingers snapped the clasp of Leorino's cloak open. Peeling him out of the cloak, he inspected Leorino's uniformed body.

"...Huh, so you work for the Palace of Defense. Who would've thought they hired beauties like you nowadays. Now imagine being stuck up in mountains like we are most of the time."

"...Don't touch me."

"I guess you're right, if Ebbo gets violent with us, death is definitely not off the table."

But as he said this, the man's fingers wandered teasingly around Leorino's chest. Those very same fingers began to undo the clasps on his collar.

"...Don't touch me!"

"Easy now."

He could hear the clasps coming undone one by one.

Leorino couldn't move, not even his hands or feet, feeling that if he provoked the man now, something terrible would happen.

"So I know the risks, but what a waste it would be to let you go. You're just so pretty."

The men audibly gasped at the sight of Leorino's fair neck peeking out from his shirt. The man's hand crawled up to his now exposed, slender neck. The man sneered at his trembling throat.

Lightly choking him, the man slipped his pinkie finger under his collar and traced his prominent collarbone. The sensation was so disgusting that Leorino could no longer hold back.

"...Stop!"

The sight of Leorino shaking off his hand and glaring at him while trembling seemed to awaken something sadistic in the man.

"Hey... Is Ebbo *really* coming back?"

Leorino didn't have the mental capacity to maintain his lie and averted his gaze before he could think better of it. The man grinned at him and cupped Leorino's small chin in his hand.

"...Oh, I see how it is. I guess that was just the best thing you could come up with, huh?"

"...Don't touch me..."

The man pushed Leorino's shoulder.

It was the exact spot Ebbo had just squeezed too tightly. He staggered at the pain and was pushed to the ground. Then the man slowly climbed on top of him.

"...No... Stop...!"

He quickly thrust his hands out, but his resistance was in vain, and before he knew it, both of his hands were in the man's grip.

The man covered Leorino's mouth. With that, Leorino was left without the use of his voice, nor his hands.

"Nnn... Ngh...!"

"Shh, hush now. Someone might hear you."

The other soldiers laughed, closing their ranks around him.

"Just humor us for a while. We won't take long."

Is this my punishment?

Punishment for deceiving Dirk and Josef and acting without their knowledge. Punishment for gouging Ebbo's old wounds. Punishment for continuing to lie to the people he cared about.

Leorino's eyes filled with despair.

Ebbo slipped out into the hallway and headed for the waiting area where many soldiers gathered after training.

His heart was still pounding in his chest.

He was still haunted by the young man who had suddenly appeared before him with news he could hardly believe.

First he was amazed by his extraordinary beauty, and then he was simply stunned by the unbelievable truth of what happened eighteen years ago.

It was as if the handsome young man was a ghost who had come back to haunt Ebbo with his past. He wondered if he had returned to condemn Ebbo for abandoning his friends and surviving. And yet.

"I'm so glad you're alive…!"

With those words, his slender body clung to Ebbo, tears streaming down his face. His body was warm. He told Ebbo of his regrets and apologized, but more than anything, when he said he was glad to see him again, he conveyed warmth.

Leorino's violet eyes and every word he spoke brought Ebbo back to the past in an instant.

Unlike the healed over scars left by the events of Zweilink, the scars from the hell Ebbo saw that day were still fresh inside him.

He still suspected that Leorino was trying to deceive him as part of a scheme of some sort. At the same time, he was convinced that he was the reincarnation of Captain Ionia. Ebbo had begun to trust him not with his mind, but with his heart.

*　*　*

The young man *must* have been the reincarnation of his beloved captain, Ionia Bergund.

Those eyes, that anguish. Ebbo would have never mistaken the eyes of the man he had fought alongside; the man he had nearly died with that day.

No matter how much his appearance may have changed, Ionia's soul had returned to Ebbo, begging him to fight once more.

Then the young man told him the shocking truth.

Edgar Yorke, the only other survivor, had been the traitor. He was the one who had taken Captain Ionia's life that day. If that were not enough, there was a mastermind behind him, and he was still a central figure in the kingdom's politics.

Everything the young man had said shook Ebbo to his core. He struggled to wrap his mind around it all. But Captain Ionia had come back to life and placed his trust in Ebbo.

Ebbo had already made up his mind by then.

When Ebbo returned to the waiting area, a fellow soldier approached him.

"Oh, Ebbo. Where have you been? Let's get back to our quarters already. Take off that armor and give it to the pages."

"…Yeah, I'm about to."

Ebbo emerged from his thoughts.

He removed his training breastplate and greaves. Handing them to the pages fulfilling their chores, his gaze swept across the room. It was then that Ebbo noticed something.

"Hey, where did David and the others go?" He asked his colleague.

The friends who had been with him just a moment ago were missing.

"Huh? Oh yeah, I guess they said they were going to look for you."

"…What?"

"They were grumbling about something when they left. How you were having a good time, or whatever."

When Ebbo heard this, his hair instantly stood on end.

"…Hey! Ebbo! Where are you off to now?!"

In an instant, Ebbo roughly threw his armor to the ground and bolted out of the waiting area.

No! They wouldn't...!

Praying that his instincts were wrong, Ebbo bounded with all the speed his body was capable of for the room where he had just left the young man.

Gravis had of course known that Leorino would be visiting the training grounds today. He had personally authorized Dirk to escort Leorino.

Both Lucas and Dirk were at the training grounds. In addition, one of the royal family's personal shadows was assigned to watch over Leorino. With so many people tasked to protect him, Gravis thought that Leorino was unlikely to find himself in any danger.

And yet Gravis had paled during a meeting at the royal palace when the message from the shadow materialized in his mind.

Leorino had run off alone at the training grounds and disappeared among the soldiers after their training. If that weren't enough, the shadow told him something absolutely preposterous: that Leorino approached one of the soldiers from the mountain troops and that they had entered a room together.

Unable to report on the situation inside the room, the shadow had asked for permission to enter. But Gravis rejected the request.

"I have some urgent business to attend to. This meeting is adjourned."

The general suddenly stood from his seat, and everyone present looked at him with astonishment.

Gravis could not help but confirm Leorino's safety personally. He was worried. At the same time, he was furious with Leorino for breaking their promise.

After how much I told him to keep himself out of danger... What a fool!

Breathtakingly beautiful as Leorino was, men were tripping over themselves to assault him the moment they saw him.

Still, to let him mingle with ruffians still reeling from the excitement of combat training without even a guard at his side was beyond reckless.

Moreover, it would be ludicrous to leave him alone with a soldier of the mountain troops, the boldest and most savage of the Royal Army.

But there must have been some explanation for Leorino's sudden activity. Leorino never acted without reason. If it was something concerning his secret, Gravis absolutely needed to know.

Twice before, Leorino had unknowingly communicated to Gravis that he was in danger. That had been the same mind speak offered by certain abilities. But Leorino never displayed even a hint of any special ability and seemed completely unaware of having used mind speech.

He didn't know if it was the royal blood flowing through Leorino that allowed him access to it. It could have been that Gravis was simply one-sidedly catching the cries of his mind.

In any case, Gravis doubted that Leorino would be able to consciously activate his mind speech as long as he was unaware of it.

At the moment, Gravis still couldn't hear Leorino's voice.

Still, he felt terribly uneasy.

So Gravis leaped toward the training grounds, where he met up with Dirk and Josef.

They now chased after him as he headed downstairs.

"I sincerely apologize. It was my fault for taking my eyes off him. I will accept any punishment."

Gravis turned around at Dirk's apology.

Gravis's expression was as cold as ever, but having known him for a long time, Dirk instantly realized that his superior was livid. Bold as he was, the thought that this ire was directed at him sent a cold sweat down Dirk's back.

"Taking your eyes off him was certainly a grave mistake, but you're not to blame this time."

"...What do you mean, sir?"

"Leorino *chose* to vanish from your sight."

Dirk and Josef gasped.

"H-he did...? Why on earth would he do that?"

Why did Leorino, with his strong sense of self-control, choose to disregard Lucas's order and run off on his own?

"Leorino went downstairs of his own accord and approached a certain man. I don't know what he intended."

But what was even stranger was how Gravis, who should have been back in the royal capital, was aware of Leorino's actions at all.

They were both confused and terrified in equal measure by the man's unfathomable power.

"Once we speak with Leorino, everything should fall into place."

Josef had had a bad feeling about this from the moment he learned Leorino had lied about the dagger's history. His premonition now confirmed, Josef bit his lip.

Master Leorino must have had his reasons... Some valid reason, surely...

But would those reasons be understood by the man before him?

Josef's legs trembled at the thought of how he might punish Leorino.

Having finished their training, the soldiers were gathered in the corridor on the first floor.

Their gazes were drawn to the tall man who suddenly descended the staircase. The man's imposing presence resonated through the soldiers' already heightened senses.

"Your Excellency..."

One after another, the men fell to their knees in a show of respect.

For most of the soldiers, this was the first time they had seen their general in person. But witnessing his overwhelming authority, perfect beauty, and unique eyes the color of darkness flecked with gold, it took but a glance to recognize him for who he was. The men were shocked by the general's sudden appearance.

Gravis ignored the kneeling soldiers, scanning the area with his glowing eyes in search of something.

Dirk and Josef were still staring at Gravis with a mixture of fear and awe.

* * *

With the men on their knees, his view was clear. Gravis pointed to the fourth door at the end of the corridor.

"...There. Leorino is in that room."

"Right... Josef, let's head in."

Nodding at Gravis's instruction, Dirk and Josef turned on their heels.

Then, suddenly, a huge soldier barreled into the room Gravis had just pointed at.

"...? What?!"

There was nothing normal about the man's ghastly appearance.

Gravis and the guards immediately tensed.

"Now!"

Josef was the first to react.

He took off like a wild animal and dashed into the room first. Gravis and Dirk followed.

A man's roar came from inside the room.

When they finally arrived, the scene that unfolded within was both the worst-case scenario, and yet somehow unexpected at the same time.

As soon as he thought he heard the man's roar, Leorino's hazy vision suddenly cleared.

The man who had climbed on top of him suddenly vanished.

"Captain...!"

Ebbo... You really came back...?

He should have left, and yet he was here.

Ebbo threw the man who had been tormenting Leorino to the corner of the room with his superhuman strength. His heavy body hit the wall with a tremendous noise.

"Ebbo...! He actually came!"

The other men had been holding Leorino down, but now rushed away to escape Ebbo's grasp.

The sheer might of Ebbo's special ability was incredible.

Once upon a time, when the wagon carrying Ionia and the other heavy soldiers had lost a wheel, he alone lifted the wagon with the passengers still inside as if it was no effort at all.

If Ebbo were to throw a man with full force—even a soldier of the mountain troops—every bone in his body would be shattered. The soldiers surrounding him now were well aware of Ebbo's inhuman strength.

The man he had thrown against the wall did not even twitch. Wrath emanated from Ebbo's entire body.

"…You bastards… You're dead to me!" Ebbo roared again.

Leorino sat up unsteadily, and Ebbo extended his arm to support him.

"Captain… Thank god."

"Ebbo… You came back for me…"

"I heard they'd followed me… Those pieces of shit."

"I should have been more careful… I'm sorry."

Leorino squeezed Ebbo's hand in gratitude, feeling the skin notched with scars under his.

It all happened so quickly from there.

"Master Leorino!"

Josef suddenly burst into the room. His eyes met Ebbo's.

The moment Josef saw Ebbo supporting Leorino, he instantly drew his sword, his hair standing on end.

"You bastard! Get your hands off of Leorino!"

Josef lifted the blade and charged at Ebbo.

"…Josef, no!"

"What…? You're the bastard who just came running, huh…?!"

Ebbo immediately rolled to the side, Leorino still in his arms. Josef clicked his tongue and adjusted his grip.

Josef had cast off his usual aloofness and wrapped his slender body in deadly intent.

"Let go of Master Leorino…or I *will* slay you where you stand."

Leorino realized that Josef had misunderstood. With Ebbo's help, he got to his feet.

"No! Josef…! Stop this! Don't hurt him! This man saved me!"

His master's desperate cry threw Josef for a loop.

"What... Lord Leorino?"

Confusion filled the room. The men who had cowered in fear at Ebbo's appearance were further startled by the sudden addition of this intruder.

"It's true. This man saved me. So sheathe that sword..."

That was when everyone in the room felt an indescribable pressure at the door and turned toward it.

An ice-cold presence entered the room.

"...Why are you...?"

Leorino couldn't even finish his sentence at the sight of the man.

"What the hell...? Why is the general here?!"

The soldiers quickly realized who the man was...

The extraordinary aura silently surrounding his entire body singed their battle instincts.

The experienced soldiers were not physically inferior to Gravis, but were nearly brought to their knees by the intimidating air he produced.

Ebbo was no exception.

"Dirk, close the door."

"...Yes, sir."

The adjutant closed the door behind him as ordered. Dirk then stepped in front of his superior and raised his voice.

"All of you, stand at attention for His Excellency the General!"

At Dirk's sharp command, the well-practiced soldiers immediately stood upright.

A painful silence fell over the room.

Gravis silently scowled at the soldier who had collapsed in a strange position by the wall, at the soldiers of the mountain troops who had presumably attacked Leorino, and at the hulking soldier who stood supporting him.

Finally, he looked at Leorino. The coldness of his gaze made Leorino's knees tremble.

He feared that Gravis already knew about his reckless behavior.

Leorino couldn't have known how awful he looked. All the fastenings of his jacket had been undone, and the shirt he was wearing underneath was open down to his stomach, revealing his fair skin. The marks of strangulation were clearly visible on his throat.

Her hair was disheveled and his cheeks tearstained. His battered appearance was clearly that of a victim who had narrowly avoided violent assault.

"Dirk, take all these men into custody."

"...Yes, sir."

Standing at attention, the soldiers trembled at these words. From their perspective, they were just hoping to have a little fun with the handsome young man who had come to visit Ebbo. It was a whim, nothing more. Their bodies had all been aroused from training; they only wanted to let off some steam.

The young man was so weak and helpless. They were convinced that as long as Ebbo didn't find out, no one would mind. When Ebbo came hurtling in, furious, they thought that as long as they calmed him down, they could still get away with it.

Only allowed to move their eyes, they looked to the general. The general's gaze was fixed on the young man.

"Leorino, why did you leave without a guard?"

The beautiful young man paled. The general and the young man must have known each other.

The men's knees began to shake as they realized they might have trifled with someone far beyond their rank.

Consumed by panic, one of the soldiers broke out of his stance and began making excuses.

"I—I only did it because David made me... Ghaaaaaa!"

The man shrieked. He could not continue.

Standing several meters away just a moment ago, the general instantly appeared in front of the man. In a flash, the general's fist shattered the man's jaw.

Everyone in the room was shaken by the punishing blow that came far too easily to the general. The men were some of the most skilled soldiers in the Royal Army. They did not expect the punishment to be so severe and so sudden.

"Aaaagaaahhhh…!"

As the man writhed in pain, Gravis shook off the few drops of blood that sprayed onto his fist.

"Save your excuses. I want no animals that break rules and attack the weak in my army."

His dark, glowing eyes passed over the men shivering in fear.

Then they caught Leorino's gaze once more.

Leorino shuddered.

Vi's not mad at these men… He's mad at me…

"Dirk, all the men gathered here are to be severely punished according to protocol. No exceptions."

"…Yes, sir."

Dirk bowed deeply at the general, as he stated his orders matter-of-factly, despite the piercing glint in his eyes.

Leorino was shocked by the order. He rushed toward Ebbo on trembling legs, as if he intended to protect his huge body, still standing at attention.

"Please, anyone but him! This man saved me…!"

Gravis spoke directly to Leorino for the first time since his arrival.

"…Leorino, I believe I told you what would happen if you put yourself in harm's way again."

Leorino despaired at his dismissive words.

But of course. He should have learned his lesson with the incident at the Palace of Defense. Even Sasha had been punished, despite being on Leorino's side. Once again, Leorino regretted disobeying Gravis's orders.

But he had to protect Ebbo at all costs. Fully aware he was inviting his ire, he desperately insisted.

"All of this was brought about by my irresponsible behavior. I will accept any punishment…but please, spare him!"

"Is this the man for whom you deceived Dirk, just so you could meet with him alone…?"

Leorino gasped. How did Gravis know that?

"B-but how…?"

"Did you think I would allow you to escape my enclosure and jump head-first into danger of your own accord, Leorino?"

When he glanced to Dirk and Josef, they also stared at Gravis in surprise.

Why... How did he know?

While Leorino stood there, trying to reconcile the facts, Gravis dispassionately relayed his instructions to his second-in-command.

"Dirk, interrogate this man first."

"Yes, sir."

"Your Excellency! Please!"

Dirk stood behind Ebbo, still standing at attention, as Gravis gestured at him with his chin. Gravis then ordered the hulking soldier to kneel and place his hands behind his back. Ebbo silently obeyed.

"You're coming with me, Leorino."

Gravis pulled him closer. The man's hands easily contained Leorino's resistance. Ebbo watched him with heartbroken eyes.

Writhing in Gravis's arms, Leorino desperately reached for Ebbo as Dirk restrained him.

"Mr. Dirk! Ebbo protected me! He doesn't deserve this!"

The arm restraining Leorino stiffened.

Ebbo... Ebbo is all that matters now...!!

Leorino cried out from Gravis's arms.

"Dirk! ...Let go of Ebbo...! He did nothing wrong! Ebbo! Ebbo!!"

Leorino struggled desperately and tried to run to the hulking soldier, but Gravis grabbed him carelessly by the shoulder.

"Aghh...!"

He hit the spot Ebbo had accidentally hurt earlier. Leorino yelped in pain and arched his back.

"Captain...!"

The moment he heard Leorino's scream, Ebbo's huge frame grew into a mountain. He pushed Dirk away, stood up, and extended his hand toward Leorino.

Leaping instantly to avoid his hand, Gravis glared at the soldier with murderous intent in his eyes.

Ebbo's eyes were those of a warrior defending his comrades.

The soldier roared at Gravis.

"Don't touch him…! Release Captain Ionia!"

It was at that moment that all the pieces clicked into place in Gravis's mind.

Why had Leorino risked so much to meet this soldier alone?

Why was Leorino so desperate to protect a man he had never met before?

And why was this scarred soldier referring to Leorino as "Captain"?

Gravis wanted to laugh out loud with delight.

Ah… Leorino, so it's true. Finally, we can move on. You really were…

He already knew the identity of this soldier. There was only one Ebbo in the world who Leorino… No, who *Ionia* had any attachment to.

"Judging by those scars…you must be Ebbo Steiger."

"Your Excellency…"

"The last time I saw you, you were fully wrapped in bandages. I see those burns scarred after all… You are the lone survivor of that unit. Your scars are those of a hero who defended this kingdom at Ionia's side."

The slender body in his arms began to tremble at Gravis's words.

Delight filled Gravis once more.

…Ah, so you've noticed. We both know your secret now.

Gravis looked down at Leorino, pale and trembling, with a shockingly tender smile.

"Ebbo Steiger, you and I must meet and speak again."

"Sir…"

"Of course, you'll be there, too, Leorino."

Noise came from beyond the door. Lucas's search for Leorino must have been in full swing by now.

Gravis picked Leorino up.

With a look of despair on his face, Leorino still reached for the hulking soldier.

"No, Ebbo… Ebbo!"

Gravis allowed no resistance.

"Dirk, this man is not to be punished, but do detain him for now. I trust you can handle the rest."

"Yes, sir. But, Your Excellency…"

"I will take Leorino with me to the royal capital… Guard, Leorino will not return to the Cassieux estate for a little while. He will stay in my palace. Let the Cassieux family know."

Josef's eyes widened at this, but he was too shaken by Gravis's intensity to speak.

Gravis held Leorino firmly in his arms once more. His gaze met Leorino's frightened violet eyes.

"Come now, Leorino."

His soft, helpless, slightly trembling body was beyond precious.

Gravis brought his lips to Leorino's shapely ear and whispered:

"It's been eighteen years… Now, whatever shall I call you?"

Come, Leorino. No, Ionia. Let's have a nice long talk somewhere where no one will disturb us.

With that, he took Leorino away.

The Soul in My Hands Once More

He was brought to Gravis's palace, to the same room as before.

Leorino was still in his arms staring at Gravis with a frightened look.

Not wanting to miss even the slightest shift in his expression, Gravis watched him, his eyes glowing gold. But despite the look in his eyes, Gravis seemed to be smiling.

"Your Excellency..."

Leorino began, but could speak no further.

It was only natural that Gravis would be furious. All of this was brought about by Leorino's own reckless behavior, but his heart was nearly bursting with anxiety at the thought of another possibility.

"...Ah!"

Gravis threw Leorino roughly onto the bed. The impact knocked the air out of his lungs. The man's large frame leaned over him. Leorino could do nothing but cower and accept Gravis's merciless, unconcerned behavior.

In a panic, Leorino rushed to raise himself and slide up the bed, but he was grabbed by the ankle and immediately pulled back down.

"Ah! ...N-not my legs... Please, anything but that...!"

Perhaps the fact he had grabbed Leorino by his right ankle meant the man was taking pity on him after all. When desperately trying to stop him yielded no results, Gravis rolled Leorino onto his back, parted his legs and pressed him into the bed with his thick waist.

With that, Leorino was completely immobilized.

*   *   *

"...Right, then, where shall we begin?"

Leorino frantically tried to push Gravis off, but his steel-like body would not budge.

"...Let's see. First, let's hear your excuse for your ill-advised one-man adventure, Leorino."

Leorino bit his lip.

"At least let me sit up when we speak... I refuse to talk in this position!"

"Why not? You were in a similar position just a moment ago."

"N-not by choice..."

"You do realize those men nearly had their way with you back there, yes?"

At these words, the full impact of how narrowly he had avoided assault finally caught up with Leorino. Looking down at him as he paled, Gravis smiled.

"Will you insist you just wanted to talk to Steiger? I could say the same. I want to talk to you."

"...You may say that, but what you're doing is no different from those soldiers. It's c-cowardly of you to use force like this!"

Gravis laughed at his naive objection.

"'Don't hurt my legs. You're a coward.' ...Hah, if asking nicely was all you had to do to get ruffians to back off, there would be no need for swords or fists in the world."

"That's not what I..."

"No matter what I seem to tell you, you keep finding yourself in these situations. What am I to do with you?"

Gravis leaned in, bringing his face close to Leorino's.

"Why did you go against my orders and put yourself in danger? I thought I forbade you from that."

"I was prepared to be punished...!"

"Is that so...? Well, look at you now. What is this, then?"

"...Ugh."

Leorino hadn't noticed, but his neck and collarbone, exposed by his ripped-open shirt, still bore the marks of the man's fingers that had choked him. His shoulders were hidden by his shirt, but they too displayed visible bruises left by Ebbo's grip.

"I told you that I would not allow anyone to hurt you, not even yourself. I told you that I would not give you any more freedom unless you accepted that you were under my protection."

Although Gravis appeared violent at first, he was holding himself back so as not to crush Leorino with his muscular body. But in his desperation, Leorino did not notice.

If anything, he was fiercely defiant toward the man who was holding him down with such force.

"...You can't hurt me like this."

Acting on impulse, Leorino dug his nails into the back of Gravis's hand as hard as he could. Blood began to seep out from beneath his nails.

Gravis narrowed his eyes slightly.

"I understood the risks! I knew I had to act, no matter what might happen to me...!"

"And when something *did* happen to you, did you not think that Dirk would be held responsible? Or how it might make your family feel?"

Leorino bit his lip at these words.

Of course he'd considered that, and more. But he'd needed to meet with Ebbo at all costs, so he'd decided to go through with it, no matter how many issues he would be causing for others along the way. Perhaps there had been a better way. But at the time, it was all Leorino could do.

He was ready to be punished.

He was scared to death when the men had nearly assaulted him, but that too was the product of his selfish ego. If that was to be his punishment, he was prepared to endure it.

"Did you think I wouldn't blame myself when you got hurt?"

Leorino's heart skipped a beat at that. At the same time, he felt anger welling inside him.

Why would I think that, when you said you don't need me by your side...?!!

Leorino had made up his mind the last time he was brought to this detached palace. Little by little, he would learn to stand on his own. He had killed his yearning for Gravis, so that he would not rely on him anymore; so that he would not grow any more attached to him. Even now, Leorino was desperately trying to suppress his desire for Gravis to accept him for who he was.

"I can't spend my entire life protected by you and my family. And in any case, it was *you* who rejected me first, saying I wasn't worthy to be by your side…!"

The large body casting a shadow on him seemed to swell with anger for the briefest moment.

"When have I *ever* said that? Is that what brought you to be nearly gang-raped by those soldiers?"

Of course not. But that had been the end result.

Leorino bit his lip.

Gravis cupped Leorino's cheek.

"Do you really hate being protected by me so much?"

"No…"

Leorino's eyes widened. He could smell the faint scent of blood.

Bringing his hand to Gravis's, he felt something wet on his skin. Looking at his hand in a panic, he saw his fingers and his nails were smeared with blood.

I did that…!

"Sir! I, ah…! Your hand…!"

Gravis, however, did not pay the wound any mind. He watched Leorino as he paled, then finally sneered.

"How do you plan to protect yourself if you tremble at the sight of such a little cut?"

Grabbing his slender wrist, Gravis pressed Leorino's hand forcefully against his own stomach.

"Once upon a time, you would have turned the enemy's body into a mist of blood and chunks of flesh—just like this, just by placing your hands on their stomach or arm."

Leorino gasped.

A trail of blood appeared on Gravis's shirt. Leorino turned sheet-white as he realized what the man's gesture meant.

"Sir…"

"You don't have to call me that anymore, do you? Just call me what you did *back then*."

Gravis lifted Leorino's hand and ran his tongue over Leorino's blood-stained fingertips.

Leorino gasped at the hot, wet sensation. The feeling that ran from his fingertips up his spine was horrifically arousing.

"Leorino... Your fingertips are so soft, so sweet."

"Sir... Th-that's not—"

"...Your fingers were much harder back then. They were the hands of a swordsman, the hands of a warrior fighting by my side."

The blood from his fingertips stained Gravis's lips red.

"Don't... Let go, hng..."

Gravis squeezed his fingers hard. Leorino winced in pain.

"Leorino...would you like me to remind you once again how easy it would be to hurt you right now?"

Gravis's eyes flashed darkly.

Leorino desperately tried to resist, out of fear and out of spite. He twisted his body with all his might, but to Gravis, keeping him right where he wanted must have been mere child's play.

Gravis grabbed both of Leorino's flailing arms and pinned them above his head.

Gravis's bony fingers wrapped around Leorino's slender wrists.

"...Come now. Is that all the fight you have in you, Leorino? I may just fall asleep."

No! Absolutely not! I refuse to yield to physical strength...!

Leorino swore as best he could at the man taunting him, the only resistance he could muster.

"...H-how are you so strong?! ...Hnnng—"

But he couldn't escape.

No matter how desperately he fought back, he was forced to give in to Gravis's strength in the end.

Ionia would have been able to free himself with a twist of the wrist. As long as he could touch something with the palm of his hand, he could shatter it in an instant and immediately regain his freedom.

Except, this wasn't Ionia's body.

That was Leorino's reality. Held in an overwhelmingly tight grip, he could move neither his wrists nor his neck pressed into the bed.

"Unf!"

Leorino moaned in pain.

Gravis closed his hands tighter around his wrists.

"...Stop struggling. You'll only hurt yourself."

Tears welled in the corners of Leorino's eyes. The fear filling him was bone-crushing.

"No... Stop..."

Gravis's large body slowly leaned onto his slender frame. Leorino was shaking now.

I'm scared... It hurts... I'm scared...

Pain was a cruel thing.

It wormed its way into all his thoughts.

The corners of Leorino's eyes twisted in pain, and before he knew it, large tears came spilling forth. His eyes grew misty and vacant.

"...Breathe."

Gravis noticed Leorino was on the verge of fainting.

He was shocked at how fragile he truly was.

In truth, Gravis wasn't doing very much at all. If he used his full force, he would easily shatter Leorino's wrists. And if he shifted his full body weight onto him, Leorino would suffocate. Even with his excited mind, he was careful not to hurt Leorino's delicate body. Still, Leorino knew little of violence— he would have hardly been able to withstand a glimpse of Gravis's true strength.

Compared to Ionia's strong body, he couldn't be more different.

"...Leorino."

Big fat tears spilled from Leorino's eyes.

As the blood rushed back to his fingertips, he became aware of the throbbing pain in his wrists. His shoulders had hurt to begin with and he had overworked his legs, and now his body felt like he was being torn limb from limb.

Leorino didn't even realize when he began sobbing.

"Ah, I went too far... I never know when to stop, do I? You're just so *weak*."

Those words alone felt like a stab to the heart. This was it, Leorino thought: Gravis had finally grown disillusioned with him. His tears of pain turned into tears of humiliation.

Gravis frowned remorsefully.

"Don't cry... Did I hurt you? My apologies."

"...I-if you're going to apologize, then let go of me..."

He could feel Gravis's lips—those same lips that had once wiped away his tears—briefly graze his closed eyelids. Leorino's face grew hot at the soothing gesture.

"...Promise me you'll never put yourself in harm's way again."

Leorino shook his head, his thoughts still refusing to focus.

I can't promise you that. If he found himself in that situation again, he was certain he would make the same decision.

He didn't want to lie anymore. He wanted to be honest.

Even frightened and in pain, Leorino still refused to break, and Gravis smiled at him, visibly impressed.

"Fine. I suppose we'll just have to repeat this exercise whenever necessary. Once you've made up your mind, you never give up... Just like *him*."

Leorino shuddered at these words. Gravis moved his hand to the back of his head and pulled him close.

"Leorino. Look at me."

Gravis's beauty was so close to Leorino now that his breath nearly caught in his throat at the sight. Gravis's lips closed around Leorino's.

"...Mmf!"

He claimed Leorino's lips hard and fast. Leorino desperately struggled against him. But gently, passionately, Leorino surrendered. He couldn't resist. The canopy of the bed caught the inelegant gasps escaping his slender throat.

"Now...let's talk about the other matter you've been keeping from me."

Leorino panicked. He tried to quickly twist out of Gravis's grip.

"...Vi— Prince Gravis! Please, let go of me...! Your Highness!! Ah! Ow..."

Leorino had turned his face away to avoid the touch of Gravis's hot lips, only for the man to sink his teeth deep into the fair skin of Leorino's exposed throat the next moment.

Leorino's eyes widened in shock. Seeing him tremble at the sharp pain and the violence inflicted upon him, Gravis ran his tongue along the bite mark of his own making, as if trying to soothe him.

The touch of Gravis's tongue summoned vivid images in Leorino's mind.

They were the memories of Ionia and Gravis's first and last night together. Leorino's heart was shaken by the feelings for Gravis carved into his memory.

"...Don't be silly. I've finally gotten my hands on you. You think I'd let you go so easily?"

"...Y-Your Highness..."

The heat of Gravis's tongue on his wound brought a sob spilling from Leorino's lips.

"I am not 'Your Highness,' silly. Call me 'Vi' the way you used to."

The man's fingers gently traced Leorino's hot, wet cheeks as if he were handling something fragile.

"Say my name...Leorino."

Leorino wanted to scream. He wanted to shout Gravis's nickname with all his might. But he couldn't.

"Your Highness, I have no idea what you're talking about..."

Gravis pulled his slender body into a tight hug.

"...Or would you rather...I call you by another name...Io?"

"...!"

Vi and Io.

The names that could only be called by each other—and no one else.

Leorino looked at Gravis.

His wavy black hair, his Prussian blue eyes flecked with gold, which so strongly resembled the night sky. His voice, so much more alluring at his current age, called his name just as he remembered it, and joy surged through Leorino's heart like an electric current.

Leorino quivered slightly as Gravis watched him with so much fondness, before finally smiling.

"...Have you noticed that you've reverted to calling me 'Your Highness' yet?"

Captivated by Gravis's smile, for a moment, Leorino could hardly process his words.

"Lucas still calls me 'Your Highness.' It's an old habit, from back when I was younger than you. Come to think of it... Leorino, when we first met, you also called me 'Your Highness' for a little while. Force of Ionia's habit, I suppose."

Something welled deep in Leorino's chest.

"Do you still insist on calling me 'Your Highness'?"

Leorino couldn't reply.

"Io... Ionia, I've missed you so much."

Ah, finally we meet again...

His familiar scent. His face. His unchanging voice. Everything about Gravis was so dear to him, and yet so confusing. Here was the man he finally got to see after eighteen long years as Ionia once more. And yet here he was, interacting with him as Leorino.

I've missed you, too, Vi.

Leorino tightly shut his eyes.

Ionia's soul engraved in Leorino's memories was screaming.

"Io... I've missed you so much. Eighteen years have passed since the day I lost you, and you have no idea how much I regretted all my choices ever since."

"...Your Highness..."

"Don't call me that... Please."

Leorino's slender body was trembling. But then again, so was Gravis.

"Please...call my name the way you used to, Io."

Leorino's throat tightened as the memories came flooding back.

He wished he could have said he was Ionia without hesitation.

But he wasn't. He was not the young man who had once upon a time been Gravis's best friend.

Leorino desperately struggled to regain control of his mind with what little ego he had left.

"Your Highness...I'm sorry. I am not the man you remember. I am not Ionia..."

As he fought back tears and the pain in his chest, Gravis tightly squeezed his hand.

"Why do you keep saying that? Why are you so adamant about denying that Ionia lives on inside you? That was why you went to see Ebbo, was it not?! That was why you'd returned to us!"

Yes. But also, no. Leorino closed his eyes.

"I admit, I was born with Ionia Bergund's memories."

A spark of joy flared in Gravis's eyes.

"Why...why did you keep this from me?"

"Because I...I am not the Ionia Bergund you seek."

Gravis only stared at him.

"I've told Lucas the same thing: I am Leorino Cassieux. A-and you...you agreed with me back then. I thought you understood."

"Nonsense. You are Leorino, of course, and you possess Io's memories; what's wrong with that? Why did you feel the need to hide it?"

"It's not 'nonsense' to me!"

Leorino groaned in despair. He lifted his throbbing hands and covered his eyes.

"...I wanted to tell you. So much, you can't even imagine. Ever since I got my memories back. I've wanted to this entire time."

Gravis frowned painfully at his confession.

"…I wanted to see you. When I came to the royal capital, when we finally met, I was so unbelievably happy…"

"Then why?! Why didn't you tell me? You must have realized how long I… How long *we* had been waiting for you."

"That's exactly why… All the memories in the world can't change the fact that…I can never be the Ionia you seek…and I wanted to escape that humiliation."

"Humiliation…? Why would you call it that?"

Gravis shook his head, unable to comprehend.

"Look…"

Leorino lifted his arms and held his hands out in front of Gravis.

"I've retained nothing from those days. My skinny body, my legs that barely move… I'm nothing like what he used to be…!"

"Io…"

Finally, Leorino screamed.

"Stop! I am *not* Io! I can *never* be Ionia again…! The man you entrusted with your back *died* that night!"

His cry of grief filled the air.

"I wanted to protect Ionia's memories… I can't be Ionia, even if you expect that of me. I can never be him, not with my body…!"

Gravis heaved a deep sigh. The sound made Leorino shudder.

"…Is that why you've hidden it for so long?"

Leorino hid his face in his hands. His shoulders shook as he choked back his sobs.

"Let me see your face, Leorino."

But Leorino refused.

"I think…Lucas and I, and our combined feelings for Io, have put you under a lot of pressure." The man continued. "We were so desperate to see Ionia once more that you thought we'd be disappointed with you… Is that right?"

Leorino could neither deny nor confirm.

He only watched Gravis's starry-sky eyes through tears.

"...You would never let me have your back."

It hurt Leorino to finally face his inferiority complex. But he desperately squeezed out the words:

"I was afraid that you would grow disillusioned with me because I was so helpless that...you could never entrust your back to me."

Gravis took Leorino's hands in his and revealed his small, tearstained face.

"...God, you're so stupid. And so, *so* stubborn."

With that, Gravis pulled Leorino into a tight embrace.

"I never thought that you would leave me for such silly reasons... Because you have no Power in your hands, because you're helpless?"

"They're not silly..."

"I'm not the one still clinging to the past. You are, Leorino."

Leorino shuddered.

"I knew you had secrets."

"...Vi."

"I decided that if you shared them with me, I'd finally say it."

Gravis raised the corners of his lips when Leorino automatically used his nickname.

"I'd tell you that I love you, and that I want to beg for your love."

"...What did you just...?"

Leorino's eyes shot open.

"I love *you*, Leorino."

Leorino immediately shook his head. He couldn't believe Gravis's words.

Gravis had told him his heart had died that day. He said he would always yearn for Ionia.

"No, you're lying... I know you said you wouldn't let Ionia...wouldn't let *me* fight by your side."

"Well, of course not. I would never let you fight."

Hearing those words, tears spilled from Leorino's eyes once more.

"You're so weak, and so precious, and I want nothing but to keep you safe. How could I ever let you fight?"

When Leorino finally calmed down, they decided to speak, and Gravis picked Leorino up and sat him down on his lap.

Seeing him so tired and weak, Gravis leaned back against the headboard and let Leorino rest against his chest.

"I'd spent half my life with you in your previous life—with Ionia. You remember that, don't you?"

Leorino remembered. He had dreamed of those memories, those feelings for so long that they were now his own.

"You knew, didn't you? I loved Ionia, and I wanted to spend the rest of my life with him. That had been the plan. Until that day."

Leorino was struck by all the emotion contained in his words.

They had won the battle. But Ionia died, leaving this precious man behind. Their dreams of a future together had come to an abrupt end.

Tears filled Leorino's eyes once more. Ionia had reached his hand to the stars, his final wish being to tell him those three magic words.

"I thought I was going to live with my feelings for him for the rest of my life. I thought I would die with them... But then you appeared, Leorino."

Gravis frowned painfully.

"At first I couldn't understand my attachment to you. When I realized that I couldn't let you go, regardless of if you truly were Ionia...I thought I was betraying him."

"Vi..."

"But I...I couldn't help it."

Gravis laughed at himself.

"I just couldn't. Somewhere along the way, I...I began to want you so badly, so maddeningly that I...I didn't want to let you out of my arms for a single moment, Leorino."

Listening to the man confess to his sins, Leorino's heart was shaken and torn to pieces.

The man before Leorino still possessed that same masculine beauty he had in the past. But it was clear he had aged. The impression Gravis gave off as a young boy, when he was somewhat restless and driven by something, had faded, and he now wore the air of a dignified, calm, mature man.

"Leorino…can my longing for Ionia not be reconciled with my love for you?"

The man's large hand smoothed back Leorino's bangs.

"If I don't throw away all my memories of Ionia, am I not allowed to love you?"

Leorino cast his eyes down. He asked himself if he wanted this man to give up his memories of Ionia.

"Ionia, whose memory you've inherited, was very dear to me. When I was forced to suffer the fate imposed on me, he was the only man I could entrust my back to. Please, don't deny me his soul and our memories… He was part of my life before I met you."

Leorino gasped.

But of course. His situation was so very different from theirs. Gravis's life had continued beyond that fateful day.

"I want you to be yourself. I never wanted you to become Ionia. I just want you to know how glad I am that Io's memories persist within you."

The man softly pressed a kiss to his fair forehead.

"…I can only ever be Leorino… A-and you don't mind?"

"I want you to be just the way you are. And together, I want us to continue honoring Ionia's memory for as long as we live. Or is that too big a burden to bear?"

Listening to Gravis's heartfelt words, Leorino couldn't hold back his tears. The words naturally followed.

"…D-did you realize today…? When Ebbo c-called me 'Captain'…?"

"No. Actually, I've suspected it for a while now."

"S-since when…?"

"I wonder… I suppose when you were crying after what happened with Lucas."

He gently lifted Leorino's hands.

"You cried that your slender hands hold no Power, and that got me thinking... Though I only became convinced a few moments ago."

Leorino's heart couldn't take it any longer. Tears streamed down his cheeks, and sobs hitched in his throat.

At some point, his sobbing had turned into wailing.

These past few months had been so difficult, riddled with lies and feelings of inferiority.

"I—I thought you'd be so disappointed... We finally got to meet again and I'm...I'm so pathetic, so—"

"Don't be silly. I could never be disappointed with you. I... Leorino, you don't even know how much I've pined for you. Don't tell me you didn't notice how obsessed I was with you."

Gravis's arms embraced him tightly.

"B-but you... You can't entrust me with your back now that I'm Leorino. You said so yourself... So I figured I didn't deserve to stay by your side..."

"When did I say that?"

Heaving with sobs, Leorino explained.

"You told Theodor...that I'm too weak to fight. That you wouldn't entrust me with your back."

At that moment, Gravis felt the strength drain out of him as everything fell into place, and he hugged Leorino tightly.

"You fool, you absolute buffoon... You were avoiding me because of that? You overheard a fragment of our conversation and jumped to conclusions... You're unbelievable."

Gravis scolded Leorino and gently pressed their foreheads together.

"...If you'd listened a little longer, you'd know I told Theodor I'd be your shield from now on."

Leorino's eyes widened.

"I don't need any guards or shields anymore. It's your turn to entrust *me* with *your* back."

"You're living life to the fullest. You are my miracle. What more could I ever ask of you?"

Hearing these tender words, Leorino covered his face and cried so hard his entire body shook.

"I wanted to be born strong enough to protect you once more… I guess it just…wasn't meant to be."

"…Leorino."

Leorino felt the hot breath from Gravis's cool lips before they closed around his own. His tongue moved soothingly inside his mouth. Once Leorino calmed down, the man slowly pulled away.

"…Vi."

Gravis smiled softly, teasingly.

"I suppose you really have been struggling to find your place in the world."

"…I thought I couldn't stay by your side if I didn't."

"Have I ever wanted anything for you other than for you to smile and stay safe?"

Remembering all that had happened, it took Leorino a moment to shake his head.

"That's all I ever wanted for Ionia, too. It was my status that forced him to choose to be my human shield. But I just… I only wanted him to stay by my side."

"And…" He closed his eyes, as if in prayer, and gently brought his forehead to Leorino's once more. "Leorino…*you* are now the reason I want to protect this country."

Leorino's violet eyes were a complex mix of joy and worry.

"When we no longer had anything to hide from each other…I was going to tell you that I want your permission to love you. That's why I kept waiting for this moment."

"Vi…"

"I will be your shield from now on. So entrust me with your back in this life."

Traces of blood still stained the back of Gravis's hand. Even someone as weak as Leorino could hurt Gravis. Indeed, Leorino had caused the man much anxiety and pain all along.

"…I'm not young anymore. To court you when we're so far apart in age might be laughable to most."

The age gap between Leorino and Gravis was a whole nineteen years, nearly enough to be father and son.

"But I don't care what they say... Let me love you, destiny and all."

Here sat a man who had set aside his position as royalty, as a general, and who now begged for Leorino's love with all his heart as a mere man.

Still shedding tears, Leorino brought his arms around Gravis's neck and clung to him with what little strength he had left.

They embraced tightly, melting away each other's boundaries.

"Please, stay by my side from now on. Don't you dare leave this world before me. It took eighteen whole years for your irreplaceable soul to return to me. I don't want to lose you again."

Leorino nodded at his words.

He wanted to respond to the man's feelings. At that moment, the words of his father August echoed in Leorino's mind.

"It's about how you want to live your life."

Of course. He would likely still struggle with feelings of inferiority and jealousy toward Ionia in the future. But he couldn't remain in his shell when the man spared no words in offering him his love.

Leorino steeled his resolve and summoned up his courage. Now was the time to acknowledge how fragile, how weak his heart truly was and finally move forward.

"...Me too."

"Leorino...?"

"I want to be with you, too."

Hearing Leorino's answer, Gravis's arms tightened around him hard enough to hurt. With that sweet pain, the anguish he had been carrying in his heart slowly faded away.

Ah... This is where my battle begins.

No longer as the man with Ionia Bergund's memories, he would now begin his fight to respond to Gravis's love as Leorino Cassieux. It would not be a test of physical strength, but of fortitude of mind, and of courage.

For that reason, he had to make peace with the past. There was one last thing Ionia wanted to tell him. So Leorino had to convey his feelings and secure their future.

"Vi...ever since you first met in the forge...you have been the only thing that mattered."

"...You speak of Ionia's memories?"

Leorino nodded.

"You were royalty, and Ionia was a commoner. And you were younger, the person he had to protect... He was convinced his feelings were all in vain."

Leorino smiled as he cried.

"But all along, in his heart, Ionia kept saying 'I love you' to you. In the snowy mountains, from the top of the fortress walls of Zweilink... Looking up at the starry sky, he never stopped saying it."

Gravis clenched his teeth.

"Even as he lay on the ground dying that day, he could see the starry sky. He reached for it and kept shouting... He screamed of his love for you."

After eighteen long years, Ionia's final thoughts had finally reached the man who needed to hear them most.

Gravis pressed his forehead into Leorino's shoulder.

"Io... Io... Ionia..."

In a muffled voice, he called the dead man's name again, and again, and again.

Leorino waited patiently until the man could speak again.

When he finally lifted his head, he saw infinite sorrow in his starry-sky eyes, and yet Gravis smiled.

"Violet eyes... That explains everything... You truly had Ionia inside you."

Leorino nodded.

He felt that his past life as Ionia and his current life as Leorino were melting together, converging into a brand new Leorino Cassieux the world had never seen before.

"Yes. But...don't call me 'Io' anymore."

"...Leorino."

Leorino watched Gravis closely.

"I think it was Ionia's feelings drawing me toward you at first. They were so intense, so…hopeless, in just the same way as Ionia in my memories devoted his blood and his loyalty to you."

Gravis's face twisted in pain. Leorino placed his hand on his cheek to comfort him.

"But that night, when you found me in the royal gardens…your scent revived so many memories that it brought tears to my eyes, and at the same time, I wanted you to see me for who I am now, not Ionia. I think that at that point I was already…hopelessly attracted to you."

The smile on Gravis's face encouraged Leorino.

"Your Excellency…Vi…I've hated myself for a long time for being so helpless."

"Leorino…"

When Gravis frowned and tried to deny it, Leorino gently pressed a finger to his lips.

"I'm hopelessly timid, and if you hadn't confessed first, I might have never had the courage to tell you how I felt."

His body was exhausted, but he gently brought his lips to the man's. It was the first time Leorino had ever sought out Gravis himself.

"Forgive me for being such a coward."

Leorino peered into Gravis's eyes with silent determination and smiled as best he could.

"But if…if you don't mind me being the way I am, then I don't want to live my life hating myself anymore. I want to believe that my heart is all I need to offer you my love."

"…Leorino."

"I love you just as much as Ionia did. Although I am much younger… much more inexperienced than you…"

He embraced him with the hands he placed around his muscular back.

"…I love you, Gravis Adolphe Fanoren. My heart and my loyalty belong to you. So…please grant me permission to love you, too."

"Leorino…"

Leorino gathered his courage and looked into Gravis's eyes. The starry sky within shone so brightly that it seemed to consume him, his heart, his everything.

"I was born to meet you. That's why...I never want to leave you again."

Leorino placed his entire heart and soul into his embrace. And he prayed.

Let me love you. I want you to finally be mine.

No matter how many times I am reborn, I want to be yours forever.

Gravis slowly embraced the precious young man, as he finally ran out of strength and fell into a deep slumber, practically fainting.

The irreplaceable person he thought he had lost forever was back in his arms.

The one soul who could overcome the difference in status and age, who with single-minded devotion wanted nothing but to be by Gravis's side. In his long lonesome life, the soul he had once lost now returned to his hands. He was ready to scream with glee.

They were two separate people, with only the feelings in their violet eyes persisting as a promise engraved in their souls.

But in Gravis's mind, they were of perfectly equal worth. They were both in the center of his heart as one and the same, yet separate and distinct.

They were as different as they could possibly be, and yet he loved them equally.

No matter how many times they were reborn, they would surely meet again and be drawn to each other.

"...I really missed you."

Gravis whispered softly in his ear so as not to disturb him. Then a small murmur, barely more than an exhale, spilled from Leorino's lovely lips.

That faint whisper. A special name that he had allowed only his late best friend to use. A name he thought he would never hear again.

Hearing that tender syllable spoken with such affection once more, Gravis's tears silently trickled down his cheeks.

A Morning for Two

When Leorino woke up, it was dim inside the canopied bed.

"Ah, you're awake."

"...Vi...?"

He felt the bed move as Gravis sat up.

Had Gravis been holding him until now? He felt strangely empty when the man's warmth pulled away, but his large body slowly enveloped him once more. Gravis's lips gently grazed against his.

"...Mmf."

His cool, damp lips pulled away before long.

Still half-asleep, it made Leorino feel unusually lonesome.

"How are you feeling?"

"Vi..."

Leorino was still barely awake when Gravis whispered to him. But he was so glad to hear his voice, he smiled at Gravis, his head empty of thought.

"Vi... I'm great."

The man laughed quietly. He placed his hand on Leorino's forehead, feeling for his temperature, before proceeding to slowly stroke his head, helping him wake up. Prompted by his touch, Leorino slowly emerged from the depths of his blissful slumber.

"You don't have a fever. Think you can get up?"

"...Yes... Good morning."

Leorino's freshly awakened mind recalled the events of the previous night. As his memories returned to him, it was not without confusion, shame, and anxiety. The last thing that emerged from the back of his mind was joy. But Leorino lowered his eyelids, suddenly anxious if he was truly allowed to enjoy this moment.

"Look at me, Leorino."

"Yes, b-but... Ah—"

The handsome man closed the distance between them once more and slowly covered Leorino's lips. He ran his tongue over Leorino's mouth, asking for permission to enter. When Leorino obediently parted his lips, Gravis's hot tongue slipped inside his mouth. As the man leisurely moved his tongue, Leorino was driven further and further from his unruly thoughts, losing himself in the pleasure.

Gravis's lips pulled away and fell back onto his time and time again. Leorino sweetly surrendered his mouth to him. He was not having trouble breathing as before, thanks in large part to the occasional breath Gravis let him take.

Gravis reveled in Leorino's adorable, frantic response to his kisses, savoring his beloved young man to his heart's content.

Finally, sensing that Leorino was struggling to catch his breath, Gravis regretfully pulled his lips away. Given the early hour, the kiss was far too intense, and Leorino could only stare absentmindedly at Gravis. He looked so precious in that state that Gravis released a contented sight.

"Ah... It's such a relief to finally have you in my arms."

"Your Excellency..."

"I thought I told you: no 'sirs,' no 'excellencies,' and certainly no more 'highnesses.' Do you need to be half-asleep to call me as I wish?"

Blood rushed to Leorino's cheeks. He remembered, of course.

Gravis pressed his thumb to Leorino's slightly swollen lips, until Leorino found it in himself to use the appropriate nickname.

"I do remember... Vi... Gravis."

Gravis looked at him fondly. Seeing that tender gaze that felt like silent praise, Leorino felt reassured and smiled shyly. Gravis's expression was more peaceful than ever, and it brought Leorino great joy. Heat slowly pooled somewhere deep inside his body.

He wished they could stay in this warm, dark, cocoon-like space together for the rest of their lives. Leorino prayed this peaceful time would last forever.

But all the wishing in the world couldn't change the fact that morning would always come, bringing reality in tow. There was only so long they could remain in their cozy, safe space. Their lives would continue beyond this moment.

Leorino slowly sat up.

"...Is it morning?"

"It's still early. You immediately fell asleep after we finished talking last night."

Gravis stood from the bed and picked Leorino up. He took Leorino straight to the washroom. After washing his face and completing his morning groom, Gravis beckoned Leorino closer. When he stepped toward him, Gravis immediately began to undo the buttons on Leorino's shirt.

Puzzled, Leorino looked up at the man.

"Vi...?"

"I'm about to bathe you."

In a few swift movements, Gravis removed his shirt. Gravis furrowed his brow harshly at Leorino's exposed body.

"...I really should have executed them on the spot."

Leorino's neck still bore the marks from where the soldiers had held him down. The bruises on both his shoulders were even more vivid. They were so pronounced Gravis could clearly make out the shape of the man's fingers.

"Did the soldiers do this to you?"

Leorino craned his neck, his gaze flitting from one shoulder to the other, and was shocked to see how visible the bruises really were. Leorino was also seeing them for the first time. It was no wonder his shoulders hurt so much.

The marks had been left by Ebbo when, surprised by Leorino's confession, he forgot to control the strength of his grip.

Leorino shook his head, insisting it was nothing.

"No, this was Ebbo... He was so shocked by my words that he forgot himself for a moment."

"Ebbo Steiger and his superhuman strength, then. I'm glad he didn't break anything at least... Try moving them."

Leorino obediently rotated both shoulders. They certainly hurt, but the pain wasn't nearly strong enough to suggest bone damage.

"I'm all right. I shouldn't have surprised him like that. Shock is the natural response when someone of my appearance says 'I have Ionia's memories.'"

Gravis nodded.

"Not to mention...he's been through a lot. The news must have deeply shaken him. I do feel guilty about it."

"I'm aware. He tried to protect you—I won't punish him. Besides, as far as marks are concerned...I've left some of my own."

Leorino's lithe arms extended from his shoulders. His wrists still bore faint marks where Gravis's large hands had pinned him to the bed.

Gravis averted his eyes in remorse.

"Your skin is prone to bruising. It's fair, and incredibly soft. I'll be careful from now on."

"It may very well be, but please don't concern yourself too much with it. I'm all right."

Although Leorino didn't seem to mind, Gravis was immensely irritated by the traces of violence the men had left on Leorino's body. He slowly stroked Leorino's slender neck down to the ridges of his shoulders.

Gravis knew that wouldn't make the bruises fade any faster, but he wanted to rid his beautiful body of the traces of other men as soon as possible. The marks on Leorino's smooth, porcelain skin were painful to look at.

If Gravis let Leorino out of the palace, he would once more be exposed to violence and men's base desires in no time. The bruises were fresh enough to fill Gravis with fear.

I don't want Leorino going anywhere. That thought resurfaced in Gravis's mind.

If only I could keep him safe in this palace, in my arms for the rest of his life...

* * *

Meanwhile, Leorino looked up at Gravis with trust in his eyes, completely unaware of what he had been considering.

Gravis reasoned with himself.

In any case, Leorino would stay with him in the palace for a little while. How long exactly? Long enough to teach the young man to whom his beautiful body and heart now belonged to.

Gravis had washed Leorino's hair and now lathered his body up with soap.

Leorino was restless the entire time, his heart pounding with awe and sweet anticipation. But Gravis did not even attempt anything indecent, simply washing Leorino's body.

I don't know if I can say we're r-romantic partners just yet, but...he's treating me like a child...

To have Gravis, a royal no less, help him bathe felt truly embarrassing and pathetic. Leorino had never actually bathed alone. So finally, he found the courage to ask:

"...Vi, do you always bathe alone?"

"I do."

"But why...?"

"You mean to say that you don't?"

Leorino blushed and cast his eyes down.

"Is that strange...?"

It was common practice for nobles of high rank to have servants assist them in bathing. There was nothing particularly wrong with it.

"No, not at all... Is that also your attendant's job? Why do I feel like I'm competing with him?"

Gravis laughed.

"You want to try washing yourself? Now's your chance to practice."

"Oh? S-sure."

"It's not very difficult. I'm certain you've managed it before. All you have to do is rub this over your body with the force you're used to. Here, try it yourself."

With that, Gravis offered him a soft washcloth.

Leorino gingerly ran it down Gravis's arm.

"Is this right?"

"Why are you washing me? Wash yourself."

"Oh, right... I'm sorry."

Leorino realized that he had misunderstood the situation. He began to clumsily wash his yet-untouched legs.

Gravis watched him with a smile. When he saw that Leorino seemed to be managing on his own, even if entirely graceless, the man began to wash himself.

"Turn around. I'll scrub your back."

Leorino nodded and turned his back to him.

Gravis gently cleaned Leorino's fair skin and continued where he had left off.

"I started bathing alone around the time I became half-fledged."

"Why was that?"

"To prevent assassination. Once, an assassin infiltrated the palace disguised as a maid meant to help me bathe. I've bathed alone ever since."

"...My, that's horrifying."

"It was all right. I can leap, after all. I could have immediately escaped, but it was rather traumatizing to be attacked when I was naked and unarmed. I've never really let anyone near me since, with the exception of those I trust when I'm vulnerable."

Leorino suddenly found it hard to breathe. The royal palace had been one of the few places Ionia couldn't protect him—and yet Gravis had continuously been in mortal danger.

"Do they still make attempts on you...?"

"No. I have no more enemies in the country. Now, foreign enemies are another matter entirely."

"Oh no. Are you not safe even in your own palace?"

"It's not nearly that easy to sneak in here. When I enter the washroom or the bathhouse, the system is set up to send out a message, increasing palace security. All the royal residences are equipped with the same system. Though I may be the only one who bathes unassisted."

"Oh..."

Learning of the daily dangers the royal family faced, Leorino was speechless.

"But that makes this the perfect place to keep you safe."

Gravis picked Leorino up, sat him down in his lap so that they were facing each other, and began washing his own hair.

Seeing Gravis's wet, muscular body up close, Leorino was flustered, his gaze darting all over the place. Gravis had a simple cloth wrapped around his waist, but Leorino was entirely nude. With his legs spread apart and body pressed close to Gravis's, the soft hair below his abdomen and his privates were in the man's full view. Comparing himself to the beauty of Gravis's muscular body was unbearable.

"Vi... Th-this is embarrassing for me."

"Why? You don't want me looking at your body?"

Leorino faltered at Gravis's question.

"I didn't say that... I'm just embarrassed to have you see *everything*."

"Yes, well, I think I quite enjoy seeing *everything*."

"Ugh... Wait...!"

Gravis mischievously wrapped his fingers around Leorino's shaft. Leorino's hand instantly shot out to stop him.

"Y-you really shouldn't...!"

"Why not?"

"B-because...I'll get aroused and end up like before."

Gravis chuckled.

"Fantastic. Let me see that arousal of yours."

With that, the man began rubbing him softly in his palm, the lather smoothing his motion.

Leorino trembled at the sudden caress.

"I—I shouldn't... We shouldn't be..."

Leorino certainly possessed Ionia's memories, but he was perfectly new to intimacy himself. He couldn't even begin to compare the contents of his memories to the real-life sensation.

Leorino could do little more than shake his head to resist his growing arousal and the pleasure it brought with it.

"Hng… Nn… Vi, you don't want to see me like that…"

"But I do. There, now you're nice and hard. And conveniently slick, too."

Lewd, wet sounds and his erratic breathing echoed through the bathhouse. Leorino took it as best as he could, his whole body writhing from the inescapable pleasure.

Gravis smiled, relentlessly pushing him closer to the edge.

"But I…I'll leak…onto your hands again…"

"'Leak'… Hah, you're adorable. That's fine, leak all you want."

The man laughed at Leorino's juvenile complaint.

Gravis worked Leorino's length tirelessly. Gravis took a moment to observe it, covered in foam and slick with Leorino's fluid.

"I must admit, it's really quite shapely. I presume you've become well acquainted with it by now?"

Stunned by the salacious question, Leorino's head nearly exploded with shame.

Before he could offer any reply, Gravis muttered in a bitter voice, "You and your damn attendant," and tightened his grip around Leorino's shaft.

"Oh… God… Ah…"

"Be honest, have you actually received your bedchamber education?"

Leorino desperately clung to Gravis's shoulders even as his hands kept slipping on the lather. He couldn't keep up with Gravis's invasive questions.

"I have… But only from books…"

"Have you ever slept with a woman? Or a man, whichever."

Leorino shook his head, refusing the question. Then, as if to prompt an answer, Gravis ran his thumb over his slit. Leorino yelped and arched his back at the intense sensation.

"Ah… There…"

"Answer me, Leorino."

He wanted to avoid defiling Gravis's hands the way he had last time. Hoping he would ease his touch, Leorino recalled the question.

"No, I've never done anything like this with anyone…or to anyone… I—I have bad legs, I never thought I could actually… Ahh."

"Right… Well, we can work with the knowledge you've got. I'd hate to have to teach you everything myself."

"I will be fine. I should be," Leorino insisted frantically, hoping to avoid any misunderstandings.

Uncertain what he meant by "fine," Gravis loosened his grip around him. Relieved that his overwhelming stimulation had ceased, Leorino rested his forehead on Gravis's shoulder and stifled a shudder.

Gasping, he desperately tried to swallow his strained breath.

"…I already know how it works. I remember everything. I more or less know what to do in these situations from Ionia's memories."

Gravis's face turned serious.

"…Then what *do* you do?"

"W-we stroke each other's members, a-and yours goes inside me and rubs my insides, and, and…"

"…Leorino."

Leorino recalled taking himself in hand in his room the night Gravis first kissed him. He remembered the ache he felt deep inside him at the time, wanting to know what Ionia had felt when he made love with Gravis, chirping about how good it all felt.

He was so incredibly aroused now that it hurt. Spurred on by the lewd memories, Leorino yearned for release, his mind going blank as he searched for the remaining amount of friction he required.

"Oh, please, I can't stand it anymore… I need more… Ugh… Hng."

Spilling his hot breath onto Gravis's shoulder, Leorino's trembling lips pleaded for the man to touch him. When that yielded no result, he moved his hips gracelessly, rubbing his tip against the man's hard abdomen.

"Would it feel good to have you inside me? That's allowed in the bedchamber, isn't it? Though I may not last very long, but please, don't stop. Please…"

"…Leorino."

Witnessing Leorino's shameless behavior, Gravis nearly lost his grip on reason.

Leorino was so young and *so* lewd.

Seeing Leorino's body shaking with pleasure in his arms, Gravis felt himself grow hard.

Gravis grabbed Leorino by the hair, forcing him to look up, and fiercely took his lips. At the same time, he moved his hand harder, faster. Leorino finally released a cry of pleasure against Gravis's lips.

"...Ahhh!"

And just like that, Leorino had bounded up the steps of bliss.

Holding Leorino in his arms, Gravis submerged himself in the tub, rinsing the soap off the both of them. Leorino leaned his head languidly against Gravis's muscular shoulder and let the man do whatever he wanted as he basked in the afterglow.

"Leorino...you're not wrong per se, but memories of Io's intimate life won't be of much use to you."

At Gravis's words, Leorino finally lifted his heavy head. With his tearful violet eyes, he asked the man why. Gravis smiled wryly.

"You've never done it before. You can't expect yourself to do everything Ionia could."

"...What must I do to do what he did?"

"You really want me so badly? ...All of me, right here?"

With that, Gravis slipped his hand between Leorino's buttocks and pressed his finger against his entrance.

Leorino gasped at the strange sensation.

He hesitated to respond to the embarrassing question, but he couldn't conceal his feelings. Flushed, he nodded earnestly.

"All right." Gravis smiled. "You truly want to learn how it feels, then?"

"...Yes. I want to embrace you just like Ionia did. Vi, I want your member to rearrange my insides."

Gravis covered his eyes and laughed out loud at the outrageous words Leorino insisted on repeating.

"I never want to hear about your 'insides' again. It'll drive me insane, in more ways than one."

"...Then what do you want me to call it?"

"Literally anything else... But that's fine. Your body is yet untouched. It won't be nearly as simple as with Ionia."

Leorino looked terribly disappointed.

"...Come now, don't look at me like that. Don't worry. With my help, you'll manage in no time."

Gravis moved the hand that had been supporting Leorino's back and brought it to his chest, running his thumb over his pale nipple.

Leorino was startled by the sensation.

"You'll...help me?"

"Yes." Gravis said, lifting the corners of his lips slightly.

His fingertip caressed his small, quickly hardening nipple, as if in praise.

"...Soon enough I should be able to pinch and lick these and offer you all the pleasure you deserve. You're likely not used to it yet, but we can address that... Like this."

"Nn... Ah."

Gravis brought his face to Leorino's chest and flicked his tongue against one of his nipples. Leorino shuddered.

"Trust me, it'll feel amazing. It'll become another source of pleasure for you, sensitive enough to make you climax with no additional stimulation."

"Vi, Vi..."

Gravis once more began to lightly tease the tip of Leorino's length with his fingers. It was still sensitive from his climax, but it slowly stiffened in the hot water.

"As for your manhood, well... I suppose it will never fulfill its original purpose, but that doesn't mean I intend to neglect it, either. In fact, I plan to wrap my tongue around it until you're begging me to stop."

Weeping at the pleasure coming from two spots at once, Leorino writhed erratically, spilling water from the tub.

"And of course...here."

Gravis brought his hand behind him, probing his entrance once more, gently slipping his fingertip inside.

"Ahh... Hng!"

"...You're small and narrow, but I can help you relax and make sure I can fit inside you without any pain."

Leorino gasped quietly.

"Leorino, it'll be quite the process, but...will you be fully mine?"

Leorino's warm body grew even hotter at the shameless question. He began to tremble with anticipation.

With enough practice, I'll be able to embrace Gravis...

He still wasn't quite sure what this practice would involve.

But all he could think of was feeling Gravis inside him as soon as it was physically possible.

"I will... So please, show me what I must do... Please."

Gravis smiled at Leorino's answer.

Don't Spoil Me

Leorino lay naked on the bed. Gravis's large, muscular body slowly draped over him.

"Vi…"

"Leorino, are you afraid of me?"

Leorino immediately shook his head.

"…I'm not afraid of you."

Now that Leorino thought of it, Gravis had been asking him that question ever since they met.

Perhaps it was a subconscious manifestation of how much Gravis cared for him. The man who was used to being feared by the people around him wanted to be absolutely sure he didn't scare Leorino.

Leorino's chest felt warm. Gravis was fearsome, but he was kind, too. He had always been like that. His cold expression might have suggested his heart had frozen over, but the sentiment he displayed for the people he cared about was deep and fierce.

Whenever Gravis asked, Leorino decided he would continue to tell him the same thing.

"I am not afraid. And I believe I already told you that I know what we're about to do."

"I see. That's a relief."

"I'll be fine. I want to acquire the necessary skill as soon as I can… I want to bring you pleasure, too, Vi."

* * *

Gravis chuckled at that.

Leorino was watching Gravis with surprising determination, despite being clearly nervous about the feeling of Gravis's skin on his own.

"You're new to this. Where's all this ambition coming from?"

But even as he asked this, Gravis already had an inkling of why Leorino was so fiercely optimistic.

"Don't concern yourself with me. You must first learn how good it can feel yourself."

"But…there's no point if I'm the only one enjoying it. I want you to feel good as well."

"Leorino, calm down."

Gravis brushed back Leorino's wet bangs soothingly.

"You said it yourself: You are not Ionia. So let go of the past. I don't need you to be an expert."

Leorino's eyes shook.

"When Io and I made love, he had already been in a relationship with Lucas. He was used to sex with men."

"Vi… I didn't…"

"Io was a warrior. His physique couldn't be more different from yours. Even with all the practice in the world, if we tried to do what I did with Io, you'd break."

Leorino looked like he was about to cry. The size difference between him and Gravis saddened him. He wished he could have been born larger, stronger.

Gravis gently stroked Leorino's crestfallen head.

"Let me be absolutely clear. I don't want you to replace Io, I want to have sex with *you*. You're more than welcome to set the pace. I don't expect you to imitate Ionia."

"Vi…will I really be able to please you?"

"Don't be silly. I'm ecstatic just to have you here."

That seemed to finally reassure Leorino enough for him to offer a stiff smile. His impatience also seemed to fade.

Leorino had said he wanted permission to love Gravis. He was likely desperately trying to catch up to Ionia, following his heart, ignoring the fear filling his innocent body.

Noticing Leorino's courage, Gravis's heart swelled with love.

"Let me tell you a little about the past."

"…?"

"When I found out that Io had started sleeping with Lucas, I was green with envy. I hated being younger than them."

In his violet eyes, Leorino saw regret, guilt, and something Gravis couldn't even begin to fathom.

Of course. A part of Ionia's heart belonged to that man, and would never be mine.

But what about Leorino? Gravis wondered.

His violet eyes were identical to Ionia's, and yet they watched Gravis with an entirely different emotion from his first love.

"…Hah, and here I thought I was *normal* about virginity."

Gravis mused to himself, and Leorino tilted his head.

"But I'm strangely glad to have you in my arms, perfectly untouched."

Leorino's eyes widened.

"Vi…"

"What I mean is, we can take our time. We'll take everything at your pace, so let me make love to you."

With those words, Leorino fully opened his heart to Gravis and allowed him to take the lead. He was finally reassured that there was nothing wrong with his lack of experience.

"…Still, I don't want to wait."

"Leorino?"

"I understand I can't do what Ionia did. But…I don't want you to hold back just because of that."

Leorino hugged him tightly. Gravis narrowed his eyes slightly.

"…Are you certain? I don't want to see you crying about how scared you are again."

"I-I'm not going to cry."

Gravis laughed, as if to say, "We'll see about that." Leorino's obstinance was astounding.

"...Very well, then. But tell me if you're in pain. I don't want to hurt you."

"O-of course... I'll do my best."

"All of those memories clearly didn't do you much good. I mean, you insist on calling it 'leaking' and telling me all about your 'insides.'"

Leorino blushed. Clearly, his vocabulary was unsuitable for intimate settings.

"Then just tell me...what words should I be using?"

Gravis brought his lips to Leorino's small ear and whispered the knowledge he seemed to crave so much.

"I can't... Oh, I really can't. That's too much... Ah, god, I'm..."

Leorino had sobbed the entire time at the overwhelming pleasure that never stopped coming. His eyes blurred with tears as he desperately pleaded with Gravis. He had been gasping for so long, he had nearly forgotten how to breathe at all.

"I'm sorry... That's too much for me."

But the man smiled and ignored his tearful pleas.

"Come now. Who said he'd do his best, and that he didn't want me to hold back?"

"Well, I did, but I...I can't...anymore."

"Can't you? I thought I told you all the words you needed to know, Leorino."

The man had already driven him to climax twice, and he was now quickly approaching the third.

Gravis was running his tongue over Leorino's tip, tickling the platinum netherhair soaked with Leorino's own fluids. At the same time, Gravis reached up to his chest and continued to rub and pinch Leorino's plump nipples.

"My chest hurts... I'm sore already... Ah, don't lick it, I'll come again. This is too much..."

"...Hah, I suppose that's an improvement from 'leaking.'"

* * *

Leorino's nipples and his length were so sensitive now that they hurt. But there was something beyond pain, too. The incessant stimulation sent sparks flying down his entire body. His body already knew where he enjoyed being touched by Gravis.

But what baffled Leorino the most was the mind-blowing pleasure coming from inside him.

"Well, how is it? ...I'm 'rearranging your insides,' just like you asked."

"Ahh... It's... It's..."

How long had it been since the man had inserted his fingers?

Leorino had had to spread his legs to allow Gravis access. Immodest as it was, Leorino obediently exposed every last part of himself to the man he loved. He endured the shame of being perceived as best as he could.

Gravis had coated his fingers with a slick liquid and initially only ran them over his balls. When Leorino gasped in fear at his touch and the strange sensation it brought, Gravis began to rub circles into his perineum with his other thumb.

He then moved to rub Leorino's entrance in the same way. Slowly beginning to find pleasure in the act, Leorino softly opened up and welcomed the man's thumb. As if on cue, the man inserted his bony middle finger.

That was when Leorino lost all track of time.

Even as Gravis caressed Leorino's entire body with his remaining hand and his lips, his fingers never stopped moving inside Leorino.

Meanwhile, Leorino was in tears from the foreign sensation and the pain of his body being stretched with each additional finger, but with an open mind and body he held on to the pleasure Gravis's fingers were bringing him.

Leorino's body was much smaller than Gravis's, and naturally it would follow that his insides were narrower as well. But, as a result of the man's continuous fingering, Leorino's inner walls swelled, soft enough for Gravis's fingers to probe deep inside.

The man's fingers seemed to thoroughly enjoy the way Leorino's flesh twitched around them. He continued to open Leorino up, leisurely moving his hand in a manner deceptively similar to intercourse. Leorino's sense of shame was long gone, erased entirely by the intensity of the sensation.

Introduced to the motion Gravis's length would eventually perform, his virgin body learned to obey and learned the method by which it would bring both of them satisfaction.

The three fingers inside Leorino had since found his weak spot, the fingertips gently rolling over it.

Gravis hardly touched Leorino's length, he only occasionally licked the flushed tip as if to soothe it. Clearly, he was attempting to lead Leorino to a third climax from the inside.

At the same time, his tongue would fall on Leorino's nipples, bright red, swollen, and painfully hard.

"Ngh... *Hic...*"

Leorino sobbed at the stinging and the pleasure it brought him. He was quickly starting to associate the touch on his chest with the pleasure he felt inside.

The squirming of his flesh around Gravis's fingers informed the man exactly how touching his chest made Leorino feel.

"...You seem to be enjoying yourself. You're *such* a good boy."

His sense of time was beyond gone.

With the curtains drawn, the bed was so dark, he couldn't tell what time it was. Leorino suddenly feared that his body might just melt away.

I'll break... I'll die...

"Ugh... Eh... Vi... T-too much..."

"It's just enough. Don't cry. You're a good boy, you're almost there."

It was Leorino who had insisted on going through with this.

Although he couldn't have imagined it would involve such a maddening amount of ecstasy.

Leorino thought that if he could loosen up and accept Gravis's length, feeling Gravis move inside him would bring him pleasure. Leorino thought that he would feel the same as what he had experienced when he took himself in hand.

* * *

But the pleasure he experienced now was entirely different.

The heavy, dull ache of pleasure that seemed to melt him from the inside deprived him of all reason.

That stifling ecstasy spread from inside him and set his entire body ablaze.

"Vi...that feels...strange..."

"You're fine, you're almost there. You know what to say now, don't you?"

"Ah... Ah, I'm...I'm coming..."

"That's it. Stay with it. Come."

At that moment, his fingertips pressed into a spot inside him harder than before.

Leorino cried in a hoarse voice as he finally climaxed with no additional stimulation.

When Leorino regained consciousness, Gravis was looking down at him with visible concern.

"Are you all right?"

Leorino struggled to pry open his eyelids, stuck together from all his crying. He had moaned himself hoarse.

Seeing this, Gravis took a mouthful of water directly from the jug and slowly poured it into Leorino's mouth. Leorino gulped down the cool water as if his life depended on it.

Repeating this twice, his throat was rehydrated, and his hazy mind slowly cleared. Gravis asked again.

"Are you in pain? How are your legs feeling?"

"...I think I'm dying."

Nothing hurt in particular, but he still felt as if his body was falling apart. He felt heavy, as if his body had been filled with mud. His nipples, his length, and his interior were especially sore from all the attention they'd received.

"I knew you'd cry."

"I'm sorry..."

"No, it was my fault. I only intended to give you a taste... I really don't know when to stop, do I?"

Leorino paled, worrying that if *this* was only a taste, what would happen to him when they made a serious attempt? At the same time, he came to a shocking realization.

"Vi...did you...put it in?"

He asked timidly, wondering what had happened after he passed out. Leorino agonized over the possibility he had been the only one who got to enjoy the whole affair.

Hearing this, Gravis looked unusually surprised, and laughed out loud.

"No, not yet."

"...I'm sorry."

Leorino felt like he had failed.

After all that effort, he couldn't even welcome Gravis inside.

Seeing Leorino wilt with a heartbroken expression, Gravis forced a smile.

"I didn't intend to insert it in the first place. It wasn't going to fit so soon, so don't let it bother you."

"...Then wh-why did you—?"

The man then inserted his fingers into Leorino once more. Remembering the sensations he had just experienced, his body obediently accepted the man's digits.

"Mm..."

"Hm, you're still nice and soft. Good boy. How many fingers do you think are inside you right now?"

"Fingers? ...Th-three?"

"Two... This is three."

As he added a finger, which fit, but not without some pain. It brought about a sense of fullness.

"Does it hurt?"

It hurt a little, but in a good way. Remembering the pleasure he had just experienced, Leorino moaned sweetly in his hoarse voice.

"...It's tight, but it feels good."

"That's good. Now if I add another..."

"...?"

With that, Gravis nudged another finger against his narrow hole that had already been stretched to its limit. Feeling the fourth finger partially enter him, Leorino was instinctively afraid and began to tremble.

He'll break me...!

When Leorino turned to the man with frightened eyes, Gravis quickly withdrew his fingers.

"Leorino, touch me."

With that, Gravis placed his hard shaft in Leorino's hand. Timidly gripping his hot flesh, Leorino shuddered at its sheer size. That was when he realized what Gravis was trying to say.

"...Do you see now? You're still too tight to accommodate me. That's normal, but without more practice, you'd tear."

It certainly made sense.

He also appreciated that Gravis cared about his body and was patient enough not to force himself into Leorino before he was ready.

Still, Leorino was melancholy.

"But Vi, I...I can't please you until...I'm stretched far enough."

Gravis laughed at his beloved young man, half-exasperated.

"Don't get discouraged. Bringing you pleasure feels amazing in its own way."

"Still..."

"It's fine. Your body is obedient and eager to learn. Not to mention you seem to really like it when I touch you like this. A few more times, and you'll be ready to take me in."

With that, Gravis inserted two fingers inside him once more.

His hot, soft, wet flesh relaxed as he felt Gravis's hard fingers sliding in and out of him. Leorino's cheeks flushed and he gasped at the pleasure.

"Ah... Ahh, mmm."

"See, you like that, don't you? You just need more practice. You'll feel even better...soon."

"...All right."

Leorino was happy to see his practice paying off already.

"I've waited eighteen years. I can wait a little longer. Though ideally not another eighteen years."

"What can I do to help you...achieve release? Oh, could I use my mouth? Would that bring you pleasure?"

Gravis laughed in exasperation.

"You and your secondhand knowledge. Did you also get that from Ionia? Honestly... Do you think you can fit *this* in your mouth?"

Panting from the pleasure of being fingered, Leorino cautiously assessed Gravis's erection.

He silently gave up before he could even attempt it. No amount of effort on his part would make it fit inside his tiny mouth.

Seeing Leorino lose heart once more, Gravis forced a smile for the nth time. He caught Leorino's pout between his fingers.

"You're fine, I'll teach you how to use your mouth in time...but for now, let's see. For now, let me borrow your legs."

Gravis withdrew his fingers and poured a thick liquid onto Leorino's thighs.

"Huh... Wh-what's this?"

"It's just lubricant meant for intercourse. It's commonly used; you can relax."

"Right... Ah, huh?"

Gravis had him close his legs and held them together over one shoulder. He stroked himself several times in front of Leorino's eyes, and then inserted his member between Leorino's closed thighs.

His impressive length, too long and girthy for Leorino's hands, began to move back and forth between his slick thighs in a steady rhythm.

"Wait... Vi!"

"I'm just going to borrow your thighs... Ah, that's good... Your skin is so soft."

Gravis's shaft brushed the underside of Leorino's sensitive nethers as it came and went. Leorino arched his back at the stimulation. Every time Gravis rocked his hips, Leorino's entire body shook.

When Gravis's breath caught in his throat and he spilled himself onto Leorino, the proof of their desire mingled on Leorino's skin.

"...Good boy, you did well."

Shivering sweetly at the hot sensation on his belly, Leorino fell into a muddy slumber, guided by a gentle hand caressing his head.

Beyond the Slumber

Shortly after Leorino fell unconscious, Gravis wrapped him in the bedcovers and picked him up.

Leorino must have exhausted all his strength. It was no wonder. He must have been physically and mentally spent from yesterday's incident at the training grounds, and from all the sex acts they had engaged in in the bath and in the bedroom first thing in the morning.

Gravis couldn't handle Leorino the way he had Ionia—he had told Leorino as much.

If Gravis were to be honest, with his remarkable physique, he preferred to have sex with men of comparable size to his own, since it allowed him to indulge his desires without all the additional fuss.

Leorino was perhaps stronger than most women, but with the size difference between them, if Gravis ever failed to rein himself in, he would inadvertently hurt Leorino. Even when Leorino sat in his lap, their eyes weren't quite level. Leorino's body was so much thinner than Ionia's. There was also the issue of his constitution, and of course, his legs.

Leorino did not stir even as Gravis carried him out of the room. Perhaps he really had fainted.

Moving into the parlor, Gravis sat down on the settee in the center of the room with Leorino in his arms. Theodor was already waiting.

"Prepare some hot water and a washcloth."

Theodor nodded and left the room. It wasn't long before he returned with several maids in tow.

The maids quietly entered the bedroom without making eye contact with their master. They too were of noble origins, schooled to perfection by Theodor himself. They showed not a hint of interest in the person sleeping in Gravis's arms.

"...Your Highness, I have prepared what you wished."

Theodor led Gravis to the washroom, where in addition to grooming facilities, stood a settee where he could rest before and after his bath. Gravis laid Leorino down on the settee and removed the covers he had wrapped him in.

Leorino's naked body was covered in traces of the previous day's violence and the passion they had shared. The marks on his fair skin were pitiable, painful, and incredibly lewd. The bruises the men had left on his upper body were still fresh, but Gravis's love bites bloomed even brighter on his skin.

Leorino's usually pale nipples were flushed, swollen up to the edges of his areolas. All across his newly awakened flesh, red marks were scattered like rose petals. The sight was so obscene, one could tell at a glance how much love Gravis had bestowed upon him in the bedroom.

From his thin waist to his fair abdomen, the proof of Leorino's many climaxes stained his skin. His modest platinum netherhair clung to itself from the filth. His length beneath was a pale pink from Gravis's excessive touch, looking rather painful. The skin around his nethers was also peppered with love bites.

Leorino was now defenseless and unconscious, his slender limbs hanging limply off the settee.

Gravis felt a powerful urge deep in his chest.

There was something heartrending about Leorino's helplessness, his inability to resist. The sight of him aroused Gravis's immense protective spirit, and yet awakened his sadistic side as well.

Theodor brought Gravis the hot water and washcloth he had asked for. He deftly wrung the cloth out and handed it to his master. Gravis began to cleanse Leorino's body with a soft touch.

"Shall I do it, my lord?"

"No. I'll do it... Bring me another washcloth."

Gravis gently lifted Leorino's legs and parted his thighs.

The inner sides of his thighs and his nethers were covered in the lubricant Gravis had used. His fair skin was wet, glistening with obscenity. Gravis smiled at his slightly swollen, reddened entrance.

Gravis's fingers appeared thin and elegant, but relative to the size of Leorino's body, they were thick and long. Even in his sob-filled daze, Leorino's body bravely accepted Gravis's digits one by one.

Without a little more practice, Gravis's length would still struggle to fit, but for his first time, Leorino had done admirably. His entrance was now beautifully closed and modest, as if Gravis had never been there.

In the end, Gravis had helped himself to Leorino's thighs. His legs were as slender as the rest of his body, with little meat to them. But Leorino's inner thighs, though slim and with little muscle, were maddeningly soft for a man. This too must have been a product of his old injuries.

Gravis had rubbed himself against those soft thighs and climaxed, savoring that lovely texture.

Leorino's body was just like his heart—honest and brave.

His entire body had told Gravis how much he loved it, how much he loved *him*. The sensation must have been far too intense for a young man who was only beginning to explore his sexuality. Pleasure brought by force could be a sort of torture, after all. Being entered for the first time and repeatedly led to climax was no small feat.

Some part of Gravis regretted it. At first, Gravis had intended to be gentle with him—god forbid he made him cry. But when Leorino told him not to hold back, Gravis had lost himself to the challenge in his voice.

Once Gravis finally got his hands on him, the sight of Leorino's crying as he clung to Gravis, his body exposed and beautifully lewd, spoke to Gravis's sadistic side. And such were the results of his slight miscalculation.

* * *

As Gravis returned the now-filthy washcloth, Theodor quickly handed him a clean one. Repeating the process until Leorino's body was pristine once more, Gravis carefully wiped him with a dry cloth one final time.

"You're unusually silent." Gravis spoke to the valet.

Theodor answered calmly. "He's earned my respect. Accepting the extent of Your Highness's affection with such a slender body requires admirable courage."

Gravis laughed.

"I thought you were going to lecture me about how I'm too old for this."

"Not at all. If anything, I'm quite relieved your body is still functional."

"Hah, yes, that's more like you. But I do worry I've overwhelmed Leorino."

"I will keep an eye on him for the time being."

"Please do... I must admit, I never thought I would cherish him this much."

Theodor could only stare at his master in surprise.

After Gravis had wiped Leorino clean, the valet immediately offered him a nightgown. It fit Leorino like a glove. Gravis raised an eyebrow at his over-prepared servant.

"Very impressive."

"These belonged to you around the time you were half-fledged, my lord. We don't possess anything else that might fit Lord Leorino. I will have a set of brand-new loungewear for him by the evening."

Gravis nodded.

Gravis gently lifted Leorino once more so as not to wake him up. When his small head was about to slip off Gravis's shoulder, Theodor gently supported it from behind and deftly maneuvered it back into place.

Gravis nodded at the valet in gratitude.

They had left the bed in disarray, but it was now in perfect order. Theodor, as was typical of him, carefully and deftly checked the bed to confirm that it had been prepared to standard, as well as to make sure that nothing danger-ous had been planted within. He quickly nodded toward his master.

With the bed stripped of its top cover, Gravis laid Leorino on top of it. Still in the grips of the deep, deathlike slumber, Leorino did not stir at all.

Leorino's platinum hair was dry. But as it had still been wet when he was initially brought to the bed, it was fluffy and disheveled from when he had writhed his heart out against the sheets.

Gravis's fingers gently stroked his hair.

"Bring me a sedative."

Theodor nodded, excused himself, and quickly reappeared with a cool cup of medicinal infusion.

Gravis took the medicine in his mouth and slowly delivered it directly to Leorino's lips with his own.

He spilled a little at first, but quickly grasped the necessary technique and poured it down Leorino's throat in small gulps, making sure he didn't choke. Leorino's slender throat involuntarily swallowed the medicine.

Theodor watched his master administer the infusion like a bird feeding its chick.

"...All right, that should allow him to rest for a while. Let him sleep until he wakes up on his own."

"Yes, my lord."

Gravis stroked Leorino's head one last time and stood up. Theodor immediately drew the curtains, plunging the room into darkness.

They left the bedroom together.

"Will you be heading to the Palace of Defense today?"

"Yes, I'm about to."

Theodor nodded.

The valet disappeared into the washroom and returned with a hot washcloth. He used it to clean Gravis's chest, still exposed from their liaison. Gravis's body also bore the traces of their passion. Having wiped him clean, Theodor proceeded to matter-of-factly prepare Gravis for the day the way he always did.

Looking down at the valet as he began to fasten the buttons on his jacket, Gravis asked, "Any news?"

"Regarding Lord Leorino?"

"Yes. I brought him in last night without any prior arrangements, after all."

"As of last night, we have already received a letter of protest from the Cassieux family and a request for an audience with Your Highness. Lord Gauff

Cassieux, a member of the Imperial Guard, appeared at the palace last night, demanding to see you in person. He left when I refused him."

There was no regret or hesitation on Gravis's face.

"Yes, that's roughly what I expected. It should take several days for them to get word out to the margrave. I suppose I should pay Lord August a visit myself before they turn him against me. Anything from the Palace of Defense?"

"Yes, sir. Dr. Sasha and Lieutenant General Lucas both requested to speak directly with Your Highness as of last night. Lord Lucas wishes to see Leorino and ascertain his safety in person."

Gravis curtly dismissed the request.

"Absolutely not. While Leorino is here, no one is allowed in the palace. That means no visits, either."

Theodor nodded.

"As you wish, my lord."

"But do summon Leorino's personal attendant from the Brungwurt residence. I want the most experienced man taking care of him."

Last night, Gravis hadn't had the time to inform the Cassieux family or the Palace of Defense of the situation. The Cassieux family must have been furious that he had kidnapped Leorino, the apple of their eye. They were growing increasingly distrustful and antagonistic toward Gravis, so to order his valet to call on Leorino's personal attendant was no simple request.

But Theodor didn't even hesitate when he accepted his master's order.

He would fulfill any and all of Gravis's wishes. That was Theodor's pride as a royal valet.

"Leorino will stay here for the time being, even if the Cassieux family attempts to use His Majesty against me. He's not allowed to see anyone without my permission. Is that clear?"

Theodor nodded silently at the additional instructions. He dispassionately fastened the cloak around Gravis's shoulders, the way he always did.

"You are ready, my lord."

Gravis nodded, and suddenly used his servant's childhood nickname.

* * *

"Theo, I need you to listen to me as my childhood friend."

Much like his master, the valet rarely showed emotion, but even he widened his eyes at the nickname he hadn't heard since they were little.

"I can't let Leorino go."

"...Yes, I've been aware of that ever since Your Highness brought him into your palace for the first time."

"But he is a son of the Cassieux family. The issue is, he is also of our royal blood. I can't keep him by my side as my 'lover,' but the reason is altogether different from my circumstances with Ionia."

Theodor smiled slightly.

"Your Highness. I daresay you have the *worst* taste in men."

"Hah, how dare you?"

"I say this as your childhood friend, of course. For a bloodline purist like myself, Leorino's bloodline is most appealing. I could understand your concern if he were a girl, but alas, he is not. Once upon a time, I would have been the first to object."

Gravis glanced at his valet.

"Hailing from a family with such unique circumstances certainly complicates matters. I might have asked, 'Why him, of all people?' If you were suddenly so inclined to marry, I would have certainly persuaded you to choose some princess instead."

Gravis laughed at his unusually talkative servant.

"True. At this rate, we might be risking a civil war with Brungwurt before we ever come to cross swords with Zwelf."

Gravis's starry-sky eyes were slightly downcast, as if he was considering something.

"What do you intend to do, my lord?"

"Well, what do you think I should do?"

Their gazes met, but Theodor found the answer in his master's bright eyes and smiled.

"You have made your decision. I can only abide by your will."

With that, Theodor's face regained its solemn, honest expression, and he bowed the way a faithful servant should.

"Allow me to begin the preparations to officially welcome Lord Leorino into the palace."

"Before we can do that, I must speak with him. Not to mention the range of obstacles taller than the Baedeker Mountains I must first cross. By which I mean the margrave...and the diet, of course."

"I see no issue." Theodor assured simply. "My lord. Once you set your mind on something, no person on this continent could ever hope to stop you—not even His Majesty the King."

Peaches

When Leorino woke up, it was once more to the darkness of the canopied bed. He had no way to tell how long he had been asleep or what time it was.

I must have fallen asleep after...all of that.

By which he meant after he had received Gravis's impressive length with his thighs rather than his insides. As Gravis rocked him in a powerful, constant rhythm, Leorino's body once more grew hot, until...he could no longer recall the details.

After a longer while at the mercy of the hot waves of pleasure, he heard Gravis's muffled panting followed by a splash of something hot on his abdomen that truly could have belonged to either of them.

His memories ended there.

I should apologize to Vi...

He was ashamed of having fallen asleep without ever thanking him.

Still, he hadn't expected Gravis would fiddle with his insides to that extent. And despite being given so much pleasure that he thought he might actually die, it was apparently still not nearly enough to fully accept Gravis inside him.

"Ugh..."

Why was it that whenever he recalled something embarrassing, he felt the need to groan?

Leorino agonized over how he thought he knew enough, but in truth knew nothing at all about the overwhelming reality of sex.

His body ached.

Leorino rushed to feel around his body. He tensed the parts that bothered him and moved them slightly. He checked each spot to see if there was any pain and if he could move them at will.

This had become his habit ever since the incident.

He wasn't in the best state. His entire body felt heavy, and the parts of his shoulders Ebbo had gripped still hurt. Not to mention, the spots Gravis had paid extra attention to—especially his entrance—felt strange.

But nothing seemed particularly injured. He had overused his legs in several ways since the previous day, but he could still move them and didn't feel any pain. Perhaps it had been thanks to Gravis's thorough care, but Leorino was at least relieved to know that his legs could withstand sex.

Still...it does sort of hurt. Or it prickles, perhaps.

He was dressed in an unfamiliar nightgown, and every time his nipples rubbed against the fabric, he felt a painful chafing that made him shudder.

There was also a prickle between his legs.

Leorino softly palmed his now limp length through his nightgown. It felt somewhat hot and sore. Still, nothing seemed to be wrong with it.

Relieved, Leorino then gingerly poked at his swollen nipples.

"Eep!"

He had barely touched them, but it felt like an electric shock had run through his chest.

Wh-why do they hurt so much? Don't tell me they're going to fall off...?!

* * *

Leorino paled at the thought. He reached for his nipples once more to be absolutely sure they would stay put.

"Have you awakened, sir?"

"Ah...! Y-yes!"

Leorino sprung upright at the voice suddenly appearing from beyond the closed canopy curtains.

"If you'll excuse me, sir."

With that, the curtains were drawn back, and there stood Theodor with his usual solemn expression.

"Can you get up? How do you feel, sir?"

"S-sorry, I'm fine."

Leorino didn't know why he was apologizing or why his hands were resting on the top covers, as if trying to prove his innocence.

Of course. This was no time to be sleeping.

Leorino attempted to bring his heavy body into a sitting position. Theodor quickly placed a helpful hand on his back. Struggling to get up on his own, Leorino accepted the help with gratitude.

"Thank you."

"No need, sir."

"Um, where is Vi... I mean, His Excellency?"

"In the Palace of Defense. He was hoping you could get some rest, sir."

Leorino's cheeks flushed, and he cast his eyes down.

Theodor must already know what Vi and I were doing...

Not only did he know, but Theodor had seen his nude body after they had finished. Though, of course, Leorino couldn't have known that.

His body felt clean under his nightgown, even though he recalled being covered in all sorts of filth. As Leorino wondered who had washed him, his head snapped to Gravis's valet in disbelief.

"Is something the matter?"

"N-no, not at all."

He knew better than to ask Theodor about it.

"Mr. Theodor, may I have the time?"

"You needn't call me 'mister,' sir. It's nearly evening."

When Leorino glanced out the window, the sun was indeed beginning to set.

Had he actually slept the whole day away?

"I apologize… I shouldn't have taken up His Excellency's bed for this long."

"No need to apologize, sir. His Excellency told me to let you rest as long as you needed, so I didn't attempt to rouse you. Can you stand, sir? I have prepared a change of clothes for you."

"Yes, thank you. Oh, but…these aren't the clothes I was wearing when I arrived."

"Indeed, we have prepared these for you instead. I hope they are to your taste."

The clothes that Theodor prepared were of a simple design, but tailored with fine fabrics that felt silky smooth to the touch. How had he managed to procure clothes of such a high quality that fit Leorino so well when he had only arrived yesterday?

Leorino was bewildered but decided to accept the thoughtful gift. He wasn't about to frolic around in a nightgown.

"I love them. Thank you."

"Allow me to assist you."

Leorino had mixed feelings about having Theodor help him get dressed, but his whole body was so tired that he gratefully accepted the offer.

As he was about to get up from the bed, he looked to the floor only to see the man had also prepared a brand-new pair of shoes. They too seemed to be a good fit for Leorino's feet.

He wondered how Theodor could have known his exact measurements, but that too was a product of having seen him naked.

Leorino hadn't eaten anything since yesterday afternoon. When Theodor learned of this, he immediately prepared him a meal.

The food was exactly what Leorino expected of a palace belonging to royalty. It was the finest meal he had ever seen.

But as soon as he made a start on the appetizer, Leorino realized that he was not only not hungry, he had hardly any appetite at all. He doubted he would be able to make it to the main dish at this rate.

He apologetically declined the remaining dishes before they could go to waste. Theodor seemed upset for the briefest moment, but silently accepted Leorino's request. After the appetizers, a soup and soft bread, both gentle on the stomach, were brought to the table.

Relieved to be served something he felt he could manage to eat, Leorino thanked him.

Hundert would have given me a stern talking-to... Right. I must send word home. My brothers must be worried.

Leorino forced his fuzzy mind to think. He had many things to consider, but his mind struggled to cooperate.

He took his time bringing the soup to his mouth and began to think about the reality of all that he left behind at the training grounds.

He began to wonder if he should inform Gravis of the secret he had confided in Ebbo. To tell him about Edgar's betrayal and the mastermind behind it would mean recounting the details of the night when Ionia was killed in battle.

Ionia's death was etched in Gravis like a scar of regret and despair.

Telling him would only reopen old wounds.

But Leorino didn't want to hide it anymore. Not to mention the roots of the betrayal must have still been spreading throughout the kingdom. Hiding the truth of what happened eighteen years ago could even put Gravis's life in danger.

The key to the secret likely lay in the Marquis of Lagarea.

I don't know if he'll believe me...but I'll tell him about the Marquis of Lagarea as well.

"Lord Leorino, your hand seems to have stopped. Please eat before the soup grows cold."

Leorino's thoughts were brought to a halt by Theodor's remark. He had been so lost in thought that he had entirely forgotten about the plate before him.

"Of course, I apologize. I'll have some more."

Leorino devoted himself to finishing the food before him.

Seeing that Leorino was satisfied with his meal, Theodor offered him the seasonal fruit for dessert, the pfirsich.

"Whoa, peaches!"

Peaches were a rare fruit that could only be found in the south during the early summer season. They were delicate and easily damaged, making them difficult to transport over long distances and preserve.

In the cool northern region of Brungwurt, they were considered a luxury.

As Leorino gazed at the pink fruit with bright eyes, Theodor smiled.

"Do you enjoy peaches, sir?"

"Yes. Back home, peaches are a rarity. My mother's greatest regret when moving out from the capital was how hard it was to find peaches in Brungwurt."

"Oh, is that so?"

Although he was full after finishing his soup, Leorino was thrilled to enjoy the peaches for the first time in so long.

"Um, when will His Excellency be back?"

"Unfortunately, His Highness doesn't inform me at what time he plans to return."

"...Oh, I see."

That was not ideal. This was no time to be relaxing over a leisurely meal. If he didn't make plans to go home soon, he would have been staying out without permission for more than an entire day.

He needed to calm down and think things over.

He asked to use the washroom and shut himself in there. He washed his face with cold water to clear his head.

"Hah..."

Wiping the water dripping from his wet bangs with the back of his hand, Leorino took a long, hard look at his face in the mirror.

What stared back at him was his same old reflection.

The special time he spent with Gravis had not turned Leorino into something special.

A tired-looking young man with dark circles under his eyes peered back at him from the mirror with a somewhat lost expression. Leorino was relieved and yet a little disappointed to see himself looking the same as always.

He placed his hands on the washbasin and watched as the water dripped from his wet bangs.

He would wait until Gravis returned, speak with him, and then go home.

Even if Leorino couldn't tell him everything today, he was certain Gravis would make time for him if only he asked.

I must first go home and apologize for staying out...and then clean up the mess my reckless behavior has caused.

He had left everything at the training grounds.

He wondered how Ebbo was doing. He wanted to believe he was not being punished when he didn't deserve it. Not to mention he had betrayed Dirk and Josef with his selfish scheme. Josef must have been worried sick.

But there was another man to whom he owed an apology more than anyone.

Luca... I must speak with Lucas.

Now that he had confessed to Gravis that he had Ionia's memories, he also had to tell Lucas the truth.

Leorino clenched his fist on the washbasin.

Suddenly, he was embraced from behind.

Leorino looked up in surprise and saw the man he loved reflected in the mirror.

Leorino's heart filled with joy.

"Vi! Welcome home."

Instead of responding to the smile blooming on Leorino's face, Gravis pressed a kiss to his platinum hair.

"How's your body? Feeling all right?"

Leorino's cheeks flushed.

"Y-yes, I'm fine."

"I hated leaving you this morning."

"Me too... I hated not getting to thank you after everything."

Gravis's smile deepened. Leorino was utterly captivated by his masculine beauty.

"Your bangs are wet."

Leorino's mind snapped from joy back to practical thought.

Gravis didn't miss the melancholy that flashed in his violet eyes for the briefest moment. He narrowed his eyes slightly.

"...Leorino."

Leorino's heart skipped a beat at the sight of his beauty closing the distance between them. Gravis tilted Leorino's head back and captured his lips.

"Mnf... Vi..."

It was a slightly painful position, but the man deeply savored Leorino's lips. Leorino did his best to keep up with the kiss that felt too long and obscene to be a mere greeting. Before long, all of his strength drained from his body, and Leorino clutched at the man's chest, trying desperately to keep himself upright.

By the time the man's tongue had finished exploring every inch of his mouth, Leorino's knees were practically buckling. His reason was slowly eaten away by the steady flow of pleasure, his mind turning into a blur.

Gravis smiled at the sight, picked up the drained Leorino, and left the washroom.

Theodor was already waiting in the parlor when Gravis asked:

"How has he been today?"

"He was asleep for most of the day. He appears fatigued, but I believe he is in good physical condition."

"Has he eaten?"

"Yes. Not enough by my estimate, but he was enjoying some peaches after his meal."

"Good to know."

Gravis nodded in satisfaction and gave Theodor some instructions. Theodor nodded in turn.

"Please inform me when you are ready. I will bring it to the bedroom."

Still in Gravis's arms, Leorino was so dazed, he could hardly follow their conversation.

Gravis gently lowered Leorino onto the bed and got to his knees, straddling his thin body.

The large bed creaked quietly under their weight.

"Vi... Oh, um... Will we do it again?"

"Yes, we will."

Leorino was barely keeping himself together from the intense kiss, but his head was slowly clearing.

"Vi...before that, could we have some time to talk?"

"Yes, we must talk. But not tonight. I want to be the only thing on your mind for now."

"But I...I've left so many things unfinished...Vi!"

Straddling Leorino, Gravis began to peel himself out of his military uniform.

"...Wait, please!"

Taking notice of Leorino's confusion, Gravis met his gaze.

"I told you, now's not the time."

He tossed the clothes he had just freed himself from onto the floor without hesitation. Once he was down to his shirt, he turned his attention to Leorino's clothing.

"Ah... Vi... But I'd like to speak with you."

"Do you really want to waste your energy resisting?"

Leorino desperately tried to curl up and protect his lower half, but there was very little he could do to stop Gravis as he undressed him one garment at a time.

In the blink of an eye, Leorino was stripped of everything but his shirt, leaving him shivering and vulnerable before the man's gaze.

Leorino was upset. Some part of him wanted to simply lose himself to pleasure once more, and yet another felt guilty for even thinking that.

"Please. Please, let us speak."

Gravis ignored Leorino's plea.

"There is only one thing you need to be doing now, and it is focusing on accepting me inside you."

Leorino's eyes welled with tears of confusion and fear.

Gravis reached down to his chest, still covered by his shirt, and squeezed one of his sensitive nipples from over the fabric.

"Ow... That hurts..."

His body jerked back at the sensation. When Gravis rubbed circles into the plump bud, it stiffened at an impressive speed.

Gravis smiled at how his flesh grew to meet his touch.

"Why, you seem to be raring to go."

"No, it's just... Everywhere you touched me this morning still prickles."

"That's just a product of your heightened sensitivity. I'll make you feel much better in no time."

Gravis slid both palms down his body until he reached his bare buttocks. He spread him open with one hand and with the other, he began to prod at his entrance. Leorino squirmed on the bed, unable to resist the lewd sensation.

"Ah... Ahh, really, can't we talk?"

"We can talk literally any other time."

Gravis ripped Leorino's shirt open, sending the buttons flying across the room. Leorino shuddered.

His fair, radiant skin was laid bare before Gravis. Upon it, the marks he had left this morning were scattered like flower petals. His small nipples and areolae were both nice and plump, making their lovely shape known.

"...I'd take you right this instant if I could."

"Vi..."

Leorino could hardly keep up with how quickly arousal was filling his body. Leorino was ready to cry from the anticipation and anxiety of the pleasure to come. The sight only appealed to Gravis's sadistic side.

Gravis knew he had to speak with Leorino.

But not now. He didn't want to worry Leorino with concerns of the outside world.

Until Leorino was his in both name and substance, Gravis had no intention of letting him out of his arms.

Gravis brought his lips to Leorino's earlobe, traced its small, delicate outline with his tongue, and whispered.

"…Let me touch you, Leorino."

"Vi… Vi, but I—"

"I want to make love to you. I want to make love to you *so* badly."

He poured his honey-sweet words into Leorino's ear, stealing away what little remained of his reason.

His tongue traced the path from his ear to his neck, awakening his erogenous zones one by one. Leorino's breath gradually turned sweeter and heavier.

Gravis's lips finally reached one of his nipples. It was red and swollen.

When he covered it with his mouth and gently nipped at it with his lips, a quiet sob spilled from Leorino's mouth.

"Leorino…are you afraid of me?"

Leorino knew the answer.

That was why Gravis always asked. To make sure that what followed was a product of Leorino's will.

Biting back his shaky breath, Leorino frantically answered.

"…I'm not afraid of you."

Gravis smiled. Leorino's slightly parted lips revealed a hint of a peach-colored tongue.

But even as his tongue moved as if he wanted to say something, Leorino did not speak.

Once again, Gravis savored the forbidden fruit of his sweet lips. Their combined juices spilled from his small mouth. As Gravis lapped it up, Leorino opened his lips a little further and fully surrendered himself to Gravis, asking for more.

Gravis relished the way he filled Leorino's mind and body. A fruit ripe for his picking. The man's body welled with the immense desire to possess him.

"Do you remember how many of these you need?"

Gravis made a display of licking his fingers before Leorino.

"Answer me."

"F-four…?"

Leorino's eyes were blurred with fear and anticipation, as the man held out his long, slick fingers in front of him.

"Yes, good boy. Now...let me finally enter you tonight."

Gravis slowly sank his finger inside him, Leorino's body already aching in demand at the promise of pleasure.

Leorino sat on top of Gravis's muscular body, enjoying the pleasure Gravis poured into him.

The man's tongue and finger were penetrating Leorino's upper and lower holes in a steady rhythm.

Gravis's tongue, entwining with and sucking on his own, felt so good it brought tears to Leorino's eyes. The feeling extended to his entrance, and despite the soreness from their morning activities, he couldn't help moving his hips in embarrassingly needy motions as the wet finger pulled back and plunged into him.

Gravis enjoyed the sight of Leorino's slender frame writhing on his hard body. With his free hand, he gently massaged Leorino's silky-smooth buttocks. Gravis absolutely adored the texture of his small, round cheeks.

The way Leorino subconsciously swayed his hips in time with the movements of his finger was beautifully lewd. Gravis watched him with fondness as he played with Leorino's tongue.

"You like that, don't you?"

"...Nn... Yes, hng."

Leorino nodded, sobbing at the slowly mounting pleasure.

"...Ah... Eep!"

The moment Leorino's chest touched Gravis's body, he shuddered and jerked back. His nipples must have been sore.

Leorino had anxiously complained that his inexperienced body had become fragile and overly sensitive after their morning tryst. Leorino was genuinely concerned his nipples might fall off. When Gravis tried to pinch them lightly, Leorino jerked away and burst into tears. Not wishing to hurt him, Gravis was careful to avoid the area.

But his obedient body had already made the connection, and while being fingered by Gravis, his nipples immediately stiffened.

Whenever Leorino lost himself to the pleasure, he ended up brushing his nipples against Gravis's hard chest and immediately jerking away.

Another part of Leorino was also erect. It was rubbing against Gravis's hard abdomen, slowly dripping onto his skin.

At first Gravis had tried to suck him into his mouth and show him a new dimension of pleasure, but Leorino protested. It was also sore, and he didn't want it touched anymore.

That was how Gravis had found himself exploring the inside of Leorino's body to bring him pleasure. But, sensitive as he was now, that alone was more than enough for Leorino.

Gravis added a finger. Leorino's body obediently accepted the second digit.

"Mm..."

"Does that hurt?"

"N-no, it's fine... I just..."

"You just?"

"I don't know, with every finger you add, I feel this sensation deep inside... I don't know what to do."

Gravis stifled a laugh at Leorino's answer. Not even Gravis could solve that problem.

Gravis sat up, Leorino still in his arms.

Carefully repositioning himself so as not to injure his legs, he gently rested Leorino's back against the headboard.

"Now open your legs."

"R-right..."

Leorino nodded and gingerly opened his legs before the man, exposing the bare skin of his buttocks. Gravis gave Leorino's fair cheek a stroke of praise, and—for some unknown reason—left him in that state, slipped off the bed, and disappeared into the parlor.

Leorino was on the bed, his body spread open to the evening air, shivering, waiting for Gravis to return.

He was scared. The shame of it all brought tears to his eyes.

Gravis reappeared very soon, carrying a lamp.

"It's too dark to see. There, much better."

"Ah...!"

Once on the bed again, Gravis pulled Leorino's hips down onto the mattress. He slipped a pillow under his slender hips, lifting his buttocks off the bed.

Leorino turned a deep shade red and flailed about at the embarrassing position. It exposed his aching entrance, his stiff flesh, and his modest balls, putting his body on full display before the man's eyes.

Leorino immediately protested.

"Th-this is far too embarrassing!"

"What have you to be ashamed of?"

"What?"

Gravis flatly rejected Leorino's complaints, and instead made an even greater demand.

"Can you hold your legs open for me?"

"What...? Ah."

"Hold your knees. Here... Like this."

He took Leorino's hands and brought them behind his knees to hold them in place.

Leorino had tears in his eyes at the compromising position.

"Vi...this is embarrassing. I've never done this before. I don't like it."

"You're all right. I've already seen every last part of your lovely body. What's there to be ashamed of now?"

"But...but we didn't do this in the morning."

"You do realize sex doesn't look the same every time, yes?"

Those words seemed to come as a genuine shock to Leorino.

Why did intercourse have to require *this* many steps? But Gravis didn't seem to be making fun of Leorino, either.

"So I presume I have to...?"

"Yes. It's fine, everyone does it."

Would Ionia have done this, too? Despite his doubts, Leorino bit back his shame and placed his hands behind his knees as Gravis requested.

With that, Leorino offered every last embarrassing part of himself to the man.

"Ow...! Agh... Ugh."

The third finger had entered him without issue, but even with thorough, careful preparation and a large amount of lubricant, Leorino still struggled to accept the fourth digit.

When the fingertip sank into him, he felt as if he would rip from the combined girth. He was quite narrow given the overall size of his body, and his tense nerves made it difficult for him to relax any further.

Even when he tried his best to ignore the feeling, he couldn't help but groan in pain and tense his body.

Leorino was crying at his failure now.

"I'm sorry...I'm sorry I couldn't do it."

"Don't apologize. I don't want to cause you pain."

Gravis stroked his head and kissed his tearstained temples.

"Your body is pliable and eager to learn. But if my fingers are too much for you, you'll have to forget about the rest of me for now."

Gravis forced a smile.

Leorino tried to argue his case through tears. "No... No, I can do it."

"Yes, you will eventually. Just not today."

The man's heat pulled away from him.

Leorino bit back a sob.

Gravis had done everything right, and Leorino still couldn't rise to the occasion. How utterly pathetic of him.

All of this when Gravis's body so clearly desired him. Leorino was the one receiving all the pleasure and giving nothing in return. It upset him so much that he pleaded with Gravis.

"At least let me do it with my mouth."

"Don't be silly. You've never done it before."

Leorino shook his head frantically at Gravis's exasperated response, insisting he could do it.

Leorino heaved his heavy body upright and brought his face to the kneeling man's groin as if to prove his resolve.

"Come now, you really don't have to."

Gravis gently grabbed him by his bangs to stop him.

The rejection made Leorino look like he was about to burst into tears.

"I know I don't have to... I *want* to. Please let me. I m-may not be any good at it, but I want to bring you pleasure, too, Vi."

"...Leorino."

"Please... Don't shake your head at me. Please let me do it."

With that, Leorino brought his face to his length.

Gravis sighed.

Leorino's small tongue began by licking his tip.

Up close, Gravis's hard member was so huge, Leorino thought they might as well be different species.

It was so voluminous that Leorino held it in both hands as he sucked at the tip. The round, taut tip was smooth to the touch, surprisingly frictionless.

Though certainly intimidated by its sheer size, Leorino began to pour his affection into his beloved's body.

"Leorino...you're truly..."

Gravis looked up to the heavens at Leorino's reckless attempt, as the young man clearly thought nothing of bedroom manners or setting the mood or anything at all, for that matter.

In the end, he decided to let Leorino run wild until he tired himself out.

"Nn... Nn..."

There was no skill involved at all.

He didn't even try to fit him in his mouth, only licking at his flesh as if his life depended on it. It was little more than a tickle, but watching this angelic beauty lace his tongue around Gravis's arousal so eagerly was quite the visually stimulating experience.

His breathing only slightly heavier than before, Gravis decided to teach him a little about the art of oral sex.

"Open your mouth. Can you suck it?"

Leorino nodded earnestly and made a valiant attempt.

But his small mouth could hardly contain the head alone. He did not know how to open his mouth wide enough, let alone his throat.

He desperately attempted to suck on it, but eventually lowered his eyebrows in silent apology and shook his head weakly in surrender.

"I'm sorry... I'm sorry."

Finally, he burst into tears in earnest. He looked so pitiful that Gravis couldn't help the chuckle as he thought they would both be better off if only he allowed Gravis to bring Leorino all the pleasure he was capable of.

"That's fine, you can lick it. And rub it with your hand...like this."

Gravis stroked himself lightly, setting an example.

Leorino nodded, watching intently, and again laced his tongue around the tip. He then began rubbing the shaft with both hands. It was an improvement, but not nearly enough to get Gravis any closer to climax.

"You're not very good at this, are you?"

Gently scoffing at him, Gravis stroked Leorino's small head as it bobbed back and forth.

Leorino looked up at Gravis, his face flushed with arousal.

His chin was filthy with drool, and potentially traces of something else, too. There was something thrilling about the thought that it was Gravis's own fluids staining Leorino's angelic beauty.

After wiping his mouth with his finger, Gravis plunged the same digit into Leorino's mouth.

Leorino was puzzled, but obediently accepted the finger into his mouth. At the same time, his eyes seemed to ask what the man was doing.

"Hah... Where's all this knowledge of yours now?"

Leorino hadn't the faintest idea how obscene his partner's request really was.

Such a perfectly pure, perfectly lewd angel.

Gravis smiled.

He ran his finger over Leorino's soft tongue, in and out, and Leorino's breathing began to waver as he remembered the excitement of having his insides rubbed in the same way.

"Oh, you find that arousing?"

"Um... Vi, please... I want you to put it inside me. I really want to fully embrace you."

As he attempted to fellate Gravis, Leorino was so consumed by this desire that he no longer cared what might happen to his body, and now desperately implored Gravis.

"Please. I want to feel you completely and utterly like Ionia did, Vi... So please."

"I told you to stop comparing yourself to Ionia."

Leorino pleaded with Gravis with all his might.

"Please, I want to!"

"God, you're so stubborn. I already said no."

"Vi...! Please. I don't care if it hurts. I want to make love with you. Please?"

Gravis looked down at Leorino without a word.

He placed his hands on Leorino's sides, pulled him up without much effort, and sat him down in his lap.

Leorino pleaded with the man with tears in his eyes.

"...You're serious about this, aren't you?"

Leorino nodded frantically.

"I don't want to hurt you."

"You can hurt me, I don't mind. I don't want to leave without fully embracing you."

It was a baseless fear, since Gravis wasn't planning on letting Leorino leave his palace anytime soon. But unable to know what Gravis had in mind, Leorino was terribly serious.

They had been embracing, skin against skin, making love with their hands and lips, but instead of romantic, the situation felt somewhat comical.

Gravis laughed at the love that welled up from the bottom of his heart.

The young man was asking him to make up his mind in a completely different way from Ionia, and Gravis could hardly resist.

Leorino was eager to show how different he was from Ionia, even though Gravis never expected that of him.

"Don't laugh... I am serious."

Incredibly enough, Leorino brought his face to Gravis's groin once more. Gravis hastily stopped Leorino as he extended his tongue to arouse him.

His violet eyes looked up at Gravis sadly, as if asking him why. His eyes were like that of a desperately pleading puppy.

Stroking his small head, Gravis sighed. There was only so long he could resist that courage of his.

There was still a way to grant Leorino's request, though given his lack of experience, it would likely make him cry.

"Will you do whatever it takes?"

Leorino smiled in excitement.

He didn't know what that meant, but he nodded enthusiastically before Gravis could change his mind.

"Yes! Anything... Please, I want it so much."

Leorino didn't know when they would get to be alone again.

The thought made him afraid to leave before he could become one with Gravis.

Pleasure Amplifier

Leorino stared at the object Gravis was holding.

"What? ...Vi, what is that?"

Gravis pulled a tool out of a basin of hot water. Warmed to the temperature of human skin, it was made up of large, egg-shaped pearls connected by a thin string. It looked a little like an unfastened necklace. At first glance, it appeared to be some type of jewelry.

Leorino was frightened by the sudden appearance of the mysterious tool. Clenching his hands, he began to tremble.

"Vi... What is it? ...Tell me first... Vi, I need to know."

"It's all right. We need it to get you ready. I'll make it quick, I promise."

Gravis generously applied lubricant to the toy and pressed the first bead against Leorino's entrance.

But Leorino had tears in his eyes, fearing the unknown.

"...I—I don't know about this. Can't you just use your fingers?"

"Leorino, I told you that without proper preparation, you'll get hurt."

Leorino felt like there was something deviant about inserting a foreign object inside him.

"...Th-that's all right, I don't mind getting hurt... But that's just bizarre. I only want you inside me, Vi."

"It's fine. I'll pull it out as soon as it does what it needs to do. Didn't you say you'd do anything? I'm going to make you feel amazing, just be patient."

Gravis pressed the rounded tip against his entrance and pushed the bead inside.

Leorino felt his hair stand on end at the sensation.

"Ngh, I'd rather you did it, Vi... Ahh."

It felt strange, but it didn't hurt. The warm bead was actually quite soothing on his raw insides, opening him up more gently than Gravis's fingers. Leorino was taken aback by the way his body had come to enjoy this sort of penetration.

He watched Gravis through a veritable sea of tears. Gravis softly ran his fingers across Leorino's entrance before pressing another bead against it.

"I...I really don't know about this..."

"It'll just help you relax. It won't take long, I promise."

Noticing his apprehension, Gravis reassured Leorino and slowly pushed the linked beads into him one by one.

Slowly, his abdomen grew heavier and fuller.

Finally, Gravis inserted the last bead. He carefully observed Leorino as he adjusted to the toy.

"Ngh... That feels strange."

Leorino was confused. They had never gone this deep before and his body seemed to close around the toy. This caused the beads to roll erratically inside him. The powerful sensation slowly began to bring him an unbearable amount of pleasure.

It nearly drove him mad. Gravis had placed him in this position, but he was also the only person to whom Leorino could cling right now. Leorino was crying as he reached toward Gravis for help.

"Oh... Vi, do something... It's so good, I don't like it."

He let Leorino pull Gravis on top of him. Gravis opened Leorino's trembling lips and laced his tongue with Gravis's to soothe him.

"Mnf, mm..."

"Almost there... Just a little longer. You're doing great."

Every time Leorino moved, the beads must have been kneading his insides, overwhelming him with pleasure.

Bringing his fingers to Leorino's twitching entrance once more, Gravis sank three digits into him with ease. The beads were pushed deeper inside. Leorino arched his back, a wordless cry spilling from his lips.

His entrance was nicely opened by the beads, but still appropriately tense. Gravis moved his fingers easily, slowly opening them and carefully creating the necessary space inside Leorino.

"...Here's that fourth finger, Leorino."

"...Ahh..."

Gravis inserted a fourth digit inside him. Leorino groaned through tears.

"Oh god... I'll break... Ah, ah... Ahh."

"It's fine, I'll make sure you don't. You're a good boy, you're taking it so well."

Leorino genuinely thought he might actually break. Stretched to its limit, both his entrance and his insides felt tight. And yet he felt incredible.

"Look, they're in."

Heaving irregular breaths, Leorino did all he could to hold onto the sensation.

"...Shouldn't be long now."

"Vi...what?"

Gravis gently pressed down on Leorino's abdomen from the outside, as if searching for something. When he found the beads under Leorino's thin skin, he began to massage them softly. At the same time, he gently moved the fingers inside Leorino.

Leorino's body was slowly stimulated from within and without at the same time.

"Ugh...ugh..."

Slowly swayed from the inside and outside, a maddening sensation began to well from within his body. It should have hurt, and yet it brought him breathtaking ecstasy.

"Ahh...agh, ah...ah."

Leorino was tossed about by waves of conflicting sensations that set his body ablaze.

"...God, I can feel them inside... Ah... Ahh... Ahhh..."

"It's fine. Go ahead and come."

Leorino's body began to soften as if he was melting away. Gravis teased the entrance with his thumb as he slowly deepened the movement of his fingers to mimic the motion of intercourse. It was a slight movement, only about as deep as a knuckle. It stimulated Leorino's inner walls more than anything they had done before. An obscene, wet sound came from deep inside him.

Leorino's slender hips swayed coquettishly, chasing the unmistakable pleasure.

He slowly reached heights he never thought possible. It was no longer just the sensitive spot inside him that brought him pleasure, but every inch of his flesh surrounding it. Leorino was in a daze when he was slowly pushed to climax.

"...I...I think I'm dying... Ahhhh!"

Pushed as deep as they could go, the beads hit his back walls in a strange motion. That was when Leorino finally climaxed.

"Ah...hah, hah..."

His entire body convulsed as if something inside him broke. Slowly, Gravis withdrew his fingers.

"...Agh, ah... Ahh."

"Well done. Now stay there... Hold onto that feeling and relax."

Attempting to soothe his twitching body, Gravis gently brought his lips to his nipples. Synchronizing with the movement of the tongue, he slowly removed the beads, carefully, so as not to ruin Leorino's bliss, and to show him how good pulling out could feel in itself.

Listening to Gravis's command, Leorino was unable to come down from the heights of his climax and continued to drown in the pleasure with each removed bead, tears streaming down his face.

"Ah...ah...ah!"

Once all the beads had been removed, Gravis pressed himself against this throbbing entrance.

"I'm going to enter you now... Just keep relaxing."

He slowly thrust into the soft, wet hole. It was narrow and tight. Even with all the intense practice, Leorino barely endured his overwhelming size, turning his head away as he sobbed.

"I knew this was a bad idea... Let's not."

"N-no, no, don't go, don't stop, please..."

Gravis clenched his teeth at these words, steeled his resolve and forced the head inside Leorino.

"Augh!"

Leorino's body stretched to its limits, accepting the girthiest part of Gravis. Leorino was still shedding tears. Gravis let out the breath he had been holding.

"...Well done."

"...Huh?"

Leorino could hardly process what was happening to him anymore, but he seemed to faintly understand he had finally been able to fit Gravis's flesh inside him. A hazy sense of euphoria welled within him.

"Hold on just a little longer."

Gravis moved his hips forward almost too carefully, driving himself deeper into Leorino's warmth. Gravis's massive length reached Leorino's vulnerable spot almost as soon as it entered him. Gravis did not move in and out, only gently swayed his hips to stimulate the spot with the head.

"Ah... There, yes... Ah..."

"Hold on. I suspect you'll enjoy this."

Gravis assured him and rubbed the spot with his tip a little harder.

Leorino released a quiet moan at that moment and weakly spilled himself onto his skin.

"Ugh... Hah, hah..."

"You came again? Well done. You're a natural."

Gravis softly caressed Leorino's balls as he praised him. At his gentle touch, Leorino wriggled his hips, Gravis's length still inside him.

Gravis didn't move his hips for a longer while, only slowly kneading Leorino's balls in his palm, and Leorino sighed at the gentle pleasure.

The sensation of his flesh wrapped around Gravis's arousal slowly grew sharper.

Leorino's fair skin glistened with sweat as he melted in bliss.

"Yes... That's so good..."

"What's so good exactly?"

"Every...thing, ah... There..."

Gravis closely observed Leorino as he slowly lost himself to the pleasure.

"Mm... Ngh..."

Even his inner walls, tightly coiled around Gravis's hard flesh, somehow grew softer. Gravis was pleased. He could tell that Leorino's body had completely surrendered itself to the pleasure. Gravis advanced his hips a little further, sinking roughly half of himself inside Leorino. Leorino moaned in pain, but Gravis slowly let Leorino get used to the size of him.

Then, when he noticed Leorino was ready, he slowly began to rock his body in regular motions. After a while, Leorino began to chirp sweetly like a kitten at the waves of pleasure crashing over him.

Gravis wasn't thrusting, he only slowly rocked his hips to teach Leorino the motion he could expect of intercourse.

"Yes... Ah, ah... Vi..."

Leorino's entire body was flushed, every part of him beginning to ripen like the sweetest peach.

The sweet scent of his sweat and the carnal smell of their flesh enveloped them every time the man used his hips to sway his body.

"Ah... Ngh, ah...ahh... Vi... Vi!"

"Leorino... You're doing great."

His body was truly amazing.

The last thing Gravis wanted to do was hurt Leorino. After all the pleasure Gravis brought him, Leorino cried, begging him to put it in, but his body was too inexperienced to fully accept Gravis yet.

That was why he had used the toy to hasten the process. It must have been quite frightening for Leorino to have a toy inserted into him when it was only his second time in the bedroom.

But even through his confusion and apprehension, Leorino desperately held on. He accepted the necessary preparations as best he could.

As Gravis continued to slowly rock his hips, Leorino's inner walls grew accustomed to his presence, became flushed and supple, and began to savor Gravis's flesh, sweetly molding around him. Sweet, wet sounds spilled from within.

"Ah... You're so soft. Good boy. You like that, don't you?"

The fear and confusion in Leorino's eyes had disappeared without a trace. He was panting sweetly.

"Mm... Yes, that's... Mmm, so good..."

The fact that Leorino's body was so relaxed was proof of how much pleasure the penetration was bringing him.

Gravis gently caressed the area around Leorino's areolae, so as not to hurt his already sore nipples. Leorino had already made the connection between his chest and the rest of his body.

The more Gravis touched his chest, the more Leorino wanted Gravis inside him. Leorino was quickly beginning to understand that about his own body. Leorino could never obtain that sort of pleasure with his manhood alone. In Gravis's embrace, he was learning all sorts of things about himself.

Leorino chirped sweetly when Gravis touched his plump nipples. At the same time, his insides seemed to grow ever softer.

His body was exceptional; narrow and tight and still softly squeezing around Gravis. He was subconsciously suckling on the man's arousal.

With some more practice, how much more pleasure could they both obtain from intercourse?

Gravis was filled with love and excitement at the thought of his lewd scheme to awaken Leorino's sexuality.

The slow rocking seemed to allow Leorino to remain conscious.

With sweat beading on his forehead and tears staining his cheeks, he met Gravis's gaze and offered a dizzyingly lovely smile.

The man was transfixed by Leorino as he shed his shell of purity and awakened into an innocent yet lewd creature, arousing Gravis's senses.

His tearful eyes seemed strangely seductive.

"Did you put it in? ...Is it already in? Are you inside me...?"

"Yes, you're doing great. Just look."

Gravis nodded and moved his hips lightly to make his presence inside him clear. The movement made Leorino gasp in pleasure. He was begging for more, and Gravis made an effort to hit the sensitive spot inside him.

Leorino felt filled to the brim, but in truth, Gravis had only inserted roughly half of his shaft. Gravis wanted to bury himself deep inside Leorino and take him like a storm, but this was about as far as they could take it for Leorino's first time.

Even now that Gravis was finally inside him, Leorino was still too narrow and tight. But his insides were luscious, so hot and thick that Gravis thought he might just melt inside him. Wishing he could stay inside Leorino forever, Gravis made love to his beloved to his heart's content.

Leorino was shedding big fat tears of pleasure.

Semi-erect, he continued dripping cloudy fluid onto his skin.

"I'm glad… I'm so glad, ahh!"

Leorino's breathing grew shallower by the moment. His arms clinging to Gravis could hardly hold on anymore. Gravis knew what this meant.

"You did well…but we should end this."

Leorino stared at the man, his face flushed, his gaze needy.

"But Vi, what about you? Did you…come? Did I manage to bring you pleasure? Did I?"

Intense love for Leorino and a savage desire to conquer him surged within Gravis.

With a long sigh and a shudder, he suppressed his bestial urges. He couldn't allow himself to lose control and hurt Leorino.

Gravis partially pulled out, keeping the head inside Leorino, and stroked his own shaft with his free hand.

Leorino's entrance and his flesh boldly engulfed the man's tip.

"Vi…are you, oh, ah…"

"Leorino…"

Gravis quickly worked himself, savoring the sight of hot flesh wrapped around his tip and the adorable lewdness of Leorino writhing in pleasure.

With one last gasp and shudder, Gravis poured the hot proof of his desire into the passage that had accepted him for the first time.

Gravis held Leorino's unconscious body in his arms, his eyes empty as he stared into the void.

He knew Leorino had wanted to talk. But just for tonight, Gravis wished to forget all his sorrows and indulge in the presence of his beloved.

That was why he had insisted on it so fiercely.

Every time he gazed at the wet, tearstained face of the young man in his arms, love filled his heart.

At the same time, he knew they both had bonds that would keep them apart; bonds that could not be broken with pure love alone.

He didn't want to hurt Leorino the way he had hurt Ionia.

But there were still so many issues left to resolve before their love could conquer all.

Gravis pondered the events of the day.

Bonds

He hated leaving Leorino behind, but too much responsibility rested on Gravis's shoulders to neglect his professional duties in favor of love.

Gravis materialized in the center of his office only slightly behind schedule. Dirk, his second-in-command, was already waiting.

"Good morning, sir."

Dirk greeted him with a stiff expression. As Gravis expected, he looked like he had a great deal of questions occupying his mind.

"Your Excellency...about yesterday—"

"Wait. Before we get into that, tell me what I have planned for today. I'd like to adjust my schedule for the afternoon."

Dirk's face instantly changed to that of the competent adjutant he was.

"There are several requests for your immediate approval. Also, Alois would like to speak with you as soon as possible. There's been a skirmish, a rather major clash even, between the Francoure naval forces and the Gdaniraques in the port of Gdanis."

"When was this?"

"Some four days ago."

Gravis frowned slightly.

"Summon Alois immediately."

"Yes, sir... He also said he would like to consult Chancellor Ginter as to whether our kingdom's intentions should be communicated to Francoure from the Palace of Administration or the Palace of Defense. May I also summon the chancellor this afternoon after you receive the report from Alois?"

Gravis immediately shook his head.

"Cancel all my afternoon plans. I'll be leaping to Brungwurt."

Dirk stared at his superior, wide-eyed.

"Your Excellency...you don't mean..."

Gravis ignored his second-in-command even as he seemed to have something to say.

"Back to the topic at hand, the clash may have taken place on the trade route between our kingdom and Francoure, but as it was in the port of Gdanis, the Palace of Administration must not send an envoy. That would mean formally declaring our intervention in the dispute between the two countries."

"...Yes, I would agree. Though I'm certain Francoure would love to see us intervene."

"We would practically be announcing to them that we're already aware of Zwelf's connections to Gdaniraque. It's too early for us to step in. Send a messenger from the Palace of Defense. Be sure that Francoure understands what's on the line. Let Alois handle it as one of my adjutants. No need to bother Ginter."

"Yes, sir."

Gravis finally took his place at his desk.

"Beyond that, the lieutenant general and Dr. Sasha would like to speak with you, sir...about Lord Leorino, that is."

"Yes, Theodor told me as much. Indeed, I must speak with them. But it won't be today."

Dirk steeled his resolve and broached the topic.

"Sir... May I ask you something? About what happened at the training grounds..."

Gravis indicated with his eyes for him to continue.

"What do you plan to do with Lord Leorino?"

"I thought this was about the events at the training grounds?"

Dirk looked serious.

"In the end, all my questions come back to Lord Leorino."

"If you mean to ask if Leorino will continue serving at the Palace of Defense, I haven't decided yet."

"No, that is not what I meant to ask."

Gravis smiled at his subordinate for a change, and smoothly changed the subject.

"How did Leorino manage to outwit you yesterday? I never thought you the gullible type."

"...Oh, does our good general have gaps in his knowledge after all?"

Dirk looked terribly chagrined. Gravis stifled a laugh.

"I love your sarcasm as much as the next person, but I regret to inform you I'm not omniscient."

"Lord Leorino and I were initially at the observation platform. Right below us, Josef and Kelios Keller were taking part in the training, and Leorino asked the lieutenant general if he could get a closer look. He was watching them so eagerly he was practically hopping in place in excitement."

Gravis could easily imagine it. Leorino idolized Ionia's strength; he must have been thrilled to see the battle training up close.

"But when the training was about to end, he suddenly lurched out of the window. I worried he might fall, but then he told me he dropped the dagger he kept in his chest...and now that I think of it, he must have dropped it on purpose...but he said the dagger had been a gift from his father, the margrave, and he couldn't afford to lose it."

Gravis seemed exasperated.

Dirk shrunk back under his superior's gaze. Gravis proceeded to heave a deep sigh.

"...I'm sorry. I fell for Lord Leorino's scheme. Looking back, I should have taken him with me, but I thought it imprudent to bring him somewhere teeming with ruffians...and that was clearly an error in my judgment. So I left him there alone, and...when I returned, he was gone. God dammit..."

"Do you still have that dagger?"

Dirk nodded and pulled the dagger from the top shelf of the cabinet. Gravis took it and inspected it from every which way.

* * *

"A decent dagger, very practical. I suspect Leorino lied about receiving it from the margrave, though such a blade would certainly suit Lord August's aesthetic."

"I thought so, too. It fell just downstairs from where we were, as you must already know, and I...I suppose I let my guard down. I have no excuse. I deeply regret what happened."

"What can I say? You were careless, but for the most part, Leorino is to blame for all that happened yesterday. I trust you to reflect on your shortcomings. That's all."

Dirk seemed more depressed than reassured by Gravis's words.

"I think I would rather be punished. That's what Lord Leorino is facing, after all, isn't he?"

"You mean punishment? Hmm. Yes, I suppose he's been *punished* sufficiently for keeping things from me this entire time."

"I realize this is out of line, but as your second-in-command and as Lord Leorino's friend, I must ask," Dirk addressed his superior with a grave expression. "What exactly do you intend to do with Lord Leorino, sir?"

Seeing Dirk's gaze, Gravis decided to answer just as seriously.

"I suppose I also have something to tell you."

"...And that is?"

"Why Leorino had done something so reckless. And...the truth."

"...The truth?"

Gravis insinuated something but didn't answer his adjutant's question. Dirk grew impatient.

"But if you're going to learn of it, I believe it should be from Leorino himself. So I'm afraid you'll have to wait for now."

Dirk nodded reluctantly.

"...Yes, sir."

"Let me answer your question instead. I have not yet decided whether or not I will let him continue working at the Palace of Defense."

"...Yes, you just said that. What I was asking was—"

"If you mean privately, I've already made up my mind. I plan to officially welcome him into my palace."

* * *

His superior's shocking statement left Dirk speechless.

"...B-by 'welcome,' you don't mean...?"

"I can't have the son of the Cassieux family as my paramour, now can I? Not that I ever intended to put him in that position."

"So you...you intend to officially take Lord Leorino as your spouse?"

"I do."

Seeing his superior act like it should have been obvious, Dirk was lost for words.

Dirk wasn't intimately familiar with the world of royalty, but even he knew that most royals married early, so for Gravis to remain unmarried at the age of thirty-seven was certainly a rarity.

Dirk surmised that if he refused to marry to continue his bloodline despite being the second in line to the throne, it was entirely a product of his own choice.

From what Dirk knew of Gravis, he was not the type to become attached to any single person. The only person he had ever been truly attached to had likely been Dirk's late brother.

As far as Dirk knew, Gravis had never had any long-term partners, although he did occasionally sleep with both men and women as he saw fit. In that sense, he had been as cold as ice.

Dirk had suspected that Gravis would likely remain a bachelor for the rest of his life.

Dirk had never expected that very same man to suddenly declare he wanted Leorino for his spouse.

Dirk certainly realized that Gravis cared about Leorino. In fact, his superior was uncharacteristically keen for him.

But Leorino was only eighteen years old. The young man had only just reached adulthood and was still little more than a boy. Even if he possessed a beauty rarely seen on the continent, let alone in Fanoren, he doubted that Gravis—who himself was an incredibly handsome specimen—would ever concern himself with the likes of physical appearances.

In any case, the news truly came like a bolt out of the blue.

"Sir, if I may...since when have you and Lord Leorino, you know...?"

"You're actually asking? How very bold of you."

"I apologize. I promise it's not just, well, curiosity, it's just…"

"I know. You mean to ask me when he caught my romantic interest."

"…Yes. No. Well…"

Gravis chuckled.

"I know what you're trying to say. I'm old enough to be his father. Once upon a time, if I had married my then-fiancée as planned, I might have had a child or two of his age by now."

Dirk was surprised.

It must have been a long time ago, but the man had once had a fiancée after all.

"From the moment we met."

"…Sir?"

"From the moment I met him, I wanted him to be mine. And when we met again, I got the distinct sense that he would eventually be mine."

Dirk thoroughly considered this. He wasn't quite sure when they had first met, or when they had met *again*, for that matter.

"…Come now, you could at least act surprised when I swallowed my shame to tell you."

"No, it's just… If anything, I'm so shocked, I'm beyond speechless."

"You must think it laughable for an old man like me to be so absorbed in romance."

"Not at all, sir. I'm only surprised to learn you were so infatuated with Lord Leorino."

"And here I thought I was rather obvious about it."

Dirk considered this.

Looking back, Gravis's heart had always seemed to be made of ice, except when it came to Leorino.

How many times had Dirk seen him looking at Leorino with that gentle, tender gaze that he had never shown to anyone else?

Gravis had held Leorino in his arms, carefully handling him so as not to frighten him, even when using a surprising amount of force.

And then there was yesterday.

Gravis still possessed unfathomable power that even his second-in-command didn't know, and must have taken steps to put layers of protection around Leorino so that he would be able to sense if Leorino was in danger.

Dirk quickly realized Gravis had been carrying a torch for Leorino from the very beginning.

Except something wasn't adding up.

"But wait. I thought royals weren't allowed to marry members of the same sex?"

Gravis brought his hand to his chin at that.

"Our laws do not forbid the royal family from marrying a person of the same sex, no. There has simply been no precedent for it."

"Oh, that's good to know."

Same-sex marriage was legal in Fanoren. It was only that people of a certain status necessitated a successor, which made opposite-sex marriage the standard.

"I'm certain that *some* busybodies would kick up a fuss, trying to find me a woman the moment they learned I was looking to be wed, but strictly speaking, they have no authority to interfere in royal marriages. All I need is the diet's approval."

"But Lord Leorino is a son of the Margrave of Brungwurt."

The corners of Gravis's mouth lifted slightly.

"That he is. Leorino is the first member of the Brungwurt family to be released into the world in several generations. The bloodline purists would be beside themselves with joy to have him marry into the royal family. If he wasn't a man, that is."

"Right. We spoke of it when discussing Lord Julian."

"Oh, that lout will be out of the picture from now on. He will not be graced with as much as the sight of Leorino's shadow."

Dirk felt sorry for Julian, wondering what would happen to him after hearing those chilling words.

"No, I worry the Cassieux family will pose a greater issue."

Dirk connected the dots with a start.

"That's why you're going to…"

"In short, yes. I could exercise my royal privileges, but for Leorino's sake, I don't want to resort to that. I'm going to personally speak with Lord August before he learns some twisted version of the events."

With that, Gravis smiled wryly.

"At least, that's if I want Lord August for my father-in-law, which I do... Ha-ha, I never thought I'd be the one discussing such matters"

Dirk was taken aback by the rare laugh of his usually stoic superior.

At the same time, he was shocked by Gravis's willingness to speak with Leorino's parents when things seemed to be moving so suddenly.

"...May I ask if Lord Leorino feels the same way?"

"Oh, yes. You should have heard him chirping just this morning."

Dirk blushed at those words. He was not seeking information on their intimate life.

He wanted to curse himself for imagining the slender, innocent young man in the bedroom at the mercy of his large, handsome superior. The scene that flashed through his mind was too salacious to consider.

"There's one more thing I'd like to ask, sir... Does Lord Leorino know that you're, um, going to speak with his father?"

His superior inclined his head as if he didn't know what Dirk could have possibly meant.

"I don't see why I should have to tell him."

Dirk's bad premonition had been true.

"What do you mean 'why'...?"

"I don't want to bother him with such matters."

"...Um, Your Excellency, no. That's not what I meant... I think most people would actually like to be bothered like that."

Dirk had no idea what had happened overnight, but most people in love would likely not appreciate their partner visiting their parents to arrange their marriage without their knowledge.

Leorino appeared fragile but was surprisingly stubborn. He would likely oppose Gravis's forceful approach.

"What if Lord August objected to it right then and there? Leorino would feel hurt."

"W-well, yes."

Dirk was astonished that Gravis seemed so keen to protect Leorino's feelings.

"Still, as long as you were there together, wouldn't he be able to accept whatever response came?"

"It's not as simple as you think. If he becomes royalty, he will likely never get to live a normal life like he desired."

"Whatever do you mean?"

"Don't you understand? Leorino's burden will grow even heavier. As my spouse, if anything should happen to me, he will have to handle both Fanoren and Brungwurt on his own."

Dirk groaned.

His superior wasn't so head over heels for Leorino that he had forgotten all about reality.

A royal like Gravis marrying Leorino of the Cassieux family would be no ordinary marriage. Considering their status, it was inevitable; even if they genuinely loved each other, it would take a great deal of political consideration for them to marry and have their union universally recognized.

Dirk pitied his superior.

Once again, Dirk felt blessed to be a commoner who could enter relationships simply because he liked the other person.

Still, Gravis would surely make Leorino his eventually. He must have made up his mind to marry Leorino the moment he laid his hands on him. By now, he had no other choice.

As expected, Gravis's face was not that of a man spellbound by love.

Dirk heaved a deep sigh.

"Sir...you don't exactly look like a man about to secure a marriage to the person he loves. Perhaps some more enthusiasm would be in order?"

Instead of offering some words of comfort or his blessing, Dirk made a lighthearted remark. Gravis forced a smile.

"I told you, there is still something I must tell you."

"Yes, sir. You did say that."

"How I wish we could simply end this with a happily ever after."

"...What do you mean, sir?"

Gravis then abruptly changed the subject.

"How is Ebbo Steiger doing?"

"We're housing him in the private quarters in the Palace of Defense instead of the commoner district."

"I need to speak with both of you together."

"Speak about...what, exactly?"

"Our past bonds are too heavy for us to enjoy our marital bliss just yet. That goes both for me and for Leorino."

Who Decides What Happiness Looks Like?

In the margrave's study at Brungwurt Castle, Gravis faced August himself.

"Your Excellency. Seeing as you have graced me with your physical presence, I presume it is to discuss one of two things."

"Lord August."

"So do I owe this visit to Zwelf...or to Leorino?"

His voice was calm, but the expression on the aging margrave's face was uncompromising. He glared at Gravis with his blue-green eyes.

August's unusually intimidating presence was certainly befitting of the major feudal lord who reigned over a strategic position on the continent. Gravis remained undaunted, but still felt the need to focus his strength in his core. The ruler of Brungwurt carried himself with the sort of aura that could rival royalty.

"Which will it be, Your Highness?"

"...It's Leorino. I have come for your permission to accept him into the royal house of Fanoren."

August heaved a long sigh and pressed his palm to his forehead.

"...Would it kill Your Highness to be a little less forthright?"

"Knowing you, I decided embellishments would do me no favors. So then...may I have your blessing?"

"Absolutely not."

August made himself clear. Gravis raised his eyebrows.

* * *

"Our family refuses to use Leorino as a political pawn. We want him to be happy in his own right."

"I promise you that he will not be harmed in any way, body or soul."

"Do not make promises you cannot keep."

"...Excuse me?"

When Gravis retorted in a low voice, the margrave lifted his eyes resolutely.

"How could he ever live a peaceful life as your spouse?"

"Lord August, do you doubt my power?"

"I do not. But I am not speaking of the past. He has lived his entire life here in the countryside, but once he takes center stage, his appearance and our bloodline will make him far too conspicuous. That frail boy becoming royalty? ...You cannot be serious. Carrying the blood of Fanoren and Brungwurt is too heavy a burden for him to bear."

"I will not deny that becoming my spouse will place him in more danger than ever before. But I will not force any royal duties on him. I can promise you that."

The margrave's expression only turned harsher at Gravis's sincere words.

"A royal marrying someone who cannot give them children would certainly be unprecedented. Being a boy weakens his position at court."

"Being of the female persuasion does not guarantee children, either. Not to mention no one expects an heir from me by now. They have Kyle. In that respect, your fears are completely unfounded."

The two men waged war among themselves that went beyond words.

"...And where is my son now?"

"He's been in my palace since last night."

The margrave had remained physically fit and hardly looked his age. His surprisingly muscular frame now swelled with wrath.

"...Don't tell me you've already laid your filthy hands on him...!"

Gravis did not deny it.

"If you're asking if we've done the deed to completion, the answer is no. Although he's not a woman, so I don't see how it should matter... In any case, everything we did was with his consent."

"You scoundrel! If you think you'll get away with it just because you're royalty, think again...!" August roared like a lion. "You good-for-nothing

Fanorens...! You deign to wage war with Brungwurt? I'll gladly accept. If you wish to split this country, I can't imagine anything simpler!"

The walls of the study shook with the thundering sound of his voice.

Gravis did not blame August for the hint of a threat he gleaned in his response.

"I wish for no such thing. That is why I am here to ask for your blessing."

"You jest...! You must be keeping him in your palace by force—how else could such an unworldly boy grow so fond of you over such a short period of time?!"

Gravis watched the trembling man intently, his starry-sky eyes narrowed.

"It's the truth. I've been waiting for Leorino longer than you could ever know. He's my soul mate. I may be of Fanoren and he may be of Brungwurt, but I will not let that be an obstacle."

"Your *soul mate*? Your Excellency must have completely lost your mind."

"It's the truth. I realize it sounds strange, but...he's my destiny. Please, have a seat." He urged August. "It's a long story, but I want you to know the truth. It's about me, Leorino, and...a certain other man."

With that, Gravis began the tale of his life, and love long lost.

After Gravis finished, August remained stunned speechless for a longer while.

The king's brother had met the son of a blacksmith when he was still a boy. The boy had grown up to be Gravis's human shield and eventually died in battle at Zweilink. And August's son, born the morning after the tragedy at Zweilink, had inherited the young man's memories.

"...Your Highness, you can't possibly expect me to believe that. My son is the reincarnation of a soldier who died at Zweilink...? You must realize how deranged that sounds."

It all sounded bizarre, beyond August's wildest imagination.

"I realize how it sounds, but it's true. Leorino said that he has been seeing Ionia Bergund's memories in his dreams since he was half-fledged. He seems to remember everything, even that final day at Zweilink."

"…No… He couldn't possibly…"

There was a tinge of sorrow in Gravis's eyes.

"…Please, believe me. He's been keeping it a secret, suffering in silence all these years."

August widened his eyes with a start.

"You don't mean…the incident six years ago?"

Gravis nodded.

"Possibly. I suspect that incident is also somehow related to the Zweilink invasion of eighteen years ago. Yesterday, while observing some military drills, he saw a man who had once belonged to Ionia's unit and went off to see him alone with no concern for his own safety. I'll spare you the details, but he was nearly assaulted by some soldiers."

"E-excuse me…?"

"Rest assured. Fortunately nothing happened. Leorino is safe. But that was what convinced me he was the reincarnation of Ionia."

August covered his mouth, speechless.

"…My god… But that's…"

"Leorino is likely following the trace left by Ionia's memories and searching for something in the capital. I suspect he hasn't told me everything yet. I don't know what he might do if I left him alone. That's why I'm keeping him in my palace."

"…Then you saved him not twice, but three times?"

Gravis recalled the incident of six years prior.

"No… I couldn't save him six years ago."

"What are you saying? You saved him by bringing him here."

"But if only I had gotten there in time… Regardless, I failed him when he needed me, and as a result, he was grievously injured. I've regretted it since. I'm sorry I couldn't save him."

"Your Highness…"

"That day, I heard Ionia's voice, just like I had eighteen years ago… That's why I leaped to Zweilink," Gravis confessed to August.

"So that's why…?"

"Yes, but when I arrived, I found Leorino. And then my gaze met his violet eyes. I saw those eyes, the exact same color as Ionia's, and at that moment, I felt this shock… It must have been fate."

August could hardly keep up.

"Lucas had told me the same thing. He suspected Leorino might be the reincarnation of Ionia. And if he is, what would that mean?"

The lieutenant general was also somehow involved, then.

August had no idea these soldiers had been pondering Leorino for six years now.

He was left in shock by the revelation.

"But at the time, I…I denied what I felt; ignored my intuition. I was so busy with political affairs that I subconsciously turned away from Leorino's existence, so as not to taint my memory of Ionia."

Gravis tightened his fist.

"I wasted six years of my life until I was reunited with Leorino because of my unresolved feelings for Ionia. I left him all alone during the trying time when he was dealing with the memories of his past life and the serious injuries he had sustained."

August had just learned how the man who was supposedly Leorino's past incarnation had died. August remembered what Zweilink had looked like after the attack. The sight was beyond gruesome. Numerous corpses, friend and foe alike, lay in the burnt fields.

One of those corpses belonged to the man whose memories became Leorino's.

"I may be hailed as a hero, but the truth is, I'm always one step too late to save the people for whom I care the most. I'm pathetic."

In his mutter, Gravis's deep anguish at being unable to save his best friend, the only person to whom he had ever entrusted his back, was evident.

And Leorino was the reincarnation of that same man.

At long last, August understood the significance of Gravis's attachment to Leorino.

"Your Highness… That soldier named Ionia, you…"

Gravis nodded simply, understanding what August meant to ask.

"I loved him. Not as a best friend, but in the same way I love Leorino. But he was a commoner; my human shield. We could never be together."

August listened as Gravis went on.

"I was nineteen at the time. My father's health was failing and the struggle for succession intensified by the day, and then Zwelf attacked. But even if we could not be wed, I was prepared to abandon the struggle for the throne after the war with Zwelf, to be disowned by the royal family if it came to it, all so that I could spend the rest of my life with Ionia. I promised Ionia as much... without realizing that such naive fairy tales could never come true."

August recalled the young prince at the time; the way he always appeared trapped by his circumstances.

"I was the one who sent Ionia's unit to Zweilink."

"...Your Highness."

"One mistake was all it took to lose him forever...but before that tragic day came, I had always dreamed of one thing: a future with him."

"I once took Leorino to Zweilink when he was very young," August recalled. "He couldn't have been older than three at the time. He was so well-behaved since he was little... He was a veritable angel of a child, almost unbelievably so for a son of mine... Small, fragile, the most adorable thing, really."

Gravis smiled faintly at these words, perhaps imagining Leorino in his youth.

"I took him to Zweilink along with his brothers for what I thought would be little more than a field trip, thinking that he would eventually join us for the annual ceremony. It happened as soon as we arrived. Leorino started crying as if he had caught on fire."

"...You think that's—?"

"He was three at the time, still hardly speaking, but he shrieked 'Close the gates!' as if someone was skinning him alive."

"...No."

The old man released a quivering breath.

"I couldn't understand what happened. No matter how much we tried to soothe him, he wouldn't stop crying. He bawled something about being hot, tearing at his body, until at last he passed out in my arms."

Gravis hid his expression as quickly as he could.

The image of his beloved's corpse flashed through his mind, looking nothing like he once had. Gravis had found his body more ash than flesh on the scorched field where he breathed his last breath, the familiar sword still in his charred hand.

Gravis could still taste the despair he felt the moment he saw Ionia, and could still hear Lucas's blood-curdling roar.

"Now that I think of it, that too must have been the product of Ionia Bergund's memories... And yet, six years ago, I took him back to that fortress, and..." August covered his face. His boulder-like body was shaking.

"Why didn't he tell me anything...?! Why did he choose to bear such awful, harrowing memories all alone...?!" The old margrave lamented. "Was it our fault?! We only wished to give him a happy life, to keep him from hardship... Did we force him to feign happiness for our sake...? Why? Why did we make him suffer so...?"

"Lord August, that can't possibly be true!"

August's eyes were wet beneath his drooping eyelids.

"...Damn you. God damn you for bringing up the past, for exposing our sins..."

Gravis could only silently watch August as he trembled with remorse.

"...But I do realize the person who has suffered most for these eighteen long years was you. And that Leorino...or rather, Ionia, the man who came before him, suffered too."

Suddenly August flexed himself into a deep bow.

"Your Excellency...! I understand that Leorino and you are bound by an inseparable bond from a previous life. But knowing that I must still ask... Please, stand down."

"...Lord August."

The old man's rock-like back was shaking.

"Please, pursue my boy no longer...!"

August begged, his forehead nearly touching his knees.

"As the head of the House of Cassieux, I am making a once-in-a-lifetime request to the House of Fanoren. I want my son to be free."

Gravis gasped.

"I say this knowing the memories he had to suffer through. That man, Ionia, may have been strong enough to fight by your side. But Leorino, he... he's too weak to be your spouse. Please, please let him go."

Gravis clenched his teeth.

He could understand August's plea. It was selfish of Gravis to desire Leorino so desperately.

August had understood the depth of Gravis's feelings and still begged him to set them aside for Leorino's sake.

The father's heartbreaking request anguished Gravis.

"Are you saying I should forsake my future with Leorino?"

August answered with silence.

If Gravis let him go now, Leorino would be freer and happier. Perhaps even with Julian.

Living with Gravis meant living in a world more tightly protected than ever, including in the physical sense.

But could they truly say Leorino wasn't prepared for as much? Could they choose his future for him simply because he was sheltered and supposedly couldn't think for himself?

"I'm sorry I made you wait eighteen years," Leorino had said.

"My heart and my loyalty belong to you. So...please grant me permission to love you, too."

Leorino had entrusted him with everything with such clear resolve—Gravis wanted to believe in his strength.

Perhaps it was just a way for him to make sense of his own desires, but Gravis couldn't give up so easily.

"Lord August, your son... Leorino is not a weak man by any means."

"...Whatever do you mean? How could that be?"

"His body may be frail and sickly, and his legs don't fare much better, but his heart is strong."

The margrave widened his eyes at those words.

"Without a doubt, he is blood of your blood, a boy of the Cassieux family."

August gasped.

"He is a sincere, loyal, courageous, strong man. And I...I want to believe in Leorino's courage."

"Your Highness..."

Gravis must have been thinking of Leorino as he spoke. August was deeply moved by the gentlest expression he had ever seen on Gravis's face.

"He apologized for making me wait eighteen years. He asked for permission to love me. And he swore his heart and his loyalty to me."

"...He did all that?"

Gravis nodded emphatically.

"Considering our age difference, we likely won't be blessed with much time together, but I will protect him with all my might. So I ask again...will you allow me to live the rest of my life with my beloved?"

"Your Highness... You truly..."

"Just once in my life, I want to be with the man I love; not concealed by the darkness of the night, but walking with him in the light of day."

August felt an intense pain behind his eyes.

How much loneliness had Gravis endured throughout his life?

This royal had bared his heart to August and candidly, fervently spoke of his love for Leorino. August was so struck by Gravis's quiet, prayer-like sentiment, he had no further objections.

As a father, as a man, and as a warrior, August did not possess the words to tear apart the two men brought together by a twist of fate, reunited at last.

"I understand your concerns as a father. You may loathe me if you wish. But I couldn't possibly give up when my destiny is alive and right before me... I'm sorry, August. But please," Gravis asked August with sincere eyes.

Here stood a man who had set aside all his pride as royalty.

"I wish him to be my husband. Let me receive the heart and loyalty he so kindly offered me."

Whom Does Love Kill and
Whom Does It Keep Alive?

In the end, the Margrave of Brungwurt gave no clear answer.

However, Gravis was relatively relieved by the fact August hadn't refused him outright. After the frank conversation, August must have understood how serious he was. At the very least, he had managed to avoid starting a civil war over Leorino between Fanoren and Brungwurt.

In order for the royal to marry Leorino, the margrave set three conditions.

The first was that Leorino should return to the Brungwurt residence in the royal capital within a reasonable time—which in practice likely meant as soon as possible. That must have been August's way of saying that no conclusion would be reached regarding the offer until they could confirm Gravis was not coercing Leorino into anything, and he wanted this just as much.

Except Leorino still knew nothing of the matter... Gravis had already begun to consider how to discuss the future without upsetting Leorino, given how many secrets he was still keeping. At the latest, he would have to speak with Leorino before returning him to the Cassieux family.

Secondly, if he were to marry Leorino, it would have to be through official channels and following due process. In practice, this meant preparing everything to perfection, ascertaining that Leorino would be given the status he deserved so that his position would not be damaged in the slightest.

Gravis had no objections to this demand. He had already been privately devising the means to obtain the king's and the diet's approval.

The third condition was regarding the timing. August demanded that the marriage take place after the war with Zwelf had been settled. August's intention was to wait until after he was able to assess the state of Brungwurt, which would of course depend on the outcome of the coming war.

Gravis had objected to this.

He had no intention of losing the war with Zwelf, but by being wed ahead of time, if something should happen to Gravis, Leorino would be safest as a member of the royal family.

But the margrave's insistence was not without merit.

If the war with Zwelf were to start in Zweilink, and in the event that Zweilink were breached, the war would quickly consume Brungwurt.

The Zweilink fortress on the border would be defended by the Royal Army, but the territory of Brungwurt was under the protection of the Autonomous Army led by August. The lands of Brungwurt were an autonomous territory where the Royal Army was not welcome. That was the unwritten rule between Fanoren and Brungwurt.

But few people carried the Cassieux name. Depending on the outcome of the war, the number of people who could inherit the blood and name of the Cassieux family could drastically decrease. For that reason, it was necessary to protect Leorino's family name as a potential heir.

This was due to Fanoren's marriage law. A male member of the royal family was not allowed to divorce his spouse unless he abandoned his royal status. Instead, they were allowed to have multiple concubines. Nobles and commoners, on the other hand, could not enter a union with several people at once, but were allowed to divorce and remarry.

In practice, this meant that Leorino could marry Julian Munster and change his family name, and in the case the Cassieux line was about to be severed, he could regain the Cassieux name through divorce. However, if he married into the royal family, Leorino would become a Fanoren forever, never to lay claim to the Cassieux name again.

Behind August's request, there was a hint of a father's reluctance to give his beloved son to a man who was going off to war.

Becoming royalty was likely the highest honor for the nobility of Fanoren.

But the Cassieux family had its reasons. From August's perspective, Julian was a much more secure candidate for Leorino's spouse, if only because he wouldn't partake in any fighting.

In August's mind, the calculations of a major feudal lord hailing from a long-standing bloodline and the fatherly love for his son were intricately woven into one.

Julian was the heir to a major noble family who could protect his beloved youngest son and was also the best man to entrust the Cassieux name to in an emergency. He weighed Gravis and Julian against each other with this in mind.

In the end, Gravis agreed to the third condition. In exchange, they would announce their engagement as soon as the formalities were completed. The only reason for this was to eliminate anyone who might consider getting their mitts on Leorino in the meantime.

This alone would keep any scoundrels from flocking to Leorino, and as Gravis's fiancé, he would be treated like royalty and afforded protection befitting that position.

Gravis would not allow the future August feared to come to pass.

Even in the event of a war, he had no intention of handing over even one blade of Fanoren grass to Zwelf. He certainly wasn't planning on dying in battle, either.

He would exterminate any fool who tried to invade his lands, no matter who they may be.

He would accept nothing but victory for his kingdom.

He would maintain the peace in which Leorino could spend the rest of his life with a smile on his face. That was the only future waiting for Gravis.

Beasts That Cry of Loneliness

Having spent a significant part of the day in Brungwurt speaking with the margrave, Gravis finally returned to the Palace of Defense around dusk.

Normally, he would have stayed up late performing his official duties, but today of all days, he wanted to be sure Leorino was doing well, since he had left so soon after their morning tryst.

But when he returned to his office, he found two men waiting for him there.

"Who gave you permission to come in?"

"...I did, sir."

It was Dirk who answered in a firm voice.

The only person with constant access to the office in Gravis's absence was the general's second-in-command.

"...Lieutenant Colonel Bergund, I'll need you to leave."

Dirk was about to say something when the other man gave the order. Given his strange behavior, Dirk hesitated to leave him alone with his superior.

"I would like to speak with His Highness alone."

"...But that's—"

"I don't care. Leave."

Gravis stared back blankly into the amber eyes that glared at him with a gaze that seemed intent on killing him with its intensity alone.

"Dirk, wait outside."

"...But, sir—"

"I'll be fine. He's not as crazed as he appears."

Gravis's starry-sky eyes flashed.

"I suppose the time has come for us to have this conversation at last... Isn't that right, Lucas?"

The other man waiting for Gravis was Lieutenant General Lucas Brandt, who now tightly clenched his fists.

"I understand your concern, so I'm happy to inform you that Leorino is safe and sound."

Gravis sat down in one of the chairs and motioned for Lucas to sit opposite him, but Lucas refused. He remained standing with his arms crossed and his lips pursed.

"And here I thought you came here to speak with me?"

"Lieutenant Colonel Bergund has informed me of what happened when I took my eyes off Leorino."

"...And what of it? Have you come to tell me that Leorino should be punished for disobeying your orders?"

At these words, anger filled Lucas's large, boulder-like frame. Gravis continued dispassionately: "He was under my protection to begin with. He will be placed on house arrest under my watchful eye for the time being. No need to punish him further."

Gravis felt he could hear Lucas grinding his teeth.

"If he's under house arrest, why not keep him in the Palace of Defense...? Why did you feel the need to bring him back to your palace?"

Gravis curtly replied: "You can't expect me to leave Leorino in the Palace of Defense without security, now can you?"

"Are you saying the Palace of Defense can't keep him safe? Hah, that's bold coming from the man who *runs* this place."

"I'm not pleased to admit it, now am I? As long as Leorino can't accurately assess danger, I can't afford to take my eyes off him for even a moment."

Lucas clenched his fists and asked in a barely contained voice:

"Your Highness...you once said that if the boy truly is the reincarnation of Ionia, then he will be yours."

"...I have said as much, yes."

"When I arrived at the scene, I found Ebbo Steiger in that room, the only survivor of Ionia's unit. Leorino disobeyed my orders and went to see Steiger, did he not? Or am I missing something?"

Gravis looked at Lucas. In his gaze, Lucas noticed the truth, and raised his voice.

"...Must I spell it out?! Why else would that sheltered boy go against my orders and risk his life to go see Steiger? Is that... Is that not proof enough?!"

"...Proof?"

"Yes! Proof that Leorino is Ionia!"

Lucas's roar echoed through the office, and soon his ragged breathing followed like an echo.

"That's what this is, isn't it? That's why you brought Leorino back to your palace. All of this can mean only one thing!"

"...You might recall, I also said that even if Leorino *was* the reincarnation of Ionia, that would change nothing."

Lucas squeezed his trembling fists even tighter, struggling to hold back his raging impulses.

"...Let me see Ionia."

Gravis furrowed his brow.

"Don't call him that."

Lucas's veil of reason finally fell away.

He grabbed Gravis by the shirt—a royal and his superior, no less—with no intention of backing down.

It would have been easy for Gravis to avoid his hand. He could simply use his special ability to effortlessly move through space. But Gravis remained where he stood on purpose.

"...Will learning his secret bring you the satisfaction you so desperately seek, Lucas?"

"It's not just that. But we must start somewhere."

Their gazes collided with so much force, it nearly sent sparks flying through the air.

"...Fine. Leorino was born with Ionia's memories. That's why he went to see Ebbo Steiger."

Lucas moaned in delight.

"...So it's true, then... He really is the reincarnation of Ionia... My—"

Gravis calmly laid his palm on the man's hand, still gripping his own chest.

"Lucas, I don't want to see Leorino reduced to tears again. So please... don't call him Ionia."

Lucas pushed Gravis's hand away in indignation.

The two men were now facing each other as old friends; beyond status, beyond rank.

"Why? If he has his memories, he must remember those days and...me. *Us*. Am I wrong?"

"...Yes, I suspect he does remember."

"Then what's the difference between him and Ionia? That's why you squirreled him away, is it not?!"

"Yes, and no."

Lucas's penetrating amber eyes glared at him in question.

"...And what is that supposed to mean?"

Grabbing Lucas by the arm, Gravis slowly pulled away.

"The only reason he kept the truth from us was because of our fixation on Ionia."

"...What?"

"He...he didn't want *us* to know that he possessed Ionia's memories."

Shocked, Lucas staggered backward.

"...I don't understand. Why? Ionia wouldn't... He wouldn't ignore me...or you, when we've waited for him so long."

"Because he doesn't think of himself as Ionia."

"He doesn't...?"

Gravis nodded.

"Yes. Even if he has Ionia's memories, Leorino is not Ionia. He knows who he is. That's why he was so distressed that he couldn't be the Ionia we were searching for."

"...That can't be."

"We had placed Io on a pedestal, setting a standard Leorino could never live up to."

Gravis heaved a deep sigh.

"I don't suppose you've forgotten the way he cried."

"I haven't... But—"

"He wept all through last night. He wanted to protect the memory of Ionia in us. He was afraid of disappointing us. You should have seen the pain he was in as he bawled his eyes out."

Unlike Lucas, Gravis may have appeared calm, but he too must have been somewhat agitated by now.

He took a deep breath and regained his composure.

"I still don't know what to make of this miracle, this mischief of the gods. All I know is that he's an entirely different person from Ionia...both in mind, and in body. Ionia has not risen from the dead."

"Which means...he may have Ionia's memories, but they are simply memories of a complete stranger stored in his mind, is that right?"

In the end, all Lucas wanted to know was if Leorino was Ionia or not.

"I don't know... Would simply having his memories not make him Ionia?" asked Lucas.

"He hadn't told me how he feels in detail yet. And as for Io's memories, we still don't know exactly how many he has inherited."

Lucas groaned in frustration.

But Gravis's next words took his breath away.

"But even if they have the same soul, they must be treated as different people. Leorino fears losing his raison d'être more than anything else," Gravis continued. "Ionia's memories have brought Leorino suffering for a long time—likely, they still are. So please...don't reduce him to tears again, Lucas."

Lucas was confused and anguished at the same time.

That was when Gravis suddenly asked Lucas a question.

"Lucas. I've asked you before. I'll ask one final time, and this time, I want you to be honest with me... If Leorino isn't Ionia reincarnated, do you still desire him?"

"...That's not—"

"Do you still feel the maddening need to get your hands on him? ...To sleep with him?"

Lucas did not want to answer. He felt that if he did, all hope would be lost forever.

He already knew his answer.

At the end of the day, Lucas yearned only for that strong, graceful, red-haired young man.

If he were truly a reincarnation of Ionia, of course he would desire Leorino. However, when asked whether he could be equally attached to the boy if he were not Ionia reincarnated, he suddenly wasn't so sure anymore.

There was certainly much to love about the slender, fragile young man, and he certainly spoke to Lucas's protective instincts.

But he sincerely didn't know if he could ever feel for Leorino what he had felt for Ionia for so long.

"I... No, I don't know. Perhaps I do, well... I might, I can't say for certain."

Lucas imagined the fragile, porcelain-like young man in his mind's eye. He remembered the way he cried as he said, "I am not Ionia."

"Who do you see before you?"

Leorino had asked Lucas that question just recently.

Lucas already vaguely realized that he should treat Leorino and Ionia as two separate people.

And yet he felt like he was an arm's length away from the vestige of Ionia he had been seeking for eighteen long years.

Even knowing they were different people, Lucas's heart still clung to that hope with unfulfilled longing.

"Your Highness...I just want to see Ionia again... I just want to see him one last time...!"

Lucas groaned with his head in his hands.

The answer he had been seeking for eighteen years was right in front of him. He could nearly reach it, only for it to slip from his hands once more.

"You wouldn't understand. And of course... How could you ever understand how I feel?"

Lucas sat down on the settee with an audible thud and covered his eyes with his hands.

"...Yes, I may have been sleeping with Ionia. Physically, he was mine. But...from the day he met you to his dying breath, you were the only thing occupying his mind."

Gravis said nothing.

"He once told me. Before he was sent to Zweilink, he nearly told me something. He laughed and said, 'I'll tell you next time I see you.' He always had this stern look on his face, but in that moment, he...he looked so peaceful, more tender than I'd ever seen him."

Lucas's mutterings brought back memories for Gravis as well.

The night before Ionia was sent to Zweilink, Gravis had gone to see him at his family's blacksmith shop, and he wore that immensely fond expression.

Lucas wasn't looking at Gravis, lost in his memories.

"Perhaps whatever he had wanted to tell me was of no consequence after all. But...I was hoping for the best. I had been waiting for the ten years I'd known him. I assumed that perhaps he'd finally give me something, some... some fraction of his heart."

Lucas's square shoulders trembled, almost as if he were crying.

"But...we were not destined to speak again."

Lucas raised his wet eyes.

"In that blazing fire, Ionia was looking at you, and only at you... But I was there, next to you! I was right there...!"

Gravis clenched his teeth.

That day, Gravis had single-handedly transported countless troops to Zweilink. He had consumed a great deal of his Power, leaving him with hardly any life force.

Lucas had stopped him with trembling arms when he tried to leap to Ionia despite this.

Of course.

It wasn't the behavior of a subordinate. Lucas had likely respected Ionia's wishes more than his own feelings.

The image of Lucas roaring and breaking down in tears in front of the burnt remains of Ionia's body was still vividly seared into Gravis's mind.

"I called his name as hard as I could...but the entire time, he looked only at you. I...I never learned what he wanted to tell me, and he died without offering me the smallest fraction of his heart!"

The roar came from the depths of the soul of a man whose undying love would never be requited.

At that moment, Lucas must have wanted to run to his beloved's side more than anyone else. But Lucas had sworn to Ionia to protect Gravis, and protect Gravis he would, even if he lost everything that ever mattered in the process.

"...You could never understand the anguish of the have-nots."

Gravis silently accepted the man's denunciation.

"I was hoping against hope...that perhaps he had always intended to give some fraction of his heart after all... I'd been waiting for those words for so, so long."

The words Ionia had wanted to convey to Lucas.

Lucas had loved Ionia selflessly and completely, and those words he was supposed to hear seemed to be the only thing keeping him alive.

"You may think me sentimental, but I thought that if Leorino was his reincarnation, he would give me the words Ionia promised me... He would smile at me like he did that day and give me the answers I've been waiting for... That's all I could ever hope for."

It was hard to blame a man who had loved Ionia so much that his feelings had turned into such deep-rooted delusion.

The loss of Ionia had also created a bottomless swamp of obsession within Gravis. And in that swamp lived a beast with the savage urge to devour Leorino, the sacrifice, to relieve his loneliness until there was nothing left of him at all.

With the sacrifice in the form of Leorino, the beast may have found the path to salvation. But the beast inside Lucas was still roaring for the other half of his soul that was lost forever.

"I should have never met Ionia."

"…Your Highness."

"If only I had not met him in that forge that day…I'm certain you would have found each other eventually and lived happily ever after."

If he had wanted Ionia to be happy, he should have stayed away from him after they met at the blacksmith's shop.

But at the time, Gravis couldn't have known.

That loving someone often meant letting them go.

He was starved of human warmth. He wanted someone who could understand him regardless of status. Their meeting had been a miracle for Gravis.

But here was the result. Ionia and Lucas, both of their lives ruined.

Gravis had made a decision eighteen years ago.

He would never apologize to Lucas.

If Lucas was going to hate him, it should be with no holds barred, a deep and true resentment, if only it meant the hatred would give Lucas a reason to keep going.

But this betrayal was different.

"Lucas…"

Flooded with emotion, he called his friend's name. Then he called out to the beast inside Lucas.

"Lucas, I owe you an apology."

Lucas's face crumpled.

He already knew what Gravis was going to say.

"I thought you and I were going to spend the rest of our lives with Ionia in our hearts."

"…Your Highness."

"I thought that our relationship would remain the same forever, until the day we at last found our way back to Ionia on the other side."

"Your Highness, please…say no more."

Lucas and Gravis were mirror images of each other.

Lucas had loved a man, a commoner, only following the call of his heart.

Gravis seemed to have it all, but was shackled with the burden of never having the freedom to love anyone.

Like the sun and the moonless night, the men were opposites in every way: their standing, their environment, their personalities, their appearances.

The only mirror that could contain them both was the red-haired young man.

The two men had been facing each other for a long time with Ionia as the mirror between them.

"I had hoped that the end would come soon...and that in my final days I would have the chance to talk about Ionia with you."

"Your Highness Prince Gravis... Please. Please keep Ionia in your thoughts. Please don't forget him."

"I will not forget him. How could I ever?"

"Then..."

"But...I'm sorry, Lucas."

Blood trickled down Gravis's lip.

"I've fallen in love with Leorino."

At these words, Lucas despaired.

Eighteen years had passed since Ionia's death. Lucas had spent far longer connected with Gravis by the bond of their love for Ionia than he had spent with Ionia himself.

This too had been a sort of love-hate relationship between them.

At that very moment, the bond was severed, throwing Lucas into despair.

"How is that not killing what remains of Ionia...? You are trying to kill him all over again!"

Gravis accepted the beast's scream without averting his gaze. For all the accusations of betrayal, he still wanted to get something across.

"Yes. I'll be the one to kill what persists of Ionia within Leorino. For Leorino to live, I will never call him 'Ionia'... Never again."

"You..."

The corners of Lucas's eyes were wet as he glared at Gravis with the unhidden desire to slay him where stood.

"Feel free to resent me, Lucas."

"You bastard... You utter piece of filth."

Lucas shuddered, groaning in despair.

"I wouldn't blame you if you killed me. If anything, you're the only person deserving of that privilege."

Gravis approached Lucas and pulled him into an embrace. He pleaded directly into the trembling man's ear.

"...But please, Lucas. Don't let your feelings for Ionia destroy Leorino."

The corners of Lucas's mouth twisted.

"Destroy...? If I did that and still wanted him for myself, what would you do?"

"If you try to destroy Leorino, you'll live to regret it."

Lucas was silent, until finally he laughed dryly.

"...At the end of the day, you truly are royalty. No one can hold you accountable for your natural arrogance, and so you will continue to live... always getting what you want."

Gravis stifled the urge to argue. Never in his life had he ever gotten what he wanted.

But no. Gravis corrected himself—he *had* gotten Ionia's loyalty.

The man who occupied his heart, and the man who occupied his body.

His best friend, and his significant other.

Which of them was truly deserving of Ionia's hand?

But the red-haired young man was no longer there to give them his answer.

"How...how could you have done something so horrible...? Ionia, Ionia..."

"...Lucas."

"No amount of hatred in the world...could make me kill the man Ionia loved most of all... Your Highness, how arrogant, how cruel you are."

Soon, Lucas's strength drained from his massive frame.

"Your Highness... I..."

Lucas muttered, all emotion drained from his face, as if he had finally let go of the burdens he had been carrying for so long.

The corners of his eyes were wrinkled with eighteen years of heartache.

* * *

"I may loathe you, but I would never betray you... I could never betray the man Ionia loved, the man he died to protect."

The man's despair and the strange blend of love and hate pierced Gravis's chest.

"And believe me, I loathe you. But if it wasn't for my love for Ionia, I wouldn't also..."

His eyes were fixed on Gravis.

"Your Highness Prince Gravis... God damn you."

This wasn't the first time Gravis had heard those words that day.

"But in his stead, my blood and loyalty...will be yours forever."

Lucas's amber eyes were filled with a thin film of tears.

"Until the day either of us perishes, I will take on Ionia's burden... Your Highness, my allegiance is yours."

Gravis returned to his palace where his beloved awaited him after a far-too-long day.

He was exhausted.

He was told Leorino was holed up in the washroom. When he opened the door, he found his beloved peering into the mirror.

When he embraced Leorino from behind, he saw a smile bloom on his face in the reflection.

Here was his other half, reunited at last. His blissful smile sent a shiver down Gravis's spine.

But his violet eyes were somewhat dark. There, he caught a glimpse of the anguish brought on by Ionia's memories.

Lucas was likely part of that anguish. No matter how much Gravis loved Leorino, as long as he possessed Ionia's memories, some part of Lucas would always exist in Leorino's mind. He would never be able to change that.

Gravis endured the pain in his chest and embraced the slender body in a frenzied impulse.

My blood and loyalty...will be yours forever. I will take on Ionia's burden.

Lucas's gut-wrenching words still tore at Gravis's heart.

Why did he have to sacrifice so much to be with the person he loved? Why couldn't he just love someone without hurting anyone else?

But Leorino was just one person. Sharing him with Lucas was not an option.

He never wanted to fight over someone ever again. If it came to it, this time the beast nesting inside Gravis would devour the beast on the other side of the mirror.

Gravis didn't want Leorino to see their deep-seated delusions. He wanted Leorino to live a long happy life to the fullest, the life Ionia never got.

Gravis would do anything to give him that.

He closed his eyes as if in prayer.

The Price of Lying

The morning after making love with Gravis, Leorino fell ill.

"Leorino, are you all right?" Gravis asked, noticing that Leorino was panting heavily, in agony from a fever. But Leorino did not open his eyes, only kept breathing in short gasps, sweat beading on his forehead.

Gravis regretted his choices.

They had gone slow, but unable to resist Leorino's pleas, they went through with the deed after all, mostly to Leorino's detriment. In a constant state of excitement since the day before yesterday, Leorino must not have realized he had reached his physical and mental limits.

If not handled with great care, Leorino would easily break. Gravis took that to heart.

It wasn't quite dawn yet, but Gravis reluctantly called for his valet.

The servant soon appeared, not daring to keep his master waiting. He was dressed as immaculately as always. Clearly Theodor still had some secrets of his own—such as when he slept.

"Is something the matter, my lord?"

"Leorino has a fever."

"…May I see him?"

Theodor received permission and entered the bedroom. Royal attendants were expected to have some medical knowledge, so he should be able to assess Leorino's condition to some extent.

Theodor quietly approached the bed and placed a hand on Leorino's forehead as he tossed in his sleep, to check his temperature and then his pulse. Finally, he brought his ear to his mouth and listened to his breathing for a while.

Leorino didn't stir at any of this.

Having examined him, Theodor stood up.

"His fever is quite high. But his pulse is stable, and there is no wheezing in his chest. There is no sign of illness in his lungs."

"Good to know."

"I suspect it is an issue of exhaustion. Or perhaps your bedchamber affairs were a little too intense for him... Did you end up using it last night?"

The valet indicated the discarded toy on the bedside table. Gravis nodded in response.

"I'm certain it didn't hurt him. His legs should be fine as well."

The valet nodded at his master's answer without concern.

"Much has happened recently. The mental and physical shock of it all must have brought out the fatigue all at once. Lord Leorino's physical condition appears to be quite unstable."

"Yes, I have heard from the margrave that since the incident six years ago, he has become very frail."

"I see. Then I think it would be best to have someone who is familiar with his constitution look after him."

"Have you brought his attendant?"

Theodor nodded.

"We shall nurse him back to health, but the hour is still early. May I move Lord Leorino to another room?"

"Why can't he stay here?"

"Well, sharing a bed in his condition may put a strain on both of you, my lord. Not to mention, Lord Leorino's attendant would be forced to enter your bedchamber."

Gravis shook his head at the valet's suggestion.

"No, I want him here."

"...Your Highness, we have already prepared the adjoining room. It will belong to him eventually."

Theodor argued matter-of-factly. Gravis raised an eyebrow, but finally shook his head.

"I want to watch over him until he gets better. You can bring his attendant here. I can worry about everything else later."

Theodor bowed, left the room, and quickly returned with the elderly servant in tow.

"This is Lord Leorino's full-time attendant. He will take care of him from now on."

The thin, elderly attendant bowed his head deeply, carefully avoiding eye contact with Gravis.

He must have been nervous about being in the presence of royalty, but he was without a doubt a servant of the Cassieux family. He was doing his best to maintain his composure.

Leorino's attendant appeared relieved when Theodor led him into the parlor and hurriedly headed for the bedroom where his master slept.

Feeling a familiar hand on his forehead, Leorino exhaled.

"You have a high fever, my lord."

Guided by the gentle voice, Leorino woke up from a dream of blood and soot.

"...Hundert...?"

"Yes, I'm right here, my lord."

Leorino found it hard to breathe and could hardly see anything in the darkness.

He didn't know what time it was or, in fact, where he was at all.

Leorino felt the smoldering heat all over his body and couldn't keep himself from writhing in agony on the bed.

"I'm hot... So hot..."

"You have a fever, my lord. You must be very tired."

"Fever... But the flames..."

"We shall cool you down, but you need to get your rest. When you wake up, you'll take your medicine."

Seeing his attendant for the first time in two days, Leorino smiled in relief, even as sweat dripped down his forehead.

"...Hundert."

"Yes, my lord, I am here. You're in good hands now. Please, rest at ease."

Hundert patted him on the shoulder from over the covers. Then something cold was placed on his head.

Hundert's presence brought Leorino no small amount of comfort.

"You should get some sleep."

The canopy curtains were drawn closed once more and Leorino was left alone in the darkness.

I don't want to go back to Zweilink.

With this thought in his otherwise vacant mind, Leorino once again lost consciousness.

Eventually, Leorino emerged from his slumber.

A fever was smoldering inside his body. Leorino felt as if he had been thrown into a blazing fire.

"Hot, so hot…" He groaned quietly.

As he writhed in discomfort, the canopy curtains were soon pulled back, clearing Leorino's vision.

"Lord Leorino…can't you sleep?"

"So hot… I want to speak with Ebbo…"

Hundert spoke slowly and soothingly to his master.

"I'm sorry, my lord, who is Ebbo?"

Leorino shook his head.

"I can't tell Vi…or Luca…"

"Lord Leorino, you're speaking with Hundert."

"I dropped it on purpose… I want to apologize…to Dirk. I must apologize…"

Hundert had no idea how to help his master as he writhed on the bed, clutching onto the covers.

Leorino seemed to voice every thought that came to mind. When Hundert placed his hand on his master's forehead once more, his temperature seemed even higher.

Whenever he succumbed to fever, Leorino began to whine like a child. He was usually so reticent—this was the only occasion when everything he suppressed came to the surface.

"Call Josef… I want to apologize."

Hundert was at a loss. Of course, Josef was not there.

Speaking of Josef... Hundert recalled the events of the past few days.

The night before last, Josef returned from the training grounds alone. Dirk Bergund, who had chaperoned Leorino in the carriage in the morning, accompanied Josef for some reason.

Leorino was nowhere to be found.

The family members waiting for Leorino's return were then presented with a shocking revelation:

Leorino had caused some issue at the training grounds, and was in the custody of the general, His Royal Majesty the King's younger brother.

When Johan learned of this, he was livid.

Johan, the mildest of Leorino's three older brothers, glared at Dirk with eyes that seemed ready to kill him on the spot. He strongly protested that detaining a member of the Cassieux family without a charge was scandalous.

In no uncertain terms, he ordered that Leorino be returned to the Cassieux family at once. Furthermore, he said that this was no longer a matter of the Palace of Defense, but an issue between the royal family and the Cassieuxs, and threatened Dirk with what could certainly be interpreted as a declaration of war.

Dirk did not apologize, but with sincerity convinced Johan that his anger was undue.

Leorino's stay at the palace was not an unjustified detainment, but rather a form of protection. In addition, there were many mysteries surrounding the events at the training grounds, and Leorino was in the position to help them get to the bottom of the situation. Dirk repeatedly and politely explained to Johan that the general was responsible for Leorino's safety and that he should rest assured that Leorino would be taken care of and provided for.

When Johan reluctantly sheathed his metaphorical sword in response to Dirk's sincerity and persuasion, the red-haired man smiled slightly in relief. Johan then promised that he would send a messenger from the Palace of Defense to the general's palace as soon as he could.

But the members of the Cassieux household were still concerned about Leorino and spent the night in anxiety. Unlike the last time, they had not received any official notice, which only worried them further.

The next day, the royal attendant of the king's brother, who introduced himself as Theodor, appeared at the Brungwurt residence.

It was highly unusual for a royal attendant to personally deliver messages.

Johan did not hide his aggression toward the messenger. Of course, Theodor was of higher status than Johan in terms of their position in the royal court. He may have been a valet, but an attendant of the royal family was nothing like a mere servant of the nobility. It was a high position in the royal court, and Theodor was the equal of the crown prince's attendant, second only to the king and queen's attendants.

The Cassieux family, however, was not bound by any visible royal court hierarchy. Unlike Leorino, Johan fully understood the power of his family name.

A long conversation took place in the study, which no servant was allowed to witness. The household members all waited impatiently.

Then Hundert was suddenly summoned by Johan and ordered to make preparations to head to the general's palace and look after Leorino. Hundert had countless questions, but did as he was told as long as it meant seeing his precious master safe and sound.

He hurriedly prepared the bare necessities such as Leorino's clothing and personal care items. He asked the other servants to prepare whatever he couldn't carry so that he could come pick it up later.

Theodor then invited him to the carriage he had arranged and brought Hundert to the detached palace of the king's brother.

Seeing the massive palace for the first time, Hundert was overwhelmed, shaken by its grandeur. Last night, he had been shown into a room so luxurious that it couldn't have been intended for a servant and was told to remain there until called for. But Hundert was not allowed to see Leorino and hadn't slept a wink.

Then, just before dawn, a knock suddenly sounded on his door, summoning him to nurse his master through a fever.

"Now, my lord, let's drink our medicine, shall we?"

"No, I shan't… You're so mean, Hundert. The medicine is always bitter."

"You're all grown up now, my lord, please be brave."

Then a large man approached his bedside.

Avoiding looking directly at the man, Hundert backed away, bowing in a panic. It was His Highness, the king's brother himself.

Gravis leaned down, peered into the bed, and seeing Leorino's bangs stuck to his forehead, gently brushed them away.

"I'll get him to drink it."

"Your Royal Highness, I…I wouldn't dare to ask that of you."

"It's fine… Theodor, hand me the medicine."

The valet passed his master the teacup with the medicinal infusion.

Gravis sat Leorino up and leaned him back against his chest. He took the teacup and brought the spout to Leorino's gasping mouth.

"No… I told you, I don't want it…"

"My lord!"

To Hundert's great surprise, Leorino tried to push away the hand of His Royal Highness. He very nearly yelled at his master for disrespecting a member of the royal family, even if he was in a daze due to the high fever.

But Gravis didn't seem the least bit bothered by Leorino's reaction, only patiently trying to get through to him, his lips by his ear.

"Oh, hush. Less complaining, more drinking. You have a high fever. You'll only exhaust yourself like this."

"No… It's bitter, I don't want it."

"It's not *that* bitter."

"No, I know it is… Hundert always lies to me."

"…Can't you tell who I am?"

Hundert was sweating buckets now.

He had no idea how he would explain Leorino's childish behavior.

"You're an adult, perhaps act like it. I thought you had things to do… Now drink up."

Gravis tried to pry his mouth open and pour the medicine down his throat. But, weak as he was, Leorino struggled and resisted. Still, the man's hand was firmly fixed on Leorino's chin, and he couldn't as much as turn his face away.

"Hng… I don't want it… No."

"I don't care. Drink."

But Leorino stubbornly closed his lips and tried to resist.

After a while, Leorino finally gave in, opened his mouth obediently and swallowed the medicine bit by bit, though not without groaning his complaints in the process.

The servants, watching this play out, released a breath of relief at the sight.

Leorino wrinkled his nose as hard as he could to express his great displeasure.

"I knew it... It *was* bitter... Ew."

"'Ew,' my ass. You'll feel better once your fever goes down. You're too old to be acting like this. Get it together."

His eyes were moist and bloodshot, his gaze unfocused in his daze. Leorino weakly raised his head and glared up at Gravis. He suddenly had tears in his eyes.

"What's wrong?"

"Vi... I'm sorry... I lied to everyone."

"I know."

"I must see him..."

"See whom?"

Leorino rested his head on the Gravis's chest and looked at someone who was not there.

"...See Luca."

"You will." Gravis said and gently cradled Leorino's small head in his arms. Big fat tears trickled down Leorino's cheeks.

"Luca... Luca, I'm sorry... Luca."

Gravis wiped his tears away and brought his lips to his sweaty forehead.

"Neither Lucas nor anyone else can blame you, Leorino."

Leorino shook his head.

"When I told them Ebbo would come back, they said I was lying... They're squeezing my neck. I can't breathe... Help."

"...Leorino."

"They said I should humor them... That it wouldn't take long... I'm scared. But this is my punishment... I deserve this."

Leorino could barely catch his breath. Gravis's hand gently wiped the sweat from his forehead.

* * *

"It's all right. You will never see those men again."

Leorino's feverish mind may have made sense of the conversation, but it was completely incoherent to the average listener.

But Gravis could understand.

Every word Leorino moaned in his delirium showed him a glimpse of the anguish he had been suffering from.

Leorino's high fever was a product of the weight of the secrets he had been keeping. He wanted him to let it out, to ease his mind.

"Ebbo was crying... He said it can't be true... His horrible scars are my fault... I'm sorry, Ebbo."

Leorino apologized through tears.

Gravis only held his thin body close.

"I need to speak with Ebbo... I couldn't get it right."

"You couldn't speak with Ebbo?"

"No... With Vi."

"I really don't understand a thing," Gravis muttered and smiled softly.

Gravis continued to slowly rub his shoulders, comforting Leorino's slender, painfully feverish body.

"...We've spoken a lot by now. What couldn't you do?"

"...The eggs... I told you, I don't like them."

"Eggs...? Oh...that? All right, good to know."

Gravis laughed this time. He didn't expect Leorino to suddenly mention the sex toy.

Meanwhile, Hundert was astonished by the intimacy between the two. When cranky with fever, Leorino was so troublesome to deal with that even Hundert, who loved doting on his master, quickly lost his patience.

But the king's brother, although exasperated, was patiently keeping him company.

Although listening to their conversation, which at least the two of them seemed to understand, Hundert wondered what eggs Leorino was referring to.

"...Vi, do *you* like the eggs?"

Gravis chuckled. He then glanced at Theodor in surrender. Hundert also ventured a surreptitious glance at the royal attendant standing next to him.

Theodor, however, seemed unbothered by their glances, maintaining his perfect blank expression.

Perhaps irritated by Gravis's lack of response, Leorino complained further. He was like a bad drunk.

"Y-you're so mean... I was so full, too."

"No, you were fantastic. You did well."

"...Will you use them again? The eggs...? So mean."

"Hard to say at this point. It'll depend entirely on you."

Leorino's feverish eyes filled with tears again. The fever must have loosened his tear ducts.

"No... I can do it... I...I want to be worthy enough to stay by your side, like Ionia."

Gravis embraced him a little tighter than before.

"You're plenty worthy already."

"I'm sorry for keeping things from you... But...no more eggs."

Gravis looked up to the heavens and drew a long breath.

"Yes, fine. Enough about the eggs."

"...All right. But I'm going home. Everyone's worried about me... Josef, I'm sorry, Josef..."

"Perhaps that's enough talking. Get some sleep."

Wiping away Leorino's tears, Gravis placed his palm over his eyes.

"It's dark... I don't want to sleep."

"Oh, no, I think you do. You'll feel better soon. Close your eyes and you'll fall asleep."

"Vi... We have to talk..."

"Yes, we'll talk when you wake up."

His heavy breathing calmed a little, and his voice gradually became more drowsy.

The medicine seemed to be kicking in at last.

"I'll have that dream again... I don't want to sleep... I'm scared, it hurts... Not that dream..."

"You'll be fine. No more dreams."

"You're lying... I hate you, I hate you."

"Hah... I love you so much. Don't say that."

His eyes still covered by the large hand, Leorino nodded.

His breathing was labored, but he seemed to be smiling slightly.

"Yes... I won't lie anymore."

"Good."

"Vi...I love you."

"...Yes, me too. I love you, Leorino."

Leorino's incoherent mumbling stopped soon after that.

None of the men spoke, patiently watching Leorino.

Eventually, Leorino's breathing made it clear he was fast asleep.

Under the men's watchful eyes, Leorino once again fell into a restorative sleep.

"...Is he always like this when he has a fever? It certainly tests your patience."

Gravis sounded exasperated as he said this, but the man's hand stroking Leorino's forehead was terribly gentle. His calm expression made his low voice sound even fonder.

Meanwhile, Hundert was shocked to his very core by their exchange.

He could hardly believe his ears when he realized "Vi" was meant to refer to His Royal Highness.

"F-fever tends to...bring out his inner child."

With some trepidation, Hundert made excuses for his master, which Gravis acknowledged with a small smile. He gently laid Leorino down on the bed and stood.

From far, far above, an assessing gaze fell on Hundert.

Shuddering under its pressure, Hundert fell to his knees.

From Hundert's perspective, Gravis was a far nobler man than he could have ever hoped to encounter. If it weren't for his beloved master, he would have simply remained prostrate on the floor.

"Hundert, was it?"

When Hundert hesitated in his response, Theodor answered in his stead.

"His name is Ivan Hundert, Lord Leorino's full-time attendant."

"I see. I'm glad you came. I know you are new to my palace, but please make sure that Leorino is taken care of."

Hundert never thought that a royal and the famously heroic general of the Royal Army would speak to a mere servant like himself with so much kindness.

"Y-yes, sir... By all means."

Hundert deepened his bow.

"If you have any questions, I'm certain Theodor would be happy to answer." With these words, Gravis left the bedroom.

After seeing his master off, Theodor insisted Hundert stand up.

"His Highness may seem unapproachable, but he is a very kind man. Do not shrink away from him simply because he is royalty. You may tend to Lord Leorino as you usually would."

"Of course. In fact, tending to my master is about all I can do..."

"If you have any questions about the palace, you're more than welcome to ask me. Later, I will introduce you to the maids who will be serving Lord Leorino under your command."

"Thank you, sir."

"You may leave everything outside this room to the maids. You should devote your undivided attention to Lord Leorino."

At these words, Hundert bowed deeply again.

Hundert was relieved to learn that his master had been treated with great respect in the palace.

"Thank you for your kindness."

"May I ask, is there anything Lord Leorino might be in need of?"

Hundert immediately assumed the expression of a loyal servant.

"I have brought the necessities with me. I plan to deliver everything else later on."

"I see. Then I would like you to tell the maids his food preferences and regular portion sizes for when he feels better."

"Yes, sir. I suspect he will only be eating soup for a while, so I would appreciate it if the kitchen staff would take care not to prepare too much for him... My master gets rather anxious about wasting food."

Theodor considered this, bringing his hand to his chin.

"He only had an appetizer and soup last night, and I'm afraid he'll only grow weaker at this rate. I hope his fever improves soon."

"Forcing him to eat will only make him sick, which will further drain his strength. He has always had a poor appetite... I will inform the cooks of Lord Leorino's food preferences and his aversions in detail later."

"Yes, I've noticed he doesn't enjoy bitter flavors."

The attendant blushed and cast down his eyes on behalf of his master.

At the very least, this reminded Hundert of something he intended to bring to Theodor's attention.

"Lord Theodor, could you please send for the doctor, preferably as soon as possible?"

Theodor frowned.

"Is Lord Leorino worse off than we thought?"

"No, he breaks out in a fever when he is under significant physical stress, so I suspect that was the cause."

"I see."

"But I am a little concerned that his fever is higher than usual...and that the, um, intimacy may have taken a considerable toll on his body, so I would rather be extra safe."

After so many years of service, Hundert could just about tell what Leorino had experienced.

"I love you so much."

The words the nobleman said to Leorino. And Leorino responded with the same.

Their tender exchange made it clear to Hundert what had happened between them. His master had entered an amorous relationship with the king's brother, to whom this remote palace belonged. And from the looks of things, Leorino must have lost his virginity last night.

Hundert's heart ached at the thought of it. He trembled at the vision of what might happen once the Cassieux family found out.

The only saving grace was that his master did not appear to have been coerced. Judging by their interactions, the act must have been consensual. Leorino's expression showed no fear of the general, further evidenced by Leorino's complete trust in him as he held him in his arms.

In any case, the recent events were one surprise after another for Hundert.

It was only the day before yesterday that Leorino had left the house, excitedly announcing he was going to visit the training grounds.

Leorino had already been so incredibly sheltered, always kept in an environment where he was unlikely to meet anyone new, let alone fall in love with someone.

Despite this, he was confined at the remote palace after being accused of being involved in a serious incident at the training grounds, and then he had suddenly found himself in a romantic relationship. Not only that, his significant other was royalty, and they had already entered a carnal relationship.

And not just any member of the royal family, but the younger brother of the king, the second in line of succession to the throne, a man old enough to be his father.

How in the world could so much have happened overnight?

Hundert was bewildered. He felt he might just break out in a fever from the worry himself.

But there was only one thing the full-time attendant could do, and it was to take care of his beloved master as always, and now of all times, focus on nursing him back to health.

What worried him most was the fact that Leorino had sex for the first time, with a man of great stature, no less. Considering their size difference, it was doubtful that Leorino's body would remain unscathed.

It was due to that concern that Hundert found it prudent to request a doctor. He worried the fever might have been caused by a wound sustained during intercourse.

Theodor understood Hundert's concern.

Although Gravis insisted that he had checked for wounds, Theodor also suspected the intercourse must have been very physically and mentally taxing for Leorino. Not to mention he had nearly been assaulted not long prior, even if the ordeal ended before anything could happen.

"Who is Lord Leorino's doctor?"

"There is a doctor from Brungwurt named Willy at the residence."

"I see… But I doubt we can permit more outsiders in the palace."

Theodor considered his options. Gravis would be reluctant to allow any more people whom he did not know into his palace, especially when it concerned Leorino.

"Are you familiar with Dr. Sasha, of the Royal Army?"

Hundert's face lit up at Theodor's suggestion.

"Yes, Dr. Sasha is well aware of Leorino's condition."

Gravis had insisted on not letting anyone into the palace, but Theodor decided to call for Sasha anyway. Gravis would likely not fault him for that decision.

"Then I will speak with His Highness and arrange for Dr. Sasha to examine him."

Leorino was bedridden with a high fever, but the day after Sasha's visit, his fever broke.

He had recovered to the point where he could sit up in bed and talk, although his body was sluggish and worn out from the fever. Yet, for some reason, Leorino was apologetically curling in on himself.

As Hundert had feared, Leorino had no recollection of the way he had fussed in Gravis's presence.

He had been self-conscious ever since the attendant explained to him what he did. Not to mention, he belatedly realized that he had been shamelessly occupying Gravis's bed the entire time, which made him restless and dejected.

"Vi… I'm sorry…for everything."

Gravis chuckled and accepted the apology, remembering Leorino's behavior yesterday.

"It was amusing to see your attendant so horrified on your behalf."

"…I sincerely apologize… When you've been so gracious as to allow me to stay in your bed, too."

"It's fine. I feel mostly responsible for your fever."

Leorino's face turned red up to his neck. Leorino was dense in regard to romantic matters, but even he understood Gravis was teasing him.

Gravis placed his hand on Leorino's forehead. Leorino closed his eyes. Gravis's cool hand checking his temperature felt good. He loved being touched by Gravis.

"Good, your fever has gone down."

"Yes... I'm sorry for worrying you. I'm fine now. May we speak?"

Gravis nodded and picked up Leorino from the bed.

Leorino seemed to have completely let down his guard around Gravis. Leaning against Gravis, he relaxed completely.

The way Leorino naturally folded himself into Gravis's arms was as if the days when Leorino had been so stubborn in his face of inferiority, complaining about how he was too helpless and powerless for a man, were behind him. This almost concerning defenselessness made Gravis love Leorino all the more.

"Help him get dressed."

"Yes, sir... Your Highness, may I ask you to carry Lord Leorino straight to the washroom?"

In just one day, Hundert had settled in as if he had been working at the palace for years, diligently tending to his master. He was even able to remain calm in Gravis's presence.

Gravis had taken a liking to Hundert. He was quite fond of people who could simply perform their job, especially if the person excelled at what they did.

As Gravis had expected, Hundert took care of Leorino more meticulously than anyone else. Gravis also appreciated his loyalty.

Gravis sat Leorino down on the settee in the washroom and left, leaving the rest to the attendant.

"My lord... Come, allow me to cleanse you."

Hundert brought a bowl of hot water and a number of clean washcloths.

"Can't I have a bath?"

The attendant shook his head.

"The hot water will exhaust you. We must wait and monitor your condition for the rest of the day."

Leorino looked disappointed but nodded without complaint.

His master was his usual composed self now. Hundert smiled.

The servant removed Leorino's nightgown, revealing his upper body and all the marks peppered across his skin.

"Oh, wow... Ah, the mark where Ebbo grabbed me turned so dark. It's purple."

Leorino traced the particularly visible marks on his shoulders with his fingers. Hundert breathed a sigh of relief at his master's apparent lack of concern.

"Yes, Dr. Sasha was quite surprised."

"Dr. Sasha came to see me? ...He must have been worried, since I disappeared without a trace. I regret being unable to properly greet him."

Hundert then removed Leorino's underwear, exposing his slim body in its entirety.

"Are you cold?"

"No, I'm fine."

After washing his face, Hundert roughly cleaned Leorino's hair with a warm, damp cloth soaked in hot water.

Next, with a cloth dampened with scented hot water, he carefully washed the platinum-colored hair from the scalp and arranged his tangled locks into small bunches.

Having cleansed Leorino's face and hair, it was time for his body. With another warm scented cloth, Hundert began to carefully wipe his master's flesh. He also moved his joints in a familiar way to check if there were any problems with his range of motion. Wherever he encountered a stiff spot, he gently rubbed it loose.

Leorino closed his eyes, enjoying the sensation.

"The doctor looked quite furious after examining you, my lord. He said something to His Royal Highness, looking very menacing indeed... I must admit, I was also very worried when I saw the state of your body."

"Oh. You mean the bruise around my neck? ...Wait, what's this?" Leorino looked down at his chest and gasped in surprise. "Hundert, what are these red spots?"

Hundert was at a loss.

The elderly servant found it difficult to admit the marks had been left during Leorino's intimate encounter.

But he wanted his master to have accurate information, so as part of his sex education, Hundert decided to tell him the truth in an unaffected manner.

"My lord, His Highness left these marks with his lips by sucking on your skin."

"He did? But when?"

"When...? My lord, don't you remember?"

Leorino considered this and immediately remembered, his cheeks flushing slightly as he did.

"...His Excellency left these marks on me in the bedchamber, yes?"

"If that's what you recall, then I suppose so, yes."

The bright flush seemed to spread from Leorino's face to his bruised body. He then proceeded to run his fingers over each and every mark.

Hundert was relieved to see that his first time with His Highness had at least been a pleasant experience for his master.

"It's a common occurrence in the bedchamber, a type of love mark. They disappear within a few days, so please rest assured."

"Right... Is it all right for me to have these marks, as long as they are left by His Excellency? Is this something people experience regardless of gender?"

"Of course." Hundert nodded. "They can be left by anyone on anyone, but you mustn't show them to anyone besides your partner. In your case, my lord, that would be His Royal Highness."

"I understand."

"We taught you when you were little that you must not expose your body to others. The same is true for these marks. They are to be kept hidden from all but the one who left them on you."

Leorino nodded obediently once more.

"One should only engage in intimacy with the person they love. Therefore, it follows that the marks left in the bedchamber must not be shown to anyone else."

"That is correct, my lord."

Leorino smiled.

"I have heard that sleeping with the person you love is a very pleasant affair, and having actually experienced it myself, I found that it really is. It was pleasurable, it was difficult, it was a great many things, really, but I was just shocked at how it all felt."

Hundert nearly choked on his own spit, but didn't let his master notice his distress.

"And you know what? There was something I struggled with."

"Struggled with, my lord?"

"Yes. I knew we were quite different in size, but he really was so much bigger than I could have imagined. Why, his length was so massive, we could hardly get it inside me at first."

"...Lord Leorino."

Hundert was stunned speechless.

Suddenly remembering something, Leorino made a circle with the fingers of both hands. Wiping down his arms, Hundert smoothly broke him out of the gesture.

"...And, as far as I can remember, I tried to please him with my mouth, but he laughed at me and said I'm not very good at it. Hundert, do you know the appropriate technique? How do I—?"

"...Lord Leorino. I will not ask you where you have obtained such knowledge, but you must not speak of such things in good company."

"I wasn't planning to. Can't I tell you, at least?"

"...His Royal Highness is waiting for you. We should speak less and focus on getting you clean instead."

Leorino hastily nodded at the attendant's words.

"I'm sorry. I know."

Hundert bit back a sigh, silently washing his master's body with an experienced hand.

Finally, he applied the medicine Sasha had prescribed to Leorino's body, then dressed him in indoor clothes made of soft material that would not damage his sensitive skin.

Leorino only sat there quietly allowing his servant to do his job.

But while he remained silent, he seemed to have slowly become trapped in pessimistic thoughts. His emotions were still all over the place. Hundert spoke softly to his master.

"Lord Leorino?"

"...You must think me unserious," Leorino muttered in a small voice. He didn't wait for Hundert's response. "I realize this is not the time to be thinking about such things."

"My lord."

His voice was so quiet that Hundert couldn't help but say something.

"I'll do better once I leave the palace. There are things I must think about, things I must do."

Hundert placed a hand on his master's shoulder and stroked it slowly.

"You are in love with His Highness, yes?"

Leorino nodded resolutely.

"I must confess that I was very surprised...but I am nonetheless very pleased to know that you have found someone who feels the same way about you, my lord."

"Vi is royalty and a general. No matter how much we love each other, I am certain that...our feelings will not go anywhere, not even this time."

Hundert did not know what Leorino meant by "this time," but he struggled to understand his master's pessimistic thoughts.

Judging by the kind treatment Leorino had received in the palace, Hundert couldn't imagine his situation changing for the worse in the future.

On the contrary...the attendant had a certain conviction about his master's future, but it wasn't his place to share his speculation until the king's brother himself told Leorino what he intended.

Hundert stroked Leorino's shoulder with his wrinkled hand, comforting him over and over.

Due to poor nutrition and the exhaustion from the fever, Leorino was beginning to lose weight, as he had when he first started working at the Palace of Defense.

"…It's all right, my lord. There's nothing wrong with celebrating the joy of being with the person you love, unserious or otherwise. Every healthy young man of eighteen would love to lose themselves to romance."

"Is that so?"

"Of course. My lord, the excitement you feel is perfectly normal. And who would blame you? You mustn't concern yourself so much, and simply follow your heart."

"Oh… Is that really true?"

Then Leorino sighed deeply.

"I don't know what most people my age do. I don't even know how to please His Excellency. I didn't even go to school… I hate being so ignorant."

Leorino was ashamed of the deficiencies in his knowledge. Although Hundert couldn't bring himself to tell him that such sexual skills were not usually taught in school.

Hundert found something very dear about his master who could have been his grandson, struggling with his first romantic relationship.

"So you lack experience in the bedchamber, and what of it? A man must never be ashamed of his own ignorance, my lord."

"I understand. But how can I improve? How can I keep him from growing tired of me…? Or is it unmanly to even worry about that at all?"

"It's just like studying the blade. My lord, you have significantly improved with the dagger compared to when you first started, and all masters must start out as novices."

"Oh… Just like studying the blade. I guess so… Huh."

"Of course. You must ask His Highness himself. It would be best to frankly ask him for his guidance on what he might enjoy."

Leorino seemed somewhat reassured by the attendant's advice.

"All right." He nodded resolutely.

"…Then it's high time to get going. His Highness is waiting for you."

"Hundert, thank you for coming."

His master's words and his beautiful smile made all of Hundert's hard work worthwhile in an instant, just as they always did.

"Can you stand by yourself?"

"I can. Or rather, I should. His Excellency is so eager to carry me everywhere that my legs will shrivel up if I don't."

Leorino stood up slowly with a smile, scolded his trembling legs, and returned to the parlor where Gravis was waiting.

Confession

"Leorino, come here."

Leorino nodded nervously as he sat down across from Gravis. He sat like any son of a noble family should, his back beautifully straight. And yet he seemed to be struggling somehow.

His expression was calm, but he was pale and looked even more fragile than usual.

"You can sit more comfortably if you'd like."

"Yes, sir. But...Your Excellency—"

"Really? You still insist on calling me that?"

"I don't want to embarrass myself in front of you."

At these words, Gravis released a small sigh.

"Come here."

Gravis beckoned him closer, but Leorino hesitated.

"I'm fine right here."

Leorino worried that if he got any closer, he would completely fall apart and lose his opportunity to finally speak with Gravis.

Seeing Leorino's guarded look, Gravis forced a smile.

"I won't do anything to you, you've just recovered from a fever. Just come. I have reserved some time with Dirk and Ebbo in the afternoon. You're still recovering, I don't want you to exhaust yourself with stress for no reason."

"A-all right."

Leorino moved next to Gravis, shrinking back a little. He perched on the edge of the bed so that he could return to his spot at a moment's notice, but Gravis suddenly picked him up and sat him down in his lap.

"Whoa."

Gravis half-forced Leorino to lean against him, even as Leorino insisted on maintaining his posture in his lap. Leorino didn't realize it, but he could barely keep himself upright. He looked as if he was about to collapse.

Gravis furrowed his brow at how light Leorino felt when he lifted him.

"Hey… You've lost a lot of weight. Oh… Your shoulders have gotten so sharp, too."

Gravis traced the shape of Leorino's shoulder bones with his hand. His shoulders had lost their healthy roundness.

When Gravis's expression turned stern, Leorino ducked his head gingerly.

"I often lose some weight when I get a fever."

"Just because it happens often doesn't mean it's acceptable. Your health should be your priority. Starting today, you must eat properly. Can we agree on that?"

"…Yes."

Gravis's harsh words did nothing to improve Leorino's mood, given his ongoing lack of appetite.

Gravis saw a silent resistance behind the obedient answer but did not indulge him this time.

"You will eat as much as you can, yes?"

"……Yes."

Gravis nodded in approval at Leorino's reluctant but polite answer.

"Now tell me as much as you can. Though you can ignore the parts you don't want to remember. I don't want you to strain yourself."

Leorino nodded.

"…It was around the time I turned half-fledged that I had my first vivid dream of Ionia. In it, I saw the face of a red-haired boy in a mirror and realized that…he was *me*. I was in Ionia's small room above the blacksmith shop."

"Around the time you turned half-fledged, would that mean before the incident?"

"Yes. I met you when General Stolf brought you to my father's forge... I remember marveling at your starry-sky eyes."

Gravis must have felt strange hearing Leorino talk about his childhood when he wasn't much older than a child himself.

Leorino smiled at Gravis's somewhat uneasy expression.

"I remember that moment clearly. You were a very beautiful, but very sullen-looking boy. You introduced yourself as 'Vis.'"

Gravis chuckled.

"I must admit, I was quite upset with Stolf at the time, wondering why he was dragging me across the city."

"Yes, the look on your face spoke volumes."

"Io suddenly asked me if he could call me 'Vi.' I recall being shocked that some filthy commoner would speak to me like that."

Leorino looked up to see Gravis's fond expression.

"Ionia couldn't have known of your status. I remember that he simply wanted to be friends with you, to spend time with you."

Leorino was pained by the trapped look on Gravis's face as he recalled those days.

"Will you hear me out? ...This is the story of Ionia's life I'd lived through my dreams, and the secret I brought to the royal capital."

With that, Leorino slowly began his tale.

Gravis listened in silence until Leorino finished telling him all about his purpose in coming to the royal capital.

"...Do you believe me?"

Leorino looked tired. He seemed to be struggling, his face red, and his breathing labored.

"...Thank you for telling me. It couldn't have been easy to speak of what happened at Zweilink."

"Oh... No, I'm fine."

After showing his appreciation for Leorino's efforts, Gravis silently lost himself in thought.

"I want to believe you...but the idea that the Marquis of Lagarea is a traitor and that he has the power to manipulate memories sounds like wishful thinking at best."

"I can't give you any proof. I simply connected Edgar with what happened with the Marquis of Lagarea. I can only guess that the Marquis of Lagarea is the mastermind, but I have not lied about either of them. It's the truth."

"No, I see your point."

Leorino looked relieved.

Gravis's expression, on the other hand, remained severe.

"I don't remember Edgar Yorke's last words, either...even though I was certainly there... Does that mean he deprived me of my memories as well...? Then again..."

Gravis was unusually evasive. He seemed hesitant.

"It's the truth, the Marquis of Lagarea has taken my memories. Vi... Please believe me."

Perhaps out of agitation, Leorino's face flushed further. Gravis was concerned about his labored breathing. He stroked Leorino's back soothingly.

"Calm down, I'm not doubting your words."

"...Right. Thank you."

"The issue is, I'll need more than that. I can't do anything without proof. Please understand."

Leorino had no objections, and nodded in agreement.

"Of course, I understand. I came to the royal capital to find confirmation as well."

Leorino wiped the sweat from his forehead.

Seeing his pained expression, Gravis decided to change the subject.

"How vivid are Ionia's memories anyway?"

Gravis had been curious ever since he learned of it.

Leorino's ignorance resulting from his sheltered upbringing and the knowledge he gained from Ionia's experience formed a strange blend in his mind.

It was due to that blend that Leorino was sometimes overconfident in his own abilities, explaining his reckless behavior, and his incomplete knowledge also caused him much grief due to the discrepancy between his ideals and reality.

Without a proper understanding of this, he wouldn't be able to protect

Leorino's body and soul without casting further burdens onto him. Gravis also worried about the state of Leorino's mind.

Leorino pondered his question for a moment, then shook his head apologetically.

"I suspect they're not as vivid as you might expect."

"So the memories *aren't* vivid, then?"

"No...but also, yes. In my dreams, the memories are all connected. They are very vivid. I live through Ionia's life. But when I wake up, I find that many details are missing, and I only remember the most important parts."

Gravis considered this answer.

He had never heard of anything like it, and had no way of telling if that was how it was supposed to function.

"...I remember where he used to live with his parents and Dirk. But I don't remember any of the details, such as the contents of their daily conversations. I can only recall the memorable exchanges. As for his conversations at school, I strongly remember the ones concerning you...a-and, well..."

"And Lucas?"

Leorino only nodded, his eyes downcast.

Gravis couldn't quite read the complex emotion hidden in his eyes.

"I do remember much about both you and Lucas. I have dreamed repeatedly of events Ionia felt strongly about. Those memories slowly...become clearer and clearer, gradually feeling like my own memories. That is the case with Zweilink. That day is most vivid of all."

The intense memories he dreamed of over and over became like Leorino's own memories, and the rest grew progressively hazier.

Gravis tried to imagine what it must have felt like, but couldn't comprehend it still.

"That would explain why your knowledge is so patchy."

Leorino looked at a loss as he considered this, and finally hung his head dejectedly.

"...I don't understand it myself. At first I thought they were just dreams. Then I remembered Zweilink and thought that I might be the reincarnation of Ionia after all. But..."

"But?"

"It still wouldn't feel right to call myself Ionia. Perhaps I am simply in conversation with Ionia's soul."

Gravis pondered for a moment.

"...That would be the domain of the gods. Mere mortals like us couldn't possibly understand."

"You are correct, my memories are patchy. For example, I remember the blacksmith shop clearly, but I don't recall the geography of the commoner district. Though, I suppose seeing it could jog my memory."

"What else can you recall?"

"I remember what the headmaster said. I also remember the battle drill with the mountain troops. But I can't recall much about the school's facilities. I don't even remember what we learned in class. And I hardly remember any of my classmates, except for Marzel and Luca."

Leorino stared into the void, frantically rifling through his memories.

It was as if Ionia had kept only the parts he wanted to convey to them.

Gravis shuddered at the thought.

Are these truly Ionia's memories?

It felt like a long-held grudge, or perhaps a tenacity of some sort.

Gravis's heart broke all over again thinking about the painful fate Leorino had been saddled with.

"Which makes me think I might not be the reincarnation of Ionia after all. I'm sorry."

Leorino drooped. But Gravis couldn't care less whether or not he was a reincarnation.

"Leorino, I'm not trying to find a clear definition for your connection to Ionia."

"I know." Leorino smiled sadly. Gravis stroked his flushed cheeks.

"But...if it were at all possible, wouldn't you simply want him to return just the way he was? Would you not have preferred it if I had been Ionia himself? You must have been terribly disappointed to have a scrawny little child waltz into your life instead."

Gravis tightly embraced Leorino's skinny shoulders as he kept going.

"Why do you keep insisting on that? I told you, I don't need you and Ionia to be the same person."

Gravis wanted to tell him that what mattered was the fact Leorino had told him Ionia's regrets.

"I want to be honest with you. I do wish Ionia could simply come back to life."

"Of course."

"I assume the same must be true for Lucas."

Gravis stroked Leorino's downcast head.

"We both have unresolved feelings for him."

Leorino's small lips mouthed the man's words.

"Some part of my heart died with Ionia. Not even you can undo that fact."

"...Of course."

"But I also know that Io can never return to the world of the living."

Leorino looked up at Gravis and blinked slowly.

"Vi... But I'm right here?"

"And you are not Io. But that doesn't mean I'd rather have Ionia take your place."

A single tear spilled from Leorino's beautiful violet eyes.

"But I have made many irreplaceable memories with Io. That's all."

Leorino timidly looked up at Gravis, searching his eyes for the truth, and finally leaned into him.

"I know... I can't deny that Ionia is the reason I fell in love with you in the first place."

Gravis lifted his chin and met his violet eyes. Sitting in his lap, Leorino's gaze didn't quite meet his own. Gravis could truly feel how different he was from Ionia now, and that he was to be cherished and protected.

"...Do you also recall the one time Io and I made love after graduation?"

Leorino only shuddered and finally quietly replied that he did indeed remember.

"I believed at the time that one day I could be free to live with Ionia, free from the bonds of royalty."

"I had already given up hope on your wish back then... I thought it was a dream that could never become reality."

"You were older than me, and you saw things for what they were, certainly far better than I did. I know my mother—the queen dowager—went to see you back then, didn't she?"

Leorino seemed hesitant to answer. Gravis stroked the back of his hand in encouragement.

"...Her Majesty told me that for the country to see its rightful king, I must know my place as a commoner."

"Of course she did," Gravis said.

"Ionia did not regret his choice at the time. He thought you should be the rightful heir to the throne... He wanted you to have that option."

"Except I'm the younger sibling. My brother was always the rightful heir."

"Perhaps. Even so, I knew that if you chose me in a moment of passion, your noble soul would surely regret abandoning your royal duties eventually."

Gravis wanted to argue. He did not want his past feelings to be so easily dismissed, not when he had truly been ready to choose Ionia over his country.

But Ionia was likely correct in his decision.

The red-haired young man understood the nature of Gravis's soul better than anyone. Gravis had inherited responsibility toward his royal duty from his mother, the queen dowager.

Even in the hypothetical situation in which Gravis had chosen the path of happiness with Ionia and abandoned his royal duties, he suspected he would have regretted it sooner or later.

Ionia did not want to force Gravis into a choice when he was still so young and full of hope. But at the time, Gravis had been unable to recognize Ionia's concerns.

His own past immaturity and foolishness burned a hole in Gravis's heart.

"Regret... I suppose you could say that."

"...I wouldn't know. I sometimes thought Ionia was arrogant for simply deciding what your happiness should look like."

"Why?"

"There were many times when I woke up and wished...he had simply taken your hand."

This sentiment may have been a product of Leorino's noble birth.

Perhaps that was the only conclusion that a commoner like Ionia could reach in response to the reckless wish of a royal three years his junior. But the answers would remain in the past, never to be retrieved.

"Was Ionia wrong?"

"He was not wrong. No, at the time I was simply a foolish child."

Leorino considered his words.

"...Vi, I remember that you came to see me at the forge before I left for Zweilink. At that time, Ionia no longer had anything to tell you...but all along he only thought to himself how much he loved you."

Leorino rested his forehead against Gravis's shoulder.

"...He didn't need anything else. *I* was already yours then."

"I never knew. I foolishly thought I could take you away from Lucas."

"Vi..."

"I hurt both you and Lucas, didn't I?"

His face buried in Gravis's shoulder, Leorino quietly began shedding tears.

"Don't cry, please."

"I'm... I'm just... I'm sorry."

"Ionia must have loved Lucas."

Those words were Gravis's self-deprecation, his own condemnation for his crimes.

But Leorino couldn't lie to him.

"...Yes, he did. Ionia loved Lucas as well. Only, he was so consumed with his feelings for you that it took him a while to notice it."

"...I see."

Now that he had slept with Gravis, Leorino could understand. That intimate act which required surrendering every shameful part of oneself could not be done between people who did not have feelings for each other.

The relief and comfort Ionia felt every time he fell asleep in Lucas's arms remained in his memories.

When his physical relationship with Lucas began, he suffered from the contradictory messages sent by his mind and body. But as the years passed, the act became familiar and brought Ionia more emotional satisfaction than physical pleasure.

He thought he shared a physical bond with Lucas. He thought he had become his romantic partner in crime. But Lucas loved Ionia, even as Ionia dedicated his entire heart to Gravis.

Ionia was so desperate to keep himself afloat at the time that he never realized the meaning of the words of love that Lucas jokingly offered him, nor Lucas's devotion to him.

It was not Gravis who had supported him through those lonely days. Ionia wouldn't have made it without Lucas.

That was another truth engraved in Ionia's memories. Ionia loved both men in different ways at the same time.

It was the greatest secret he had wanted to keep from Gravis.

"He loved you and Lucas...separately and in different ways, but at the moment of his death, with all his heart and soul, Ionia's only thought was of you."

Ionia died for his love and loyalty to Gravis, never reciprocating Lucas's feelings.

Ionia... How cruel of you...

He forced Leorino to clean up the mess he had left of the two men in his stead, when all Ionia had ever wanted was to simply, sincerely say that he loved the man who now sat before Leorino. Ionia's memories still baffled Leorino.

"Leorino...will you also come to love Lucas eventually?"

Leorino considered Gravis's question and finally shook his head.

"I don't know."

"...Right."

"I met Luca in very different circumstances from Ionia. I don't think I could ever love Luca the way Ionia did. But..."

"But?"

"Ionia's memories were what made me fall in love with you in the first place. It was because of Ionia that I was able to meet you at all. But my love for you is mine alone."

"Yes, well... I suppose we will never know what would have happened without Ionia... That hypothetical alone is a fantasy."

Leorino's platinum hair swayed. Its soft texture caressing the tip of his chin made Gravis's chest feel tight.

"I wanted to be with you regardless of Ionia. I wished for you to love me, despite having nothing I could offer you."

"Leorino."

"But you are right. That's a fantasy. You and I met because of Ionia." Leorino clung to Gravis's neck with the desperation of a drowning man. "But this is my destiny. I wish I could have met you as nobody at all—as myself. But that dream is beyond my reach."

Gravis didn't know what to say.

The only thing he knew was that neither he nor Leorino had any way of knowing what would have happened if they had met without Ionia's influence.

Watching Gravis nod his assent, tears filled Leorino's violet eyes.

"As long as I carry Ionia's memories, I can't make any promises. I may or may not fall in love with Luca..."

"All right."

"I can't promise you anything when I don't yet know what future this destiny will lead me to. I'm sorry. I love you. But I just don't know."

"I understand. No need to cry."

Leorino nuzzled his face into Gravis's neck and continued quietly shedding tears.

"I want to see Luca... I want to tell him how Ionia felt about him. Only then will I find my own answer."

Leorino raised his tearstained face and pointed his piercing gaze at Gravis. In response, Gravis nodded.

"Then we shall make some time to speak with Lucas."

"Yes, please. I want to tell Luca how Ionia felt about him. I suspect this is another mission I inherited from Ionia."

Leorino could not finish his lunch.

He had been served a modest portion, not nearly large enough to be considered a light meal by most grown men. Owing to Hundert's consideration, he had received a mildly seasoned soup and bread, but meager as it was, he still struggled to finish his food.

Finally, Hundert noticed that his master had covered his mouth, his body heaving, and rushed to stop the meal.

Gravis's orders had clearly not served him well.

"You mustn't force yourself any further."

"But...His Excellency told me to... Ugh..."

"His Royal Highness did not tell you to eat more than you reasonably can... Now you should go lie down."

"I'm sorry, Hundert... and Theodor, you too. I'm sorry for wasting the meal you prepared for me."

Theodor was also watching Leorino with a concerned look on his face.

"No, not at all. We must prioritize your health, after all."

Leorino nodded apologetically. He was still suffering from regular bouts of nausea.

Hundert assisted him to a settee. The servant then took off his shoes and threw his feet up on the seat. Still, his nausea lingered.

"Please close your eyes for a moment or look into the distance."

As Leorino remained still in the comfortable position, the pain in his stomach slowly subsided, and breathing became a little easier.

Closely observing his master, Hundert was deeply concerned.

Leorino had always developed a fever when he was physically exhausted, but in the past, after his fever broke, he would quickly regain his energy. Following that, his physical condition would improve as well.

This morning was no different. He hadn't made a full recovery yet, but was clearly optimistic.

However, following the conversation with Gravis, his health took a turn for the worse. It was not physical exhaustion. This time it was his mind that was at capacity.

For the next half an hour or so, Leorino rested in the parlor, dim from the curtains drawn within.

"Are you awake, my lord?"

"...Yes. Sorry to worry you."

Leorino's pale complexion had improved, but now the corners of his eyes had reddened, as if the fever had returned. Hundert frowned.

"I'm afraid you'll have to cancel your afternoon plans in this state."

"...No. His Excellency gave me permission to leave."

"My lord, but is that wise?"

"Hundert, I appreciate your concern, but don't spoil me. There are things I must do."

Ever since they'd reunited at the palace, Leorino had been acting strangely. Gravis entered the room.

He approached Leorino on the settee with a stern look on his face.

"Are you not feeling well again?"

Leorino attempted to sit up straight in a panic, but Gravis stopped him in a calm voice.

"Don't move. Keep resting."

"...I'm sorry. Did Theodor tell you?"

"Yes. You couldn't eat much."

"I'm sorry. I couldn't keep my word."

"I never said you have to gorge yourself until you're sick. I'm sure you ate enough... You did well."

Cold fingers brushed back his bangs.

Leorino slowly exhaled. But the man furrowed his brow.

"You're feverish again."

Gravis glanced at Hundert, who had given them some space. Hundert understood the meaning behind the look and pleaded with him with his eyes.

"If you're not feeling well, we're canceling our plans for the afternoon."

"I-I'm fine now. My nausea has subsided, and my fever is nearly gone. I can go."

"That decision is not up to you."

Grabbing Gravis by the sleeve, Leorino desperately pleaded.

"I'll be fine. Please. Please, let me speak with Ebbo."

Gravis chided Leorino with a look of exasperation on his face.

"...Leorino. Calm down."

"I will not. I'm going... I must go, please let me go."

"Leorino."

Gravis placed his hands on Leorino's shoulders as he clung to Gravis, silencing Leorino with a slight squeeze.

"Calm down."

"Vi... B-but—"

"Get a grip! You're flustered right now."

"I am not!"

"Don't yell! Your fever will return."

Leorino remained agitated, and this time Gravis scolded him sharply. His thin body shuddered.

Gravis cupped Leorino's cheeks in his large hands and firmly met his gaze.

"...Listen, Leorino. The past you've brought up is a very serious matter. It will take a great deal of time and careful planning to ascertain its veracity. Not to mention patience... This is not a matter we can resolve today, tomorrow, or anytime soon."

"...Well, yes, but—"

"You alone are the key to uncovering the past. What if this rush of yours makes you sicker than ever?"

"...Yes, I'm aware! But I only had a few moments to speak with Ebbo. I'm certain Ebbo must be confused and concerned by now."

Gravis shook his head sternly.

"You don't need to worry about Steiger's mental state."

"You can't be serious! Of course I do! I am responsible for getting him involved at all."

"Even so. Steiger is well in his forties. He is also a member of the mountain expeditionary troops and a fierce warrior who has been through much worse during his long time in the army. What *you* must protect first and foremost is your own mind and body."

Leorino was saddened by such a brutal reminder of his own immaturity. "But...still..."

Gravis sighed deeply and placed his hand on Leorino's cheek. It must have been because he hadn't had a proper meal in days, but Leorino's already small face had gotten so small Gravis felt he could contain its entirety in one hand alone.

Wondering when he had become so emaciated made Gravis's heart ache.

He's so stubborn, yet sensitive and weak, and still he tries to bear everything on his own.

Gravis heaved a small sigh.

"There really are no easy answers with you, are there?"

"Of course not. I can be bold in my own way."

Gravis didn't believe that for a second. Every time he saw Leorino, his frailness filled him with worry.

That was why Gravis couldn't keep himself from checking in with him over and over.

"I'll be fine. I promise."

"Don't make promises you can't keep."

"I... No, I'm not..."

Leorino refused to back down and after a moment, the man sighed once more.

"...Are you certain you're going to be all right?"

Leorino nodded, his face instantly brighter.

"If you feel sick again, tell me immediately. I will be very mad if you hide it from me."

"O-of course. So you will take me to Ebbo after all?"

"Yes, I will."

"Thank you!"

When the attendants learned that the king's brother had given permission for Leorino to leave, they hastily prepared for his departure.

* * *

Leorino and Gravis were now alone.

Gravis lifted Leorino's slender hand and pressed his lips to Leorino's fingertips.

"Leorino...I ask for one thing alone: that you are happy and healthy."

"Of course." The warm sensation on his fingertips made Leorino's cheeks flush with joy. "I know you are worried about me."

"So don't make me worry any more than I must. I want to act with respect to your dignity."

Leorino was glad to hear that. He could tell the man was just barely holding back his overprotective instincts.

Leorino wrapped his other hand around Gravis's palm holding his own. Gently pulling it closer, Leorino brought his lips to the man's fingers the way Gravis had just done to him.

From index finger to pinkie, he showered them with small, bird-like pecks.

The sensation of those soft, moist lips made the corners of Gravis's eyes soften.

"I ask for the same. I want you to promise me that you'll stay safe as well."

"I'll be fine. We have more important matters—"

Leorino shook his head sadly.

"I realize I'm your priority... But still." Leorino pressed his forehead against their intertwined fist. "I can't protect you anymore."

Leorino worried about Gravis. That was why he was in such a rush. He wanted to find the enemy as soon as possible and free Gravis from his troubles.

Gravis felt something creak deep in his heart.

"Leorino. I'm quite a bit stronger than I was back when I needed your protection."

"...That's not what I meant. I believe in you...but now that I've told you everything, my heart has been louder than ever."

Gravis embraced Leorino tightly.

"If there really is a traitor, I want to find him as soon as possible. I want to eliminate everything that could cause you grief. If I could, I would do it with my own hands..."

"Does it really matter who does it?"

"Well…no."

Leorino's eyes widened at the man's question. He realized that he had unconsciously set his mind on solving the problem all on his own again.

"Now it's your turn to trust me."

"I trust you. But my heart is still filled with worry."

"Will you let me carry that worry?"

A muffled voice came from his chest.

"…I don't know. I just feel so restless."

"Leorino. I may be repeating myself, but I'm not the same as I used to be. I do not plan on dying, and I have the power to protect you."

"I know that, but my heart won't listen. I just… I can't stop wishing I had the power to protect you."

Perhaps Ionia's feelings were to blame for that.

Gravis lifted Leorino's face. The wilting flower was wistfully confronting his own memories.

Hoping to soothe some of his anxiety, Gravis impulsively covered Leorino's lips with his own.

"…Mnf… Mm…"

"…Open your mouth. Let me in."

Leorino's lips opened obediently, and Gravis's fleshy tongue slid in through the gap. Leorino gasped faintly as he was slowly swept away by the pleasure of the kiss.

In between breaths, the man whispered in his deep voice, his words sounding like a prayer. "I'll have your back from now on."

"Vi… Vi…"

"…Leorino. Trust me."

Leorino fought back tears. He knew. He knew that Gravis's words were more a prayer to Ionia.

His own mind, body, his everything was not what Leorino wanted it to be. Inside his thin body, a glowing ember of anxiety continued to smolder.

"The truth is, I would prefer to keep you in this palace."

Leorino set aside his anxiety and put on a cheerful smile instead.

"And I want to leave with you. I want to accompany you wherever you go...now, and always."

Leorino's smile was so beautiful that it made his chest feel tight. If there ever was a radiant smile, it would surely look like this.

Gravis savored Leorino's lips, fueled by the fierce possessiveness that welled deep inside him. Gravis again prodded at his lips with his tongue.

"Ah...Ngh... Vi... Mm, no more..."

"I know...just one more."

Gravis gradually regained control of his faculties as he got his fill of those sweet lips. Leorino's feverish mouth was a sweet threat to the man's reason. He wanted to hold Leorino, strip him naked, and rock his body until he cried.

But now was not the time.

Gravis regained his reason. He slowed the movement of his tongue, so as not to arouse Leorino too much.

Absorbing Leorino's arousal, Gravis gently entwined Leorino's tongue with his for the last time, a sweet purr escaping his lips. Leorino glared at him resentfully with moist eyes.

"...You're so mean, Vi. You very nearly made me want to act unwise again..."

"I'm sorry. That was a bit much."

Leorino reached his hand, clinging to Gravis's muscular neck.

"Let us stay like this until I calm down."

Gravis indulged him.

Gravis stroked Leorino's back slowly, comforting his body as it recovered from its arousal. Though that seemed to have the opposite effect.

"Ngh...stop."

"Leorino."

Far from being calmed, spurred by the hand crawling up his spine, Leorino couldn't resist and brought his lips to Gravis's. Spilling sweet gasps, Leorino begged for another kiss.

Gravis complied, urged by his small tongue.

Leorino did as his heart desired, savoring the sensation of the man's lips.

Is This a Figment of Your Imagination?

When Leorino and Gravis appeared in the archives, three men were already waiting for them.

They were Ebbo Steiger of the mountain troops, Dirk, Gravis's second-in-command, and Kaunzel, the keeper of the archives.

Kaunzel had also been a member of the mountain troops before he retired from the front lines due to his injuries. Since he and Ebbo were acquainted, he was quite surprised to see him appear in the archives with Dirk. But Kaunzel was wise and prudent enough not to ask questions.

As soon as the men saw Leorino appear alongside Gravis, they were shocked.

"Wow... Oh boy."

Dirk said the first words that came to mind. Kaunzel also donned a sour expression.

Leorino only intently watched Ebbo, looking as if he wanted to say something. Ebbo, on the other hand, could not look at Leorino directly and averted his gaze, his rugged face red.

Seeing Ebbo's reaction, Leorino's expression turned somber. But Leorino misunderstood why Ebbo looked away in the first place.

Leorino had changed. He had about him a presence that stole people's gazes to a violent degree, wrapped in a fresh sex appeal alongside his usual refined, cool air. His fair, glossy skin, lush lips, and slender, graceful limbs emanated a sweet, innocent sensuality. It was as if a butterfly had emerged from its chrysalis.

Leorino had remained in the palace for only a few days.

But the experienced men already understood what had happened to him in that time.

Leorino was unaware that his entire being seemed to be announcing that he had made love with a man. He still had the same delicate, otherworldly air about him, but there was also something intensely seductive about him that made it difficult to look him in the eye.

Dirk glanced at his superior. Gravis, having understood the meaning behind Dirk's gaze, bent down and whispered something into Leorino's ear. Leorino's eyes widened with a start as he looked up at the general. The next moment, he cast his gaze down pensively.

His innocent sex appeal faded slightly, reassuring the men.

Deep in thought for a moment longer, Leorino finally looked up. He nodded at Gravis.

"I want Mr. Dirk to know."

"Hm? Me, really?"

Dirk had thought his role was only to communicate with Ebbo, and now inclined his head. Leorino nodded.

"Yes, I want you both to hear what I have to say."

Gravis turned to Kaunzel. Kaunzel nodded and produced the key to the vault. He led the men to the door and opened it. The room still held that unique musty old paper scent of dust.

"This way."

There was a small reading desk in the back of the room lined with a few chairs.

"I shall take my leave."

Not asking any questions, Kaunzel tried to leave with the minimum courtesy.

"Kaunzel."

Hearing Gravis's voice, the keeper of the archives nodded quickly.

"...I understand, Your Excellency. Your Excellency and Lord Leorino did not set foot here today."

"That's right. Thank you."

After a brief, concerned glance at Ebbo, Kaunzel left them a lamp and walked away.

The remaining men were silent. Eventually, they heard the door to the vault close.

It was the general who broke the silence.

"Dirk, Steiger, sit down."

"Your Excellency... But..."

The two men found it inappropriate to sit down in front of the general, but sensing from his gaze that Gravis wouldn't take no for an answer, they took their seats without another word.

"Leorino, you should be resting. Now sit down."

"Vi... B-but..."

"Don't worry about me. Just talk to them."

Gravis stood behind Leorino and placed an encouraging hand on his shoulder.

"Um...Ebbo. No, Mr. Ebbo... I'm sorry I startled you the other day at the training grounds."

Leorino bowed his head.

"Captain... Please, I—"

It was Dirk who responded to Ebbo's words.

"'Captain'...? Captain Steiger, you called Lord Leorino that the other day. Whatever do you mean?"

"Dirk, shut up for a moment and listen to what he has to say. Leorino will address that, too."

But it was Leorino who trembled at Gravis's rebuke. He tried several times to open his mouth, but each time he released a shaky breath and fell silent.

The shadows of the men danced on the walls of the silent vault. The men waited patiently.

"Don't be afraid. You chose this, you can do it."

Leorino had cast his tearful eyes down, and Gravis squeezed his shoulder.

"…All right."

Leorino lifted his head, even as his face crumpled.

"Mr. Dirk…what I'm about to tell you may sound absurd. I already told Ebbo about it at the training grounds."

Dirk looked to the giant man next to him before he could help it. Ebbo nodded silently. Dirk couldn't begin to guess what this meant.

"…Mr. Dirk. I used to be very close to you."

"What do you mean by that, Lord Leorino?"

"…I—I—I mean…"

His violet eyes shook, reflecting the light on the desk. Gravis again offered a helping hand.

"Leorino, you must be more direct."

"But I'll be getting him involved in everything…"

"Don't worry. Steiger already believes you. Trust that Dirk will as well."

Leorino turned to Ebbo. The large, scarred man looked at Leorino and nodded kindly.

"Captain. His Excellency is right. It's all right, please be brave."

Leorino nodded, tears welling in his eyes.

Then he looked squarely at Dirk.

"Mr. Dirk. I was born in Brungwurt eighteen years ago, the morning after the recapture of Zweilink."

Dirk nodded and furrowed his brow.

"But I have memories from before I was born."

"Hmm…huh? You what?"

But the next moment, Dirk received a shock that felt as if a sword had pierced his heart.

"I have the memories of your brother Ionia Bergund, who was killed in the battle for Zweilink."

"…What are you talking about…?"

Dirk began to doubt Leorino's sanity.

He turned to his superior, searching for an answer, but Gravis just silently stared back at his second-in-command.

*   *   *

Dammit, what the hell...?! This is so ridiculous, it's beyond in poor taste!

"Lord Leorino, I'm rather fond of you. But...I don't know where you learned about my brother, but I honestly don't want you to speak of him so frivolously."

With a heavy exhale, Dirk strongly refused to continue the conversation. Leorino bit his lip and endured the harsh words.

"I don't expect you to believe me right away. I also thought it was just a strange dream when I first began to see Ionia's memories."

"...Dreams? You dream about my brother?"

"Yes. The first dream began when I saw his face in a small mirror on the wall of his room. A boy with red hair who...looked nothing like me, but with the same eye color, was staring back at me. I knew, even in the dream, that he was *me*."

Indeed, a small mirror had hung on the wall of his brother's room, right above where the washbowl and pitcher were placed.

"...Who told you about my brother?"

"No one told me."

Dirk glanced at his superior. Gravis shook his head.

"I've never seen Ionia's room."

That was likely true. Only his family could have known what Ionia's room looked like at the time.

"When we first met, you said you recognized my eyes and...that they looked just like your late brother's."

"That's...true."

"Look into my eyes again, Dirk."

Leorino intently watched Dirk. That unique color—purple with a spoonful of dawn. The eyes of the brother he remembered... Yes, the eyes of his brother who died eighteen years ago spoke volumes to Dirk.

"...I hate this. Someone tell me it's not true..."

"Dirk..."

Leorino extended his small, thin hand to him. Dirk immediately swatted it away and stood up.

It made a surprisingly loud noise.

Is This a Figment of Your Imagination?   447

"Dirk."

Gravis called his name in a low voice. It was a warning to treat Leorino with care.

"I apologize, sir. But I am confused. Will you please allow me to leave the room?"

Gravis's quiet voice calmed the adjutant as he treaded the verge of indignation.

"Listen to Leorino for a little while longer. Then you can do as you see fit."

"...Yes, sir."

Trembling slightly, Leorino bowed his head to Dirk.

"I'm sorry for startling you."

"No, I should be apologizing... I'm sorry for pushing you away. I'll listen to you."

Leorino bowed once more. The way he shrank in on himself inspired pity. Gravis patted him on the shoulder.

"Come, get a hold of yourself. Didn't you come here because you decided to tell them everything?"

"...Yes, I'm sorry... Dirk, I want you to believe me. I'm not lying."

"...There's nothing I can say to that right now."

Leorino looked like he was about to cry.

"...I was so happy to see you when we met in Vi's office. The last time I saw you, you were a boy, not even half-fledged... I never knew you had become such a fine, strong man."

Dirk laughed to himself at these words. He wanted to stop this farce as soon as he could.

Leorino had only just recently outgrown his boyhood himself, but was now looking at Dirk as if he were his own flesh and blood. It all felt very dramatic, but he was clearly serious. Dirk had no idea how to react.

He remained patient, just as his superior ordered. Still, he didn't know how much more he could endure.

Dirk's gaze on Leorino showed clear signs of irritation.

He...he really does resemble Ionia.

* * *

Dirk had an amicable face, but his body was similar to Ionia's. He had a beautifully muscular upper body. His long limbs also contained well-developed muscle.

Ionia's body was more toned, perfectly fit for a soldier. Dirk was a little plump, as if to represent his easygoing personality.

Perhaps Leorino should have expected as much.

The little brother from his memories would in reality soon be thirty years old. He was now older than Ionia was at the time of his death, a fully grown man that had long stopped being a youth.

"I'm sorry for hiding the fact that I had his memories until now. I was born this way, and I was afraid of what would happen if Vi, Luca, and you… learned that I was Ionia."

Dirk couldn't stand hearing Leorino call the general and lieutenant general by their pet names and quickly ran out of patience.

"I'm sorry, Lord Leorino, but I really can't do this."

"Dirk…"

"Frankly, I find it very hard to believe that you have inherited my late brother's memories."

Leorino bit his lip for a moment as if trying to hold back his emotions, but then turned to Dirk again with an intense gaze. His hands were clasped together on the desk, shaking slightly.

"I thought I would have to carry these memories alone for the rest of my life. But then I had a dream about that day."

"That day?"

It was Ebbo who reacted to his words, having silently watched the situation until then.

"Captain…do you mean Zweilink?"

Leorino offered Ebbo a small nod.

"Yes. The night of Ionia's death."

"What about it…?!"

"I remembered fighting that day at Zweilink. And…I remembered the truth of what happened back then. That's why I came to the royal capital."

For the first time ever, Dirk hated Leorino. He gritted his teeth, wishing he could tell him to stop using his brother's death for this pathetic performance.

"Truth... What is this truth you speak of?"

Dirk was proud to say that he had thoroughly researched the battle for Zweilink. The reason, of course, was the death of his brother. He had been investigating it in the archives both during his time in the academy of higher learning and after joining the Royal Army's General Staff.

Why did his brother have to die so tragically? Dirk did everything in his power to solve this mystery.

Dirk couldn't help but cover his eyes. He concealed the loathing welling in his heart.

"...Don't speak of my brother's death so casually, Lord Leorino... Please, you've said enough."

"Please. Please hear me out."

"...I can't promise that I'll believe you."

"Of course."

Dirk looked at Leorino once more.

"I'll listen to you. So? What happened to my brother at Zweilink?"

"That day, Ionia was betrayed by an ally. A man who had been under Ionia's command stabbed him in the stomach, inflicting a fatal wound."

Dirk was dumbfounded.

"...What?"

"There was a traitor on our side. The man's name was Edgar Yorke."

Dirk began to search for the name in his mind. It wasn't long before he found it.

"Edgar...Edgar Yorke. The man who was found with a serious abdominal wound?"

"The wound in Edgar's abdomen serves as proof of Ionia's final struggle."

"Wh-what...?!"

"Ionia knew of the man's betrayal and tried to kill him with what little remained of his Power. But Ionia had very little life force left in him because of the boulder he had shattered earlier. In the end...he breathed his last breath filled with regret, with no way of confirming Edgar's fate."

"I-I'm sorry... Just give me a minute."

Dirk couldn't keep up with one shocking reveal after another.

"Edgar was also responsible for helping the enemy invade the outer fortress that day."

"...Wait!"

Dirk shouted, but Leorino vehemently insisted.

"Please, listen. Edgar had also set fire to the plains of Zweilink!"

Dirk held his hand out to stop him.

"For god's sake, wait! ...Please."

Leorino finally shut his mouth and waited until Dirk's confusion had subsided.

"Is this all...a figment of your imagination?"

"No, it is one of the many truths of that day that Ionia learned, that I now must tell you all. It is neither a lie nor a fantasy."

"Even if it were true, how could you possibly know this? It happened before you were born!"

"I saw it in my dreams."

Leorino looked at Dirk with a solemn expression.

"I have lived the life of the man who was your brother in my dreams throughout my life...over and over again."

Dirk turned to Ebbo.

He wanted something to bring him to his senses.

The large, scarred man nodded as he watched Dirk with calm eyes.

In his desperation, Dirk finally looked to his superior.

"...Sir, what am I being told here?"

Gravis calmly replied. "Let your feelings answer that question, Dirk."

Dirk turned his gaze back to Leorino.

Leorino's eyes were his brother's eyes, a little sad and somewhat anxious. They looked just like they always had.

Dirk did his best to remain calm. He was beyond baffled.

But his heart was beginning to accept the truth of what Leorino was saying before his mind could.

"Are you really...my brother...?"

Leorino's smile seemed somewhat uncertain.

"I'm not exactly Ionia. I only remember living his life. I was born that way."

"How much do you remember of me…?"

Inclining his head slightly, Leorino stared into the void as if searching his memory.

"I don't remember everything. When I wake up from my dreams, most of the trivial, everyday things are missing. But the important memories are there. So, Dirk…of course I remember you." Leorino smiled calmly. "We were so far apart in age, it was difficult for me to spend time with you. Especially after I entered school."

That was true. After moving to the dormitories, his brother rarely returned to their family home.

"…Why didn't you come home?"

"I had a duty to fulfill. I had to protect Prince Gravis. And…after I killed a man with my Power for the first time, I dreamed of shattering you with my hands over and over again…"

Dirk was shocked by the confession.

"…I saw it every night, again and again. I worried that if I no longer hesitated to kill, I might one day hurt my own family. I was so afraid that one day I might kill my little brother by mistake that…I couldn't go home."

Dirk never realized his brother had worried about that.

"…My brother would never do such a thing."

"Thank you… But I also remember the good times."

Leorino smiled.

"…Dirk, do you remember Ionia's special ability? He could shatter anything with just a touch."

"Yes…but…"

"I can faintly remember. You watched when Father asked me to crush the ore when you were little, and you clapped and told me how beautiful it was."

"…You, how could you possibly—?"

Dirk vaguely recalled that his brother had magical hands that could instantly turn any object into pieces. The shattered pieces of ore were beautiful, glistening in the light.

Leorino's expression turned tender.

"You kept saying, 'Make more sparkles!' and I shattered more ore than

Father asked for, and got yelled at rather harshly. Though you were so little, I don't know if you'd remember…"

Yes…I kept badgering him about it…

He clearly recalled his brother's violet eyes smiling gently at him in that forge that smelled of metal.

Now his brother's eyes were watching Dirk.

Leorino wasn't his deceased brother, nor was he his ghost. A living being with those extraordinary eyes had appeared in the flesh before Dirk in a completely different form from the brother he remembered.

"And," Leorino muttered to himself, "the night before I was sent to Zweilink, I returned to our family home. You looked so proud when you saw me in my military uniform. You saw the sword my father had made for me and praised me. Do you remember? Did I get that wrong?"

"…You're not wrong."

Dirk recalled their last meal together.

Ionia's sword had been forged by his blacksmith father. Though unadorned and utilitarian, it was a magnificent sword.

The sword had returned covered in blood and soot, but not his brother, who had been buried in the land in which he perished. Now the sword was beautifully polished, displayed in their father's forge.

"…I said that when I grew up I would also fight with our father's sword… I was so proud of him, he was so strong, so high in rank despite being a commoner, fighting on the front lines."

A smile appeared on Leorino's tearstained face.

"I see. That's why you were so happy… Thank you."

"…A-are you…are you really my brother?"

Dirk's stunned mutter echoed through the dark archives.

Continued in next volume